Rave and Let Die

The SF and Fantasy of 2014

Rave and Let Die

The SF and Fantasy of 2014

Adam Roberts

Steel Quill Books
An Imprint of NewCon Press

First edition, published in the UK September 2015

by Steel Quill Books,
an Imprint of NewCon Press
41 Wheatsheaf Road, Alconbury Weston, Cambs, PE28 4LF

SQ003 (softback)

10 9 8 7 6 5 4 3 2 1

ISBN: 978-1-907069-80-2 (softback)

Cover layout by Andy Bigwood

Minor Editorial Interference by Ian Whates
Text layout by Storm Constantine

Contents

Introduction

When I was young and my heart was an open book, I used to say: 'the business of a review is clearly, accurately and without hyperbole to assess the respective merits and demerits of a book or film, thereby to give readers some sense of whether it is worth paying hard-earned cash for the product.' But if this ever squee-filled world in which we're livin' makes me give in and cry, it is to the extent that reviews today seem to fall into one of two camps, both rather crude in approach, neither of them appealing: gushing and unguarded praise on the one hand; scornful and dismissive dispraise on the other.

Is this really the topography of our cultural landscape? Is this what that topography has become? What I mean when I ask that question, is: has the larger culture of SF truly bifurcated into two categories defined chiefly by the vehemence with which praise or dispraise is asserted, in turn informed by a prior set of ideological investments? Us and them? And after all we're just ordinary men. And women. We might insist, I suppose, that it's always been this way. But to cast a cold eye over the landscape of SF and Fantasy as it appeared in 2014 is surely to be struck by how polarised, how ideologically and aesthetically divided it has grown. The Hard, politically conservative 'SF is about learning and respecting the inviolable laws of physics', masculinist, macho kill-and-rape video game, neo-Fascist Hugo ballot-stuffing crowd in one corner; and the Literary SF, 'science fiction is about the encounter with otherness', lovin-the-alien, polymorphous, feminist, queer, coloured, trans and politically liberal crowd in the other. I can think of many Hard SF aficionados who would not thank me for bracketing them and their tastes in with the more obnoxious end of the Gamergate and Sadrabidpuppies world, but (casting a cold eye, remember) we cannot wish away the impact those two phenomena had upon the 2014 genre landscape. I'll come to that in a moment. For now I should probably qualify myself a little. Certainly, as an aesthetic preference, a taste for Hard SF, military SF and so on is precisely as neutral as any other taste. That said, there is an element on this side of the divide that adopts a more-or-less explicit 'the laws of Physics make my political ideology correct!' line, which in turn leads to a receptivity best tagged *proscrustean.*

When I rave about a well-written literary SF novel about queer aliens rewiring our human expectations, it is because I have good reason for my enthusiasm. When *you* rave about a cookie-cutter Space Marines techno-adventure it is because you are raving mad. And vice versa: when you rave about an exciting, thought-provoking narrative based upon rigorously extrapolated science, it is because such stories expand our apprehension of the real wonder and splendour of the cosmos – because physics is true in a way ideology never can be – and because this is what SF is supposed to do. When I rave about books that deliberately muddle long-standing traditional notions of gender, sex and identity, books that show dismissive contempt of the hard work involved in mastering science, it is because I am raving mad.

I am a raver, I confess it. I am also a let-dier. Indeed, looking over my reviews of 2014's output, gathered together here, it strikes me that I'm rather more consistently a let-dier than I am a raver. So my nature is subdued to what it works in, the let-dier's hand. Pity me, then, and wish I were renewed. The polarisation of SF, and the heat this has generated in online discussion, drifting like a sterile thunderhead over genre, seems to me the main takeaway from the year 2014. Insofar as a shared discourse is patently lacking, it starts to look rather like a Differend. A study of the rhetoric alone would make a fascinating read: 'right winger' becomes 'wingnut'; 'liberals' become 'lib-tards'; the notion that either side could even conceivably be arguing in good faith is laughed derisively out of court. I have a particular dislike for discussions (on Twitter, facebook, blogs and so on) being notated with the word 'headdesk'. Headdesk means: *what you have said is so stupid, so not-even-wrong, so moronically beneath contempt, words quite literally fail me.* Let die the wingnuts, the libtards. It is an index of pre-determined unengagement. Words should never fail us. Words are all we have.

The rapid expansion of the semantic field of 'troll' is part of this. It used to mean 'somebody maliciously commenting on a blog-post for no other reason than to cause distress to the poster or the other commenters'. Now, very often, it means 'someone who has expressed a view that does not align with my own ideological preconceptions'. There are such things as trolls, of course, in the online world; and there are some comments that are so stupidly bigoted or un-thought-through that engagement would be a waste a time. But these are not the majority, even though the majority of contrary views are sincerely held.

The present volume is a collection of reviews of the SF and Fantasy books and films that were released during 2014. Some of these reviews are very positive. Some are negative, occasionally dismissively so. There's nothing special about 2014, except that it so happened I read a much higher proportion of new releases during that year than I normally do. This was because I was a judge for two linked literary prizes – the Kitschies' Red and Golden tentacle (for best novel and best debut novel). The prize itself had nearly 200 submissions from over forty publishers, and our judging policy was to make sure that as many of the books as possible of were read by all of the five-strong judging team, with absolutely every title being read by at least two judges. From the spreadsheet Glen 'The Man' Mehn, chair of judges, assembled I discover I read 107 titles during the initial run through, and then a quantity more during our whittling down process, to bring us all up to speed. I at least glanced at most of the rest. Before and after the judging period I'd say I read a couple more score of genre novels that happened not to be shortlisted for this particular award. Let's ballpark my reading at the 160 figure. It's a good number, 160. It is, for instance, both the sum of the first 11 primes, and the sum of the *cubes* of the first three primes.

The volume that follows this introduction consists of reviews of 90 titles; a little over half what I read. A nice round number. I wrote some of them on commission, in order to review titles for newspapers, magazines or the like, for that is what a professional writer does. But most of them I wrote only to get my thoughts in order about the titles themselves. I've reached the stage where it's hard for me to know what I think unless I write it out.

So: this is a small fraction of the total output of genre for the year. Something like 700 new English language SF and Fantasy titles are published annually (I do not include reprints and new editions of old classics), a number that will increase sharply as self-publication and e-books become established in literary culture. About a quarter of our Kitschies' submissions were e-book only, a quite a few of those were self-pubbed. We even shortlisted one self-pubbed title. More, a properly synoptic overview of genre in the year ought to read all the graphic novels, novellas and short stories (reading so many novels squeezed my shorter fiction reading quite sharply), not to mention go to see all the SF/Fantasy plays, and play all the SF/Fantasy games. As a starter. And that's just the Anglophone stuff.

Clearly I can make no claim to comprehensiveness, as far as 2014 in genre went. But I came closer than I usually do, by quite a significant factor. That in turn prompts me to reflect back on the year. It was an interesting year. You know that old Chinese curse about interesting years? Of course you do.

2014 was the year cancer claimed Iain M. Banks: he was widely and deeply mourned. My friend Graham Joyce also died that year, and of the same disease. On a more positive note, 2014 was the year Worldcon came to London. It's rare for Britain to host the planet's most prestigious SF/Fantasy convention, and 'Loncon' was a great success. Although, as British fandom's rejoiced, hopes for a 'the British are coming!' moment in SF were undermined by the lack of Brit winners, or even nominees, in the convention's annual Hugo awards. The year's best novel Hugo went to *Ancillary Justice*, American writer Ann Leckie's first novel. Indeed, award-wise, 2014 was very much Leckie's year. She became the first author to win the Arthur C. Clarke, Nebula and Hugo awards all in the same year. Her follow-up novel *Ancillary Sword* appeared in 2014. It advances the multi-volume story with aplomb; and if it also reads like some of the momentum is slipping, that's as much an index of the impossibility this sort of expectation puts on a writer as on Leckie's undeniable talent.

So, there were grounds for some rave reviews. And some quarters of SF fandom were full of ravers. William Gibson, Godfather of Cyberpunk ('Cyberpater'?) published his latest novel, *The Peripheral* to great fanfare. Andy Weir's Hard SF stranded-astronaut-on-Mars thriller *The Martian* topped bestseller lists around the globe and has since been filmed by Ridley Scott. Jeff VanderMeer published all three volumes of his 'Southern Reach' trilogy in one year: *Annihilation*, *Authority* and *Acceptance*, ringing dream-haunting changes upon wilderness writing, parsing the natural world of Florida through weirdness into a potent and brilliant newness. These are contemporary masterpieces, and career-defining novels for their author.

We Brits are less likely to rave (to froth at the mouth, to caper and shout) in the face of excellence, and one consequence of that is that genuinely good books will tend to get neglected by mainstream arbiters of taste. David Mitchell's hugely entertaining blockbuster *The Bone Clocks* is a case in point: sneered at by some reviewers on account of the

High Fantasy component of its many narrative-strands – the word 'hokum' was used by some reviewers. Ignore such voices. *The Bone Clocks* was one of the year's genuinely significant books, a powerfully-imagined fable about love, hope, life and death that manages to be both formally ambitious and immensely readable. Then again, perhaps publicity-generating hostility is better for an author than the sort of bald neglect under which many of the year's best SF and Fantasy languished. Dave Hutchinson's *Europe in Autumn* is set in a future Europe balkanized into a tessellation of myriad new mini-states (2014's Scots and Catalonian Independence referenda made the book seem especially timely). The legendary Rachel Pollack made a relatively unheralded return to genre with her first novel in twelve years: *The Child Eater*, an intricately imagined Tarot-themed fantasy. Simon Ings' grimly powerful *Wolves* ought to have set the literary establishment on fire; as should Peter Higgins' atmospheric and gripping *Truth and Fear*, set in a version of Russia halfway between ancient magic and Soviet concrete. Clare North garnered a little more notice – though frankly not notice enough – for *The First Fifteen Lives of Harry August*, a book that not only finds a smart new twist on time travel, but uses it to pluck some genuinely moving emotional resonances.

Grim has been the flavour of the genre for some years now, and 2014 was no exception. Tania Unsworth's clever, unsettling Young Adult dystopia *The One Safe Place* was a highlight. Lavie Tidhar's *A Man Lies Dreaming* was another, juxtaposing the horrors of the Nazi death camps with a splendidly over-the-top gumshoe adventure starring Adolf Hitler himself as a 1940s London private eye. Joe Abercrombie wrote his first YA novel, an effortlessly readable Fantasy called *Half a King*. Michel Faber's potent though downbeat *The Book of Strange New Things* fumbles its science-fictional elements rather; but is still the sort of book that haunts the mind long after finishing it. 2014 also saw the final volume in Tom Pollock's superb YA 'Skyscraper Throne' trilogy: *Our Lady of the Streets* uses Fantasy conceits and a tireless capacity for imaginative invention to map the dazzle, diversity and menace of London in ways simply unavailable to realist writers.

The long story short is: I read a great many brilliant, stimulating and entertaining books; and many more dull, numbing ones. The rubric for the Kitschies specifies three criteria by which shortlists are selected: books must be intelligent, progressive and entertaining. This was the first time I'd judged a literary prize. My main take-away from the experience is how much really good stuff is being written at the moment – especially (but not exclusively) by women, especially (but not exclusively) in YA and what we could call 'near future dystopia'. Mind you, one point of diplomatic disagreement in the judging star-chamber concerned how much weight to give the 'entertainment' criterion. My fellow judges were minded to accord it a good deal of weight. The older I get the less I find myself reading for 'sheer entertainment'. Many of the novels that have meant the most to me, that have stayed with me and that I re-read have not been 'entertaining' in any conventional sense. Certainly, I would say that some of 2014's best novels are like this. I appreciate I'm an outlier here. Sane people don't want to plug dutifully through a novel; they prefer to be carried through on a well-greased downward slide of pure enjoyment. I'm an English Literature professor. I also have less of a problem with 'duty' than some, the relict of my time labouring the mines of Nineteenth-century Literature and Culture. It has always seemed to me that duty has this advantage over pleasure: that whilst doing one's duty is often a pleasure in its own right, that moment when indulging in one's favourite pleasure becomes a duty is the moment the pleasure dies. But, look: I'm prepared to stretch the point far enough to say that whatever else reviews are 'for', they ought to be entertaining.

The process of judging the Kitschies worked towards a conclusion. Here are the shortlists we agreed on:

Shortlist for the Red Tentacle (novel)

Lagoon, by Nnedi Okorafor (Hodder & Stoughton)
Grasshopper Jungle, by Andrew Smith (Egmont)
The Peripheral, by William Gibson (Viking)
The Way Inn, by Will Wiles (4th Estate)
The Race, by Nina Allen (NewCon Press)

Shortlist for the Golden Tentacle (Debut)

Viper Wine, by Hermione Eyre (Jonathan Cape)
The Girl in the Road, by Monica Byrne (Blackfriars)
Memory of Water, by Emmi Itäranta (Voyager)
The Long Way to a Small, Angry Planet, by Becky Chambers (Self)
The People in the Trees, by Hanya Yanagihara (Atlantic Books)

After much genuine and heartfelt discussion, we decided *Grasshopper Jungle* and *Viper Wine* would gain the prize; but all these titles were in the running until the very last horse was traded. Here, for comparison, is the BSFA shortlist for best novel:

Nina Allan, *The Race* (Newcon Press)
Frances Hardinge, *Cuckoo Song* (Macmillan)
Dave Hutchinson, *Europe in Autumn* (Solaris)
Simon Ings, *Wolves* (Gollancz)
Anne Leckie, *Ancillary Sword* (Orbit)
Claire North, *The First Fifteen Lives of Harry August* (Orbit)
Nnedi Okorafor, *Lagoon* (Hodder)
Neil Williamson, *The Moon King* (Newcon Press)

It was especially pleasing to see North and Hardinge recognised there, since it was only the fact that they were themselves Kitschies judges that prevented their novels coming under serious consideration for that prize. *Ancillary Sword* took the palm, the second year running that Leckie won.

Then came the Arthur C. Clarke Awards:

MR Carey, *The Girl With All the Gifts* (Orbit)
Michel Faber, *The Book of Strange New Things* (Canongate)
Dave Hutchinson, *Europe in Autumn* (Solaris)
Emmi Itäranta *Memory of Water* (HarperVoyager)
Claire North, *The First Fifteen Lives of Harry August* (Orbit)
Emily St John Mandel, *Station Eleven* (Picador)

A good list. Its great strength, I think, is that none of these six writers have been nominated for the Clarke before. There's a sense of freshness here, a newness, and it is commendably symptomatic of a genre growing and changing. The downside of the list, I'd say, is a certain sameness of apocalyptic and post-apocalyptic vibe. *The Girl With All the Gifts*, *Memory Of Water* and *Station Eleven* are all set in lands ravaged by prior disaster, in which people eke out existences denuded to one degree or another. Eek. And one of the main themes of *The Book of Strange New Things* is the ongoing climate collapse on Earth, such that Faber's narrative plays out against a grim sense of social disaster and foreboding. They're all fine novels, although personally I don't think postapoc is really where the most exciting stuff is happening in genre at the moment. Of course I could be wrong. Then again, neither *Europe in Autumn* nor *The First Fifteen Lives of Harry August* are postapoc, although the former (very fine) novel is sort-of about the breakdown of Europe as a functioning socio-political entity, and there's a global doomsday creeping ever closer in the (wonderful) latter. The Achilles heel of *Europe in Autumn*, I'd say, is its ending, a knight's-move that points the reader rather sharply in the direction of the sequel, and which may leave some readers blinking rather hard. *Harry August* has no such problem, for although it takes a little while to pick up speed the bulk of the novel clamps an impressively iron grip upon the readerly imagination. I suppose some readers may struggle with the expertly evoked existential claustrophobia of the novel. Not me; I'd describe that as a feature not a bug. But existential claustro-phobia does characterise pretty much all the novels here, to one degree or another, on the level of timbre or mouthfeel. So it goes.

But there's an elephant in the room of 2015 award shortlists, and its name is Hugo. A good elephantine name, I'd say; like 'Jumbo' or Coco'. There's no getting around the linked issues of 'Gamergate' and 'Puppygate' in SF. Some of this spills out of its 2014 chronological box and is a matter more correctly described as 2015; but a lot of it is distressingly germane to my topic in this volume. I'm not going to list the 2015 Hugo shortlists (notionally for the best SF of 2014), because the lists were swamped by two coordinated Gamergate-ish campaigns, self-dubbed 'Sad Puppies' and 'Rabid Puppies'. Titles from the co-ordinated slates of these two overwhelmingly dominated the prize, and as a result the 2015 Hugos were a write-off.

The thing to keep in mind is that the Puppies' slates represented an efficiently executed political strategy. The Puppies campaigned within the rules of the prize, and were more successful than their self-defined 'enemy' in coordinating their followers. The response needs to be political if we want it actually to bite. This means one of two things, I'd say: either to organise an anti-Puppies slate for all future years in which the prize runs, with all the labour and cat-herding that implies. I have some doubts as to the achievability of this, and many doubts as to its desirability: for it would remove the Hugos even further from the notion that works and individuals get nominated according to their merit. Personally I think the better strategy is otherwise, essentially a *Delenda est Hugo* approach.[1]

The Puppies set out to destroy the Hugos. Let them. Napoleon thought he had won the battle of Borodino, but actually he lost it. Let the Puppies retreat through the winter wasteland of community hostility and indifference. The Puppies, after all, are not interested in winning Hugos per se; they are interested in the esteem associated with the Hugos. But that does not magically inhere in the rocket-shaped trophy. It's the other way around. The trophy functions as an index of the esteem of the community as a whole. The 2015 shortlist breaks the connection between the first of these things and the second. So it goes. It is the whole community that controls how it distributes its esteem, not any one pressure group; such esteem cannot be 'gamed' by the coordination of voting blocks. Once upon a time the Hugos were the genre's Blue Riband award; functionally they have not been that for several years. But there are other awards which are, even as we speak, producing much better shortlists: three of them are listed above. Now is the time to invest the esteem of the community as a whole in those.

Of course we have a sentimental attachment to the way the Hugos were. But the award is not an inseparable part of Worldcon; the con can continue going from strength to strength without it. And the award will of course carry on, as a sort of in-house prize for the best right-wing homophobic militaristic clumsily-written flat-character linear space-adventure of the year. The important thing is that there be an award or awards that register the genuine esteem of SF Fandom, in all its diversity and variety. Besides, the Puppies are inherently negating. They thought that by gaming their favoured titles onto the list they would sprinkle the prestige of the Hugos over these shitty novels. They discovered that the law of conservation of momentum works in such things: that rather than doing that they have instead diminished the Hugos with the taint of their shitty books and stories. So it goes.

A connected point is to do with self-promotion for awards. I've

[1] Who knows what the gender of the word 'Hugo' would be, treated as a Latin word? We might think it masculine, since Gernsback was a man (in which case the phrase ought to be '*delendum est Hugo*'). But the gender of nouns doesn't necessarily follow the 'actual' gender of the thing, and I prefer to treat the term as feminine. For several reasons.

several times expressed my opposition to the shift in SF culture towards today's situation where 'for your consideration' self-pimpage has become the norm. The last time I did this I got considerable blowback, indeed hostility, from various quarters on the grounds that a white western male advocating a 'no self-promotion for awards' position was effectively silencing non-white, non-western and non-male voices. I take the force of this argument, of course. Nevertheless, I have to point at where we are: this year's Hugo Slate makes manifest the tacit logic in all self-promotion. Because it doesn't matter how diplomatically it is framed, or what degree of passive voice is used ('if you are thinking of voting in this year's Hugos I would be honoured if you would consider my novel/short story/essay...'). Putting yourself forward for an award is inevitably predicated upon the following premise: I think my work should win this award. And that means only one thing: I think my work is the best novel/short story/essay published this year. The danger with the normalisation of self-promotion for awards is that it obscures this unpleasant truth – because of course only three types of people can make that latter claim with a straight face: bona fide geniuses; egomaniacs; and people trying to undertake Puppies-style award-list gaming. You are not the first of these three categories any more than I am; and you do not want to be the second or the third. Authors should extricate themselves from award promotion altogether and leave that to the fans. That's all I want to say about awards in this place; although I return, below, to the larger culture force of which the Sad and Rabid Puppies are but symptoms.

Reviewing the short fiction provision of *Analog* through 2015 on his blog, Alastair Reynolds noted:

'I was struck by the sense – which I think has also been articulated by Gardner Dozois – that we're starting to see the emergence of what you might call the 'New Default Future'. Bear's world is one of vanishing privacy, information for all, continued social inequality, climate change as a given, radical lifestyle changes effected by new biotechnology. You can tweak the parameters a bit, but it does seem as if writers are once again beginning to converge on a shared sense of the future. No, it doesn't necessarily involve space colonies or rolling roads or flying cars, but it's no less valid, no less fascinating.'[2]

It *is* fascinating, I agree; and a conclusion certainly supported by my reading of 2014's fiction. There is a preponderance, or drift, towards what we might call mild dystopia – although 'mild' is, I daresay, the wrong word. Centralised Orwellian nightmares are rare (though not entirely absent: see David Ramirez's *The Forever Watch*). More common are visions of a decentralised, worn-out, deracinated future: the sort of world portrayed in Gibson's *The Peripheral*, portions of Mitchell's *Bone Clocks*, Tania Unsworth's *The One Safe Place* or the earthly sections of Faber's *Book of Strange New Things*. None of these books see Tech as 'the Enemy'; and that old Frankensteinish 'unintended consequences' libel on scientific endeavour seems to have run out of steam. Monica Byrne's *The Girl in the Road* is hardly a happy shiny novel where its vision of the future is concerned, for Byrne extrapolates current-day inequalities of race, gender and sexuality into a more crowded and careless future world. But Byrne takes a common-sensical approach to the good tech can bring to the world, and most SF writers (I think) share that. Indeed, this is, I think, as much a question of tone as of hardware.

Widescreen dioramas of catastrophic alien invasion, or hurry-down-doomsdays (the bugs are taking over!) tend, like Andrew Smith's marvellous *Grasshopper Jungle*, to adopt a lighter, funnier voice. This is less paradoxical than it might seem. A new generation of SF/Fantasy writers have emerged shaped by the Bush/Blair years of lies in high places, dodgy dossiers, illegal wars and vast human suffering. It is not surprising that, by and large, they write stories suspicious of official authority that are simultaneously stories of finding solace and strength amongst one's friends. Writers begin as fans, and fandom is stronger now than it has ever been. By 'stronger' I mean more connected, linked by social media in a way that wasn't true two decades ago, let alone five; but I also mean more responsive and responsible. For a long time Cons were jolly but precarious social spaces, where women were as liable to be groped as welcomed, where disabled access was patchy and the broader culture was careless of difference and vulnerability. It seems to me that there is a collective will, now, to change those things – speaking broadly.

---

[2]http://approachingpavonis.blogspot.co.uk/2015/02/asimovs-science-fiction-february-2015.html

The big theme in SF/Fantasy, as in culture more broadly, is: change. One of the functions of art (if you'll permit me to speak instrumentally, as it were, for a moment) is to help us live better in the world; and the world has changed in very significant and irreversible ways over the last half century or so. If we concentrate for a moment on the West, social mores concerning the rights of women, the validity of queer, trans and other lifestyles, the vacuity of racist beliefs, the social and cultural advantages of diversity – all has advanced more in the last generation than in a hundred generations prior. Some people deplore this, but it's a fact of the world now. It seems to me that the best genre novels of the year had this in common: *Lagoon*, *Grasshopper Jungle*, *The Peripheral*, *The Race*, *The Girl in the Road*, *Memory of Water*, *Europe in Autumn*: in diverse ways these books all interrogate how human beings deal with radically changed and changing worlds, what revolves during a revolution, how we adapt (or fail to adapt), how life's dome of many-coloured glass refracts new wavelengths and hues. Perhaps the most significant example of this is VanderMeer's *Southern Reach* trilogy, one of the few titles reviewed in this book assured, I'd say, classic status. Here Nature itself enweirds; humans try their best to comprehend, but are always running after the strangeness and newness that is the true idiom of things.

Not everything is about change so centrally, of course; and one common complaint about genre writing is that it is too often comfortable only with the familiar – shared tropes (robots, time machines, space marines) and cosily familiar narrative and character shapes. 2014, for instance, saw a great many books still working away at the tired old vampire and zombie templates, books cluttering up the landscape with their metaphorical apprehensions of – respectively – the repellent-irresistible lure of sex, and the flattened effect of late capitalist living. Authors write these stories because readers are still reading them, but there's little new to be said about either topic I'd say. M R Carey's *The Girl With All The Gifts* comes closest to this novelty, for it is a zombie novel full, ironically enough, of life.

Zombies also cluttered up the landscapes of 2014 more broadly, in a meta-sense. I'm talking about 'Gamergate', the shadow of whose ferocity fell like a blight across the sunlit uplands of fandom in 2014. It would be disingenuous of me to pretend impartiality when it comes to summarising this. Here's my best shot: Gamergate was mass-action outrage and aggression by (mostly) male fans of video games, motivated by a belief that the forces of 'political correctness' had combined in a malign conspiracy to censor, outlaw and demonise certain games for being insufficiently feminist. In point of fact, nobody has called for the outlawing of all '18-cerificate' video games, even assuming such a thing possible; and there is a surely a structural problem in a movement championing freedom of speech by aggressively working to close down, via death threats and intimidation, the speech of people with whom you disagree. It is not a coincidence that the object of this latter campaign of online lynching, doxxing and threats were overwhelmingly women.

A starting point for the movement was a sense shared by some gamers that games journalism was 'corrupt' – meaning, as I take it, that reviews of games were thought compromised by undisclosed private interests. Such a circumstance is certainly possible, even likely, although 'corruption' is really not the right word for it. Similar situations can be found in all small-scale, vigorous fan communities, and is best addressed by agreeing social codes of transparency and by contributing more disinterested and objective reviews to the discourse. Rather than adopt this strategy, Gamergate instead decided to go down the 'threatening female journalists with rape, torture and death and forcing the shut-down of public debate by warning that mass shootings would ensure if women are given the stage' road. At any rate, by 2014 this notional kicking-off point was a dot in the distance, and 'it's about ethics in games journalism!' had become a mere punchline, a badge of laughing-stockiness. The haptic gloves were off, and 'Gamergaters' revealed their true target: Social Justice Warriors.

When I first started seeing this label appear on social media, usually shortened to 'SJW', I had to pinch myself. Has a movement ever chanced on a *less* felicitously-chosen name for its opponents? If you're defining yourself *against* the Social Justice Warriors, then what are you – Antisocial Injustice Cowards? I'm reminded of that Mitchell and Webb sketch when an SS Sturmhauptführer, noticing as if for the first time that his uniform is all black and accessorised with skulls, wonderingly asks his comrade: 'Hans – are we… are we the *bad guys*?' ('Of course the *Americans* are going to think we're the bad guys!' his friend reassures him. 'But they didn't get to *design our uniforms*, did they,' the Nazi returns). Gamergate's tin ear for slogans, though trivial enough, does go right back to the beginning. For all I know, Adam Baldwin really thinks that 'Watergate' was a 1970s campaign against attempts to deprive people of water, or perhaps a brave challenge to the power of the evil Social Justice Water-Board. At any rate it would be foolish, this late in the day, to pretend we don't know what hatred of 'SJW' expresses. It has nothing to do with the question of whether gamers will still be 'allowed' to play games in which realistically-rendered avatars of women are stripped naked, raped and killed as sidebar plot-points of narratives about male heroes' bloody quests to blah blah blah. The issue is about a much larger and more important question: the evolution of society so that it becomes more accepting of the various diversities that necessarily comprise it. To be a little more specific, Gamergate is about the (I'm pleased to say: inevitable) de-straight-white-male-ification of culture more generally. That this is inevitable has nothing to do with the actions of female games journalists, valuable and interesting though their writing often is. It has to do with the larger forces of society. At root the change is a consequence of education. In the old days, when white men dominated culture, they were able to do so mostly by ensuring that women and other ethnicities did not have access to the same social possibilities they did themselves. To use the jargon, this was a hegemony that depended upon Ideological State Apparatuses rather than, say, the police and the army. If women and blacks are not educated, are denied the tools by which they can effectively take charge of their lives, then there's little they can do to change the ingrained structures of things. If such education as they *do* receive stresses their unfittedness for the large, difficult and dangerous tasks of running the world and making the money, then that reinforces white male de facto domination. But by the same token, once women and people of colour are given access to equal educational opportunities, then they will start to use the tools that education provides to take charge of their own destinies. That's the real shift, and it's not the kind of thing that online hate campaigns can stop. It's also not something any straight white male (and I speak *as* a straight white male) has cause to fear. The outcome will not be the establishment of a dystopian tyranny of Women and Queers in which white men are corralled behind barbed wire, forced to play *Sex and the City* tie-in games and swear allegiance to the original SJW: Sarah Jessica, er, Warker. Rather it will be a world in which we all have a much wider resource of human ingenuity, wealth-creation and compassion on which to draw.

Culture panic is a strange thing. The first flush of 1960s/1970s feminism and Civil Rights advances led to an alarmed kick-back by white men, who predicted that such destabilisation of society would lead in short order to catastrophe. Books like William Luther Pierce's *The Turner Diaries* (1979) took this perceived threat very seriously, and agitated for an armed Aryan white-race revolution. Some of the reaction was comic and satiric, at least in intention. The popular BBC comedy show *The Two Ronnies* ran a serial in 1989 called 'The Worm That Turned', set in a dystopian 2012 in which women rule Britain. Conventional 20th-century male and female gender roles are reversed, with the men having women's names and the women men's. Men are housekeepers and wear women's clothes, and law and order is managed by female guards in boots and hot pants. It wasn't very funny even then, and nowadays would look staggeringly insulting and objectionable. But it speaks to one interesting symptom of the panic, a kind of all-or-nothing logic that can see culture and society only in monolithic terms. Either white men are in charge, or they will be enslaved! Of course this is nonsense. We sailed right past 2012 without women assuming totalitarian control of life. There's little danger of the straight white males, the 'Swhims' as we might call them, losing their dominance any time soon, culturally or indeed politically. Gamergate and the forces of political reaction are not fighting to prevent the overthrow of the swhims; they are fighting to prevent us swhims losing so much as an inch of our ancient, hereditary privilege. Speaking as a swhim myself, let me say to them: please stop. You're embarrassing us.

Though they sought, as a damage-limitation exercise, to distance themselves from Gamergate proper, the Hugo Puppies are symptoms of exactly the same larger cultural anxieties. Sad and Rapid Puppies professed two rationales for what they did (and by 'what they did', I mean 'shit all over the Hugo Awards'). The first was that they claimed a left-wing conspiracy had secretly taken over the Hugos process in a concerted attempt to get lefty 'literary' sf by women, gay people and people of colour onto the ballot and to prevent (as they saw it) good honest right-wing space adventures by white men from being rewarded. In this they are simply wrong, something quite easily demonstrated: in the wake of Puppygate a great river of blogposts went over the stats on this, looking at the spread of nominees and winners over many decades. There's been no shortage of right wing white men honoured by the

Hugos; works of SF that prioritise left-wing ideologicaly preaching over literary and aesthetic qualities have not won the prize. Indeed, for myself, as a left-wing writer of 'literary' SF who has never been nominated for a Hugo, I have to say that if there *were* a secret cabal dedicated to getting such folk on the ballot, I'd want to go stand behind them and say 'ahem!' loudly.

The second rationale has a little more merit to it, though not much: it's that the Hugos have increasingly rewarded the sorts of books (highfalutin literary and experimental work) that doesn't reflect the kinds of SF most SF fans actually read. This is probably true: core SF Fans buy 'traditional' action adventure SF with the emphasis on likeable heroes, hissable villains and page-turning plots served up with lashings of gosh-wow SF sense of wonder. Last year's Hugo winner, *Ancillary Justice*, gave its readers some of that, but was also quite a sophisticated experiment in defamiliarising its readers' assumptions about gender. The year before, Scalzi's *Redshirts* was a playful metafiction deconstructing the logic of *Star Trek*. Both novels sold pretty well, but if you measure their Goodreads ratings (for instance) then they score less well than many more old-fashioned SF.

Personally I don't see this latter situation is a problem: the Hugos never were a mass plebiscite of all of SF Fandom; you have to care sufficiently to buy a worldcon membership ($40 for non-attenders, considerably more if you actually want to go) in order to get a vote, so the constituency of voters is proportionately small. Indeed, it is precisely this that enabled the Puppies to 'game' the vote so effectively. So the Hugos don't pretend to represent the whole of SF – a vast and very diverse body of people ranging from people who read several SF novels a week to people who never read novels and are interested only in (say) games, comics, movies, TV and cosplay, and every variation in between. There could never be a definitive judgement by this larger community as to what single thing is 'best'.

The problem the Puppies have, it seems to me, is twofold. One is that collating these two grievances – one party-political and inarguably wrong, one demographic and at least arguable – has resulted in the whole process becoming tainted with a monstrously divisive ideological bar-brawl between right and left. Everybody loses. Two, related to this, is the question of how close the 'Sad Puppies' (run by a number of politically conservative authors who, though I disagree with them, do represent a large body of fans) and the Rapid Puppies (run by 'Vox Day', one of the most noisome and despicable individuals on the scene today, a militaristic pro-Hitler homophobe, misogynist and racist). The former really don't want to be associated with the latter, yet the Puppies debacle has fixed them together in everyone's imagination. Wait. Hold up. Listen… Can you hear? You'll need to turn off all other noise, and attend very carefully with your ears. That tiny, tiny, sound? It's me, playing the world's smallest violin in sympathy at their plight.

Books are half the picture; the other half of my SF/F life in 2014 was cinematic and televisual. Here my experience was much less positive. I'm constrained a little by practical circumstances when it comes to new releases, since I have young kids. Sometimes the exigencies of accompanying children to the big screen pays off: *Big Hero 6* (dir. Don Hall and Chris Williams) was enjoyable enough, and the middle act of *Maleficent* (directed by Robert Stromberg) hits some highs. Sometimes, though, it is does the very opposite of paying off. It pays, er, on: *The Hobbit: The Battle of the Five Armies* (directed by Peter Jackson); *Teenage Mutant Ninja Turtles* (directed Jonathan Liebesman) and worst of all *Transformers: Age of Extinction* (directed by Michael Bay) were startlingly, shout-aloud, weep-bitter-tears bad. They were very bad indeed. Even *Guardians of the Galaxy* (directed by James Gunn), certainly a cut above these other movies, tended to smother its charming central buddies-together vibe in a great spuming froth of unearned grandiosity.

This, of course, is not a phenomenon new to 2014. Big Screen SF and Fantasy has been defined by a process of debilitating visual inflation for years now: the 'scale' gets bigger and bigger, the SFX more and more lavish, the films themselves get longer. In each case the stakes are ramped up – the entire universe is threatened! – in a manner that ensures such stakes become purely notional.

That I only review one SF play in the present collection (Susan Gray's excellent *Sum*) does not reflect the burgeoning world of often brilliant and stimulating SF drama. In the event I saw only three plays this year, an observation that again reflects the restrictions of having small children (indeed, the other two of our theatre 'outings' in 2014 were with the kids in mind: *Emile and the Detectives* and the *Slava Snowsnow*, both at the South Bank). And I can be honest. This indexes a bias, or prejudice, by which, my sensibilities having been shaped by cinema and (especially) TV, I prefer my acted drama in screen form. I sometimes joke with my friend Dan Rebellato, Professor of Theatre at Royal Holloway University of London no less, and a man who feels his day incomplete if he doesn't see three separate avant garde theatrical performances at three different dramatic spaces – that I find his love for the living stage incomprehensible. And he jokes in return that my obsession with science fiction strikes him exactly the same way. But where the joke is, I suspect, close to the truth for him, I'm not really baffled by his love for the theatre. On those rare occasions where I do see a play, and a story is told in the sweat and breath of present actors, I am always struck by the power of the occasion. In fact, it is probably that very power that disinclines me from going to see more live plays. It's like William Empson says, in his *Essays on Renaissance Literature*:

> It was quite frequent on the sands for one of the kids to bellow because Punch was too hard to take, and this unfortunate would be carried away by its nurse; but the elder children, when I was one, proud that they could take it, would laugh on till the final hanging of Punch as their Victorian parents had done at the same age. I have been secretly afraid of the theatre ever since, but I feel I know what it is about.

Both my undergraduate degree and the subject of my PhD were English Literature/Classics, and in both cases the Classics side was heavily inclined toward the theatrical: my UG dissertation was 'colour terms in Euripides' (exciting, no?) and my PhD looked at Robert Browning and (mostly) Aeschylus and Euripides. The thing about the Athenian stage is that it was a holy ritual as well as being the performance of a diverting narrative; and the heart of the holy ritual is fear – a timor divini either elevating or a debilitating, depending on the individual. People gather together and recite their resonant rote-learned lines in church, and in the theatre, and in both venues they do so to ward something off. It's the thing being warded that scares me, I suspect; though I wouldn't go so far as Empson in claiming quite so vehemently to know what it is about. The intervening screen (televisual, or cinematic) filters out much of this ancient numinous potency. Indeed, many of our screen texts are dimly aware of this fact, and respond by ramping up the volume. To capture the merest glimmer of the awful wonder of Lear's pentuplet 'never' thousands must die on screen, disaster and catastrophe must be hyperbolically bodied forth in global disaster, city-obliterating explosions and the like. It's a losing game, of course, and the more cinema increases the intensity the less we feel it. This, incidentally, is an occasion for relief rather than anything else; if we really felt the force of the deaths in *The Battle of the Five Armies*, *Guardians of the Galaxy* or *Transformers* we'd be catatonic by the end of the performance.

Still, if it seems to me that movies are losing heft and weight in direct proportion to their increasing running-times, I'm hardly the only one. Does it matter? Or put it this way: does it matter more for science fiction than for other branches of culture?

I'm tempted to say 'yes', if only to be consistent with myself. A decade ago I wrote the *Palgrave History of Science Fiction*, in which I argued (inter alia) that *Star Wars* represented a major Rubicon in the evolution of SF. Before that, and speaking very broadly, SF had been a literature of ideas, of extrapolation and transcendence rooted primarily in verbal texts, popular only with a relatively small group of aficionados who called themselves 'fans'. After that, through the 1980s and 1990s, SF shifted about on its axis to become a mass-culture phenomenon, much more widely consumed but (and this is the rub) as a visual mode. Relatively few people buy and read SF novels and short stories; everybody watches *Dr Who* and goes to see *Avatar* and Marvel Comics Universe films. This shift has, I think, advantages and disadvantages to it. Read as visual texts, movies like *Jupiter Rising* are, visually speaking, extraordinary and beautiful, even as they are (judged by such non-visual criteria as narrative, character, cogency and conceptual eloquence) muddled and bad. The eclipse of the latter categories by the former is not inevitable: *2001: A Space Odyssey* or *Stalker* are as visually stunning as they are content-rich and intellectually stimulating. But that eclipse does seem to be a feature of genre, and culture more largely, going forward.

This is part of a larger phenomenon, of course. Marshall McLuhan's is the name most often associated with this, but, for myself, I prefer the work of Walter J. Ong, cultural critic and Jesuit priest. Briefly, Ong argued that, just as the shift from orality to literacy in the ancient world produced vast structural changes in the logic of society and culture, so the on-going shift from literacy – script – to what Ong calls a new 'oral-electric' culture primarily visual will result in similar change. One consequence of the original shift from oral to literate culture was the stratification of those who had command of the new technologies (scribes, Ong calls them) and those that don't: the illiterate, now disenfranchised. But the advantages of literacy over orality are so manifold – in terms of clarity and distinctness, archiveability and facility – that Ong goes so far as to say that Christ came into the world at the time he did *in order to* take advantage of this shift: born into a culture still primarily oral but one on which the alphabet existed to give the Word, the *Logos*, its necessary social robustness and endurability: 'the precise time when psychological structures assured that his entrance would have the greatest opportunity to endure and flower.'[3] I bring God into the matter here not for theological reasons, but to contextualise what Ong says about a hoped-for return to an older model of orality. He yearns for it because he considers it sacred. Frank Kermode summarises: for Ong 'visuality and typography, desacralized the world. The oral Word is a Presence, the written word is not; the oral Word presents an interior, the typographical word a surface.'[4] What I like about this is its sense, contra McLuhan, that the present day's intensification of the logic of the visual is a *development* of the typographic world of the 20th-century, not a departure from it. The question is whether our culture is morphing into newer, less 'alphabetic' forms. Does the affectless post-Pomo flatness of *The Hobbit* trilogy, or the scrambled visual kaleidoscope of the perfectly empty *Transformers* franchise move genre in some new direction? Perhaps there is a return here to a mode of more immediate access that in turn informs a sort of *faceless* orality: what we might associate with social media like Twitter. Online interactions lose the alphabetic sequential rigour and logic; they function as emotional rather than intellectual megaphones. Poke your head into online interaction – about the new Star Wars movie, Dr Who's representation of women, Gamergate, the 2015 Hugos, anything you like – and what comes across most strongly is that people feel intensely and are moved to express those feelings with a vehemence that cannot comprehend that others might feel just as strongly in a different way. 'The characteristic mental disorder of alphabetic societies,' according to Ong, 'is

[3] Walter J Ong, *The Presence of the Word* (Yale Univ. Press 1968), 191

[4] Frank Kermode, 'Father Ong', in *Modern Essays* (Fontana 1971), 105

schizophrenia, but of analphabetic societies it is anger and polemicism. Old oral was very angry.' Since I can't really think of a neater encapsulation of the online culture surrounding genre in 2014 than 'Anger and Polemicism', I find myself wondering whether we aren't moving, in some sense, to a combination of oral choler and typographic flatness. Renaissance and Reformation scholars attacked one another with furious rage over things they believed mattered intensely – God in the world, how we are saved, how we must live. People today employ the same furious rage, and many of the same rhetorical tactics, over the issue of the crossguards on the lightsabre glimpsed, for less than a second, in the trailer to the forthcoming *Star Wars 7: The Force Awakens*.

Why do we get so worked up? Because, presumably, it matters to us to a degree larger than our capacity for tact and courtesy. Perhaps the communities surrounding SF and Fantasy *aren't* angrier and quicker-to-take-offence than they used to be. But they feel that way, to me. The Gamergate-Puppies is one reflection – a reaction, an intemperate kick-back – against a broader logic. I'm put in mind of something Orwell wrote (actually, the opening to the very last review he composed) of *Brideshead Revisited*:

> Within the last few decades, in countries like Britain or the United States, the literary intelligentsia has grown large enough to constitute a world in itself. One important result of this is that the opinions which a writer feels frightened of expressing are not those which are disapproved of by society as a whole. To a great extent, what is still loosely thought of as heterodoxy has become orthodoxy. It is nonsense to pretend, for instance, that at this date there is something daring and original in proclaiming yourself an anarchist, an atheist, a pacifist, etc. The daring thing, or at any rate the unfashionable thing, is to believe in God or to approve of the capitalist system. In 1895, when Oscar Wilde was jailed, it must have needed very considerable moral courage to defend homosexuality. Today it would need no courage at all: today the equivalent action would be, perhaps, to defend antisemitism. But this example that I have chosen immediately reminds one of something else – namely, that one cannot judge the value of an opinion simply by the amount of courage that is required in holding it.

That last sentiment is the really crucial one. SF and Fantasy have, it seems to me, been at the forefront of dramatising social, cultural and sexual diversity and difference as an imaginatively comprehensible possibility. That the rights with which people are endowed to life, liberty, the pursuit of happiness are not contingent upon their gender, the colour of their skin or their sexual orientation is so staggeringly obvious an observation, and (after a long hard-fought struggle for these rights) now so widely accepted by society, it hardy requires courage to believe it. And yet so many of our shared narratives are premised upon physical courage! So many of the stories we pretend to value put such premium on the ability and the will to fight, to maim, to kill. This is truer of games than other narratives, but it's true in films and books too. It may not be co-incidental that there are people who, realising on some level that supporting sexism, racism, homo- and transphobia and so on, requires *courage* in this day and age, then make the leap to believing that courage itself validates their odious opinions. What other values do games inculcate, apart from persistence and the ability to move your fingers really fast? But now I am in danger of simply repeating the points I make in my review, below, of Michael R. Underwood's inadvertently revealing portrait of 'geek culture': *Attack the Geek: a Ree Reyes Side-Quest*, reprinted below, so I'll move on.

I want, speculatively, to return to the question I posed above. Something in this stuff genuinely touches us. Something about it matters intensely to us. I wonder what? Permit me to hypothesise why, and what, by looking at Young Adult writing, one of the continuing cultural dominants of 2014. Although in fact, to excavate why this matters so much to so many, I think I'll need to go back beyond my year a little way. Because the focal point of YA passionate fandom is occupied, I'd suggest, by three texts, each of which became major cultural events (in genre, but in the wider world as well). I'm talking about the prodigious global success of *Harry Potter*, *The Hunger Games* and *Twilight*. Of these, the first interests me the most. The sheer scale of its popular success is, perhaps, only more staggering now that it's starting to wane and we can look back upon the phenomenon with a more objective eye. What was it about these novels that made them so huge? 'Because they're relatable,' says my thirteen-year-old daughter and she has a point: kids at school read stories about kids at a school (except, a better, more wonderful school where kids learn magic) and connect with them. But actually I wonder if there's something more particular going on here.

I have sometimes wondered if there is an unresolved contradiction in the *Harry Potter* books' attitude to 'pure blood' as a value and source of power. On the one hand, there is in these books a sustained, commendable critique of those Voldermortians (Voldermorticians?) and Malfoyers who believe that being 'pure blood' makes a person superior to mudbloods and muggles. Rowling makes the point repeatedly that they're idiots for thinking this; and quite right too. Plus you have Dumbledore's commendable and repeated insistence that a person is defined not by their birth but their actions. A bloodline is not some magic passport to special-ness or power. On the other hand is the fact that Potter's early life has been protected from being Death Ate by, precisely, his blood; or more precisely his mother's blood. And his aunt's. And Voldemort is undone by the same magic substance. 'He took your blood and rebuilt his living body with it!' explains Dead-Dumbledore; 'your blood in his veins, Harry, Lily's protection inside both of you!'[5] So it turns out a bloodline is a magic passport to special-ness or power after all. It just has to be the right bloodline! Which, when we come to think of it, is precisely what the pure blood brigade have always claimed.

I still think this is a problem, only now I think I'd frame it slightly differently. It's going to sound oblique (and in order to explain it I'm going to quote C K Chesterton at length, which may simply put you off), but bear with me. So: I think that, amongst other things, Rowling is trying to do a Dickensian something with her YA fantasy, not just formally but in terms of an agenda of social justice: girls are as clever as boys; racial purity is a noisome and destructive lie; fairness, decency, friendship and love are as important on the social as the personal level. I'd even be prepared to believe that Rowling is self-consciously 'doing' Dickens: big novels, bursting with characters and incident and so on. But actually I think that Rowling doesn't have the heart of Dickens. I think she has the heart of Scott. And to explain what I mean, here comes the long passage from Chesterton's 1906 book on Charles Dickens. It's one of my favourite pieces of critical prose, actually, with

[5] Rowling *Harry Potter and the Deathly Hallows*, 568

respect to Dickens but also, really, tout court; so I'm not going to apologise for the length.

'Of all these nineteenth-century writers there is none, in the noblest sense, more democratic than Walter Scott. As this may be disputed, and as it is relevant, I will expand the remark. There are two rooted spiritual realities out of which grow all kinds of democratic conception or sentiment of human equality. There are two things in which all men are manifestly and unmistakably equal. They are not equally clever or equally muscular or equally fat, as the sages of the modern reaction (with piercing insight) perceive. But this is a spiritual certainty, that all men are tragic. And this, again, is an equally sublime spiritual certainty, that all men are comic. No special and private sorrow can be so dreadful as the fact of having to die. And no freak or deformity can be so funny as the mere fact of having two legs. Every man is important if he loses his life; and every man is funny if he loses his hat, and has to run after it. And the universal test everywhere of whether a thing is popular, of the people, is whether it employs vigorously these extremes of the tragic and the comic. Shelley, for instance, was an aristocrat, if ever there was one in this world. He was a Republican, but he was not a democrat: in his poetry there is every perfect quality except this pungent and popular stab. For the tragic and the comic you must go, say, to Burns, a poor man. And all over the world, the folk literature, the popular literature, is the same. It consists of very dignified sorrow and very undignified fun. Its sad tales are of broken hearts; its happy tales are of broken heads.

These, I say, are two roots of democratic reality. But they have in more civilised literature, a more civilised embodiment of form. In literature such as that of the nineteenth century the two elements appear somewhat thus. Tragedy becomes a profound sense of human dignity. The other and jollier element becomes a delighted sense of human variety. The first supports equality by saying that all men are equally sublime. The second supports equality by observing that all men are equally interesting.

In this democratic aspect of the interest and variety of all men, there is, of course, no democrat so great as Dickens. But in the other matter, in the idea of the dignity of all men, I repeat that there is no democrat so great as Scott. This fact, which is the moral and enduring magnificence of Scott, has been astonishingly overlooked. His rich and dramatic effects are gained in almost every case by some grotesque or beggarly figure rising into a human pride and rhetoric. The common man, in the sense of the paltry man, becomes the common man in the sense of the universal man.

He declares his humanity. For the meanest of all the modernities has been the notion that the heroic is an oddity or variation, and that the things that unite us are merely flat or foul. The common things are terrible and startling, death, for instance, and first love: the things that are common are the things that are not commonplace. Into such high and central passions the comic Scott character will suddenly rise. Remember the firm and almost stately answer of the preposterous Nicol Jarvie when Helen Macgregor seeks to browbeat him into condoning lawlessness and breaking his bourgeois decency. That speech is a great monument of the middle class. Molière made M. Jourdain talk prose; but Scott made him talk poetry. Think of the rising and rousing voice of the dull and gluttonous Athelstane when he answers and overwhelms De Bracy. Think of the proud appeal of the old beggar in the Antiquary *when he rebukes the duellists. Scott was fond of describing kings in disguise. But all his characters are kings in disguise. He was, with all his errors, profoundly possessed with the old religious conception, the only possible democratic basis, the idea that man himself is a king in disguise.*

In all this Scott, though a Royalist and a Tory, had in the strangest way, the heart of the Revolution. For instance, he regarded rhetoric, the art of the orator, as the immediate weapon of the oppressed. All his poor men make grand speeches, as they did in the Jacobin Club, which Scott would have so much detested. And it is odd to reflect that he was, as an author, giving free speech to fictitious rebels while he was, as a stupid politician, denying it to real ones. But the point for us here is this that all this popular sympathy of his rests on the graver basis, on the dark dignity of man. "Can you find no way?" asks Sir Arthur Wardour of the beggar when they are cut off by the tide. "I'll give you a farm... I'll make you rich."... "Our riches will soon be equal," says the beggar, and looks out across the advancing sea.

Now, I have dwelt on this strong point of Scott because it is the best illustration of the one weak point of Dickens. Dickens had little or none of this sense of the concealed sublimity of every separate man. Dickens' sense of democracy was entirely of the other kind; it rested on the other of the two supports of which I have spoken. It rested on the sense that all men were wildly interesting and wildly varied. When a Dickens character becomes excited he becomes more and more himself. He does not, like the Scott beggar, turn more and more into man. As he rises he grows more and more into a gargoyle or grotesque. He does not, like the fine speaker in Scott, grow more classical as he grows more passionate, more universal as he grows more intense.'

The response the beggar gives Sir Arthur Wardour (from *The Antiquary*, of course) is so brilliant and powerful, Chesterton is absolutely right to pick it out. Sends chills up my spine. But the properly salient passage here is this one: 'Scott was fond of describing kings in disguise. But all his characters are kings in disguise. He was, with all his errors, profoundly possessed with the old religious conception, the only possible democratic basis, the idea that man himself is a king in disguise.'

This, I think, is the ground of the strange 'relatability' of Rowling's globally popular novels: not class, or race, or gender, or school experience or anything like that; and neither because of any quasi-Dickensian textual campaigning against social injustice, creditable though that aspect of the novel-series is. It's that Rowling says to her child readers, repeatedly and eloquently: you are kings in disguise. You possess magical validity and force. And her child-readers grok it, because kids understand the Scottian insight better than adults do. Maybe that's because they are closer to the time when all human beings share perfect, imperial elevation and power, when the whole of creation bends its efforts to placating and maintaining them – when we are babies, of course. Or maybe it is a more Chestertonian 'old religious conception', the same numinous if unconscious awareness that Wordsworth ascribes to childhood in the Immortality Ode. At any rate, it goes some way to explaining (I think) why Harry has to be the central character, rather than Hermione. Hermione is too obviously special: too clever, too multi-talented and self-disciplined and grounded and so on. Potter is the chosen one not despite but *because* he is so ordinary; because (the novels are saying) mere common ordinariness, like yours, like mine, is the absolute ground of magical royalty. We are all kings in disguise.

I think the equally popular, equally enduring Narnia books say the same things, for (where Lewis was concerned) equally Chestertonian reasons. Lewis' ordinary English children are kings and queens of Narnia, not because Lewis thought representative parliamentary democracy delinquent and wicked, but because his faith told him that we are all of us, the entire demos, kings and queens of Narnia.

The *Hunger Games* books naturally take a less monarchical view of the same state of affairs. Katniss is a US President in disguise, the old American conception of possibility given new dramatic bite by exaggerating the nature of the obstacles that stand between the Log Cabin and the White House. *Twilight* is the least progressive of the triad, because the only royalty it is interested in is the inward-looking private life version in which a girl is crowned, and set on a pedestal, by a special boy. But the case can be broadened. This, or something close to it, is what our most beloved SF and Fantasy gives us. 'Man,' Hazlitt said in *Characterstics* (1823), 'is an everlasting contradiction to himself. His senses centre in himself, his ideas reach to the ends of the universe; so that he is torn in pieces between the two.' Hazlitt concludes gloomily ('there is no possibility of it ever being otherwise') but SF disagrees. In this literature alone are there ideas that actually do reach to the ends of the universe, physically and temporally, become actualised as stories *about us*. And this is what gives SF its power: its imaginative capacity to harmonize and heal this everlasting human contradiction. That's worth raving over, surely.

We've moved, rather, away from the business of establishing protocols for reviewing. To rave about a title, in a strange way, is to belittle your subject; the reader of the review will obtain a clearer sense of the reviewer's froth and enthusiasm than of the book under consideration. By the same token, writing a killing critique of a book or film may well provoke the sympathies of your reader for the object of scorn: it's natural to want to come to the aid of somebody who's receiving a kicking. Surely it can't be *that* bad. The middle line is the most effective, in terms of conveying the pros and cons of a given title. Going back over these reviews, in order to tidy them, modify them and generally titivate them for publication in volume form, I was struck by how often I use the phrase 'your mileage may vary', or alternatives thereof. This is not to suggest that value judgements are inevitably subjective. Rather it is to recognise that different kinds of books are written for different sorts of audience, and that I – a middle-aged, balding man – am not being specifically addressed by many of the YA, girl-focussed titles published in 2014. I could, perhaps, have done more to uncover my inner 14-year-old girl, but this was a task for which I simply didn't have the energy. Beyond that, of course, reviews must strive to be fair: to approach the book without prejudice, to review the book as written and not condemn it for differing from the way you might have written it yourself. But coeval with fairness is truth, and a review must above all be truthful. Bad books must be reviewed as such, and not excused (because the author is a friend, because you're a fan of the author's other stuff and really wanted this one to be good, because you think the book is in some sense 'important', to articulate tribal or ideological loyalty or affirm affiliation… and so on). Good books should be lauded, in order to bring them to the attention of as many readers as possible. In both cases the review must proceed not by mere assertion, as should not rely only on the authority or otherwise of the reviewer. I admit I break this last rule myself a few times in the reviews that follow: not that I ever expect you to trust my judgement simply because I'm me, but that in some of the shorter pieces I haven't given myself enough room to adumbrate the evidential base, the quotations and analyses, that lead to the judgements. In most cases, though, I do.

There's an obvious problem with the truth criterion, though. Peter Porter says somewhere: 'in all truth-telling there is waste of art'. A review needs to be truthful, but it needs art too: it has a duty to being readable, entertaining piece of prose in its own right. This last thing is the hardest to achieve, not just because writing (for example) comic prose is much harder than you might think, but because the converse to Porter's aphorism comes into play. To more art one works in, the more dilute the truth-telling becomes. A happy medium is desirable, though not always achievable.

There's one other thing I want to say before I bring this overlong introduction to an end. It is to stress again the partiality of reviewing. I don't just mean in the obvious sense, that the opinions expressed in these pages are only one person's opinions (that you should triangulate them with other opinions for a better sense of the books under discussion – or, indeed, quadrilate, or –ilate them to geometrical figures of more sides even than that). This goes without saying, of course. I mean partial in another sense – to speak of the inevitable belatedness of reviews. Here's something Northtrop Frye once said:

> The basis of critical knowledge is the direct experience of literature, certainly, but experience as such is never adequate. We are always reading *Paradise Lost* with a hangover or seeing *King Lear* with an incompetent Cordelia or disliking a novel because some scene in it connects with something suppressed in our memories, and our most deeply satisfying responses are often made in childhood, to be seen later as immature over-reacting... As a structure of knowledge, then, criticism, like other structures of knowledge, is in one sense a monument to a failure of experience, a tower of Babel or one of

> the "ruins of time" which, in Blake's phrase, 'build mansions in eternity'.[6]

I think this resonates so strongly with me partly because science fiction was something I fell in love with as a child-reader. I still love it; still write it and write about it. But I'm increasingly conscious of the ways in which the exercise is based upon a kind of structural hermeneutic inadequacy. 'Our most deeply satisfying responses are often made in childhood, to be seen later as immature over-reacting' is almost a too perfect thumbnail of the adult apprehension of SF; and SF criticism always a kind of running-to-catch-up uttering various post-facto justifications. What's neat about this Frye quotation is the sense it conveys that, actually, all criticism is in the business of doing this. And the reviews in this volume are no exception.

Adam Roberts,
June 2015

[6] Northrop Frye, *The Critical Path: an Essay on the Social Context of Literary Criticism* (Indiana University Press 1971), 27

Joe Abercrombie
Half A King

Half a review. Prince Yarrrvi, descended perchance from pirates, is set the task of regaining his Aberkingdom by an Abercruel fate. Though born an Abercripple (and thus considered the titular 'half' mentioned in the book's title) Yarrrvi must use his Abercleverness and his one Abercapable hand to regain the Abercrown he never Abercraved in the first place, overcoming abadversity, hardship, double-Abercrossing and the general Abercrappiness of the Abercosmos' attitudes to mortals. Trust no one; for even those Aberclosest to you can betray you into slabery, sorry, slavery. In a nutshell, this is a lean, chilled, typically well-abercrafted tale. The world Joe has Abercreated is Abercrisply evoked; the Abercharacters work well; the violence, though Abercranked down a notch from *First Law* (this being YA), is Abercrimson enough for most palates. Most of all it's immensely, rather disgracefully readable: gripping and twisty. An Abercracking yarn. If I had one Abercriticism to make, it would be that

Nina Allan
The Race

This is one of the best novels published this year, in any genre. I can't think of a pithier way of putting it than that.

I'll tell you what I consider the acid test where such judgement is concerned: having read the novel, and been very impressed, I've waited several months before jotting down these review thoughts. The book is still fresh in my mind. *The Race* worked its way under my skin – metaphorically, I mean; not literally. That would be gross. Allan's writing is controlled, evocative and effective; her emotional intelligence as a novelist is second to none; the story is very readable and narratively satisfying. But there's something more, and it's the something more-ness that makes this novel stand out. Linda Hutcheons' venerable contrast between crime fiction as epistemological (because fundamentally fascinated by questions and answers, finding stuff out, uncovering secrets and so on) and science fiction as ontological (because fascinated in the being of thing, worldbuilding, describing the possibilities of alternate existences) still has some purchase, I think, in 21st-century genre. If I say that Allan has written something more hauntological than ontological it's not because I want to try and peg her as an aridly Derridean writer. I mean that our sense of the world she creates is as much shaped by its revenant apparitions as its solidities. I don't just mean the past, though that's part of it. Allan is nonpareil on the way the present is riddled through with the might-have-been and wonder-where-she-is-nows that we might call regret, but which has a much more plangent force in her view of the world. She knows that it is the reverberations of affect that define us, not this event or that. *The Race* is a masterclass in the potency of juxtaposition.

On the simplest level of structure, this means that the novel is built out of a series of distinct but overlapping narratives, set in their own realities, like those tricks with differently-coloured spotlights all being focussed on one point on the stage and becoming white. We start in a near-future and I think alt-reality England, somewhere on the south coast – the town Sapphire, based on Hastings apparently, though I (having grown up in East Kent) got more of a Folkestone vibe. Jenna Hoolman earns her living making the specialised gloves worn by 'runners' in the lucrative but at best semi-legal business of smart-dog racing. These dogs are genetically engineered to be clever and have a bond with their runners There are hints that they were developed as weapons of war, and further research has been banned by the government so the whole industry has a twilit, semi-legal quality. Jen's rather brutal brother Del is a smartdog trainer, and the story of this first section is driven by the kidnapping of Del's three-year-old daughter Lumey. We are led to believe that she has been taken by one or other underground dog-racing syndicate over Del's unpaid debts; but we also learn that Lumey is a telepath, able to communicate without the tech-devices (for instance, gloves) that most runners use. The trauma of Lumey's disappearance is extremely well evoked on those left behind; Del is thoughtless, violent and occasionally worse without ever becoming a cartoon monster or quite losing our sympathy; but best of all is Jenna, a superb piece of characterisation.

One thing *The Race* absolutely gets inside is the feel of life lived as a working-class woman in modern Britain. That this should be so remarkable is itself a fact that does not reflect glory upon the novel today. Science fiction is (rightly) fascinated by diversity and alterity, and many writers work to explore what life is like from other than straight, white, male perspectives. Alterities of ethnic, gender and sexual experience are commonplace: women writers, writers of colour and LGBT writers are finally being recognised – a recent development in our culture, this, and very welcome. Class, though, is the Cinderella still at home in amongst the ashes. Where the culture industries used to be almost exclusively the domain of straight white middle-class men, they are increasingly being permeated by middle class women, middle class artists of colour and middle class figures of LGBT orientation. There are practical reasons for this: it is simply harder today to make a living as a writer than once it was. The result is that, broadly speaking, people who write do so because they have the financial security to do so, independent wealth, a day-job, a supportive partner or patron, government subsidy. I'm not suggesting there's anything wrong with being middle class per se: I am myself the most middle class person imaginable. I'm saying that it is culturally distorting; that it tacitly established the middle class worldview as default, and middle class anxieties and concerns as the real drivers of art. Nick Mamatas only exaggerates a little when he says that there are only two working class

SF writers working in the USA today: himself and Saladin Ahmed. The situation is certainly no better in the class-bound United Kingdom.

We rightly prize diversity of outlook in our SF, and *The Race* gives us precisely that. Not characters whose financial context is mysteriously always already provided for (as in Jane Austen), nor characters creeping like Beckettian tramps through a landscape of dystopian hyperbolic awfulness. But working class characters doing their best with limited resources, getting by from day to day. Dog racing is well chosen as a community focus here. Royal Ascot for the upper classes; Sandown Park for the middle and dog-racing for the proletariat. But the whole world of Kentish quotidiana is beautifully written.

A separate yet hauntologically related story is set in present-day Hastings, and concerns a writer called Christy Peller, returning to the town in which she grew up following a bereavement. Through her reminiscence we get a translated version of the first narrative: a bright woman growing up with a controlling sometimes violent brother Derek, coping with the stress of everything by creating her own imaginary version of the town inside her head. Derek was engaged to be married to a girl called Linda, with whom he was smitten. Her disappearance still haunts Christy, decades later: did Derek murder her, because she was seeing someone else, or because she wanted to escape his stifling and controlling personality? Or did she manage to get away? She speaks to a journalist called Alex Adeyemi, who also grew up in Hastings. He dated Linda before she got involved with Derek. A third section in the novel gives us his narrative, memories of the pervasive low-level racism that blighted his childhood, his failed marriage, his fears for his own daughter. Finally the novel ends with a return to the alt-England of section one: in the north of the country, kidnapped Lumey is now a young woman called Maree with no memory of her former life. She sails the seas to 'Thalia', wherever that is, where she and other 'new race' empaths will fulfil the shadowy pseudo-scientific programme for which they have been raised. She interacts with her fellow passengers, and worries about the giant leviathans that live in the deep and that have smashed some previous ships to fragments.

The beauty of *The Race* is the way it sets-up a straightforward reading (that this novel is Christy's story, bookended by two examples of the Sapphire-set fantastika that she writes) in order to shuffle about our assumptions. I don't mean the Metafiction 101 sideshuffle –

though Allan is a writer who does live in Hastings, and we can assume that in part this is a novel in which she looks back upon her young life. I mean something more carefully balanced. My sense of reading the novel was to take Sapphire as the baseline, and to explore the oddities of contemporary life (those limitations of empathy of our non-telepathic species that manifest as sexism and racism, for instance) as the salient aberrations. But this is to respond to this excellent work in too clumsy a manner. It is not about the priority of these different worlds, but their juxtaposition; not about writing but about reading and understanding and unsealing one's eyes; not about the corks bobbing on the surface but the gigantic telepathic cetaceans slipping magisterially through the waters beneath. A tremendous novel.

Scott K. Andrews
Time Bomb

First instalment in the forthcoming YA 'Time Bomb' trilogy, this is a genre yarn best described as okay-ish. Various young adventurers from various time-periods are dragged into our era, and thence to the English Civil War. It's a book low on original ideas, although high-enough on incident to keep itself readable. But it bogged down for me in a couple of writerly clumsinesses. There was stylistic clumsiness of the too-many-adjectives, too-many-adverbs sort:

> Dora cracked open the **heavy oak kitchen** door, poked her head out into the **stone-flagged, wooden-panelled** corridor, and listened **intently**. [11]

Three adjectives for a door is three too many; and the urge to replace simpler terms like 'opened' and 'looked out' with what one fondly imagines to be more vigorous, vivid ones like 'cracked open' and 'poked' is, broadly speaking, to be resisted I think. Then there are clumsinesses in the 'keeping the reader in necessary suspense' stakes:

> Kaz turned his gaze to Steve. 'And you?'
> 'I plead the fifth,' said Steve, with an apologetic shrug. 'It will all become clear eventually, but for now I have to remain enigmatic. Sorry. Look there'll be time for a full explanation later but basically you two can travel in time.' [63]

This might bother me less if the clumsily deferred explanation, when it came, were a little less *bleeeeuuuurgh* ('They found an asteroid out in the Kuiper Belt. It was composed of a kind of substance that messes with time somehow' [237]). So that's: *messes with time somehow*. Okey-dokey.

Adam Baker
Impact

Sentries manned the wire.

Thrillerland. Zombietown. The Literocalypse has come. No time now prosewise for bells, whistles. Main verbs. Prepositions. Personal pronouns. Fuck that. It's clipped sentences, now. Manly sentences.

A pretentious Literary Novel climbed the chain-link. Pages streaked with purple prose and similes.

'Look at him. Fucking Proust.'

The rotting canonical text had reached the razor wire. Barbs tore its binding.

'Give me some red tip. I want to light this fucker up.'

Standard full-metal jacket rounds swapped for a clip of incendiary cartridges.

'Proust? No zombies in *that* fuckheap.'

'No last minute flights in an antique B-52. No plan to drop an atom bomb to wipe out the source of the zombie virus. No plane crashing in Death Valley leaving the crew exposed to heat, infighting and the endless zombie threat in that pile of memorious shit.'

'It's all madelaines, madelaines, *fucking* madelaines. Far as the eye can see.'

Crank the charging handle. Cross-hairs centre on the spine of the book. Complex emotions and nuanced writing. Pitiless like a shark.

Lower the cross-hairs. Centre on his open page.

Gunshot.

Skullburst. Book blown apart. Paper confetti and magnesium fire. Proust's fucking silly writing landed on the grass in pieces.

'Give me a drink.'

'All we got left is Bud.'

Tab-crack. Head thrown back.

'Fucking piss.'

Can crush. Belch.

A fresh survey of the crowd of literary fiction pushing at the fence.

Cross-hairs centre on a James Joyce short story, couldn't be more than 10-pages long. 'We should hose those fuckers in aviation fuel and toss a match. Save some ammo.'

'Fucking connecting particles. Fucking James Wood. Bollocks the lot of it. Main verbs! Nuance! Who needs it? Fuckers.' *Blam!*

Leigh Bardugo
Ruin and Rising (The Grisha: Book 3)

This book is not aimed at people like me. Middle-aged men with thinning hair and bags beneath their eyes. Professors of literature and old farts who have read Pushkin, Tolstoy and Nabokov and think that's how 'it' (let's say, for the sake of argument, Russia) should be done. There are people – other people than I, young people, eager people – for whom books such as this *are* written. People who don't experience a sinking of the heart at the dead facility with which commercially successful franchises can be mashed together (of *Grisha* Book 1, *The Stylist* magazine lamented 'it's like *The Hunger Games* meets *Potter* meets *Twilight* meets *Lord of the Rings*.' Wait. Did I say 'lamented'? I meant: *gushed enthusiastically*). There are people for whom Bardugo's Fantasy-Russia 'Ravka' makes a refreshing change to Westeros and District 13 and wherever it is Divergent is set (Chicago, is it?). People who find the Goth intensity and doomed love story of the main character Alina dreamy and wondrous, not cloying and shallow. Bardugo's villain is called 'The Darkling', and it's nothing to do with Keats' bird. It's because he's *dark*; and Evil in this universe is *a literal darkness* ('The Shadow Fold') and Good is manifested as a hero with the skills of a 'Sun-Summoner', like the refrain from that song by the cockernay Chimney Sweep in *Mary Poppins*. Because some people don't find crashing literalness of imagination deadening. They think it's cool. Good luck to those people. May they enjoy this turgid, drawn-out, talky finale to the Grisha trilogy. May they likewise enjoy their lives, and the company of their fellows; may they laugh and dance and drink wine together in the sunshine.

Gregory Benford and Larry Niven, *Bowl of Heaven*

Two big names in SF collaborate on a Big Dumb Object novel. The titular 'bowl' is a titanic construction built around a red star and travelling through the galaxy collecting life-forms. It is, in effect, half a Dyson sphere. Appropriate to this conceit, Benford and Niven have here written a half-arsed novel. Less BDO, more *BOOO*!

The thing is, I've a soft spot for these kinds of rude *Rama* retreads – 'Re-rendezvous With Rama' – and even Niven's hilariously cack-handed writing and plotting can't spoil the original *Ringworld* novel for me, where traces of grandeur still manage to cling, like wisps of morning fog, around the main idea (I say nothing of the myriad sequels, which are all terrible). BDOs are cool; scale and sublimity and the chance to let yourself wander, imaginatively speaking, around a varied and beguiling environment. *Bowl of Heaven*, though, is lamentably bad. There are two different levels on which it is simply not yet ready to be published. One is the level of story. We start with a sub-light interstellar spaceship called *SunSeeker*, on its way from Earth to a planet called Glory. Key crewmembers are woken from hibernation because the ship's trajectory, in a co-incidence the scale of the cosmos licenses us to call 'bollocks', has crossed paths with the Bowl of Heaven. Since there's some question as to whether supplies will last the rest of the *SunSeeker*'s voyage, on account of whoever supplied said supplies Earthside being obviously an idiot, the crew decide to fly their starship, complete with its sleeping cargo of thousands of human settlers, into the Bowl. This they do by nipping up the superheated plasma stream of the BDO's exhaust. You see, the 'bowl' has a big hole in its base, and mirrors in its concave inner surface focussing the starlight back on a spot on the star, which in turn shoots out the colossal plasma jet that moves the whole thing through space. The motion forward exactly counteracts the tendency of the bowl to fall into the gravitational well of the star, keeping the system in equilibrium. On the other hand, late in the book some of the Earthers see a sort of home movie of the Bowl being built, and there's no explanation of how the structure is kept in its orbit during the eons-long construction. No matter. Surely we can agree that flying up the stellar exhaust pipe is a stupid thing to do.

Of course, we know that Benford and Niven (I like to think of them as 'Nivbenford', the result of a tragic matter-transporter malfunction) need to get their human characters aboard ~~Rama~~, ~~Ringworld~~, ~~Orbitsville~~, the Bowl of Heaven as soon as possible, so they can have Adventures. Let's give them a bye for that. The problem is once the characters are there the story gets flushed down the cosmic toilet-bowl of heaven in short order. Nothing very much happens. The characters are so flat and interchangeable that not even the authors are able to keep them distinct. The landing party is a group of ten people [87] that immediately splits up, main character Cliff Kammash taking four with him, and Beth Marble taking, er, five with her. What? Sometimes the authors forget that Cliff is called Cliff and call him Carl [for instance on p.327]. Individuals specified as being in one group are casually referred to as being in the other group. One character is killed by native life forms, watched helplessly by other characters from the far side of a towering transparent wall. Those same characters later refer back to the event as if there had been no wall. Several events happen twice in quick succession, with slightly different characters, as if Nivbenford was trying out alternate possibilities only to forget to delete the less favoured one. The captain leaves the bridge, and a few pages later leaves the bridge. No sooner have the landing party arrived than they spend literally days trying to open a closed hatch (to, unless I misread, outer space) by burning it with seemingly inexhaustible lasers. It turns out they can't; but I don't know why they were even trying. There's little overall shape to the story, and only at the end do we discover (hah! ahaha!) that there is no end to the story either, for it is to be continued in an indeterminate number of sequels.

I mentioned two things, and the second is the worldbuilding. This is more deplorable, in a way, since the novel really only exists to display the cool BDO. But Nivbenford seem to have run out of space on the back of the envelope they used to plan this structure. It's big: 'bigger than the orbit of Mercury' [34]. To be precise 'it covered a perimeter about the size of Earth's orbit' [247]. Which is certainly bigger than the orbit of Mercury. It rotates in nine days [247] except on p 315 where it rotates 'in about ten days'. How is the implausibly earth-like atmosphere kept inside? A barrier is stretched across the inside of the bowl, like clingfilm. Imagine the size of the roll they must have used! Ah, but how does the bowl *steer* itself, slow down to pick up new life forms, stop etc? We're not told, presumably because it can't. Out of what improbably rigid material is the bowl made, to prevent it breaking-up? Again we're not told, though we are vouchsafed that the construction of the Bowl entailed 'girders... scaffolds... crossbars... joists and brackets the size of planets' [242]. Pull the other one. Nivbenford's imaginations have failed them, and they've reverted to an Empire State Building sized construction rather than a solar-system sized one. This novel puts the 'ow!' in 'bowl' and the 'heave' in 'heaven'. If I were you I wouldn't touch this Bowl of Heaven with a barge-pole. Of heaven.

Robert Jackson Bennett
City of Stairs

There's a writer who's sure all that glitters is gold
And he's writing a city of stai-airs.
When he gets there he knows, if the bookstores are closed
Go online, he can get what he came for.
Oo-oo-ooh, oo-oo-ooh, and he's writing a ci-i-ty of stairs.

[*Jangle-jangle-guitar-strummy*]
Ooh, it makes me wonder,
Ooh, it makes me wonder.

It does make me wonder, too: in a good sense. This enjoyable and absorbing novel is set in a Fantasy-ized sort-of-Russia, chief city Bulikov: a land whose spiritual reality has been ripped from it during a war with their former colony, godless Saypur (a Fantasy-ized sort-of version of the materialist West). And if I finished the book wondering whether its very strengths don't go to prove that Worldbuilding Alone, no matter how cool and intricate, cannot carry a novel the whole distance...? Well; that's probably just me. In case saying so makes my praise looks like the faint-and-therefore-damning variety, I'll reiterate it, unfaintly: the worldbuilding here is exceptionally cool.

In olden Bulikov, the gods were real, and divine magic sustained the social and material infrastructure of life. Once Saypur found a way to kill off the six divinities, not only did things like medical care and the sewage system stop working, reality itself fractured. Mass death, famine, invasion: fast-forward some decades to the start of the novel and the new Saypur ruling class have declared it illegal even to mention that there were once gods. Bulikov is now a strangely dislocated cityscape, filled (*vide* the book's title) with stairs that go nowhere, disjunctured walls, massy blocks of unconnected architecture, only partially re-fitted to supply the exigencies of city life for the surviving population. The land is poor and oppressed and the people are chafing under the imperial yoke. The opening chapter is set in a courtroom, where a Bulikov trader is being prosecuted for displaying a symbol that might be interpreted as the sigil of one of the unmentionable, vanished gods.

But proceedings are interrupted when (*duh*! *duh*! *DUHRR*!) a famous Saypur scholar of all things Bulikovian, one Efram Pangyui, is discovered murdered.

An investigator is dispatched by the Saypur authorities to get to the bottom of the crime: a woman called Shara (in a slightly strained, even melodramatic touch it turns out that she is the great-granddaughter of Kaj, the Saypur warrior who somehow managed to develop the wonder-weapon that effected the deicide). Shara has a bodyguard, Sigrud: a barbarian of few words (rather Groot-like in some scenes; though in others somewhat more talkative) who seemed to me a little too self-consciously pitched at us as a 'future fan favourite!' I assume Bennett chose 'Bulikov' as a name for his city to honour Mikhaíl Bulgakov; that's pretty bold, if so. Certainly the novel never quite rises either to Master or even Margarita levels of powerfully strange. I also assumed, when reading, that Bennett was inspired by Piranesi's Carceri:

That's what kept flashing onto my mind's eye, at any rate, as I read. That, and a grittier, more Russian version of this:

One reason the worldbuilding works so well is that it gets not only the material details and consistency right; it gets the atmosphere right too. The story takes a little while to pick up momentum, but once it does it rolls very nicely along. Good book.

There are some problems, though, too. At its beginning *City of Stairs* perhaps reads too derivatively like a Fantasy version of *Gorky Park*: Shara investigates, overcomes inertia and opposition, pushes on despite high-up warnings, survives assassination attempts and so on. She runs into (another slightly strained co-incidence) her old college boyfriend, now a wealthy Continental trader with factories producing a rare and valuable commodity: stainless steel. There's a deal of procedural stuff. Then after 100 pages or so of that the tone and pace shift a little jarringly: not all the gods are dead; revolution is in the air; magical artefacts are being stored in secret *Raiders-of-the-Lost-Ark*-last-scene warehouses that nobody knows about except that actually everybody seems to know about them.

Shara keeps 'calling' her aunt, who coincidentally is the head of Saypur Intelligence Services, with a magic viewer that's supposed only to be used for dire emergencies. There are attempts at metaphysical profundity that don't quite work; although at the same time the pace picks up from the rather sluggish opening. Bennett only partly squares the circle of bringing his readers up to speed with the complicated backstory and worldbuilding; which is to say, he can't quite resist the infodumpy aside, the as-you-know-Bob (or as-you-know-Boris) dialogue. There are a few too many moments when Shara stops to recapitulate what has happened so far and why it is important; or draws up lists – seriously, itemised and numbered lists – of her options for proceeding. It is sometimes wondrous; and sometimes a little jingle-jangly-strummy as it moves from set-piece to set-piece.

I recommend it, though: I enjoyed it plenty. Although I can't quite work out whether the symbolic translation from West/Former USSR into Saypur/Bulikov is muddled in an imaginatively debilitating way, or eloquently complex and tangled. The novel elides, I fear rather inchoately, our sense of 'Russia' as both *more* spiritual/mystic/religious than the West, and at the same time less so: godless Communism; dialectical materialism; Stalin's famines and gulags. The loss of the gods of this realm channel the 21st-century sense of all those towering Soviet Heroes, whose statues were literally pulled down, leaving a country dislocated, prey to mafia (Bennett calls them 'warlords'), confused about its past. But at the same time, it is Communism itself that dislocated the ancient, god-haunted land of Russia. The West, likewise, occupies a blurry double-state. We're told that Saypur was forced to develop materially and scientifically because it didn't have gods: that on the Continent the gods simply magicked the cities' sewage away, but on Saypur they had to dig proper sewers. So, when the gods disappeared Saypur was well-placed to survive, and the Continent struggled. But the notion that Asia somehow 'had it easy' whilst Europe and the USA put in the hard graft inventing civilisation is a pretty rum one; as is the symbolic identification of the West with atheistical materialism (no Jesusland?) and Asia with soft-eyed reality-bending religious submission. We might call that, oh I don't know, pick a word, 'orientalism'. Are we take 'materialism' here as a cipher for consumerism, against which the USSR held out with the support of their nomenklatura, until the wall fell and their lives went to shit? Seems like an odd position, considering (for example) the fact that modern Russia has exactly the same Gini coefficient as the modern US. But, see, this is precisely the problem. I should stop trying to think through the implications of Bennett's worldbuilding, and just enjoy it for itself. So I do that. Even if it means the novel thereby drifts into a pleasant-pastime space, rather than a something-interesting-to-say-about-the-world space.

Big Hero 6 (dir. Don Hall and Chris Williams)

There's a lot of love 'out there' for this movie, so I'll sound merely grumpy when I record that I liked it but didn't love it. The Japamerican design work is certainly cool; and there are some laugh-aloud moments (I laughed! *Out loud*!) in the middle portion, all of them associated with the Baymax character, and the loudest laughs in my corner of the cinema provoked by a sequence where low battery power renders the medical robot, in effect, drunk. Ah, but. But: I thought the throughline story weak, the moral Bildungsfilm of 14-year-old protagonist Hiro Hamada abrupt to the point of jerkiness (in his anger he reprograms his robot to *kill* the villain! Then he instantly realises the ethical delinquency of this action, and *changes it back*! That's it!) and unconvincing, and the action sequences weirdly uninvolving. But that's just me. Everyone else loves it. You will too.

And to double-down on my grumpiness by adding-in spoilers: the 'villain' is driven to villainy by the fact that his daughter has vanished into the weird dimension between the two matter transporter portals. He's reputedly the world's smartest scientist, yet he decides to don a kabuki mask and terrorise the city rather than, let's say, look for a way to retrieve his daughter? We assume from the cues the movie provides that he's been involved in developing said portals, and he's for instance able to resurrect one and set it to destroy a university: but it doesn't occur to him to at least take a peek inside? In a related grump: are we to assume that the Baymax floating inside the mystery dimension, having gifted its green 'good' programme chip back to Hiro, is left only with its kill!-kill!-kill! karate *red* chip inside it? So that's a killer evil Baymax floating through the mystery dimension to... wait, really? And here's a more personal snark: in the movie's big car chase sequence, humour is generated by the fact that the driver of the car in which our heroes are fleeing the bad guy is an obsessive-compulsive neat-oid type, who stops at the red lights despite the imminent peril behind him and so on. I, the author of this very review, put exactly that scenario into the central car chase of a novel, published some years ago, called *Yellow Blue Tibia*. I daresay the film-makers never read that particular book. I daresay.

Not just personal grump, though, I think: too much of this movie felt second hand, in a tired way. Hiro flies Baymax through the clouds whooping with delight, and it's all a bit *How To Train Your Dragon*. Other bits strike too *The Incredibles*-y, or *Wall-E*-y, or *Cloudy With A Chance of Meat Ballsy* vibes. But, never mind what I say. The film has enjoyed the second-best opening weekend, in terms of gross, of any Disney animation, behind only the juggernaut that is *Frozen*. So you'll probably love it.

Marie Brennan,
A Natural History of Dragons

There's a certain odour of *How To Train Your Dragon* about this novel, with the cod-Viking milieu replaced with a Fantasyland version of Edwardian England, and the cartoonish humour swapped over for a detailed (frankly, rather too detailed) evocation of the curiosity of the natural historian. The result is a gentle and, to some extent, absorbing yarn; although one that lacks any properly draconic fire or force. The narrator, Lady Trent, nurses a by-the-standards-of-her-sexist-time unladylike interest in dragons from an early age. She learns from the cook how to preserve a dead 'sparkling' in vinegar (a dragon so small some categorise it as an insect). She grows up reading the copy of the *De draconum varietatibus* in her father's library – I can't say I trust the Latin here, since Lewis and Scott insist the genitive of *draco* is *dracontis*. Or perhaps Latin works differently in Brennan's imaginary locale. After all, Lady Trent grows-up in Edwardian luxury in 'Scirland' not Britain, and she travels from this large set of islands off the shoulder of the mainland continent not to Albania/Transylvania/ somewherelikethat-ania but rather to 'Vystrana'. What Brennan gains by setting her tale in this arbitrarily constructed Fantasy realm isn't clear to me.

Anyway, not to get ahead of myself: Lady Trent grows to maturity and gets married the kindly Jacob, a less oppressively patriarchal husband than Isabella might have been lumbered with. Jacob risks social ostracism by permitting his wife to attend him on a scientific expedition to the valleys surrounding Drustanev in assuredly-not-Albania/Transylvania/somewherelikethat-ania in search of dragons. There are a couple of rather slackly told adventures: our heroine kidnapped by colourful bandits, who despite her fears that they might 'outrage her honour' in fact swiftly return her to the expedition. She goes on to encounter ancient tombs, statues, legends of the mythical half-human-half-dragon king Zhagrit Mat, and a variety of actual big-as-a-bus dragons, which Isbaella sketches. The illustrations, notionally hers, are one of the high-points of this otherwise rather underinflated story. Nothing very much happens; the cod-Edwardian tone is too broadly pastiche-y and Down-Abbeyesque properly to work and the whole flavour is, well, cosy. Though Isabella carries on her shoulder the scar of a childhood encounter with a Wolf-Drake (half wolf, half duck! Or, no, wait a minute: *actually* a kind of large dragon...), and though she's always tumbling through into subterranean caves, being stalked by wild beasts etc, it never generates any tension or terror. On the plus side, the dragons are treated as examples of naturally occurring wildlife, rather than as feeble McAffreyish ciphers for housecats or horses. But on the down side, the dragons are treated as examples of naturally occurring wildlife, and the minute itemisation of their anatomy and behaviour is a little... well, dull.

Eric Brown
Jani and the Greater Game

The scene is set in a Steampunky, alt-historical India: British Raj, 1920s vintage. A mysterious energy source called 'Annapurnite' has enabled Britain to maintain a boosted global empire. Jani Chatterjee, precocious teenager and the daughter of an Indian government minister, is returning home from Cambridge University via airship when the Russians attack. She is saved from Russian violation and murder by a weird creature: 'long and thin, its skin deathly white... its features were almost human' (is it an alien? a Frankenstein's monster? Peter Crouch?) From there-on it's a series of diverting adventures in Brown's alt-Raj: dastardly plots are afoot; life-size mechanical elephants are there for the riding; Annapurnite is not all it seems. It's enjoyable stuff, if perhaps a little underinflated, narratively speaking. Sometimes it reads like a jolly novella expanded to novel length; and few of the twists surprised me. Still, Jani is an appealing protagonist, and the pastiche Edwardian-y ripping yarn style is fun.

Tobias S. Buckell
Hurricane Fever

This is a sort-of sequel to Buckell's previous spy-malarkey thriller *Arctic ~~Roll~~* sorry, *Rising* (2012), which I haven't read. So, you know: I may be missing some nuances. I'm just not convinced that 'nuance' is really the name of the game in this sort of novel. It's bang-bang-bang, thrills and tension, fight and flight and more fight. They call this sort of book a 'thriller' for a reason. And that reason is: Marketing. Not that there aren't some nice touches. There are. I liked the near-future globally-risen sea levels, flooded streets and hurricane afflicted Caribbean. Or Ca*RIB*-beun, as I believe the Americans like to say. It was nice to see that part of the world treated as a proper setting, rather than just an exotic locale for incidental adventures. The story is efficiently plotted, and written with the sort of unembellished directness its genre mandates. That story concerns ex superspy 'Roo' Jones, dragged back into the 'game' after a former colleague is killed. A secret package turns up, and he's on his boat (having to babysit his teenage nephew) whilst a wonder weapon that could Destroy The World is somewhere in the offing. It's a good job Roo is on the case. All the time steering his boat to avoid the titular hurricanes. Truly, he Roo, Roo, Roos his boat.

I'm going to pause for a moment, to let the odour of that dissipate.

Right.

So, there's a lot of rapid-fire action, and some rather too neatly disposed global conspiring too. It's a spy-thriller with a strong maritime component and a dusting of near-future imaginary tech. In other words it's yet another example of the Oft-Discovered Bond Spree, from whose Bourne/No trad Le Car-Returns, and Catcher in Jack Ry-/An makes Missions quite Impossible. Not to, you know. To get carried away. **clears throat** Thus Copying doth make Cowards of us all.

My problem is generic, not specific to this novel. That problem is that certain readers, and the writers who supply them, believe that fighting is more interesting than talking, that shooting is more interesting than being, that violence is more interesting manifested physically in the outside world than internally in the psyche (indeed, who believe that the former doesn't really entail the latter at all, though the latter is where all violence actually comes to rest), that explosions are fireworks rather than massively accelerated entropy, that Bond, James Bond is better than Henry James (Henry), and in sum that characters in action are more fun than action in character. Whereas I tend to believe the exact opposite. But that only means I'm probably not the idea reviewer for this title. Which is bound to happen, from time to time, in this reviewing lark.

Charles Burns
Sugar Skull

What an odd standalone *Sugar Skull* would make. Imagine reading it without knowing that it was the third in a trilogy of graphic novels: first *X'ed Out* (2010), then *The Hive* (2012), now this. Or then again, maybe it wouldn't make much difference. It's an oblique and puzzling and suggestive work, but then the whole trilogy is that. Doug is a performance artist, given to wearing masks and hanging out at countercultural events. He met his girlfriend Sarah on this scene, but her psychotic ex-boyfriend is also lurking about. Parallel to this *vie* more-or-less *quotidienne*, and intercut with it, is a Burroughsian alternate reality in which Doug's alter-ego, Nitnit, has a series of discombobulating adventures in a run-down city populated with mutants and freaks, and also in an underground breeding hive, where lizard-like humanoids patrol the corridors and seemingly human women give birth to gigantic slimy eggs. Nitnit is the reverse of Tintin (black quiff instead of blond, creepy-gross adventures in a deformed and baffling land rather than uplifting action shenanigans in the exotic hotspots of the world), and much of the beauty of this book inheres in the clever distortions and exaggerations Burns inflicts upon Hergé's *ligne claire* style. Sugar Skulls are the name of the skull-shaped sweets Nitnit is compelled to buy in *The Hive*'s very last frame; and there are plenty of skulls in this volume too.

The protocols governing 'spoilers' perhaps don't apply as they normally might in a work as oblique and deliberately puzzling as this. Accordingly, though still proceeding in a *caveat lector spoilerōrum* fashion, we might note that the skull in question is Doug's, sugared in the vividness and high-calorie, low-nutrition buzz of its imagined universe, and sugary also in its fragility. He gets mugged by Sarah's ex and suffers a head wound bad enough to hospitalise him (hence the plaster Nitnit is always pictured as wearing). His visions are a direct reaction to this trauma. We can also trace the various hideousness connected with childbirth, dwarfs, miniature monsters, piglets and so on to the fact that Doug got Sarah pregnant and then ran out on her, leaving her to raise the kid alone The male guilt, squeezed between unhappy memories of his unhappy Dad on the one hand, and his own complete delinquency as a father on the other, inform the queasily ghastly mood of the whole trilogy, I think.

It makes compelling reading, certainly. Maybe one or two of the grotesquenesses are a little too, I don't know, *obvious*; and certainly they depend too strongly (I'd say) on a buried revulsion at female physicality as such, female flesh in its obstetric mode but also female sexual allure in a broader sense. And there's a slightness to the overall telling, although this may be more feature than (ugh! squash it squash it!) bug. The imagined world is pretty nightmarish, but the nightmare is different in details not in kind to the actual lived life; and Burns is good on illustrating that old saw of psychiatric medicine... that though madness is a particular problem for a patient's family and for society as a whole, it is a particular solution for the patient him/herself. If the solution looks extreme, then think how severe the underlying pathology must be...

Monica Byrne
The Girl in the Road

This is a really good novel. Hard to summarise, and at times hard to like, it is always written with courage, vividness and power.

It starts out more-or-less near-future SF conventional: Meena, one of our two heroines, wakes in Mumbai with snake-bite wounds fresh on her chest. Convinced she is being targeted for murder, she flees; and her slightly paranoid, cycloptropic character is very well drawn as she makes her way across India to Africa. This entails crossing the Arabian Gulf on a bridge known as 'The Trail': a pontoon made of cleverly designed blocks to harvest wave-energy (walking, and indeed living, on The Trail is supposed to be illegal; but that doesn't stop people). Meena's journey is full of colour and incident, much of it sexual; but it becomes plain early on that she is an extremely unreliable narrator, and that the mysterious trauma from which she is fleeing more complicated than we at first think. The other heroine, Mariama, is younger and a little more reliable; crossing Africa towards Ethiopia, escaping the repeated rape of her mother by the man who insists he owns them. She joins an overland caravan transporting oil and falls under the spell of a beautiful woman called Yemaya. This grown woman engages in sexual acts with child Mariama, and Byrne's handling of this element is rendered hard to read by a refusal to repeat the narratives structures of uncomplicated outrage that usually frames accounts of sexual activity with children. That's doubtless Byrne's point (her view of the ghastly consequences of sexual exploitation and abuse is, otherwise, clear-eyed and unsentimental). Saying so doesn't make it any easier to read. *The Girl in the Road* understands how sex can be oppressive, and also how it can be liberating; understands how vast the human forces and energies are that it channels. This certainly adds nuance to the story, although it also perhaps muddles the whole. 'How beautiful and revolting sex was,' one character comments, late in the novel. 'How its juices are both nectar and poison' [193].

More than that about the book is hard to lay down in a short review, partly because Byrne doubles down on her point-of-view characters' unreliability and partly because much is told via a complex network of mythic and magical allusions (snakes figure a good deal) dreams and magic. The novel goes out of its way to avoid being too pat or obvious, and Byrne's energetic and sometimes over-energised writing style refuses to let the reader settle into any kind of complacent groove, reading-wise. That's a good thing, by and large. We assume that Meena and (the rather more likeable) Mariama are going to meet, or at least that their storylines are going to intercept, even though it becomes apparent that the narratives are set at different times. Byrne's future-third-world felt real to me, though I hold up my hand and confess I'd be the last person to be able to judge the accuracy of portraiture of places and cultures I have never, myself, visited. Byrne's prose is a superior instrument, and she is *mostly* in charge of it (she's especially good on descriptions of landscape and the natural world; and her dialogue is snappy and well flavoured). I like the bright-eyed way the novel handles its future tech; none of that *Frankenstein*-syndrome bollocks here. It's people who cause other people hurt, not tech, in Byrne's world. All in all this is a remarkable novel, made more remarkable by the consideration that it's a debut. The road goes ever on.

M R Carey
The Girl With All The Gifts

On the upside, this is a sharply written, well-plotted, grippy-read-y thriller. It builds a workable post-apocalyptic world, keeps its momentum going and pays off nicely. The central character, the titular young girl, little Melanie, is an especially noteworthy creation: a highly intelligent child kept in a cell, who is strapped into a chair and muzzled in order to be wheeled through to her schoolroom with her peers. Why is she treated this way? Ah, that's the hook. Her perspective on the classroom experience (something there's not enough of in contemporary culture: it's a shame it only occupies the early sections, here), on adult attitudes to childhood, and on the arbitrary and often cruel way she and her kind are treated, all this is brilliantly done.

On the downside, it's yet another zombie story.

To return to the upside, the rationale for zombification (a toxoplasma gondii-like neural fungus) is kind-of new, and people never use the 'z'-word, because, you know: the one thing you don't want to do when zombie apocalypse has destroyed almost all humanity is to trip-yourself into using worn-out terminology like a square. So it's 'hungries', not zombies. There's a creditable primary focus on female characters and female interactions here, that doesn't exclude or merely demonise the men in the story; and there's nicely-handled light dusting of mythic resonance: Pandora's box, *Iphigenia at Aulis*.

On the downside, though: it's yet another zombie story.

I don't want to underplay the upside. This is a smart, readable book. It plays cleverly with our point-of-view assumptions when it comes to this mode of story; it has some interesting things about humanisation and dehumanisation, about parents and children. True, the middle section was a bit wandering-about-y, and I kept getting flashes of Cronin's *The Passage* (oo-er missus!), which though it also has its problems, is a heftier, richer version of the same thing. Still, this isn't aiming at epic sweep; it's trying for something more emotionally engaging.

On the downside, though: it's yet one more example of that egregiously over-supplied contemporary sub-genre known as 'the zombie story'.

So upside: readable, engaging.

Downside: another another another fucking zombie story.

That's the thing about zombie stories. It never BRRAAAAAINS but it pours.

Adam Christopher
The Burning Dark

Hard to know how to factor in the inevitable element of subjective reaction where reviewing is concerned. Christopher has many fans, and his latest novel comes with some impressive back-cover endorsements ('a riveting sci-fi mystery reminiscent of Shirley Jackson's *The Haunting of Hill House*' says Martha Wells; 'Creepy and Compelling' says Gareth L Powell; 'not to be missed' says James 'James' Lovegrove. Also Scott Sigler says 'Christopher puts Sci-Fi in a Metaphysical choke-hold – *The Burning Dark* makes reality tap-out', which may be praise. Or not. To be honest I'm really not sure what Sigler means). To say I did not find it so is to register that my organ-of-spookage was not tickled, the hairs did not raise at the back of my neck, I neither cared not was scared. Or was scarred, but then the novel probably wasn't trying to do that. Your *eeek*!age may vary.

The novel is, I believe, the first in a series called 'The Spider Wars', after the supersize cyborg villains against which future-humanity is fighting a galaxy-wide war. This novel, though, has relatively little to do with the Spiders, apart from one flashback at the beginning (in which some Spiders are literally devouring an entire planet: I didn't believe it for a minute) and some later-in-the-novel spoiler-redactedness. Most of the novel concerns Captain Abraham Idaho Cleveland, a decorated war veteran about to retire, and referred to throughout as 'Ida', in what is either a clever piece of gender-subversion or else an irritating distraction. The world of the novel is bounded by the 'Fleet', the military organisation prosecuting the war, piloting all the space ships and dismantling the space station U-Star Coast City. This Fleet is somewhere between Star Trek's Star Fleet and the army-as-fascist/utopian-model-of-society familiar from Heinlein. Christopher doesn't really capture the aura of neo-Prussian authenticity that makes Military SF so popular Stateside. He's certainly not as ideologically moronic as Heinlein; but it's a pretty old-fashioned set-up nonetheless. Old fashioned verging on stale. That said, Christopher's focus is clearly on the haunted house story, not militarism, its ethos and praxis, so maybe this matters less. But not being able to suspend my disbelief in the military diminished my investment in the spooky story the novel wants to tell. Long story short: I was not scared by the strange noises, things going bump in the night, sudden chills etc. Accordingly the couple of hundred pages devoted to this stuff didn't ratchet up the dread and the tension, it just bored me... Too much exposition, too much faux-tough dialogue and blather. To quote the Raven: nevermore.

The Scare is subjective. What scares one person will leave another scratching his bald patch and pulling a slightly pained face. The star around which U-Star Coast City shines with a weird purple light; but instead of putting me in a *Solaris* frame of mind, it made me think of those fly-zappers you see in butchers. A mostly deserted space station just doesn't have the same vibe as a haunted house, because ghost stories have to be about a malign form of groundedness, a poisonous kind of belonging (fundamentally: death that is so linked to life that it can't, quite, leave it) and space stations are all, and this one a fortiori, temporary structures... it's being dismantled as the story is being told. The tone of voice of Abraham Idaho Cleveland, hard-boiled, sweary, blue-collar American brogue, never rang true for me: not quite *Go-Bakda-Joisey-Ya-Moron*!, but not far away. But then again I have an imagination, and can use it to imagine a reader who is drawn into the atmosphere and tension, and for whom the novel generates real Spook. You pays yer money, you takes yer choice, you dismantles yer space station.

John Darnielle
Wolf in White Van

I might say 'I enjoyed this', except that 'enjoy' doesn't seem the right word, exactly. For a first novel it's a very accomplished piece of work indeed: sensitively, evocatively and occasionally alarmingly written. It is eerie and weird and sticks in the mind after reading, like a piece of pungently delicious food sticks in the teeth. Quite apart from anything else, it offers a portrait of the inward oddness of the SF fan (the crossover between SF and gaming especially) a healthy distance away from the rather self-congratulatory cosiness of Jo Walton's Hugo-winning *Amongst Others*. There's little to love and much to recognise in this portrait of what it means to be a geek. *Wolf In White Van* shares with Walton's book a deliberately aimless structure, and little actually happens in it. A better book, though, I think.

Story: our narrator, Sean, lives alone in Californian suburbia, coping with the consequences of some terrible incident in his youth that left his face hideously disfigured. A nurse calls four times a day to check on him and top up his treatment. The rest of the time he runs a retro-style, postal-only role-playing game called 'Trace Italian'. People write to Sean detailing their next move in the post-nuclear-disaster dystopia of his game-space, and he writes back with personalised details as to how their game is going. The novel is structured, in a sinuous sort of way, backwards: so we start at the end, rewind through the story of two teenage players of Trace Italian who confused the game and reality and suffered (one died, one badly hurt) as a result, and we end up with the initial trauma that wrecked Sean's face. Along the way are some beautifully written excursi on solitude, imagination, science fiction and games – the stuff on the porousness of game-players' sense of game and world struck me, post-Gamergate, as prescient (Sean has a thing for Conan, and also for John Norman's Gor novels, although not to read, just to stare at their 'shameful and garish' covers, 'pornographic, but in an almost dishonest way': 'I didn't need to hear the stories the books were trying to tell me: their skins haunted me enough' [49]). Sometimes these excursi drag a little, but often they are marvellous embedded essays on the side of being a genre Fan upon which *Amongst Others* prefers not to dwell. Sean is keen not to be thought a creep and a freak, and works hard not to be; but there is something creepy about him nonetheless, and as you read through the novel it starts to dawn upon you that this freakishness is nothing to do with his ruined face or hermit existence. It's the freakishness he shares with you: the combination of desire to escape and desire to control, the passion, passivity and hatred of being passive, the strange potage of imagination, generosity, anger and perversity that is mixed in the head of the true science fiction geek. I know whereof I speak.

It's a novel about SF rather than a SF novel, without even the set-dressing of magic that made *Amongst Others* Hugo-acceptable. Darnielle is, perhaps, a little too obviously coy about withholding the precise details of the 'event' that led to young Sean Phillips' disfigurement. Sometimes the prose strays into mere whimsy (though this is rare). But it's a very good novel for all that.

Glen Duncan
By Blood We Live

Vampires are creatures that enjoy unnatural long life, sustained by ruthless predation upon other forms of life. Vampire novels are, formally speaking, the same. On and on the genre goes, sucking the lifeblood out of everything from Bram Stoker and Anne Rice to the 'Count of Sesame Street' and that girl from *Adventure Time* to maintain a pale not-quite-life of its own. On and on, never seeming to die. Werewolves have a similar postmodern hoover-it-up, wolf-it-down wearying endurance quality to them. Of course, Duncan is very far from the first writer to think it might be a nifty idea to combine the two. *By Blood We Live* is the third in a trilogy that began with *The Last Werewolf* (2011) and continued with *Talulla Rising* (2012), and it certainly embodies its premise, formally speaking, insofar as it goes on and on and on and will not lie down and die already just wrap it up my god you've already had 900 pages to tell your story do you really need another 450?

I'm not suggesting Duncan is a bad writer. On the contrary, Duncan can clearly write, and write very well. But what he's written here wearied me a great deal, partly because the plot is too choppily structured, partly because my nonreading of *Last Werewolf* and *Talulla Rising* left me more than a little puzzled as to the meaning and/or point of it all, but mostly because it's just really tiring to read so many ripely-written sex scenes, so much goresplash and so many endlessly purpled interior monologues. That all this is pretty adolescent, really, isn't exactly a criticism, because Vampires and Werewolves are fundamentally adolescent imaginative constructions. It's just a little wrongfooting to find such stylistic effort and panache expended upon 'like a warmth going through him and it was like the warmth of coming home and his face had felt so full and tender with this feeling of ashamed homecoming that even then he'd known would never be free of rage and boredom and sadness and he'd never be anything except alone and what he was' [232], not to mention 'Madeline with her snout in the girl's flank and her ass in the air, legs spread, the smell of her cunt was sly and sweet and full of tortured willingness, and me with a hard-on that could've broken a piano in half' [285] (though I am compelled to confess my doubts as to whether 'tortured willingness' is actually a smell), and let's not forget 'my fingernails went so easily through the soft flesh of his throat... I got a grip on the wet tubing of his throat and pulled. A lot of it came out. His eyes couldn't open wide enough to fit this surprise in. Miles away, his legs were kicking. I felt my thumbnail go through a big slippery vein. An artery I guess. Blood went through the air like a Spanish fan' [385] and pretty soon you're thinking: 'as Tithonus came to regard his own eternal life, so I look now upon the endless stream of neverending vampire/werewolf novels. ἀποθανεῖν θέλω.'

And ever when the moon is low,
And the shrill winds are up and away,
In the white pages, to and fro
We see the randy werewolves play.
But when the moon was very low,
And wild winds bound within their cell,
The shadow of the vampire fell
Upon his bed, across his brow.
He only said, 'This genre's dreary,
Goes on and on,' he said;
He said, 'I am aweary, aweary,
I would that it were dead!'

Graham Edwards
Talus and the Frozen King

Some time ago, prompted I think largely by the global success of Ellis Peters' *Brother Cadfael* novels, many writers cast about for historical periods into which to embed their investigating detectives. For a while a great many whodunits got themselves written starring Victorian, Tudor, eighteenth-century, Ancient Roman and so on detectives. Then the vogue fizzled out – Peters died in 1995, and the historical whodunit form has largely gone out of fashion (*Death Comes to Pemberley* style exercises aside). Still, even when this kind of sub-genre was in vogue I don't think anybody thought of writing a prehistorical detective, conceivably because the elevator pitch sounds, well, stupid.

Graham Edwards' *Talus and the Frozen King* has decided to plug that gap, whether or not you realised it was a gap that needed plugging: 'Introducing the World's First Detective', declares the cover shout-line. Now, Edwards is a veteran writer of genre Fantasy, and knows how to put a story together – it's not Nabokov, but neither does it shirk its storytelling puzzle-box responsibilities. Talus is a sort-of rhapsode, travelling about with his companion, Bran. Once upon a time fire rained from the sky, ruining his left hand; Bran saved his life and now they have a special Caveholmes-and-Wats-*ugh*! thing going on. In this case, the mystery is a Warrior King frozen to death on a mysterious island called Creyak. The murderer could be any one of the king's six scheming sons, or perhaps one of the other prominent islanders. Talus investigates. Edwards' idea here is that detection is a matter of telling oneself stories, and that Talus has a more advanced story-telling lobe in his brain than many of his fellow cavecitizens.

It's not entirely to Edwards' discredit that his imagined prehistory feels underpowered compared to a book like Kim Stanley Robinson's recent *Shaman*. It's bound to, of course. This is not a matter of specific historical anachronisms; it is a matter of tone – characters chatting on with one another like Agatha Christie ciphers in bearskins, saying deeply unNeolithic things like 'is it true what they say, that Love survives death?' [14] and 'our work here is done' [265] or Talus doing a Columbo impression ('Just as the morning fog was folding itself around Cabarrath's retreating form, Talus called, "Actually, I have just thought of another question''' [151]). That's all fine. Puzzle-whodunits are a game, and it's boorish to complain about the rules. If you don't want to play, don't play. Still: I retain my reservations.

I'm assuming from the style of the title that Edwards is planning a long string of 'Talus and the…' murder mysteries set in prehistoric Scotland. Who knows; it could become a Thing. The problem I have with this novel is the problem I had with Brother Cadfael, back in the day. It is, fundamentally, a Foucauldian problem. The structures of detection are part of a larger episteme of mass surveillance and discipline. The lone detective figures, paradoxically, not as a solitary genius, but precisely as the epitome of the larger social forces of industrialisation and embourgeoisification, and the carceral episteme they entail. That's the name of the game, and it misfits a pre-bourgeois world as glaringly as if Talus rode onto Creyak on a unicycle smoking a cheroot and singing an a capella version of Depeche Mode's 'Master and Servant'. The detective – the Holmes, the Poirot, the Rebus – is the externalisation of the principle of imprisonment; he (and usually, it is he, for reasons to do with the close structural connections between patriarchal authority and Capitalist society) intervenes in the free play of libidinal anarchy represented by the murder, and imposes the narrative-deductive grid that is his defining feature. It is entirely uncoincidental, given this discursive logic, that successful whodunit writers end up manufacturing a great quantity of mass-produced items – the seemingly endless production line that churns out Poirot novels, Cadfael novels, Maigret novels, not to mention the myriad 'Inspector X and the Y' style novels. 'Is it surprising,' Foucault asked rhetorically, in *Discipline and Punish* 'that prisons resemble factories, schools, barracks, hospitals, which all resemble prisons?'

Hermione Eyre
Viper Wine

This is a genuinely charming and engaging example of historical fiction, given added vim by a number of wittily handled pomo touches. Mostly it is simply an entertaining read, although intermittently it becomes more than that and achieves palpable greatness. What it isn't is a Fantasy or time-travel SF yarn, but that's hardly a hanging offence.

The two main characters are actual people, and the core of what happens has historical sanction (Eyre is fond of quoting chunks of the *Dictionary of National Biography* to shore up the on-going narrative). Here is Sir Kenelm Digby, seventeenth-century aristocrat, natural philosopher, Catholic, alchemist and all-round old-fashioned English eccentric. More compellingly here is his wife, Venetia Anastasia Digby (née Stanley), one of the most acclaimed beauties of her generation. Which, if you're a fan of tiny mouths, wide-set-eyes, and a ghostly forehead fringe of hair that spells out 'dSygg666' like a captcha, she may well have been:

Sir Kenelm's multifarious interests, and his wife's anxiety at her fading charms, are rendered by Eyre very skilfully: the whole book is energetic, fluent and readable stuff. At the same time, it's all interleaved by the present, in ways that speak to a – strange to say – rather quaintly old-fashioned postmodern vibe ('vibus postmodernicus'). Early in the book Digby is interviewed by various gentlemen, amongst them Paxman, 'a soft Irish man called Wogan' and 'Jonathan Ross, a fool with weak "R"s' [34]. The author herself pops up ('a woman with a notebook marked "Viper Wine"'[37]). Kenelm notes ideas down under headings that include 'Cosmographie', 'Thaumaturgike' and 'Nanobiotechnology' (though when he looks again 'he could not remember what was meant' by this latter [249]). He gets garbled html messages from somewhere:

response.setContentType("text/html")

and the like ('the letters seemed to [Kenelm] like a spell or symbolism more than a story: hieroglyphs' [179]), and he instructs that the message 'One Small Step For Man One Giant Leap For Mankind' be painted along the wall of his long library: though the calligrapher slopes off leaving only 'One Small Step For Ma' actually on the wall [165]. All this is very beguilingly done, threading the tricky path between hard core literary experimentation on the one hand and frou-frou whimsy on the other, only occasionally straying into either. It's scrupulously researched, too: I read with a pedant's eye for errors and found almost none (there's a 'by the by' on p.113 that should be 'by the bye'; and some Latin on p.222 that's not quite right). There is a class problem, not unusual in novels like this: we gad about with people of the caste of the Digbys and Van Dycks and other assorted posh nobs, whilst the 99% are background colour (one exception is an interleaved first-person narration by a poor Wessex lass; but it hardly counterbalances the posho bulk of this novel's 17th-Century).

It's in the nature of this kind of project, perhaps, that it's liable to go on too long, and to register a proportion (I'd gauge this, using my complicated actuarial equipment, at 22%) of misses in amongst all the hits. More debilitating, perhaps, is the way the almost-whimsy degrades the novel's scenes of pathos: the way Eyre draws out Venetia's vanity into something more existentially eloquent; and Venetia's abrupt, early death, in which the titular 'viper wine' (another actual thing from actual history, a potion made from snakes supposed to keep a woman young looking) is implicated; and the profound grief of her husband. All this is good, and Eyre does interesting thematic things with Digby's interest in 'curing wounds at a distance' (he thought the trick was not to treat the wound, but to apply magic powders to the thing that caused the wound, no matter how far away it was from the wound it had caused). Overall, a notable novel.

Michel Faber, *The Book of Strange New Things*

Faber is a novelist I esteem a great deal; but this novel left me pulling my 'lost dog pondering a sign-post' face. It's not badly written, or wholly uninteresting; but by the same token I can't honestly say it really works, or that I liked it, or that it struck me as ultimately worthwhile. I'd be tempted to peg it as falling down in the ways familiar from previous 'literary' novelists deciding to have a go at genre sf; except Faber's debut *Under the Skin* was a proper SF novel, and a very good one. So what goes wrong here?

I'll qualify myself straight away and say that some elements here go very right. The core of the novel is a portrait of a happy marriage, that between Peter Leigh and his wife Bea, that is put under the strain of enforced separation, and that's very precisely and movingly worked. I also liked very much the way Faber treats the Christian faith of his Peter and Bea. This central to their senses of self, and it's quite properly handled in the novel with great scads of earnest Christian evangeloid and soul-searchy discourse, as they both try to comprehend and do what they take to be God's will. Like the marvellous BBC series *Rev.*, *Strange and New Things* manages to give a sense of Peter's life as a vicar in England as one defined by external stresses and practicalities without losing sight of the inward, sustaining faith. It's rare to see that in contemporary fiction. (Of course, the fact that strangeness and newness have always struck me as the crucial Christian salients, howsoever obscured by centuries of tradition and the affection people have for tradition, doubtless helped Faber's representation of Christianity strike home for me where that was concerned). One of the novel's best moments, I thought, is when Peter recalls the day he proposed to Beatrice, 10.30 on a morning of sweltering heat, as the two of them were standing at a cash machine in the high street prior to doing a supermarket shop.

> Maybe he should have gone down on one knee, because her "Yes, let's" had sounded hesitant and unromantic, as though she considered the proposal nothing more than a pragmatic solution to the inconvenience of high rents. [203]

Everything in the day goes wrong: their bank card is swallowed by the machine; when they go to the branch to get a new one the teller is rude and insulting and Bea storms out in a rage; outside they discover a vandal had scratched a swastika into the paintwork of the car; Bea's phone loses battery; the first garage they visit is shut, the second quotes a huge sum for the work to repair the scratched paintwork; then they discover the car exhaust is shot and will need replacing, none of which can they afford. When they eventually get home Peter realises the lamb chops they had bought had spoiled in the heat. He is about to throw them out in fury, but changes his mind. He finds Bea on the balcony of their flat, gazing at the brick wall opposite.

Her cheeks were wet.

> 'I'm sorry,' he said.
> She fumbled for his hand, and their fingers interlocked.
> 'I'm crying because I'm happy,' she explained, as the sun allowed itself to be veiled in clouds. 'This is the happiest day of my life.' [204]

It's a moment more-or-less nicked from Flaubert's *L'Éducation sentimentale* of course, but never mind that. It works very well.

So, all right, but here's the problem: all this stuff is prologue and backstory only. The main focus of *The Book of Strange New Things*, and the reason why Peter is separated so painfully from Bea, is that he has accepted a job with a commercial corporation called USIC to work as a Christian missionary on a distant planet, Oasis. Most of the novel is set here, a hot, rather barren world with 72-hour-long night, constant rain and a spongy surface that soaks all the water up. How the water thereafter convects back into the sky to fall as rain again is not explained. Indeed, throughout these sections, the SF fan's imagination taps Faber's writing to find it not ringing true. Peter agrees to go despite knowing absolutely next-to-nothing about the distant world (Earth as a whole seems improbably uninterested in this habitable, populated planet with its English-speaking aliens), and even less about the organisation that is taking him on. He doesn't even know what 'USIC' stands for. On the space flight to his destination, and upon arrival, other characters drip-feed him (and us) information, but the notion that he'd be parcelled off on this epochal journey without training or briefing simply boggles the mind. There is some hand-wavy intimation that the hyperspace jump has scrambled his memories, so that he's forgotten stuff he was briefed on, but it's not very convincing. When Peter arrives on the planet he's left to his own devices by the other members of the colony; oddly offhand behaviour by his otherwise cost-conscious new employers, given that the expense of transportation means every coke he drinks costs hundreds of dollars and every email he sends his wife (and with nothing else to do he sends a lot) cost them $5000 a pop.

Eventually Peter makes his way to a village of aboriginals – humanoid in shape and wearing hooded abayas, the main difference to us being that their faces look like 'two foetuses curled up'. Whatever that looks like. Peter discovers, which fact nobody had bothered to tell him, that there was a previous missionary called Kurtzberg who has subsequently disappeared; and that the otherwise opaquely baffling aliens are desperately enthusiastic to receive more Biblical teaching, readings from what they call the 'Book of Strange New Things'. So Peter sets to; and his learning the world is interspersed with epistles between himself and his wife in which she details an increasingly desperate climate collapse on the home planet, and slowly grows apart from him.

The further I read, the more I began to wonder if the weird conceptual ellipses and apparent clumsinesses were going to be explained by some clever final reveal. But, no. They're not. The rather infuriatingly leisurely telling finally works its way to an end, whereupon the reader pauses to reflect how debilitatingly second hand the whole SF element is. This is Blish's *A Case of Conscience*, without the focus or imaginative steel; and without Blish's deep engagement with the problematic of the human, rather than alien, incarnation of Christ in the gospels. It's Mary Doria Russell's *The Sparrow* (a much inferior book to Blish's) with only the blandly nice aliens and not the rapist feline overlords. The result is *The Book Of Depressingly Familiar and Old-Fashioned Things*.

Nor, despite some lovely passages here and there, is it an especially well put-together work. Faber's novel starts slowly, and then drifts through hundreds of pages that detail Oasan agricultural routines and Oasan funerary practises and the Oasan habits of shitting in the streets without breaking stride. It picks up some emotional heft again towards the end, though the actual ending itself, avoiding spoilers, is very anti-climactic. When he wants to represent the Oasans speaking their own language (and the difficulty they have speaking English and pronouncing our 's' and 'd'), Faber goes fontbonkers:

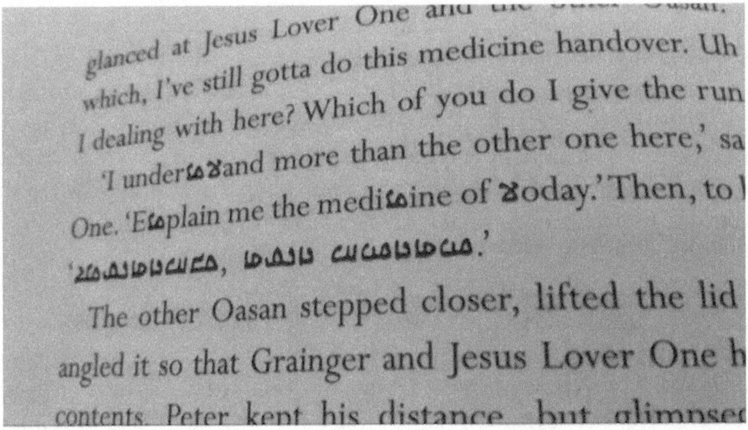

> glanced at Jesus Lover One and
> which, I've still gotta do this medicine handover. Uh
> I dealing with here? Which of you do I give the run
> 'I under[illegible]and more than the other one here,' sa
> One. 'E[illegible]plain me the medi[illegible]ine of [illegible]oday.' Then, to
> '[illegible], [illegible] [illegible].'
> The other Oasan stepped closer, lifted the lid
> angled it so that Grainger and Jesus Lover One h
> contents. Peter kept his distance, but glimpsed

These letters look distinctly Arabic, though in garbled form. I stop short of accusing Faber, with his bernouse-wearing, crumple-faced, shitting-in-the-street, yearning-to-hear-the-true-Gospel, white-protagonist-can't-tell-them-apart, village-dwelling, Arabic speaking aliens, of trading in racist stereotypes. But I'm standing right on the line, there. Who knows? Maybe he uses Arabic font because it's available on the MS Word font menu, and so was ready-to-hand. I'm unsure, though. (Near the end of the book, he refers to one of the alien's hoods as a 'hijab', so maybe it's all deliberate).

The real problem, it dawns on you as you read, is that Faber just isn't that interested in his alien Others. His story is about the strain placed upon a loving marriage by distance and other difficulties. That in turn makes the alien worldbuilding, the planetary colonisation plans, the aliens themselves pasteboard, set-dressing. A shame, all in all.

I have a worry of personal bias, thought in this judgement. My peculiar perspective means that the Christianity/Aliens thing looms out disproportionately large for me. What I mean is that when I wrote *The Palgrave History of SF* what I found is that seventeenth- and eighteenth-century SF was absolutely obsessed with the question of whether space aliens were saved by the blood of Christ or not. William Empson has a great essay on this (called, rather wonderfully, 'John Donne the Spaceman'): because, as Empson points out, if they are not saved in Christ then they are inevitably damned, which seems heartless of the Creator; but if they *are* saved in Christ then the unique specificity of Christ's atonement on our world becomes fatally diluted. If there are a million worlds, were there a million Christs, all crucified in various ways – ten-armed alien Christs crucified on asterisk-shaped crosses? and so on. That was intolerable to Christian sensibilities (people got burnt at the stake for suggesting it), and the double-bind was one reason why the Catholic Church hung onto the Ptolemaic solar system so long in the teeth of scientific evidence to the contrary, something not generally true of other branches of science. Indeed, for a long time the only way out of the double bind was the one proposed by C S Lewis in his SF: that there are loads of alien life forms scattered through the universe, but only mankind fell into sin, so only one Christ (ours) was ever necessary. All this strikes plenty of modern people as angels-on-a-pinhead, I don't doubt; but it really did dominate and shape attitudes to outer space two centuries ago. And so I was excited that Faber had tackled it. But he does nothing with it whatsoever. Indeed, for all the earnest Christian proselytizing in the novel it is a theologically really unimaginative piece of work. But where does that leave us? If its SF is tired and stale and its theology is unimaginative, that's two thirds of the book rendered rather pointless. Bah.

Tana French
The Secret Place

A Dublin police procedural, set almost entirely on the grounds of a posh private girls' boarding school where a handsome but flirty and selfish boy called Chris (from a neighbouring boys' school) has been found with his head bashed-in. The murder weapon was a hoe from the groundskeeper's hut, but the groundskeeper has an alibi. The murder was investigated, not solved, and so shelved. A year later, on a noticeboard in the school called 'the secret place' (a board on which people post anonymous messages of the 'I stole your cake!' 'I fancy so-and-so', 'I hate so-and-so', 'I want a boob-job' sort, a pressure-valve for the high strung schoolgirls) a person or persons unknown has put up a card that reads – 'I know who killed him'. This restarts the murder investigation. Ambitious young Stephen Moran, our narrator for half the tale, is handed the card; he gets together with ball-busting Murder Squad detective Antoinette Conway. They go to the school. 500+ pages later the mystery is solved.

That's one problem, there. The novel really doesn't need half a thousand pages to tell its story. The prose is well-formed and readable, the dialogue (including a pleasingly high number of uses of that splendid Irish word 'bollix') mostly lively, the class tensions well drawn, and the murder absorbing. But it all goes on too, too long. There are far too many repeated scenes of the detectives interviewing teenage girls, too much (I'm sorry to use the word, but) padding to do with seeming apparitions of the ghost of Chris. The intention I'm guessing is to paint the closeted high-strung world of the girls' boarding school with some of the hues of Miller's *The Crucible*; but although French strains pretty much every pip in her writing to achieve this, it simply doesn't come off. Feels told rather than shown, not helped by French leaning too heavily on the 'ohmygod!' 'that's totes freaky', 'um, hello, like, actually I didn't kill him, all right?', 'whateva' idiom for her central group of girls. I'm not saying this is badly observed, where teenage girls are concerned; only that this idiolect becomes monotonous in such a large dose, and that this monotony is aesthetically counter-productive.

There's one other element in the tale, but the fact that I've left it to this last brief paragraph indicates its semi-detached relationship to the rest of the novel. Interleaved with the police procedural chapters are flashback chapters in which the main group of friends bond over midnight trips to a nearby field, and discover they have actual magic powers. This 'fantastika' element is worked-in to the solution, but never felt very real to me. It needs to be uncanny and unnerving; but it reads more like a blander version of that 1996 movie *The Craft*.

Diana Gabaldon
Written In My Own Heart's Blood (Outlander Book 8)

Read in my own eyes' weariness.

Steven Galloway
The Confabulist

A fictionalised life of Houdini (lots of stuff about touring his stage act, with Galloway painstakingly explaining how Houdini achieved all his illusions; beefed-up with extra spy action-adventure flummery in Rasputin's Russia, and a diffusely paranoid subplot about hostility from the American spiritualist community) is plaited with a second story about Martin Strauss – an old man in present-day America whose tinnitus is actually a symptom of some rare brain disease where all cognitive function remains healthy but memories start disappearing to be replaced by 'confabulations' of fictional memory. The main thing about Martin is that, in his youth, he was the geezer who punched Houdini in the stomach when the magician wasn't prepared, thus rupturing his appendix and killing him. Being the man who killed Houdini haunts Strauss

This is a promising-enough set-up; and the novel's tag line ('I didn't just kill Harry Houdini. I killed him twice!') points us towards the revelation that Houdini's death from peritonitis might not be everything it appeared – the insurance company paid out double indemnity following the death, after all. And there is a twist ending, which is reasonably enough handled (hint: Houdini's faked death was not actually about insurance fraud). But the shadow of Priest's peerless *The Prestige* lies darkly over this book. It's considerably feebler than the prior text, not only blandly written and very meagrely characterised (the two main characters never come alive at all), but too eager to explain as it is going along, too unsure of its own tone – too declarative, insufficiently negatively capable. Priest's book uses its trick plotting to frame eloquent points about doubles and deceit, about fictions and truths. Galloway only pads out a shaggy dog story with lots of details from Houdini's many biographies (one of which, I was pleased to see, has the triply exclamative title '*Houdini!!!*'). Bottom line: *The Confabulist* just doesn't really work. Less Houdini, more Who-cares-y.

In other news: *Priest's Peerless Prestige* sounds like a late Victorian emollient lotion. Buy some today!

William Gibson
The Peripheral

Reviews that are about the process of writing the review rather than about the title under consideration are exceeded in annoyingness only by reviews that are about the process of *not* writing the review. So I apologise. My usual practice is: I read a book and write a review straight away, partly to get my thoughts in order, and partly because then it's fresh in my head. But pressure of other things meant that I wasn't able to do this with Gibson's much-anticipated new novel. I read it. Then I left it a week. Now that I have some time to turn over to it, I've already read a number of other reviews, by critics whose judgement I respect. They all like it a great deal. The most recent issue of SFX talks of 'the Return of the King', as if this novel marks a glorious renascence. I find myself out of step. It makes me doubt myself.

I guess I could still write an arrow-to-target review, I suppose; or I could spend a whole review fretting around the peripheries of the novel. What you gonna do? **sniffs**

It's not that I hated it. I didn't hate it. I didn't especially love it either. The first 200 pages set up the novel's bivalve premise in rather trudgy fashion; the remaining 250 pay it off, slowly, and with a good deal of characters-explaining-things-to-other-characters. Its bivalve premise? Well, one part is a near future rural USA where main character A, Flynn Fishers, lives hand to mouth picking up piecework (her brother is a frazzled army veteran who persuades her to take over his job, which he tells her is beta-testing a new immersive video game. It's not though.) The other part is a further-future, set after a perfect storm of environmental collapses known as 'the jackpot'. We're in London, where the super-rich are enjoying themselves under the distant, light-touch tyranny of the Chinese. Main character B, the dreadfully-named Wilf Netherton, is a PR/minder figure for pop celebrities. He has a problem: the sister of his client has been murdered. The two chambers of the novel are linked with a time-travel remote viewer powered by handwavium. People in the further future are communicating with people in the nearer-to-us-future, and vice versa. When Flynn thought she was beta testing a game she was actually flying an observation drone around further-future London; and what she thought was a bit of in-game assassination was an actual murder. So she's a witness, and accordingly some ruthless people in the further future are after her. As regards the time travel conceit, Netherton at one point asks 'can't you just jump forward and see what happens? Look in on them a year later, then correct for that?' and is told 'No, that's time travel. This is real.' [92] I quite liked the chutzpah of that, except that subsequently the explanium leaked, rather, from its containment chamber:

> When we sent out our first email, we entered into a fixed ratio of duration with their continuum, one to one. A given interval in the stub [*the novel's name for the past being contacted, because it's assumed to be a bifurcated alt-historical divergent line going nowhere important*] is the same interval here, from first instant of contact. We can no more know their future than we can know our own, except to assume that it ultimately isn't going to be history as we know it. [92]

It struck me as a rather high-handedly arbitrary and contrived premise. We might wonder whether there are reasons of pseudo-physics, rather than merely reasons to do with the exigencies of plotting, that mean the further-future can't send a *second* email to a later time in the stub? Or have an AI send a million emails and sketch out the shape of the stub? (Maybe each email would open a new stub; but then the further-future make multiple contacts with Flynn and each just carries on the story of their interaction). But, wait: I speak too soon. The passage goes onto directly to address the question of why 'time travel' is configured this way:

And, no, we don't know why. It's simply the way the server works, as far as we know. [92]

Well. That's clear, at any rate.

But all right: I'm not going to review the plot, except to say that it struck me as intricate without being complex, which is not praise. And I'm not going to review the characters (sophisticated agalmai humanised with one main flaw, like Wilf's alcoholism or Flynne's, uh, blandness) or the pacing, except to say that whilst individual chapters (these are many and short) were okay, the pacing of the whole seemed to me too slow. On the other hand, there's a '3D printing' thread that runs through the whole, and I can see that the novel, towards the end, pulls together its components in a way reminiscent of the way 3D printing works: initial elements that seem weirdly decontextualized slowly, even painstakingly, reveal themselves as part of a larger whole. As to why it takes so long, and moves with such ponderous grace: I'm not sure. It's half-way through before Flynne gets uploaded, avatar-like, into a further-future waldo robot thing – the device is called a 'peripheral', hence the novel's title. It's not that the first half lacks incident or interest. Not exactly. It's more that I got the impression the to-and-froing was there to show-off the Gibson vibe, the patent Gibson 'kick-ass' prose.

As far as *that* goes, I was unpersuaded. It is very far from being badly written, of course. Indeed conceivably that was my problem: it reads like prose that has been rather too assiduously written and rewritten. It isn't a question of obliquity, although Gibson takes an evident and rather sweet pleasure in making his readers work, or at least wait, for the full comprehension of all his slang, clipped allusions, specialised vocabulary and so on. But that's fine: stubs, hate Kegels, the klept ('not funny at all', 322), flu (not in the sense you think), artisanal AIs, battle-ready solicitors, autonomic bleedover, continua enthusiasts and haptics. Bring it on. Not that, but rather a sense of effort in the prose itself, a something that stops it moving with the smooth fluency it needs to. Hard to pin down, actually.

Let's agree that 'The sky above the port was the color of television, tuned to a dead channel' is a great opening sentence: eloquent, atmospheric, calibrated to wrongfoot the reader by precisely the right amount. And let's agree, hell why not?, that: 'the future is there, looking back at us; trying to make sense of the fiction we will have become' (from *Pattern Recognition*, and perhaps the kernel of this new novel) is a good sentence. The opening sentence of *The Peripheral* is: 'they didn't think Flynne's brother had PTSD, but that sometimes the haptics glitched him.' That's not as good a sentence, I think: the uneuphonious tangle of consonants with which it ends; the back-breaking comma. Starting a novel by telling us something that unnamed individuals did *not* think is rather a turn-off. And all the way through I found myself snagging on sentences that didn't quite solder together their idioms of expressive insight with their flavours of proletarian stylised suspicion-of-intellectualism-as-elitism inarticulacy. I mean all the too-cool-for-school stuff: the 'shit in that game. She hated that shit' [52]; 'What you been doing?' 'Fucking the dog.' [43]; 'Not worth it, Conner.' 'Fuck-all ever is' [56]; 'I don't give two shits where he's from' [405] stuff. There's a lot of that stuff in this novel.

To be clear: I'm not trying to imply Gibson thinks working class people are actually inarticulate and unintelligent. I'm suggesting he's aiming to reproduce a distinct proletarian idiolect, as spoken by the sort of people who (to quote *Mona Lisa Overdrive*) 'have grown up in white Jersey stringtowns where nobody knew shit about anything and hated anybody who did.' Bobby in *Count Zero* is described as having repudiated religion:

> religion was now something he felt he'd considered and put aside. Basically, the way he figured it, there were just some people around who needed that shit, and he guessed there always had been, but he wasn't one of them, so he didn't.

It's the mode of expression that interests me, here, rather than the sentiment: qualifiers that work to emphasise the unruffled rejection of fancy speech and complexity through an implicit 'YMMV/whatever' textual strategy both distancing and ironizing. 'Basically', 'the way he figured it', 'that shit', 'he guessed'. There's a good deal of this in *The Peripheral.* Indeed, one of the key ways Gibson generates his aesthetic effects is by rubbing that kind of thing close up against a completely different idiom, informed by a kind of decadent pseudo-poetic oddness eloquence. One the one hand tech might be 'no shit? a drone? Serious-ass sensing capabilities' [328]; on the other hand, tech might be a 'vaguely Egyptianate, milkily translucent giant sperm of a cam' [392]. It means that scenes might be set with prose like this:

He was trying to sleep on a granite beach in the tall cold hall of Daedra's voice mail, while trains, or perhaps mobies departed, dimly announced by gravely incomprehensible voices. [440]

Or like this:

> The house had floodlights trained on it, bright as day and ugly as shit. They'd painted everything white, she guessed to tie it together, but it didn't. [292]

It can work. It has worked for Gibson before. It didn't really work for me, this time. But shit, man. You know? **shrugs**. YMMV. Whatevs.

David Gilbert
& Sons

This was published in January 2014; I didn't read it until November. So, coming to it a little late, I found the paperback I picked up already weighed down with big-name endorsements, like the chains draped around Marley's ghost – 'magisterial', 'singularly brilliant', 'caustic, comic and clever' – this last from James Wood himself. All of which interpellate me into a grumpy, contrary place: because I really didn't like it. It seemed to me an arch, laboured and frankly irksome piece of work. But when the praise is as big-gun as this, it's hard not to feel that I'm missing something.

What though? Does literature really need yet another big, baggy Foster-Wallace-wannabee, faux-Franzen novel about the eccentric interactions of a narrow clique of patrician New Yorkers? Not, I'd hazard, if it's as hit-and-missy as this one. But, look: why would you trust my judgement? Consider all the big name critics who have praised this novel. I daresay your own experience will align with theirs rather than mine.

& Sons is based about a Salinger-y writer at the end of his life. In his youth A. N. Dyer sold millions of copies of his novel of adolescence *Ampersand* (hence the '&' of Gilbert's title); but now he's a creaky, cranky recluse. He has a couple of sons from his marriage, and a much younger third son from a late life dalliance with a much younger woman, and the book is about these father-son relationship (hence the 'sons' of Gilbert's title). The narrator of this rather strenuously tricksy narrative is a different son, the offspring of Dyer's best friend, Charles Henry Topping. The novel starts with Topping's funeral, to which Dyer has been coerced into attending to deliver the eulogy. But Dyer, panicky and hating being out in public, fluffs his speech badly. From there the narrative spirals out into a variety of filial stories. Philip Topping, our narrator, has a rather unhealthy fixation on Dyer, whom he hopes will endorse and otherwise facilitate his own stalled literary career. Dyer's oldest biological son is an ex-druggie, now drug counsellor moving into the world of cinematic screenwriting; which gives Gilbert the opportunity to write scenes set in the world of movie pre-production, about all of which I could – as I believe they say in

America – care less. The second biological son Jamie is wilder, more damaged individual with a fixation on death and disaster. The teenage third son Andy is fixated upon losing his virginity before he hits eighteen, since losing it *after* that landmark birthday would be, somehow, demeaning.

It aims, as I say, at a certain Foster Wallaceness. It does not hit that elusive target. This is partly because what it has to say, beneath the flurry of its *look-ma-no-hands*! prose, is pretty banal: 'when you have grown up sage and comfortable, you often find yourself admiring the poor and desperate, as if they are somehow more honest' [76]; 'so much happens to us without our knowing' [153]; 'you can never really know something' [309]. Okay then. But what sank the novel for me were the similes. Occasionally these are good, like this one:

> The windshield carried the grimy aftereffects of snow, the wiper blade describing an arc similar to an open book. [71]

Others were less so ('Richard kicked the ground with his breath', 382. Say what?). And most were bad, poorly judged or ill-thought-through, straining for that comedy zing but instead of zinging only zanging, or zoinging, or sometimes *zzz*-ing. 'Andy and Emmett jingled the ice [in their drinks] like a nest of exotic but short-lived creatures' [278]; 'his face was colored with almost exotic damage, like a psychological tan. He. Had. Lived.' [50]; 'The fire said Fuck you and Richard said Fuck you back before he laid the wet towels on top and there was a hiss and a mini mushroom cloud' [411]; 'one of those awful airport restaurants that reeked of disinfectant, as if Mr Clean were decomposing in the corner' [149]; 'Eyes so shrunken a blink might tear the skin' [233]; 'his expression [was] so flinched as to be flinchless' [206]. They keep coming, *say-what*? after *say-what*? Since the whole novel depends from the hook of Gilbert's chatty, simile-sprawly style, too much of this kind of thing slayed it for me. There's also, as a bonus, some genuinely dreadful sub-Updike descriptions of vaginas: 'her pussy – Jamie wondered if this was being disrespectful to the dead or if the dead begged for these memories – but her pussy was perfect, with its mitten of dark blond, its interior the impossible smooth of a conch.' [146] We get long quotations from *Ampersand*, and Dyer's other books, none of which leads me to believe his literary reputation would have been what

Gilbert repeatedly tells us it is. It turns out Topping is an unreliable narrator, with a distinct streak of curlywurly-cuckoo about him. All in all: Bellow's *Seize the Day* this is not.

Philip Larkin used to review jazz records for *The Daily Telegraph* back in the 1960s. I have no interest in jazz, but enough interest in Larkin to have at least browsed these pieces, collected in *All What Jazz: A Record Diary 1961–71* (1985). One review particularly struck me: it was of an early Beatles LP, and it read (I quote from memory) 'the jazz content of this record appears to be nil'. I love that, and am tempted to re-apply it in modifed form here. I can't, though; because the SF/F content of this novel is not actually nil. There's a [SPOILER, I suppose] midpoint revelation about paternity that draws on some mildly speculative genetic engineering, very handwavily introduced. Little is made of the 'palingenesis' pseudo-cloning point; some characters refuse to believe that it explains Andy Jr, others use it to riff on the same-but-different nature of the whole patrem-filius dynamic. And actually, if I think about it, there are clearly *some* jazz inflections, howsoever faint and background, to early Beatles records. Taste the SF mouthfeel of this novel: the Larkinesque judgment still holds.

The Grand Budapest Hotel (dir. Wes Anderson)

This film having been nominated for the 2015 Oscars, and with the fact that it popped up (conveniently) on the TV again, I decided to re-watch it. It really is a splendid piece of work: charming, witty, laugh-out-loud in places, gorgeously framed and designed and acted. Fiennes' Gustave is a beautiful performance (boo to him not getting Best Actor nod), and I would hazard the only character from any of this year's films who will enter popular consciousness in a longer-term sense. There's also the sheer pleasure of seeing Anderson make his most Andersonian film yet, and registering all the little tropes and signatures of which he is so fond: the uncondescending absorption in kitsch, the use of models, the sly but telling staging of generational misdirection and love. Charm, I have had occasion to say more than once, is really very hard to fake, and this is a thoroughly and deeply charming movie.

The question is: is it anything more? I've read criticism suggesting it is style over substance, all icing and no actual cake. Suggesting it isn't really *saying* anything. There is lots of running around and some artfully staged gags and set-pieces, but to what end? The first time I saw it, last year, I wondered if it was saying something about American attitudes to Europe, specifically that other-side-of-the-Atlantic sense that there is something old and elegant and a bit faggotty but above all something out-of-time and doomed about the mitteleuropäisch world. Which is fair enough, if a little shallow and caricaturing.

Rewatching it, however, was a revelation. The whole movie erects its filigree gorgeousness across a chasm, and only a fool (like me, evidently) could fail to grasp the nature and depth of this abyss. The repeated scenes, like visual rhymes, in which the old-school cultured European is on a train that is stopped in a field. Peering through the window and wondering 'why are we stopping in a field?' A whole movie structured across a tacit divide: we get the pre-war elegance and the post-war Sovietised shabbiness and downbeat melancholy. But what is the gap, exactly? What story does the film keep telling, in its various ways? Deputy Kovacs, played with swaggering elegance by the Jew, Jeff Goldblum, tries to execute the legal will of his deceased client and for his pains is murdered by the thuggish, skull-faced Jopling (played by the Aryan, Willem Dafoe). Serge X (played by the Jew, Mathieu Amalric) helps Gustave and Zero by packing 'Boy With Apple' for Gustave with the true will in the back, is also murdered by Jopling. Zero himself (played as a young man by the Guatemalan actor Tony Revolori, but realised in old age by the splendidly Semitic (I thought him Jewish, but it turns out his parentage is Syrian Christian and Italian) F. Murray Abraham) relates how his whole family has been murdered, and faces several close brushes with death himself. He survives, but everyone he loves vanishes into the abyss between the pre-war and post-war iterations of the movie. The Nazis are never mentioned; but they, and the Holocaust, are the invisible centre of gravity around which the whole film bends. This is not to suggest it's in any way a gloomy or morbid movie. On the contrary the lightness and humour with which Anderson tells his story is not only wonderful in its own right; it is a very clever way of narrating the Holocaust. As M Gustave says of the perfect lobby boy, he is completely invisible, yet always in sight. I have heard the eternal footman, or in this case, lobby boy hold my coat and snicker. What happens to Gustave in the end is that 'they' shoot him. As the man himself puts it: 'You see, there are still faint glimmers of civilization left in this barbaric slaughterhouse that was once known as humanity. Indeed that's what we provide in our own modest, humble, insignificant... oh, fuck it.'

I was put in mind of a sentence from Nabokov's 1948 story 'Symbols and Signs', perhaps my single favourite short story. The characters are two elderly Russian Jews, living in New York after the war and trying to find the wherewithal to keep their deranged, paranoiac, possibly suicidal son in the institution that cares for him. At one point, the mother pulls out a photograph album and looks through the photographs. Her attention is mostly on her son, of course; but the sentence I'm talking about is the last of this quotation, the one concerning Aunt Rosa.

> She pulled the blind down and examined the photographs. As a baby, he [the son] looked more surprised than most babies. A photograph of a German maid they had had in Leipzig and her fat-faced fiancé fell out of a fold of the album. She turned the pages of the book: Minsk, the Revolution, Leipzig, Berlin, Leipzig again, a slanting house front, badly out of focus. Here was the boy when he was four years old, in a park, shyly, with puckered

> forehead, looking away from an eager squirrel, as he would have from any other stranger. Here was Aunt Rosa, a fussy, angular, wild-eyed old lady, who had lived in a tremulous world of bad news, bankruptcies, train accidents, and cancerous growths until the Germans put her to death, together with all the people she had worried about.

There's a whole novel in that sentence (I often think Nabokov doesn't get enough credit for the extraordinary *tenderness* with which he can write). Rosa was right to worry, we might think; it's just that she worried about the wrong things: she fussed at the near-by trivia and did not see the storm-front rearing over the horizon. I'm not sure that's right, though. We live our life close at hand, after all; the people we care about tend to be near, and they matter a great deal. It's reasonable to hope that the huge impersonal forces of death and horror pass us by, but it's a mistake to obsess about those things. In its attention to detail, to the surface textures and delights of life, even unto the icing, *Grand Budapest Hotel* understands that. It also understands the abyss, into which the middle years of the century shovelled literally millions of Jewish and Queer corpses. It just doesn't put that centre-frame. When I watched it first I thought the movie charming but lightweight. Now I wonder if it isn't a masterpiece.

Mira Grant
Symbiont

This, the second volume in Grant's 'Parasitology' dyad, turns out actually to be the *middle* volume of an on-the-hoof refashioning of Grant's "Parasitology" series into a trilogy. Maybe vol 3 will turn into a two-part conclusion, which in turn will yield four instalments and so on. I don't know. At any rate, the premise here is that near-future humanity all have special 'SymboGen' tapeworms in their guts to enable them to combat disease, obesity and so on. The tapeworm in question is called 'The Intestinal Bodyguard', which I don't believe would get past the product development Beta Testing stage, name-wise. Personally, I'd have suggested 'Gut Lord', and licensed that Blur song for advertising purposes. Anyway, not to get distracted: the iron law of Frankensteinian Unintended Consequences means that these tapeworms malfunction, become self-aware, clamber up through their host's bodies, killing some people and turning hordes of others into zombies. The z-word is, naturally, never used: the afflicted are called 'sleepwalkers'. But don't let the terminology fool you. This is pure AFZN, an acronym which here stands for *Another Fucking Zombie Novel.*

Grant deserves credit for the sheer boldness and oddity of writing a tapeworm/human interspecies romance. The thing is, she doesn't take proper advantage of the weirdness of this conceit. Repeating the phrase 'a tapeworm in a human suit' is as far as the novel goes by way of flagging up the David-Cronenberg-ish yuk! potential. In the telling the fact that our narrator is 'a chimera of human and tapeworm, a dead body piloted through the world by an invertebrate' [359] is handled in a clean-as-clean-can-be fashion. The reader is given great wodges of talking, exposition, padding, running about, pseudo-science and hand-waving:

> 'the science was all gibberish delivered by people wearing white coats and serious expressions. The fact that I was actually a tapeworm in a woman-suit made no more or less sense than anything else' [63].

Bottom line: the book stands or falls on how far it convinces you of the resonant pathos of its central conceit, viz.: 'I would love him until the day I died and we would never be the same species' [367]. It's an emotional swipe that completely failed to land, for me. Your wormileage may vary. 'And don't forget I'm... I'm also just a parasitic flatworm of the genus Platyhelminthes Cestodea, standing in front of a boy, asking him to love her.' Without that emotional piquancy, I found reading this long narrative increasingly wearing. It's a book with the texture of cotton wadding, the dialogue is flat, the scenes where the characters are in peril from the zombie sleepwalkers are unexciting, there are various holes in the plot, and I was left with no desire to read volume 3. Thog might like it, though:

> His affronted expression [was] melting into guilt. [30]
> There was a hand on my shoulder. I didn't want to think about it. Thinking about it would have meant admitting that I had a shoulder. [49]
> As with the gurney from before, I was strapped to the surface that I was on top of. [158]
> I swallowed hard, trying to convince my salivary glands to do their job. [159]
> Sherman's eyes raked dispassionately over the three men. [192]
> Gunshots. They came quick and efficient, one after the other, like someone running a hand along a typewriter. [273]
> Her bare skin [was] humping up into goosebumps as the air-conditioning rolled over it. [364]
> 'I don't know,' I said, shaking my head until my hair whipped against my forehead like a hundred tiny, stinging lashes. [365]
> The hot/cold slush in my belly was beginning to melt, becoming a warm, solid mass of resignation. [406]
> I shook off the veil of disgust that had settled over me. [434]

My favourite of these is probably the Ernie Wise-ish one from p.158. And so ends the review what I wrote.

Susan Gray
Sum

I saw Susan Gray's excellent science fiction play *Sum* at the Bread and Roses, in Clapham, on Saturday 20th November 2014. It is a play about the early days of a hivemind, set in a blasted near-future and tracing, through a sinuously threaded string of intense set-piece scenes, the tension between assimilation and individuality. The direction, by Chris Callow Jr, very effectively focuses attention where it needs to be: on the performances and the words; and the acting of the all-female cast is uniformly excellent. Where so much of the dramatic force depends on the integrated work of the whole company it would be invidious to single performances; but, that said, Lydia Kay as Carrie/Lan did extraordinarily well with the technically tricky business of acting two rather different characters at once; Melanie Crossey brought real electricity to Syne's hopes of becoming the 'head' of this new acephalic entity. Gray's play is at once an imaginative new intervention into a venerable SF trope, and a meditation upon theatre itself. Callow, who trained at the Athenian Stage in Greece, knows very well how the interaction between individuated 'characters' and a group-mind 'chorus' determined the very shape of drama in Aeschylus, Sophocles and Euripides; and *Sum* feels in one sense like a modern re-evaluation of the core structures of theatre itself. Highly recommended.

Daryl Gregory
Afterparty

Smart near-future thriller about designer drugs is smart. Lots of lovely 'woh!' and 'mmm?' and 'aha!' moments here, and a likeably quippy alt-culture narrator. The big sell is the notion that 'the Numinous' (which Huxley, following Rudolf Otto, usefully pinpointed as the salient where religious belief is concerned) might be something a pill makes neurologically manifest in people. Not a brand new notion this, in terms of SF, but it's interestingly handled here. There are various other cool speculative drugs, some nifty future tech (like miniaturised living farm animals you can keep in your bedroom), some rather gratuitous fighting and torturing, and a good deal of running about.

It wouldn't be the first novel of which one could say 'it might have been better if the author just laid out his cool ideas rather than trying to realise them in novel-form via storyline, characters and all that'. But it would be, eh, 'a' novel. Of which one could say that. If you see what I mean. The 'ideas' part is super-cool, the character interactions intermittently cool and the overall story not really very well handled. I had problems with the worldbuilding too. In our not-future-at-all present many people buy their drugs from dealers; but even now there are plenty who are happy to grow and/or mix their own. After all, Jesse Pinkman is perfectly capable of running-up passable meth; what Walter W. brings to the party is the extra quality that comes with his Respecting The Chemistry. Fast forward to a future where everybody has 3D printers and concoction machines, surely most people would be downloading recipes from shady online sources and cooking their own? But Gregory's crime-story plot needs a sub-culture of dubious dealers, fences and cooks, pursued by law enforcement of several stripes, so that's what we get.

Mind you, one thing I liked very much was the novel's emphasis on the affective rather than the logical component of its Big Theme. This, after all, is what drugs are about. People talk about 'smart drugs', but the reality is people take drugs, from alcohol to heroine, from LSD to speed, to alter their affect, not their intellect. And this is right for religion too. One of the mistakes Dawkins-gang atheists frequently make, I would say, is treating religious faith as a set of rational (to them:

irrational) truth-claims about the cosmos. That kind of thing is a vanishingly small proportion of actual religious praxis, I think; and Francis Spufford is surely right that whether or not religion makes cognitive sense it does make surprising *emotional* sense.

I might dilate upon this for a moment, actually; because an older, eighteenth-century brand of atheism (the one that shaped Shelley's *Necessity of Atheism* pamphlet, for instance) starts from precisely this position, and uses it to make points rather more compelling than Dawkins does. It is *because* the truth of faith is felt, not rationalised, that by definition religion's reach is limited. People are often capable of rationalising a belief after the fact; but it's really not possible to force oneself to feel something one does not feel. The Jehovah's Witness people leaning on my doorbell are working against the insurmountable friction of that fact when they try to draw me across to their view of the cosmos. But the flip-side of this is that Dawkinistas are just as surely on a hiding to nothing in trying to convince people who *feel* faith to abandon it on merely rational grounds. Faith is a species of love, after all; and the more earnestly and rationally a third party strives to *prove* to you that the person you love is unworthy of your affection, the more you're liable to dig your heels in. When it comes to love, you feel what you feel.[7] Gregory understands this basic aspect of religious pretty well, I think. At one point the Vincent, a CIA expert in stress techniques, mulls over the old 'right and wrong' question. What is the difference between those two things?

---

[7] I don't want to derail the review by banging on about this, but the parallel interests me. It's the circumstance of the proselytising atheist that is so fascinating. Person A loves God. Person B loves Dennis. I think person B could do better: Dennis isn't actively abusive, but he isn't the kind of the person I think merits so profound a human emotion as love (it doesn't matter, for our purposes here, why I think this: maybe Dennis is a bit of a slob, or deadbeat; maybe his politics are 'wrong'; maybe he just strikes me as inconsequential). The point is this: what kind of individual would I have to be to try and intervene into Person B's life to persuade him/her that s/he really *shouldn't* love Dennis? I suppose it's possible that my strawperson Dawkinista considers Person A's 'relationship' with God to be abusive; and indeed, if Person B loved a violent, emotionally controlling or otherwise abusive person I might feel moved to intervene. But it's hard to see how a non-existent person could be abusive. What it boils down to is: I don't see that Dennis is loveable, which is an index of the fact that I don't love Dennis. That's a pretty thin reason to try and drag Person B across to my view. Similarly, what grounds do I have for meddling with Person A's love?

> 'I know in my head,' the Vincent said. 'And what I've learned is that it's not *knowing* what's right or wrong, it's *caring*. Feeling the wrongness... Your morality is not *rational*, or handed down to you on stone tablets by some divine cop, it's wired into your nervous system.' [89]

It's possible the novel leans a little too hard on the 'just because it's imaginary doesn't mean it's not real!' [340] angle. But it's good stuff. You should try a toke.

Bethany Griffin
The Fall

Griffin's fourth novel is no great departure, concept-wise, from her second and third (*The Masque of the Red Death* and *The Dance of the Red Death*) – that is to say, it is a novel that briskly spins its hand-whisk in the thick cream of Edgar Allan Poe, producing something recognisably Poe-like that is, at the same time, considerably less dense and rich. ('Cream of Poe' is like regular cream, except that is, you know: black. And tastes of mausoleums. Goes well with over-ripe strawberries.)

So, this aerated and rather temporary concoction is *The Fall of the House of Usher* turned into a novel-length Gothic-y YA yarn. As such it's all about the mood; Madeline Usher, our point-of-access beautiful, doomed young heroine, wakes up inside a coffin ('tears wet my cheeks. I cannot breathe. I cannot breath. Blood trickles down my fingernails and I am choking' [3]) as per Poe's original story. Indeed, without a knowledge of this original text it seems to me this rather oddly structured tale wouldn't make a great deal of sense. The problem is, with that knowledge, it feels a little redundant: why do we need this novelisation, when we have the original? Griffin mixes the timeline up (chapters are all named after Madeline's age, and hop about: 'Madeline is sixteen', 'Madeline is nine', 'Madeline is seventeen' and so on); but the novel drags its heels. Its stacked, black, vinyl heels. The whole is 420 pages long, and could easily have lost 200 or more from the middle without missing them. But, sure: the rather repetitive plotting isn't the point. The mood is the point. I readily concede that sour middle-aged male university professors are not the target audience for this book. The most I will say is that I did try, when reading, to unlock my inner emo teenage girl, and that I failed. On the plus side, props to Griffin for actually opening her novel with 'It was a dark and stormy night'. (Strictly speaking, this is the start of chapter 2; but that's close enough for government work, especially since chapter 1 reads like a kind of prologue):

> Wind and rain, lightning and thunder, a storm throws itself against the House of Usher, rattling every window, including mine. Thunder pounds the earth and the house groans. [5]

And so on: the whole is written in this rather gnashing manner throughout (it's less fruity than Poe's prose, though; which is a good thing. Although more fruity than Poe would be hard to achieve. He is the fruitiest of the fruity. Hence – the cream.)

There ought to be a name for the – I think, genuinely recent – cultural logic by which a short, powerful text is expanded into a longer mode, because 'we' respect length in a way we don't brevity. I'm thinking of things like: the, we can agree, dreadful, movie version of *The Cat in the Hat*; or the many famous short stories ('We Can Remember It For You Wholesale' pops into my head) made into lengthy movies, and often then translated back into lengthy prose form as 'novelisations' of the original movie. What would we call this, I wonder? And what does it say about us? One thing that strikes me is that this cultural-evaluative bias towards length ('epic' as a term of praise, and so on) is happening at a time when or attention spans are supposed to be getting shorter, when our online reading is supposed to be shaped by a twitter-esque logic of tl;dr. What's up with that?

Guardians of the Galaxy (directed by James Gunn)

Quite jolly, but hardly the Second Coming, and *surely* not (as I have seen bruited about) the best Marvel movie ever. The plot was varied, there were lots of inventive details scattered about and some of the banter was funny; but by the same token there was never any real tension or drama, since nothing was ever really at stake. The more hyperbolic the macguffins (infinity jewels that could destroy the galaxy!) the less we believe it, and clearly none of the team are going to snuff it. Still: it would be out of place to carp. Fun was had. The special effects were very detailed and professionally done. Groot was sweet. It bothered me more than it should have done that Drax the Destroyer's inability to comprehend simile or metaphor ('nothing goes over my head' and so on) was so inconsistently applied: many things are said to him in this film of the 'you defeated him single-handedly!' kind that didn't seem to bother him in the least. More debilitating from a dramatic point of view is that the villains all lacked menace. Karen Gillan's Nebula looked like she was auditioning for the mirror-universe's Blue Man Group; Lee Pace's Ronin was camp without ever managing scary camp (which is totally a thing, by the way) and the only evil thing about Josh Brolin's Thanos was his enormous chin. Really: Jimmy-Hill-worthy chinnage.

Big old chin.

One other thing occurred to me as I watched the big SFX-splurgy conclusion, and it was this: when will big budget Hollywood find a way of ending SF movies that doesn't involve crashing enormous planes into a New York City analogue? *Avengers*; *Star Trek Into Darkness*; this film. Which is another way of asking: when will that trauma no longer be so overwhelmingly dominant in the US cultural subconscious?

John Gwynne
Valour

Valour is Grimdark Heroic Fantasy. Doesn't that look like an oxymoron, though? Even perhaps a triple oxymoron? ('triximoron'?). Heroism depends upon a culture in which ideals are widely shared; Grimdark upon a world in which everybody is cynical and jaded and out for number one; and Fantasy depends upon threading a path between the stifling ideals of Right Action All The Time and a demeaning nasty-brutish-and-short-ness.

I'm overthinking this. *Valour* is volume two of John Gwynne's ongoing saga *The Faithful and the Fallen*. The first volume, *Malice*, was a reassuringly or depressingly (pick whichever term you prefer) familiar High Fantasy fable-cum-potboiler: Corban, growing to adulthood, begins to comprehend he that is the Chosen One as his cod-medieval kingdom is George-R-R-Martinned around him. *Valour* continues the story. For those desirous of orienting themselves, the publishers have provided the following jacket text:

> The Banished Lands is torn by war as High King Nathair sweeps the land challenging all who oppose him in his holy crusade. Allied with the manipulative Queen Rhin of Cambren, there are few who can stand against them. But Rhin is playing her own games and has her eyes on a far greater prize... Left for dead, her kin fled and her country overrun with enemies, Cywen has no choice but to try to survive. But any chance of escape is futile once Nathair and his disquieting advisor Calidus realise who she is. They have no intention of letting such a prize from their grasp. For she may be their greatest chance at killing the biggest threat to their power. Meanwhile, the young warrior Corban flees from his conquered homeland with his exiled companions heading for the only place that may offer them sanctuary - Domhain. But to get there they must travel through Cambren avoiding warbands, giants and the vicious wolven of the mountains. And all the while Corban must battle to become the man that everyone believes him to be - the Bright Star and saviour of the Banished Lands. And in the Otherworld dark forces scheme to bring a host of the Fallen

into the world of flesh to end the war with the Faithful, once and for all.

Also provided is a map.

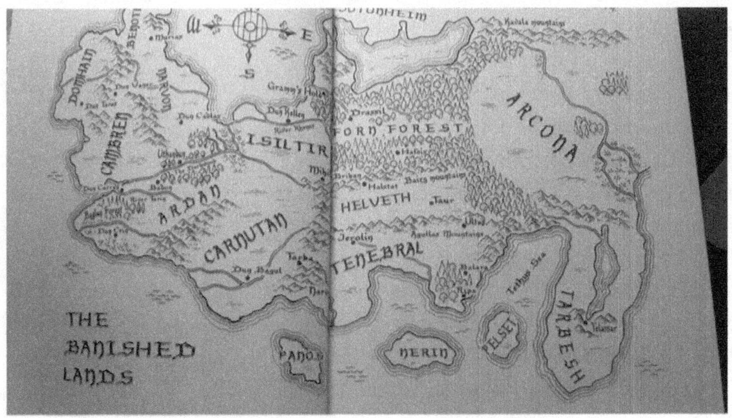

Not a bad map, as these things go. Then a poem:

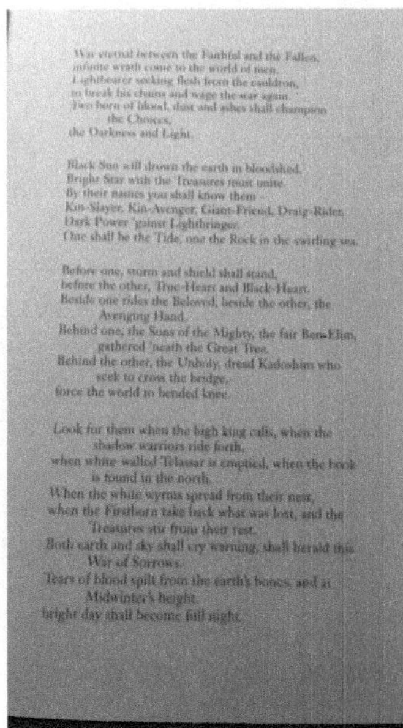

War eternal between the Faithful and the Fallen,
infinite wrath come to the world of men.
Lightbearer seeking flesh from the cauldron,
to break his chains and wage the war again.
Two born of blood, dust and ashes shall champion
the Choices,
the Darkness and Light.

Black Sun will drown the earth in bloodshed,
Bright Star with the Treasures must unite.
By their names you shall know them –
Kin-Slayer, Kin-Avenger, Giant-Friend, Draig-Rider,
Dark Power 'gainst Lightbringer.
One shall be the Tide, one the Rock in the swirling sea.

Before one, storm and shield shall stand,
before the other, True-Heart and Black-Heart.
Beside one rides the Beloved, beside the other, the
Avenging Hand.
Behind one, the Sons of the Mighty, the fair Ben-Elim,
gathered 'neath the Great Tree.
Behind the other, the Unholy, dread Kadoshim who
seek to cross the bridge,
force the world to bended knee.

Look for them when the high king calls, when the
shadow warriors ride forth,
when white walled Telassar is emptied, when the book
is found in the north.
When the white wyrms spread from their nest,
when the Firstborn take back what was lost, and the
Treasures stir from their rest.
Both earth and sky shall cry warning, shall herald this
War of Sorrows.
Tears of blood spilt from the earth's bones, and at
Midwinter's height,
bright day shall become full night.

Not a good poem, as these things go.

Then: a five-page list of dramatis personae. That's *five full pages* packed tight with names like 'Dath', 'Gar', 'Heb', 'Rafe', 'Vonn', 'Kai', 'Morc', 'Rhin', 'Rath', 'Jael', 'Wolf', 'Bos', 'Walk', 'Tanc', 'Flai', 'Jam', 'Nitti', 'Grittay', 'Tolkien', 'Tutti', 'Bois', 'Frum', 'Dee', 'Bigg', 'Bad', 'Citi', 'Dissis', 'Djamhodt', 'Dissis'... Look, I'm making these up now, I freely confess, and have been doing so since 'Bos'. But at least 'Bos' is an actual character in this book. There are also two individuals called 'Fray' ('Giant, companion of Uthas') and 'Ventos' ('a Helveth travelling merchant-trader') who, one earnestly hopes, come together in the main narrative to sell meat pies.

Then: a cauldron!

The cauldron was a hulking mass of black iron, tall and wide, squatting upon a dias in the centre of a cavernous room. Torches of blue flame hung upon the walls of the chamber. Uthas of the Benothi giants strode towards the cauldron...

Now that I have 'pies' in my head, I can't read 'Benothi' without salivating. Mmm! Anyway:

> ...strode towards the cauldron, his shadow flickering on the walls. He climbed the steps and stopped before it. It was utterly black, appearing to suck the torchlight into it, consuming it, reflecting nothing back. [1]

None more black. This gives you a flavour of the whole: unafraid of a bit of cheesy Gothic melodrama. When the story gets going it's all about the many characters all travelling from place to place and scheming and fleeing and fighting. Perfectly serviceably done. You, for instance. Yes, you. You may well be looking for a huge swamp of a narrative in which you can lose yourself, like sinking into a warm bath. If so, then this is for you, It's utterly unoriginal, full of violence, lots of things happen and it doesn't really go anywhere. Me, I found the prithee sirrah idiom hovered uncomfortably between too wincingly archaic ('"Did you see Akar fall?" "Aye. Calidus spoke true. A giant did slay Romar"' [19]) and frankly not archaic enough ('Textual inconsistencies are remarkably rare in the giants' histories' [316]). There's every dramatic cliché you can think of, as well as most of the stylistic ones, and that irritating convention by which characters' inward thoughts are rendered onto the page in slabs of italics. *Aye*, he thought to himself, *that has always annoyed me, when writers do that. What do they hope to gain?*

The world is early medieval, largely Celtic in flavour with a strong dose of Norse: giants, dragons and other monsters are real. But the worldbuilding is the usual Fantasy mishmash *omnium gatherum*: bits of French ("I'll not be a corsair for you!" [333]), Greek ('amphorae of wine' [117]), Persian (carpets are mentioned on p.141) and Indian ("Avatar of Elyon!" [179]) and so on. Chapters are short, heavy on the dialogue, threaded with detailed descriptions of stabbing, mauling, decapitating, torturing and slaying, and each ends with a mini-cliffhanger or duh-duh-DUH! revelation. The author's website suggests he plans four volumes of *The Faithful and the Fallen*, but I see no reason why it couldn't go on forever. I admit I found it draggy and stale, but your George-R-R-Mileage may vary.

Graham Hancock
War God: Return of the Plumed Serpent

Set notionally in the 16th century, during the Spanish conquistador incursions into Mexico, the world of this novel is fashioned from equal parts cardboard, laboriously infodumped historical research, and anachronistic dialogue ('they say a bird in the hand is worth two in the bush', as one 16th century Spaniard says to another 16th century Spaniard [225]). We also get: flat characters adopting a series of melodramatic postures, dramatic cliché, stylistic cliché, egregiously bloody interludes of violence and torture, more cliché and a draggy over-long telling that starts and ends in medias res, for there are more, and perhaps woe-is-it-unto-us many, many more, volumes to come in the *War God* series. Bloaty stuff. Let me put it this way: not my favourite novel of 2014.

Tom Harper
Zodiac Station

What we have here is a very competently handled Arctic thriller. US Coast Guard ice-breaking cutter *Terra Nova* is working the frozen Nansen Basin when a desperate man comes looming out of the mist, skiing across the ice. So abrupt is his arrival that he is actually shot by a startled security detail. The man lives, however, and in the vessel's sickbay tells his story: he is called Thomas Anderson, and has come from the research base Zodiac Station hundreds of kilometres away, a place full of (as Anderson tells it) high-strung scientists and administrators, a crucible of murder by conspiracy and violence. The base has now been exploded, as if by a bomb. As it happens, I have likewise planted a major spoiler in this review too, in the second paragraph, and it may well explode your enjoyment of reading the novel, assuming you haven't already read it. You have been warned. Otherwise, the authorities fly to Zodiac, and recover other survivors, who tell a rather different tale to Anderson. There are schemes and counter-schemes by climate scientists and climate change deniers in the pay of big industry, CIA involvement, freaky science, many polar bears; there's loads of zipping across the ice, exploring abandoned mines, falling down crevasses. As is the way with 'classic' style thrillers a good deal of Quite Interesting Facticity is kneaded into the running-around, exploring, shooting, threatening-and-being-threatened plotline. The reader learns a good deal about the far north, about methane and arctic fauna and how you have to lift a snowmobile's back-end off the ice before you fire it up, since if its treads have got frozen to the ice you'll burn out the engine. Which is all fine. I thought the book starts very well, and then dissipates itself in a too-many-plotlines, too-many-red-herrings middle section. It might be that the red herrings looked redder and more obvious than they would otherwise have done, set against the bright white background of the ice-pack. Then there's the ending.

So, yes: spoiler. The brighter-hued herrings swim away to their red sea, and we're left with the normal-coloured herring – *Zodiac Station* is a reworking of *Frankenstein*, taking its cue from the powerful initial and final scenes of Shelley's novel, also set, of course, on the polar ice. The *Terra Nova* is Harper's version of Walton's ship; the creature is genetically engineered instead of being stitched together from corpseparts but is still called The Creature, still stronger and cleverer than us, still a full grown adult of only a few years mental maturity and so on. Now all this is fine by me, and a fairly clever reveal; and looking back over the narrative lots of things (names, clues, quotations from Milton) drop into place. But it's tricky too. It's the two stools problem. For a SF geek like me, there's something anticlimactic about bringing in the Novum only at the very end; for I feel it ought to have been the starting point, the better to explore all its implications. Whereas a fan of straight thrillers (and Harper has written several of those, with considerable commercial and fannish success) is liable to agree with the reviewer who took to Goodreads to say: 'Good page turning thriller. A good few twists to keep you guessing. Fairly believable plot right up to the end where it does get a bit silly.' Hmm.

Nick Harkaway
Tigerman

The Harkaway thing about *Tiger(man)*
(For *Tiger(man)*'s a Harkaway thing):
Its tops are made out of Batman;
Its bottom is made out of Greene.
Its bouncy, flouncy, lit'ry, bit twee, fun fun fun fun fun,
But by far the most Harkaway thing about *Tiger(man)*
Is its tangled-yet-self-aware-complicity-with-upper-middle-class-White-English-masculine-codes-of-right-behaviour-in-a-postcolonial-context:
Po-o-o-ost
colonialcontext.

A. F. Harrold
The Imaginary

This is a lovely older child/YA fable by the impressively bearded A F Harrold, beautifully illustrated by Emily Gravett (I mean the *book* has been beautifully illustrated, not that Gravett has drawn fetching designs upon Harrold's own flesh. I've no idea whether she has done this latter thing). It's about imaginary friends, but from the point of view of those imaginary friends, troped here as real but supernatural entities. Amanda, the heroine, discovers Rudger (not Roger!) in her cupboard.

'Why's there mud on the carpet, then?'

'It weren't me, Mum,' Amanda shouted, sliding off her bed and onto her feet.

There were footsteps coming up the stairs.

She picked up the wet shoes. Actually, they were a little bit muddy, she thought. Sort of. If you looked really hard.

She stood there for a moment, the shoes dangling from her fingertips. If her mum came in and found her holding them like that, and saw the mud on their soles, then she'd leap to a conclusion. Amanda had to get rid of the shoes, and quick.

Opening the window and chucking them out would take too long. She could throw them under the bed, except her bed was the sort of bed that didn't have an under underneath it, just big drawers, and they were already cram-packed with important junk.

There was only one thing to do.

She pulled open the door to her wardrobe and tossed them in there.

They hit the boy who was still holding her coat. He said, 'Oof,' as the shoes bounced off his stomach and fell to the carpet.

8

Amanda was just about to tell him off for dropping them when her bedroom door burst open.

'Amanda Primrose Shuffleup,' her mother said in that annoying way mothers have. (They seem to think that if they can remember all your names you'll somehow feel more thoroughly told off. Since, however, they probably named you in the first place, it's never really that impressive.) 'What have I told you about taking your shoes off in the hallway before coming upstairs?'

For a moment Amanda didn't say anything. She was thinking fast, but confusion was winning.

There were two doorways. One led out to the landing and was filled up by her mum. The other, that of the wardrobe, framed a boy she'd never seen before. He looked about her own

They have splendid play-adventures together. Some delicious chills are provided by the alarming Mr Bunting, who has unnaturally extended his lifespan by devouring imaginary friends, and now has got a whiff of Rudger. Amanda is well realised; Rudger's adventures, pursued by Mr Bunting, and properly tense and thrilling; but the most moving part of the whole novel, perhaps surprisingly, is the secondary story of Amanda's mum, who has forgotten about her own childhood imaginary friend, a dog called Fridge; who recalls him, and then forgets him again. Heartbreakingly written! All in all: a very lovely novel indeed.

The Hobbit: The Battle of the Five Armies (directed by Peter Jackson)

The Defining Chapter, declares the poster for Jackson's last Middle Earth movie, *The Hobbit: The Battle of the Five Armies*. Insofar as 'definition' means *clarity* this claim is demonstrably wrong, for this movie is as muddled as you have heard: character motivation and identity a mess, narrative logic and consecutiveness hit-and-miss, emotional through-line clumsy and unengaging. Still, there's the related sense of 'definition' as *expressing the essential nature of something*, and where that is concerned the poster is much closer to the truth. *Hobbit 3* is like *Hobbit 2*, but more so – a special effects splurge of weightless, affectless fighting and running around. Frankly the whole trilogy has proved less J.R.R. and more C.G.I. Tolkien.

The pre-credit sequence is a James-Bond-style self-contained set-piece. The dragon, Benedict Cumbersmaug, sets Laketown on fire, and movie touches briefly on what for want of a better word I'm going to call its *main theme*, viz. political leaders are untrustworthy types, fundamentally uninterested in the welfare of their people. In this case it's the Master of Laketown. Played by Stephen Fry with characteristically one-note Stephen-Fryness, he loads a barge with treasure and flees coward-fashion as his town burns. For heroism we have to look to Bard the Bowman, a man whose pronounced Welsh accent would be less incongruous if the rest of Laketown didn't speak generic Cockney. Bard climbs a clock-tower with a quiver full of arrows and fires volley after volley at the Wyrm. In the first draft of this review I inserted a "How Green Is My Volley?" joke at this point, but on reflection I think we're all better off without that. Of course his shots all bounce off the dragon hide, until, arrowless, his bow broken, Bard's young son pops up carrying a gigantic metal shaft. With the same bowstring, somehow rigging the two halves of his broken bow and using the boy – absurdly – as an arrow rest, Bard shoots this last shot. Now, the requirement that momentum be conserved means that any given bowstring can propel a lighter arrow faster or a heavier arrow more slowly. Somehow, though, this shaft hurtles with increased force and celerity, and Smaug is Cumberslain. Who knows how the laws of physics were thereby circumvented? Perhaps: magic. The prologue then pays off this early, minor iteration of its main theme by having Stephen Fry squished by the falling dragon corpse.

The main body of the movie is disposed into two sections, although these relate very uncomfortably to one another. In the first, Thorin is afflicted by 'dragon sickness' and becomes obsessed with the magic jewel Arkenstone, paranoid that his fellow dwarfs have betrayed him. He breaks his word with respect to helping the now homeless Laketowners, walls up the entrance to Erebor and generally goes to the bad. This is the movie's major key iteration of its *main theme*, and is underscored when the Elf King Thranduil rides up on an elk with a troop of gold-armoured elvish warriors. It is not clear to me why a tree elf considers an elk an appropriate mount, or indeed what the elk – a beast surely more associated with tundra and open-grasslands – was doing in Mirkwood to begin with. But *Hobbit 2* has already established that Thranduil is an example of the *main theme*: a monarch whose disconnect from reality and policy of closed-borders has already been represented as short-sighted abdication of the responsibilities of leadership in the face of the reappearance of Sauron. Here we see more of his ill-judged whim-of-iron leadership. His 'motivation' is that Smaug's horde contains a certain necklace he prizes, a flimsy enough pretext for war that the film never properly explains or unpacks. Bard, now de facto leader of the Laketowners, makes an alliance with the elves in the hope of compelling Thorin to honour his word, and give his homeless people the financial wherewithal to rebuild. Dragon-mad Thorin is implacable, and war seems inevitable.

Gandalf arrives, having escaped from his imprisonment by Sauron via a set of narrative daftnesses too dispiriting to list here. Thranduil demonstrates again how ill-fitted he is to kingship by ostentatiously ignoring Gandalf's warning about a huge orc army, just over the brow of the hill. It seems war between dwarfs and elves/men is imminent. At this point Billy Connolly rides in astride a giant pig: a sentence which in almost any other context would be cause to give up writing the review altogether and instead head off to the pub, but which here strikes a note almost of sanity. Connolly is playing the dwarf king Dáin Ironfoot, and he has brought an army with him. The first half of the movie ends with these four armies arrayed against one another.

The transition into the second half of the movie is so jarringly abrupt one might almost suspect Jackson and his scriptwriting team of taking the piss – for, after all, who can touch them? The movie is guaranteed to be a box-office smash pretty much no matter what. The orc army rocks up, just as Gandalf warned they would. Whilst the four forces were squaring off, Azog somehow managed to erect a command centre on top of a nearby mountain, in plain view of the battlefield and complete with a gigantic semaphore flag scaffold, and nobody noticed. I'm going to repeat that: *and nobody noticed.* From this eminence Azog then delivers his fifth army to the battlefield via tunnels specially dug by rock-chewing cousins of Dune's Sandworms. Titantic worms dig out tunnels a few hundred yards from Erebor and thousands of orcs swarm forth. As to why Azog didn't have his titanic worms come up underneath the elvish/mannish/dwarfish armies and finish them off – or why he didn't detour past the battlefield altogether, have then tunnel straight into Erebor, snaffle all the gold and carry it away... well these profound and puzzling questions are not addressed by the film. Also unclear is where the worms go once they've dug out the tunnels. What *is* clear is that the orcs' arrival bends the movie into a wholly new and tortuously implausibly shape.

The first volte face is that the dwarfish and elvish/mannish armies immediately forget their mutual enmity and coordinate to fight the orcs – coordinate, in fact, with the kind of precision it would surely take months of Bob Fosse coaching to bring about. The very first manoeuver involves the dwarfs locking shields into a long testudo wall, and the elves leaping over this in unison to surprise the advancing orcs. The second about-turn is that Thorin abruptly cures himself of the dragon sickness (by, it seems, standing on a huge golden floor *having a hard think about things*). Newly heroic, he leads his troops into battle. There's a long interlude of CGI hewing and hacking, in which gigantic orcish warriors in armour made from slabs of pig iron prove ridiculously vulnerable to the swordplay of child-sized dwarfs wearing not very much. Still, our four forces (Thranduil's elves, Bard's men, Thorin's dwarfs and Dáin's larger dwarfish army) are hugely outnumbered by the orcs, and things look grim. Their response is the strategically jejune one of 'cutting off the head of the snake,' viz. ascending the eminence from which Azog is directing his armies via semaphore and killing him, thus making all the remaining orcs, I don't know, evaporate or convert on masse to Quakerism or something. To reach this height Thorin, Fili, Kili, Stabbi, Garoti and Dori the Explorer

(I confess my vagueness as to the actual names) mount certain giant armoured war rams that are standing nearby. From whence these rams came, why nobody else was using them, how they are able to leap up a sheer cliff: I regret to say I simply don't know.

Meanwhile, Legolas (looking spookily rather *older* than he does in the set-60-years-later *Lord of the Rings* films) and the she-elf Tauriel have been scouting the northlands. They discover an orc fortress, built in neo-Brutalist style out of angular slabs of concrete like a 1950s power station. As they watch this structure disgorges a whole new goblin army, headed by Bolg and preceded by a flock of screeching war-bats ('they are bred,' Legolas tells Tauriel, 'for one purpose only...' and you can almost see Orlando Bloom counting inwardly *one-onethousand, two-onethousand, three-onethousand*, before completing the line: '...*war*!'). These bats have almost no part to play in the battle, beyond screeching and flapping about, which makes me suspect that they were actually bred for one purpose only... *CGI spectacle.* Mind you, Legolas does grab a leg-o'-bat at one point, and use it for a leg-up, fast. Otherwise, like the rock-chewing worms and some nifty giant trolls with giant catapults backpacks, these beasts are to be gawked at briefly and forgotten about.

With the arrival of Bolg we're now dealing, by my reckoning, with six armies; but the more pressing concern is that Bolg's army will arrive first at Ravenhill and so surprise Thorin and his companions, including Tauriel's love interest Kili. So she speeds up the steep slope, with Legolas close behind. What follows is an interminable sequence of single combat scenes between Bolg and Tauriel, Bolg and Kili, Azog and Thorin and Legolas and Bolg. On and on it goes. Just when you think one of these parties is dead, s/he leaps up again and the single-combatting continues, like a video-game sword-fight version of those irritating candles waggish people buy for birthday cakes that, blown out, persistently re-light themselves. Bolg's army, meanwhile, are pouring into the valley and turning the tide of war.

It's at this point that an army of eagles arrives (so: *seven* armies?), giving the audience a two second glimpse of Radagast the Brown and a three second cameo by Beorn, sky-diving down to turn into a bear on the way. The eagles possess the ability to rake through whole battalions knocking them down with their talons like skittles (a skill they presumably lose in the later-set movies), and so the battle is decided. Legolas finally disposes of Bolg; and Thorin kills Azog, receiving a mortal wound in the process. The dwarfish king then has a fifty-minute death scene, expiring in Bilbo's arms in such a manner as to show how apt is his name of Thorin Woodenactor. Nothing remains except some too-abrupt sequences of Bilbo returning to the Shire.

Given that this movie is more tightly, or at least more conventionally structured than either the weirdly bloated and misshapen first two, it's surprising that it works so much less well. It's almost as if it was the bloat and odd shape that redeemed *Hobbits 1* and *2* from the mere dreariness of, in effect, watching somebody else play a video game. Too little is made of Bilbo's possession of the ring, except for one sequence when he wears it to slip through the battle and warn Thorin. Earlier films set up expectation of pay-off from the fact that the hobbit was keeping the possession of the ring secret from Gandalf, but in a bafflingly throwaway moment at the end of the movie it turns out that Gandalf knew all about it all along. Frankly, Jackson fluffs the significance of this artefact; for it has no rôle in this movie except to gesture forward to the Lord of the Rings trilogy. And, sadly, the film is full of this: Bilbo being given the mithril shirt for no reason (it doesn't figure in the actual battle at all) except that we know he later gives it to Frodo. Similarly, Saruman growling 'leave Sauron to me,' after Galadriel has – crazily – magicked The Evil One away into 'the east,' like Robin Williams' genie baseball-pitching the lamp containing Jafar over the horizon at the end of Disney's *Aladdin*. The most egregious example of all comes at the end: Legolas, apparently heartbroken (it's hard to tell, his face is so mask-like) at the realization that Tauriel can never love him, is instructed by Thranduil to 'seek out the ranger in the north who is known as Strider' but whose 'true name you will have to find out for yourself,' because 'you two will become best buddies in the follow-up adventure and we need to lay that groundwork here. For the fans – for *the fans*, you see.' And so, accompanied by the cracked-bell chime of this thuddingly over-literal foreshadowing, Legolas legs it at last.

Perhaps it is a mistake to judge this sort of text by such old-fashioned conceits as 'character,' 'story,' 'coherence' and so on. We might prefer to judge it as an exercise in the visual spectacular, which approach certainly offers us more by way of satisfactions; but important though Weta have been in the development of special effects many of the shots here have an airless, waxy, artificial feel to them. Or maybe it would be better to think of this movie as a species of ballet. Once upon a time, people would queue outside the cinema to watch Ginger Rogers and Fred Astaire disport themselves to music in ways that foregrounded their almost godlike grace, an elegance of motion far beyond mortals like us. Now we queue to see Orlando Bloom, or rather his CGI proxy, comport himself with similar grace – dancing through a scrum of orcs, decapitating as he goes, or leaping along a line of masonry blocks as they tumble into the abyss. What this shift from 'courtship' to 'battle' as the idiom for dance signifies, in a larger sense, I leave as an exercise for the reader to work out. One thing it does mean is that moments that are in any way internalized – say, Thorin overcoming his own dragon sickness – get played out according to the logic of dance routines (in this case, Thorin leaping around a solid gold dancefloor that in turns writhes and swirls). It also means that the battle sequences are about as menacing as the finger-clicking gang encounters in *West Side Story*.

So: none of the character motivations make any sense, with the possible exception of Bilbo: and he gets much too little screen time in this, especially considering that the movie's main title refers to him alone. Not that the film's subtitle accurately reflects the movie either. I don't just mean the numeration; I mean the 'battle' part. Some long shots of CGI hordes flowing over CGI landscapes aside, this movie has no interest in 'battles' as such. It is interested in single combats, for which war, howsoever meagre the *casus belli*, provides the opportunity. This individuation of war is part and parcel of the 'defining' nature of these films taken together. They cannot, it turns out, think the collective at all; they can only think the individual – the fan favourite, the key prop, the singular. That's a pity.

It's a pity for the logic of a film called 'The Battle of the Five Armies,' but it's a bigger pity in terms of the adaptation from Tolkien. Indeed, I wonder if this – rather than the spurious addition of sexy elvish maidens, giant rock chewing worms, and Super Mario-ish combat sequences – is the main mismatch between Tolkien's source text and Jackson's films. Jackson thinks in Romantic and post-Romantic terms, of tragic-heroic heroes and heroines; his vision is fundamentally Byronic and Gothic. Tolkien, though, is a deeply pre-Romantic writer, who thinks in terms of communities, peoples, languages and the idioms of human congregation. These are his great themes, and his evils are things (like the Ring) that cut the individual off from human community.

It has something to do with the movie's 'main theme,' I think. I daresay it's symptomatic of 21st-century attitudes to mistrust and despise politicians. Here the only good leaders are Bard (who, the film is quite clear, does what he does 'for his family' rather than through any larger sense of social duty) and, I guess, Gandalf – though the wizard starts the film caged, beaten and too weak to stand, and never really garners any authority. Otherwise the Master of Laketown is venal and hypocritical, Thorin's shift from corrupted paranoid to noble warrior is positively manic-depressive and rewarded only by death, and Thranduil's haughty camp is as unreliable as it is unreadable (although he at least survives the end of the film). It may over-stretch interpretation to read all this as a more meta transferred suspicion of creative authority – the author, Tolkien himself, who both justifies the entire undertaking and yet whose source material is so difficult to squeeze into the lineaments of modern Hollywood blockbuster form. Jackson and his team work through their confused mixture of admiration and resentment by bending and twisting that unreliable 'authority' in riotous ways. The result is not, I'm sorry to say, very good

.

Kameron Hurley
Infidel

The second volume in Hurley's *Bel Dame Apocrypha* trilogy is actually a 2011 title, and old news for true Hurley fans ('Hurphiles'?). Still, better late than never: it was finally published in the UK as a paperback in 2014. This novel, then, carries the story of Nyx, warrior-assassin for the matriarchal 'Bel Dame' Guild, past the end of the war that characterised volume one of the sequence, *God's War*. Barebones summary: Nyx is now too-old-for-this-shit, no longer a Bel Dame and working as a bodyguard for a diplomat's child. In an opening scene that reminded me, somewhat, of Tony Scott's *Man on Fire* (with Nyx in the Denzel role), she is ambushed whilst escorting her charge. Ah but the twist is: it seems the Bel Dames themselves have put a hit out against her, rather than the kid she was guarding. Throw in a wasting disease slowly killing our hero, lots of juicily repellent Bug-tech, and an incident-ful narrative more cannily paced than *God's War*, and the result is a very readable book. Hurley's descriptive chops are better in this instalment too, I thought. The whole is better crafted without losing its visceral, tearing-off-heads shock and vigour.

Downside: the narrative barrels the reader through so effectively that the post-reading experience involves reflecting back in a way that starts to notice a general thinness, literally for Nyx, figuratively for the book as a whole. Of course it is marking time until the end of the trilogy; but it doesn't move us very far forward. And the villains and their evil schemes are underdeveloped, in part because the focus is so largely on Nyx and friends. There's also a degree of individual mismatch, unavoidable in the case of books and (some of) their readers, and which will certainly not bother most. In this case it has to do with the conceptualisation of war. Hurley is unflinching in showing the horrible, sickening and bloody mess war entails; and her baseline assumptions are the post-world-war-1 consensus that battlefields are arenas of savagery shaped by the hypocrisy of leaders and the pitiable plight of the front line soldiers ('We kill a few people to stop a lot of people dying,' Nyx said. 'Wars kill a lot of people to keep a few people rich.') Not being a warmaker myself, and shaped as I am by the predominantly anti-war aesthetic of 20th-century literature, I certainly don't disagree with this; although it's enough of a consensus now (cf also: 'Grimdark') as to risk becoming deadening. And it opens up upon some dangerous side-alleys, not the least of which is the general contempt for 'politicians', a word treated as a synonym for 'corrupt leeches', as against honest salt-of-the-earth street brawlers and criminals ('I'm a bloodletter, not a politician,' Nyx said. 'I just take off heads'), which was exactly the attitude that softened the ground for the sowing of Fascism in the 1930s.

That's not my problem, though. Not really. Hurley is scrupulous in showing how much Nyx's career as a fighter has harmed her, ground her down, wrecked her body (even in a world where new body parts are easily purchased), deadened her soul. But it seems to me that the harm war does to soldiers is not the most interesting or important story to tell about war. More to the point is the harm war does to people who aren't soldiers. Both *God's War* and *Infidel* are about unaccommodated woman, the life *solus*, the costs and exhilarations of fighting and surviving. But that's easy. What's hard is not surviving yourself, but keeping other people alive. My own personal prejudices predispose me to think the most interesting stories are about people who *raise kids* in a warzone. The opening scene of *Infidel* made me wonder if this novel was going to address this; but it doesn't. Ah well. The thing about Achilles is that he doesn't have kids.[8] In one sense, better than the whole of the *Iliad* is the scene in *The Magnificent Seven* where Charles Bronson spanks the Mexican kids for despising their parents. The point of that scene is: being a parent is much harder, and requires a different, more complete form of bravery, than being a gunslinger. It's the same logic that says: the Dad in McCarthy's *The Road* is a greater warrior than Han Solo.

I hate to extend this, really quite simple point further, but I need to clarify. One of the great strengths of this novel, and its predecessor, is the way it challenges the calcified attitudes to gender and the 'proper' role of women in society. So I need to stress I'm not talking here about

---

[8] To sink into mere pedantry, I know (of course) that Greek myth attributed a son to Achilles: the ferocious Neoptolemus. But there's nothing paternal, or parental, about Achilles in the Iliad. He has his self-reliance, and his superb fighting skill, and his glory, given extra sweetness by his foreknowledge of his tragic doom; he had his lover Patroclus, his slave-girl Briseis, and that's all he wants. That and killing people. He's Nyxish, or Nyx is Achillean. One of the two.

anything procrusteanly woman-ish. I'm well aware of the deep-rooted bias in society (one that Hurley tackles head on) that women are 'naturally' nurturing and men are 'naturally' belligerent. Fuck that for a game of soldiers. My point is not that I wanted to read a story about Nyx caring for a child (blimey: can you imagine how that would even go?). Women are not to be defined by their capacity for caring for children. But human beings *are* to be defined by their capacity for caring for one another. Nyx is a warrior, indomitable and self-reliant and marvellously lacking in self-pity; but there are other, more collective and less individualistic modes of making war, and they work better. There are better military strategies than violence, too, although they may be less immediately dramatic for story-telling purposes. Gandhi made deeper and more permanent inroads into the British Empire than Hitler, after all.

Dave Hutchinson
Europe in Autumn

Young Rudi is a citizen of a future Europe that has been balkanized into a tessellation of new mini-states, of all sizes and sorts, including a trans-European high speed railway line from Portugal to Siberia that declared itself an independent nation-state as soon as construction was concluded. As the novel starts Rudi is working as a chef. After some argy-bargy in his employer's Polish restaurant involving a drunken party of Hungarian Mafiosi, he is recruited into the shadowy organisation of 'Coureurs', an apolitical group that specialises in moving information, parcels and people covertly across the spider-web proliferation of new borders. We follow Rudi's training, and then his adventures in a labyrinthine nested set of plots, counter-plots and counter-counter-plots that take him from Poland to Estonia, Germany, former ski resorts that are now nations, to London and elsewhere; from Spy Who Came In From The Cold waiting around in seedy cafes, to more Bondy shootings and explosions and severed heads in lockers.

There are times when being a writer as well as a reviewer can get in the way, rather, of the simple business of Doing The Reviewing. A writer reads slightly differently to the way a reader reads, since she always has a portion of her eye on the technical skill or otherwise with which the job has been done, like a plasterer at a dinner party, slyly checking out their host's walls. In this case, what kept getting in the way of full absorption in the story was sheer admiration at Hutchinson's chops.

This is my main take-away from the novel actually: that Hutchinson is an exceptionally skilful writer. *Europe in Autumn* is rendered with impressive fluency, precision and vividness. Hutchinson knows how to write dialogue, how to plot, how to pace, and best of all he writes characters – both main characters, and walk-on figures – that just lift off the page, alive, distinct, believable. He gets inside the variety of European settings in ways that absolutely compel belief. He is good with mood and atmosphere, and he is bold in withholding many of the satisfactions readers come to thrillers for – explanations, loose-end-tyings-up and so on. The whole book, actually, is a masterclass in how to do this sort of thing – this sort of thing being the post-Le-Carré, state-of-the-(European)-union thriller-y, adventure-y, ideas-y novel with a pinch of travelogue. I enjoyed the whole thing immensely. Quite apart from anything, it's very funny.

Europe in Autumn is also a timely novel, not only because (I'm writing this before the results of the 2014 Scottish Independence Referendum are known) national independence and succession movements have become such a prominent feature of contemporary European life, but because it is a book about Europe – and it's surprising how few such novels are written. I say surprising, because it seems to me that 'Europe' is so patently a major subject. We need more art about 'Europe', rather than just about individual European nations. Indeed, one of the great strengths of *Europe in Autumn* is its geographical capaciousness. For a long time the view from Britain has been that 'Europe' (to which we regard ourselves as, at best, semi-detached) is basically three things: Germany, France and 'the South' (Italy, Spain, maybe Greece). One of the nice things about Norman Davies insanely ambitious attempt to comprise an entire history of Europe in one volume was the attention he paid to Eastern Europe – although his Polish expertise perhaps over-played that one Eastern nation.

Hutchinson doesn't include scenes in every single European nation in his narrative (it would look forced if he did); but he gives a much wider and more convincing sweep of the whole than most writers or historians. Formally the novel is a sequence of more-or-less closely linked novella-ish chapters, each one approaching the condition of standalone. I liked this, as appropriate to the logic of balkanization the novel explores on the level of content. And the main character is a lovely piece of writing: potentially unlikeable – he is, after all, a loner, a breaker of laws – but actually engaging and fun, without ever losing the capacity to surprise the reader.

If I had to carp (carping? Oh – *Muß es sein*?), I might say that the book doesn't generate any great sense of dread. Hutchinson's instincts as a writer are comic rather than specifically Hitchcockian or Kafkaesque. Even when Rudi's plans go wrong, and he is captured and tortured, the book still reads as pleasant and funny rather than alarming or horrifying. This is not necessary a bad thing, in one sense. We might say that the geniality of mood Hutchinson creates in this novel is its own reward. But it melds awkwardly, in places, with the conventions of thriller adventure, and the result can feel leisurely and pleasant when it needs to be tighter or sparer. And the ending – no spoilers, now; you'll have to read for yourself to see what I mean – left me thinking: 'hmm, does that quite work, now?' But you know what? Probably it does.

Interstellar
(directed by Christopher Nolan)

Interminablestellar.

Emmi Itäranta
Memory of Water

Amongst the many impressive things about Emmi Itäranta's debut novel *Memory of Water* is the fact that its author wrote the book in her native Finnish and also in English. It was published as *Teemestarin kirja* in Finland in 2011; and now, like Beckett, she has become her own autotranslator, with an English version, *Memory of Water*. What's doubly remarkable is that the English is as good as it is, considerably better than many a native-speaker I could mention. Like Hannu Rajaniemi, Itäranta is capable of writing not just serviceable but actively beautiful English prose. I admire, too, the way this novel is content to tell a plain story, eschewing the *bang!-bang!-bang!* attention grabbing hyperactivity of too much contemporary genre fiction, proceeding by inflection and rather than clunking direct statement.

It is set in a post climate-meltdown world where the freshwater rivers, lakes and springs have all dried. Water is now a precious resource, and a zealous, oppressive military guard it, permitting each family only the one official water-pipe that is plumbed into their house, and from which a trickle of ill-tasting fluid drips. The narrator, Noria Kaitio, is the 17-year-old daughter of a 'tea master'; for although being set somewhere in the after-disaster Scandinavian/Baltic/West Russian area, there's a strong Japanese cultural inflection here: raking the gravel garden, respecting the elaborate rituals of tea preparation. Mr Kaitio has access to a secret and pure spring; if the military find out it'll be curtains for the whole family. Meanwhile, Noria and a friend uncover an old recording that seems to contain information contradicting the official history.

So, to stay with the good for a moment longer: the relationship between Noria and her father, written with immense sensitivity and delicacy, is genuinely touching, especially when she graduates against the odds to tea master herself and he [spoiler] dies. And the novel's world is vividly evoked, its parched people so bothered by horrid insects they can't go outside without donning an 'insect hood', rummaging through the heaps of rotting and discoloured plastic our culture bequeathed them. But *vividly*, oddly enough, doesn't necessarily equate to *plausibly* or *suspensive-of-disbelief*. And to be frank I didn't really believe it. Early on, Noria's friend Sanja buys some water from a travelling salesman, and reacts furiously that she's been conned: 'bloody sham sold me salt water! I tasted the water first, like I always do, and it was fresh' [16]. Noria explains the ruse ('a double-pipe fraud... inside the dais there's a secret container with salt water in it. The pipe has two settings...') But by this stage I'm thinking: the world clearly has no shortage of brine, for the ice caps have melted (Noria's mournfully reflects that she will never see the glorious ice packs of history). And desalination is not hard to manage; a couple of glass bowls and a transparent plastic sheet in the sunlight will do the trick. Accordingly I did not believe that the military would be able to control water distribution so totally, or that water for personal use would be so scarce.

But I know what you're thinking. You're thinking: 'why must you read in so deadeningly literal-minded a manner?' I concede the point; it is my curse, for I have a narrowly literal mind and never read poetry. And I'm certainly prepared to accept that *Memory of Water* figures more metaphorically and pseudo-poetically than it does by any of the restrictive codes of Hard SF plausibility. Water in this novel 'remembers' the abuse humanity inflicted upon the world, both in the sense that it carries the pollutants in its body, and in a more spiritual sense. And Itäranta is good on the intermittencies and strangeness of memory: 'memory has a shape of its own, and it's not always the shape of life' [92] is how Noria puts it. Although in places awkwardly done, there is something commendable in the way Itäranta structures her novel to try to reflect that queer shape. But, at the grave risk of alienating your sympathy altogether, dear reader: too often her poetic-prosy meditations on the nature of water seemed to my ear like unto the sounding brass and tinkling cymbal of pure Fotherington-Thomasness. Too many of these passages read like slogans from inspirations posters, ready to be printed over pastel photographs of morning-misty landscapes, or purple-and-cyan mountain peaks arrayed beneath a full moon starry sky.

> Water is the most versatile of all elements... Water walks with the moon and embraces the earth, and it isn't afraid to die in fire or live in air. When you step into it, it will be as close as your own skin, but if you hit it too hard, it will shatter you. [5]

It's all the way through the book:

Water is the most versatile of all elements. It isn't afraid to burn in fire or fade into the sky, it doesn't hesitate to shatter against sharp rocks in rainfall or drown into the dark shroud of the earth. It exists beyond all beginnings and ends. [221]

You may indeed, if your soul be less crusted and derelict than mine, find this uplifting and beautiful. Your moisture, that is, mileage, may vary. Water is delicate, and evaporates and evanishes; but it is also strong as a mighty tide or tsunami, when each individual water droplet says to its fellow, 'let me add my strength to yours'.

4. A new recruit for the hard-pressed crew. Aktually it is only fotherington-tomas you kno he sa Hullo clouds hullo sky he is a girlie and love the scents and sounds of nature tho the less i smell and hear them the better.

Howard Jacobson
J

First off, the novel is not called *J*. It is called *J-crossed-through-with-two-horizontal-lines*. The fonts with which my computer is supplied do not have the actual letter. The best I can do is: Ɉ; but Jacobson wants the double strikethrough, partly for emphasis, partly because it mimics what the main character, Kevern 'Coco' Cohen does whenever he speaks any word that begins with 'J': 'he put two fingers across his mouth, like a tramp sucking on a cigarette butt he'd found in a rubbish bin. This he always did to stifle the letter j before it left his lips' [6]. Kevern doesn't know why he does this. He does it because his dad used to do it.

Which brings me to S̶. Why do I put one finger across my mouth when I say this letter? Because Spoilers arouse fiery feelings in some people; irrational hatreds, ferocities. And there's simply no way to review this novel without letting some sibilant Spoilers out of the bag. I'll hold back for a paragraph or two, and then warn you again, dear reader; because the best way to read this novel is to do so blind, so that the significance of the double-strikethrough-J creeps up on you.

And in a way, the first third (or so) of the novel – before Jacobson gets more specific – is easily the best. It's a remorselessly grim, near-future portrait of Britain, focussed on our hero 'Coco' Cohen, who makes a living turning wood in his seaside cottage near the run-down, charmless village of Port Reuben. With thwunking irony, Cohen's main productions are wooden love-spoons, sold in the village shop – ironic because nobody in this place seems to know anything about love. Married couples scream at one another to eat shit; couples are either drunkenly fighting-grappling one another, or else drunkenly rutting like pigs in car-parks and up against walls. Cohen, thoughtful and sensitive, is more-or-less shunned. When he finally starts a relationship, with the beautiful, younger Ailinn Solomons, she is amazed that he just kisses her – rather than, like all the other men, punching her hard in the face. Literally. The locals are boorish, beery, aggressively quick to take offence and ready with their fists. There are references to some collective trauma in the near past, referred to as WHAT HAPPENED, IF IT HAPPENED. After this happened, if it did, a national programme called 'Operation Ishmael' was instituted, and the entire country worked to forget what happened (if it happened). Everyone changed their names to Jewish ones, drew a line under the past and looked to the future. This was not a matter of centralised diktat, or top-down authority. Indeed, there don't seem to be any actual laws in Port Rueben; just a collective sense of what is permitted and what isn't – a state of affairs (Jacobson makes a good job of persuading his reader) more, rather than less, tyrannical. 'History books were hard to come by, diaries were hidden or destroyed, and libraries put gentle obstacles in the way of research' [5]. The one thing everyone seems to agree on, sometimes violently, is that nobody has anything to apologise for. Black has been 'outlawed', since it might be confused with mourning clothes, and nobody has any reason to grieve over what happened (if it happened). Lots of things from the past, like Jazz music and foreign travel, are strongly discouraged.

This, then, is where the novel starts. The tender but cranky relationship between Ailinn and Kevern is well drawn, and their world, though in many ways schematic and sharply tendentious in its dramatization, sort-of works. Which is to say, it works as the setting for a fable, a Saramago-like milieu. A second story strand is woven in early-on, from a generation previous: a young girl called Esme Nussbaum is looking into WHAT HAPPENED, IF IT HAPPENED. Uncoincidentally she is knocked down by a motorcycle and hospitalised in a coma. A third strand, the least successful of the novel I think, centres on a series of violent murders in the village, investigated by the policeman Gutkind, much given to conspiracy-theories. These killings are there to illustrate Jacobson's belief that literally murderous violence is always bubbling away millimetres below the surface of ordinary English village life. This is also the moral, surprisingly, of the Miss Marple novels; and I have to say I don't really believe it, in either textual incarnation. And actually, to speak more practically, the murders are also there to give some narrative heave and motion to what is otherwise a pretty static piece of novel-ising.

Still, as we move into the second two-thirds of *J* the whole artifice of the book starts to stall and judder. Willing suspension of disbelief gives way to grudging suspension of disbelief, and finally morphs into *uh-oh-there-goes-my-disbelief,-crashing-down-like-a-rodeo-clown-tossed-from-the-back-of-an-unusually-skittish-colt.* There are more murders. Kevern is prime suspect. Ailinn and Kevern go on an in-country holiday, eventually pitching up in London – never called 'London' in this novel, only ever referred to as 'the Necropolis'. Esme Nussbaum, having survived her coma and grown old, now inserts herself into the life of Ailinn and Kevern, for her own frankly mind-boggling reasons. I'd explain what they are, but ~~S~~! Hmm. S… s… s.

I'm hissing like that because, from here to the end of this review, the snake-tongue Spoilers will flicker forth. Then again, you may have already guessed what the reveal is. WHAT HAD HAPPENED, IF IT HAPPENED turns out to have been WHAT HAD BEEN DONE [225]. And what was that? The mass-murder of Jews by the population of Great Britain. This, it seems, was a spontaneous ground-up atrocity. One character refers to the crucial tipping point as 'Twitternacht' – not as witty a pun as Jacobson perhaps thinks it is. We are not given any specific rationale for this new Holocaust, because one of Jacobson's main points in the novel is that such 'rationales' are always spurious. Pogroms happen, he says, because the ancestral, endless hatred the world feels for the Jews bubbles over from time to time. Pogroms cannot be explained, and no more can they be legislated against or prevented.

This second Holocaust seemed to me a fundamentally unbelievable thing. What I mean is: I do not believe there is any prospect of a second Holocaust in Britain in the near future; and I certainly don't believe that it is liable to happen out of a sort of spontaneous action of the twittering classes, suddenly deciding en masse to pick up tire-irons and anything else to hand and brain all the Jews (this is, more or less, how Jacobson portrays the WHAT HAPPENED). Mind you, and rather cleverly, my reaction is already part of the structural fabric of Jacobson's novel. His point (and it is a powerful one) is that people thinking 'it could never happen here' has always been the prelude to it happening. The Jews in multicultural, civilised 1930s Germany believed it would never happen there, and they were catastrophically wrong. Insofar as his novel acquires the kind of weight and resonance that justifies its place on the 2014 Man Booker shortlist it is by framing its catastrophe as un-rememberable, not because it is forgettable but precisely because it is unforgettable. That-which-cannot-be-spoken is the leitmotif of the book. The word 'Jew' nowhere appears in it, except that it appears with every doubly-struckthrough J, from the title page on.

The pogrom was preceded by ice-cream vans – of all things – touring the countryside.

> 'Those vans were going round the country painted with the slogan "Leave Now or Face Arrest". Bethesda Academy did the artwork.'
> 'Ice-cream vans?'
> 'Yes.'
> 'Telling people to leave?'
> 'Yes.'
> 'Which people?
> 'Come on, Kevern. You know which people.' [198]

These vans keep their chimes: 'Greensleeves'; 'You Are My Sunshine'. Jacobson is not afraid of walloping his readers pretty hard with the irony stick. Elsewhere he gives over a very long section to one of the murderers, a regular Briton, justifying his killing of a nine-year-old Jewish girl (burned to death in an art gallery because said gallery traded Jewish art) as 'necessary' and 'inevitable'. The closer it gets to its melodramatic death-plunge ending, the clunkier the novel gets.

Perhaps I say so because I'm a gentile, and complacency about the level of anti-Semitism in my homeland is my part of my white privilege. I don't think so, though. The self-evident foolishness of the dodo's 'it could never happen here!' is not the universal solvent Jacobson perhaps thinks it is. Now, it should not need saying, but always bears repeating: there is never a 'justification' for genocide. But saying that is not the same thing as insisting that the desire to murder Jews is fed by the quasi-mystic ancestral darkness that has always swirled in the violent hearts of gentiles since time immemorial. The man who murdered the nine-year-old confesses his reasons to his schoolgirl lover (he is himself a middle-aged schoolteacher) in a long speech like something out of *The Portage to San Cristobal of A.H.* He desired the girl's Jewish mother in direct proportion to how much he hated her and wished her dead. 'The more I hated her the more fascinated I became'. This Jewess is the defining Other to his gentile masculinity:

> 'It's you or them. You can't both breathe the same air. Some people are too different. I am who I am because I am not them,

> you tell yourself. That's why you fall in love at first – this clean break with yourself. Because if you are not them, they are not you. But then you realise it isn't anything about them that you love, it's the prospect of your own annihilation. They say before the executed die they fall in love with their own executioner.' [245]

He says having sex with this Jewish lover was like being 'in a sarcophagus making love to a mummy'. There was 'something ancient about her. I don't mean in appearance. I mean in what she represented. She went too far back. History should have finished with the likes of her by now.' As for his actual murderous actions, he claims 'they weren't mine alone. I was just repeating what had been done countless times before … I'd been culturally primed to do it.' The ultimate effectiveness of this novel, it seems, will stand or fall on whether you buy this. I don't. It is possible to insist that there can never be a 'justification' for things like the Holocaust whilst also insisting that things like the Holocaust happen for reasons of ideological and socio-political specificity, not out of a mystic swirl of ancestral hate. And I really couldn't piece together in my mind the circumstances in which the people of Britain would spontaneously rise up and beat all the Jews to death with tire irons. I didn't see how – let's say – outrage at the Gaza situation would scale up. (Jacobson gives us no specifics). I'm certainly not trying to pretend that there is no anti-Semitism in Britain. But I suppose I *am* suggesting that it has to jostle in the scrum alongside the pervasive anti-Catholicism, anti-Black and anti-Pakistani prejudices, not to mention Islamophobia, Euroscepticism and general dislike of foreigners. The Jew is not the only Other.

Jacobson's belief in this malign form of Jewish exceptionalism speaks to his personal situation as a prominent British Jew, of course. But his novel has to make it work as more than just the sophisticated paranoia of an individual well-versed in the last millennia European history. I don't mean that to come over as dismissive. How have moral panics actually manifested themselves in Britain recently? Take a word beginning with P: I mean the sporadic ground-up self-righteousness about paedophiles that prompted mob action some years ago, satirised so well by Chris Morris' *Brass Eye* 'Paedogeddon' episode. There was a similar group idiocy about this (attacking the houses of paediatricians because the mob didn't comprehend the difference in the two words and so on); and I daresay a tangle of psychological paradox underlining it of the sort Jacobson attributes to his Jew-murdering teacher – that is, the people who most vehemently demonize 'paedophiles' and the people who derive erotic enjoyment from ogling 16-year-old page three girls may be doing the former in order to split off their 'bad' selves from their self-acceptable identities. Of course, 'paedophiles' are defined as a group by their socially repellent actions, where Jews are defined simply by their ethnicity (the same is true of 'Blacks', 'Arabs', 'Irish' and so on). Individual Jews are good or bad, depending; Jewry is neither of those things. Indeed Jacobson makes this point in (again) slightly clunky manner early on. All the popular singers in his imagined future world are Black. Why?

No laws or duress. A compliant society means that every section of it consented with gratitude – the gratitude of the providentially spared – to the principle of group aptitude. People of Afro-Caribbean were suited by temperament and physique to entertainment and athletics, and so they sang and sprinted. People originally from the Indian subcontinent, electronically gifted as though by nature, undertook to ensure no family was without a functioning utility phone. What was left of the Polish community plumbed; what was left of the Greek smashed plates. [14]

This is aiming for a wry deadpan, I know. But even so. The problem is that Jacobson can't resist the allure of the sweeping, vatic statement; as if the business of the novel is very much *not* to give you the specific details of actual lived-experience, but instead always to extrapolate to the pretentious-general. 'Women talked of resisting love because it weakened them,' says the narrator [183]. Really? Is that what 'women' do? When his girlfriend chides him that he's not having a crisis, Kevern replies 'the behaviour of men is the proof we're in a crisis.' 'That's a tautology,' she returns [116]. Wait – really? Discussing art with a librarian called Rozenwyn, Kevern agrees that 'to be an artist is to have the freedom to think anything', including 'the freedom to think evil.' Rozenwyn agrees, and recalls a (fictional) writer called Everett, of whom she says: 'he likes to play with the idea of wrongdoing. It thrills him. He'd be another Sade if he had the balls. They all would.' [197]. Wait: *all* of us?

This is where the greatest strength of Jacobson's novel becomes, I think, its greatest weakness. That strength is in the way he has reconceptualised near-future dystopia, or post-apocalyptic writing. It has hitherto almost entirely been the case that post-apocalyptic novels, from *On the Beach* to *The Road* have predicated their stories upon an actual material catastrophe – comet collision, zombie uprising, whatever. Jacobson does something much cleverer: his catastrophe is a moral one. And he is, I think, absolutely right to insist that living in the aftermath of a moral catastrophe – like the decisions taken by the German state to murder all its Jews – is as materially damaging as any zombie-phage-asteroid-collision fantasy version would be. He's also right that this post-apocalyptic situation is a collective, rather than just a personal, one. Hence, 'dystopia. But, that said, the lineaments of Jacobson's version of this post-traumatic social logic are full of holes. 'Operation Ishmael', by which the nation collectively tried to forget what it had done, entailed amongst other things people and places abandoning their old names and taking on names like Cohen and Solomons. Is this supposed to be like the planetary settlers in Bradbury's *Martian Chronicles*? Or a counter-intuitive psychological tactic? Surely not. Un-memory doesn't work this way.

Remember the word beginning with P, above? There's another one of those unspoken P-words in this novel: Palestinian. Imagine (imagining things, after all, is the currency of the speculative writer) that Israel made the tactical decision to nuke Gaza and kill every Palestinian. It would not, I think, then institute an 'Operation Aladdin', and change everybody's name to Maħmūd and Haroun. When genocide has happened in the world, it has usually been followed by – simple forgetting. Modern Turkey doesn't consider itself defined by the Armenian genocide of 1915. Today's Republic of Rwanda (motto: 'Unity, Work, Patriotism') is building a lucrative tourist industry that depends upon rather pointedly *not* mentioning the mass murder of a million Tutsis two decades ago – the tourism board website boasts not just that 'Rwanda is a green undulating landscape of hills, gardens and tea plantations, home to one third of the world remaining Mountain Gorillas', but also that the people are 'friendly': 'Rwanda is a thriving, safe country with one of the lowest crime rates in Africa.' Maybe the repressed doesn't always return. Maybe forgetting is one of the superpowers with which we ordinary Clark Kents all happen to be gifted.

Jacobson's *J* is not about the Gaza conflict, or modern Israel (neither place is mentioned; and this absence is not freighted in the way the lack of the word 'Jew' is). Jacobson's novel is about Britain; and a very unflattering portrait it paints, a country filled with casually violent, beer-swilling, blinkered idiots and fools. Maybe that's true. But I don't think so; or to put it more precisely, I don't think that's the whole picture. It lacks nuance, and that's a problem – because Jacobson's labour in this novel is all about suggesting not telling, about the potency of inflection and the eloquence of innuendo. It has to be, because if we strip it back it might look as if the response of one of Britain's most esteemed novelist to the recent Gaza war is: 'why do you keep going on about those dead Palestinian children? It's Jews who are the real victims here. Jews are the ones at risk!' And put like that, without nuance, that looks a little, shall we say, crass.

Reading the novel put me in mind of Lyotard's *Heidegger and the 'jews'* (1990), not only because of that work's insistence (reinforced by Lyotard's deliberate use of scare-quotes and the lower-case-j) that 'jew' is a larger category of abjected and persecuted Other than 'Jew'. Jacobson's book is about not just present dangers but about the actual, measurable psychic and social violence a people does to itself by refusing to remember its history. Lyotard has a different perspective on the injunction 'never forget!' What does it mean to insist that the Holocaust must always be remembered?

> Here to fight against forgetting means to fight to remember that one forgets as soon as one believes, draws conclusions, and holds for certain. It means to fight against forgetting the precariousness of what has been established, of the reestablished past; it is a fight for the sickness whose recovery is simulated. [Lyotard, 10]

This looks more tricky, perhaps, than it actually is: for Lyotard is saying that categorical 'remembrance' is as or more distorting than the evasions and repressions of traumatised non-recollection. Genocide has been a ghastly feature of human history for millennia, but the Nazi Holocaust, of all genocides, is surely the one that most runs the risk of becoming the kind of calcified 'officially remembered' reification that Lyotard is talking about here. When, a little later he says that where trauma is concerned 'psychoanalysis, the search for lost time, can only be interminable, like literature and like true history (i.e., the one that is not historicism but anamnesis): the kind of history that does not forget that forgetting is not a breakdown of memory but the immemorial always "present"" [20], it made me wonder if Jacobson's novel isn't too terminable. This is how Lyotard's short book ends, and where he finally defines what he means by 'jews':

The debt that is our only lot–the lot of forgetting neither that there is the Forgotten nor what horrors the spirit is capable of in its headlong madness to make us forget the fact. "Our" lot? Whose lot? It is the lot of this nonpeople of survivors, Jews and non-Jews, called here "the jews," whose Being-together depends not on the authenticity of any primary roots but on that singular debt of interminable anamnesis.

'Which people?' 'Come on, Kevern. You know which people. All people.' Still, the moment I find myself asking 'ah, but is the anamnesis of Jacobson's novel sufficiently *interminable*?' is probably the moment to give all this a rest. Is this novel a masterpiece? Is it fundamentally rubbish? It's very hard to say.

Some of the most powerful bits from Claude Lanzmann's *Shoah* movie are the interviews with the Polish residents in the local villages, who simultaneously knew what was going on and somehow refused to believe that anything *had* gone on, that there had ever been a Jewish 'problem' in *their* village in the first place. And I can see Jacobson is sort-of getting at that. The 'J-under-erasure' is quite a powerful little rebus. But it's also a little too slippery. I've seen people flinch when I describe my wife as 'a Jew', in a way that doesn't happen when I describe her as 'Jewish' (what's that Jonathan Miller joke? *'I'm not a Jew; I'm Jewish. Not the whole hog'*). It's not exactly 'the n-word', but there *is* a valence to 'the j-word' that makes it tricky for use in polite society. Jacobson is saying: that's an index of disgust rather than sensitivity – or he's saying what the sensitivity is sensitive to is revulsion. I wonder about that.

In Martin Amis' *Experience* there's a bit where young Marty asks his Dad, racist old Kingsley Amis: what does it mean to be an anti-Semite? And his Dad replies the main thing is: you just really notice it when someone is Jewish. *Oh here's Doctor Cohen, the Jew.* That kind of thing. Now, since Amis *père* never actually lent a physical hand to any pogroms I can sort-of see this – I mean: I can see that this is as far as his anti-Semitism went. And the thing that strikes me about it, living as I do with a Jew, is that this is exactly what my wife does. A Jewish person comes on the screen whilst we're watching telly and she'll say 'oh, s/he's Jewish you know' (usually this will be when somebody is not obviously Jewish. 'Oh there's Scarlett Johansson. She's Jewish you know'). Or, another example: the UK's Jewish newspaper *The Jewish Chronicle.* That recognition is basically its whole stock-in-trade: 'Jew wins Nobel prize' and the like. What this has to do with Jacobson's novel is that he assumes that as a kind of universal, the unspoken yet everywhere perceived j-word. The J word under complicated erasure. But my problem is that I'm just not sure the whole world notices Jews as intently as do other Jews and mad anti-Semites. Especially in the West, where Jews are largely integrated and it's hard (look, there's Scarlett Johansson!) to tell which ones are Jews and which not. But then again, I look at the cultural prominence of Holocaust denial (I suppose another of Jacobson's targets here) and I wonder if I'm just being naïve.

Erika Johansen
The Queen of the Tearling

Second-guessing where a trilogy is going on the strength of just its first volume is, clearly, a mug's game. Nonetheless I like to think I possess at least something of the qualities of a sturdily built cup designed for consumption of hot beverages, so here goes. Erika Johansen's debut novel appears to be a High Fantasy romp of almost arthritically traditional cast; but as the trilogy unfolds I expect it to metamorphose, for good and ill, into a future-set dystopia on another planet, in which what appear to be magical, immortal, or otherwise prophetically fated elements to the story are revealed as having pseudo-scientific rationales. There: take my hostage, fortune!

In this opening episode, though, the flavour is pretty pungently Tudor Fantasyland. We start, of course, with a map: the Tearling is a peninsula some two hundred miles by one hundred, poking out into the ocean: 'Fairwitch Sea' to the north, 'God's Ocean' to the west, 'Tearling Gulf' to the south) and in many respects resembling a sort of mirror-reflected Kent, capital 'New London,' main port 'New Dover.' It is mostly forest and farmland, and though improbably densely populated – we're told at one point that two million people live there – it is very poor. Our point of view character Kelsea Glynn is the rightful Queen of this place, but she's been raised *Sleeping-Beauty*-like in the woods, to keep her out of the way of the 'Red Witch' who wants her dead. You see, to the east of Tearling is the ominously named kingdom of Mortmesne, and they have all the iron, and a large well-trained army, and a thoroughly ruthless manner. A generation earlier their queen, the aforementioned Red Witch, sent her military on a raping-and-pillaging march through the innocent Tearling countryside. The army stopped at the walls of 'The Keep' in New London, and only returned home once the old queen there had signed a peace treaty involving a regular tribute of slaves: 'two hundred and fifty people, once a month, like clockwork.' Kelsea (who, having been raised in seclusion in the woods, has the sort of ignorance that's terribly useful for a writer needing to lay out her worldbuilding to her readership) is horrified when she learns about the tribute. 'The Red Queen wanted tribute, Lady,' her bodyguard tells her. 'The Tearling had nothing else to offer' [112].

Kelsea has a bodyguard because, as the novel opens, she's finally coming of age. Soldiers turn up to escort her out of hiding and to her throne, currently occupied by her wicked Uncle – a corpulent alcoholic who keeps a beautiful naked woman chained at his feet. Evil, you see. Kelsea possesses the magical jewel that establishes her right to rule, but – as the novel's tagline has it – her throne only awaits 'if she can live long enough to take it.' Her uncle wants her dead. The Red Queen of the neighbouring superpower wants her dead. She, meanwhile, is so blithely ignorant about everything one wonders if she knows how to sit the right way round on a toilet. She doesn't know who her father is, or what her mother was like; she doesn't know that Mortmesne invaded, or compelled her land to make this terrible treaty. She basically doesn't know anything about anything, and Johansen builds the first half of her narrative as a mutual suspense-and-uncovering of the past's secrets by Kelsea and the reader, hand in hand.

Strange to say it works pretty well. Unostentatiously written, characterized in obvious and rather broad strokes, *The Queen of the Tearling* nonetheless holds the reader's attention – or at least it held mine. On her way to the throne Kelsea falls in with a Robin Hood individual called Fetch (not, as I initially misread this, Fletch, though Chevy Chase's leering phizog stayed in my mind's eye as I read his scenes), who helps her on her way. Eventually she makes it to New London, the Tearling's capital city, where she encounters the horrible truth of the Minotaur-y tribute her nation is paying. Kelsea indignantly frees all the captives at once, even though it will mean an inevitable Mort invasion and all the atrocities of war. The mother of one of the children she had freed relates the fate her daughter had so narrowly escaped:

> 'She would have died before long. The girls die much more rapidly than the boys. Used for menial labour until she was old enough to be sold for pleasure. That is, if she was fortunate enough not to be bought by a child rapist upon arrival.' Andalie bared her teeth in a grim, pained smile. 'Mortmesne condones many things.' [149]

This is a horrible enough premise, and all the more arresting in that the book is effectively being marketed as a post-Potter YA Fantasy.

The front cover of my copy comes with a 'notice me!' big red sticker announcing 'Soon to be a major motion picture, starring Emma Watson.' The flap-copy doubles down on this boast: 'Film rights have been acquired by Warner Brothers, who will reunite *Harry Potter* team of producer David Hayman and star Emma Watson.' Not that Watson will be well cast as far as this role is concerned. One thing the novel insists upon, with a weirdly insistent repetition, is how plain-looking Kelsea is: tall and dark, but heavy-set and unpretty. The handsome Fletch assures her that he's not romantically interested in her ('You're far too plain for my taste,'); and her fencing master is downright rude ("'You require conditioning, Lady. You'll never be as lithe as a dancer, but you'd move faster if you carried less weight.' Kelsea flushed and quickly turned away. She knew she was heavier than she should be, but there was a big difference between knowing something and hearing it spoken out loud" [266]).

This is a venerable *Jane Eyre*-y strategy, of course: dialling down the pulchritude of your heroine the more believably to mary-sue her. And as a strategy it has certain advantages: for since the hero isn't distracted by a pretty face, and falls in love with the heart beneath the unalluring exterior, it can work to heighten the true love pang with which the story will eventually pay off. (I'm again, mug-like, guessing here: *The Queen of the Tearling* surrounds Kelsea with gorgeously handsome men, but she has copped-off with none of these by the end of vol 1. That will surely have changed, come vol 3.) Hollywood, I suppose, is like US daytime soap operas, simply disinclined to cast actual human beings in key roles. But the point of the red sticker, and flap copy, has less to do with the rather boyish good looks of Watson herself. It is a signal to potential readers. Want more *Potter*? Buy this!

As far as that goes, *Potter* is a tricky prototype to follow. I don't just mean in terms of its globe-spanning success, or special charm. I mean that Rowling's series starts out *Young* Young Adult, and ends up, via death, torture, and burgeoning sexualities, considerably more *Adult* Young Adult. If you want to pitch your book to readers who have already worked through all seven of those books, you may decide to plump for a more *Deathly Hallows* and less *Philosopher's Stone* vibe.

What this means for *The Queen of the Tearling* is that we get faux-adult violence, sexual references, the odd f-word, and even one use of the c-word – rather jarringly so, in an otherwise entirely by-the-numbers contemporary young adult story of a teenage girl working to change her world from dystopia to better, like *Hunger Games*, *Divergent*, or *Noughts and Crosses*. (Also from *Noughts and Crosses*, I presume, is the inversion of racial roles, rather flip in this context: the pacific, oppressed Tearlingers are white, the Mortmesne invaders black. I wasn't convinced that this worked terribly well, although at least Johansen doesn't sew it onto a banner in three-foot-high letters and flap it in her readers' faces the whole time.)

The YA framing leads to a cartoon-y exaggeration of good and evil. For example: the first time we meet the Red Queen, she is in her bedroom, looking through her casement at 'the Crown city of Desmense.' She has been woken early by a nightmare, and her nightmare of course is of the threat posed by Kelsea, the Queen of the Tearling. So far, so Grimm; but this scene swiftly takes a darker-than-Grimm turn that propels it right past (crooking my little finger against the corner of my mouth) *ee-evil* and straight into absurdity.

A thick guttural sound came from behind her, and the Queen whirled around. But it was only the slave in her bed. She had forgotten about him. He'd performed well, and she'd kept him for the night; a good fuck chased the dreams right away. But she loathed snoring. [44]

'The Queen had handpicked him,' we're told, 'for his dark skin and aquiline nose, a clear sign of Mort blood. But a slave who snored was no use to anyone.' So? So she summons her guards.

> 'Take him down to the lab. Have them remove his tongue and uvula. And sever his vocal cords, just in case.' The slave screamed and struggled harder as her guards worked to pin him to her bed. One had to admire his strength... 'Once he's healed, offer him to Lady Dumont with our compliments.' [46]

Blimey. This sort of thing never happened in *Narnia*.

One way of reacting to this is to deplore the increasing sexualisation of youth culture, where the ceremony of innocence has been, if not exactly drowned, then certainly waterboarded to within an inch of its life. Johansen is not trying to shock her young-adult readers. On the contrary, she is giving them just what they expect, in our general cultural post-*Game of Thrones* darkling grimness. This is how kids are, nowadays. This is how they see the world – the more cossetted and affluent their own suburban home-life, the more horrible a place they take the larger world to be. And anyway I'm less struck by questions of moral decadence than I am of aesthetic praxis. Lewis' White Witch tempts Edmund with some Turkish Delight, and he succumbs, betraying his sisters and brother. Less being so much more than more, this generates real dramatic punch, in a way that using a slave for sex and then having his tongue ripped out simply cannot.

The novel is indicative of contemporary youth in other ways too. The Red Witch is centuries old, kept unnaturally young by magic; but as with *The Hunger Games'* opposition between the fresh-faced natural beauty of Katniss on the one hand, and the hideous overly-made-up faded artifice of the Capitol chaperone Effie Trinket on the other, there's a pervasive sense in Johansen's novel that middle-aged (= "old") people doing sex and physical attractiveness is just, like, *gross*. When she takes over her court, Kelsea meets Lady Andrews, whom the novel does not spare:

> Lady Andrews' hands had clutched into claws. The nails were long hooks, manicured a bright purple. Deep pockets of red had emerged in the fleshless crescents beneath her eyes... Kelsea wondered: how could a woman who looked so old still place so much importance on being attractive? She had read about this particular delusion in books many times. [333]

Ah, yes: the psychological delusion of refusing to act the old crone when you reach the age of... wait, how old? 'She was much older than she seemed in the dim light of the throne room, perhaps as old as forty.' GET OUT OF TOWN!

I know, I know. Forty seems impossibly old when you're a teen, and the thought of such skeletons, like, actually having sex is of course repulsive to you (your parents, like, doing it, *eew, gross*). Johansen channels that vibe very efficiently. Her teen heroine is wisecracking and sharp enough to appeal to, and vulnerable and unsure enough to connect with, her readers. There's a mildly satirical portrait of the Christian Church in Tearling (its Holy Father rules with sinister ruthlessness, although not many Tearlingers follow the faith) designed I suppose to appeal to youngsters heady with *The God Delusion*. The Mort army mobilizes on the border, and the situation seems hopeless; but in appropriately Tolkienian eucatastrophic mode, the day is saved by the magic jewel Kelsea carries with her, and from which, Frodo-like, she can't bear to be separated: 'when she pulled the chain from her neck she felt diminished. It was a dreadful feeling, like being drained' (p. 358).

The Tolkien reference, there, isn't arbitrary; the New London Keep Library contains, amongst other books, *The Hobbit* and *The Lord of the Rings*. These and a score of other artfully dropped-in references indicate that the novel is set in a possible future, not an alt-past. And that in turn brings me back to my mug-like opening predictions. I started reading this novel thinking it would be a Queen-Elizabeth-in-Fantasyland tale; I finished it believing that it was pitching itself at a rather different target. I think this series wants to be a twenty-first-century *Darkover*. Marion Zimmer Bradley's name has of course become a toxic one in SF fandom, and with good cause; so it's easy to forget how hugely popular the *Darkover* books were, back in the day. Their mix of heroic fantasy and futuristic rocketship planetary romance appealed to a huge constituency of readers. I wouldn't bet against Johansen achieving a similar success.

Debbie Johnson
Dark Vision

Our protagonist, Lily McCain, is Liverpudlian music journo (references in the novel include: Muse, made-up bands actually comprised of actual vampires, and Mazzy Star. Remember them?) Lily has a magic gift/curse: when she touches someone, or they touch her, she sees their future. Yes, that's nicked from Stephen King's peerless *The Dead Zone*. But where King sees in his premise an opportunity to talk about isolation, loneliness and the disconnection inherent in modern life, Johnson steers the same premise in a very different direction: towards rather a gooey love story in a world that turns out to be a kind of Charlaine Harris Merseyside. I know which of the two treatments of this premise I prefer.

It doesn't help that Johnson writes her debut novel in a kind of foresquare tell-it-how-it-is feisty-cum-sassy idiom, stitched out of cliché and painfully forced jollity. It also doesn't help that her own ingenuousness so often betrays her into Thoggisms ('...sipping bitter black coffee so hot my lips recoiled in protest' [16]; 'He stood tall, in fact even taller than he usually was' [31]; 'he laughed, and before I could stop him, stroked my face with the speed of light' [54]; 'Gabriel's eyes [were] sparking a bruised shade of purple... I felt a thud of disappointment hammer through me' [128]; 'my throat was so parched I couldn't even have swallowed my own non-existent spit' [217]; 'it was just a pillow now, and I carved out a moment to feel sad about that' [218]). There's a good deal of blushing by our streetwise but virginal narrator, especially in the first half, and a heavy dose of The Celtic, myth-and-magic-wise. Time travel of course takes us back to the Beatles playing The Cavern in late '62. Where else? A bit frantic, especially in its battle-of-gods-and-mortals conclusion. You might very well enjoy it.

Graham Joyce

On the 9th September 2014 my friend Graham Joyce died. He was 59, far too young for anyone to die; but with Graham it was especially shocking, especially grievous. He had always been so emphatically alive. He lived life with what we could call an unforced, mature joy. That wise quality infuses his writing too. My happiest memories of him are of our team, which always lost, at the highfalutin 'pub quiz' held intermittently at the Century Club on Shaftesbury Avenue: James Barclay, Rob Grant, Simon Spanton, myself and Graham. I think it was at the last of these that he tried to persuade me to join him on the 'England Writer's' football team that toured the Continent. I promised him I was a rubbish player. 'You think I'm not?' he countered. 'You should definitely come; it's a laugh.' I wish I had, now.

He taught creative writing at Nottingham Trent University, and at some point decided it would be useful for his career to have a PhD in the subject. So he submitted work for a PhD by Publication (he put in *Leningrad Nights* and *Smoking Poppy*, together with a specially written critical commentary). To ensure impartiality Nottingham appointed two external examiners: myself and Farah Mendlesohn. Since the creative work was to all intents and purposes flawless, we concentrated our attention on the critical commentary and gave him a pretty rigorous viva and some key re-writes. But of course he was awarded the PhD. Later *Private Eye* published an article accusing Nottingham of corruptly gifting one of its employees a soft PhD. So I wrote them a pompous letter, which of course they printed, insisting upon the scrupulousness with which the process had been carried out (as indeed it had been), and informing them that PhD by publication is a standard pathway in the sector. Graham thought the *Eye* article was hilarious; but he thought my pompous rebuttal even funnier. He was as far from pompous as it is possible to get. Some time after that viva, he was my interviewer at a BSFA night, and with the best grace in the world put me through the ringer. I don't know anyone in the writing or publishing world who didn't love him dearly.

But most of all, this. I daresay it's a symptom of the narrowness of my horizons of judgment; but since I am a writer, this is the highest praise I can think of (and it applies with tremendous force to Graham): he was a superb writer. You must go and read his books.

Tim Lebbon
Alien: Out of the Shadows

The cover-stress on novelty here ('an original novel'; 'official new novel'; my copy came with a little silver sticker declaring 'All New Story') bends the truth a little, without fracturing it entirely. But that's okay: we understand the drill. To put it more precisely, the *sjuzhet* here is new, or new-ish, though the *fabula* is as old as Dan O'Bannon's 1970s screenplay, and I daresay as old as *Beowulf* and *Gilgamesh*.[9] Indeed, come to think of it: even the *sjuzhet* is rather second-hand. There's a mining spaceship operated by a varied crew; Ripley joins them; they land on a planet and go underground (in this case, into a mine to get some magic fuel); uh-oh, there are Aliens™ down there! Tension; gore; hard-bitten dialogue; tension; gore. Ash, the Ian-Holm-android turns up. Ripley survives. Done. That Ripley survives is no spoiler, for the story is set between *Alien* and the sequel movie *Aliens*. So the reader does not doubt Ripley's immunity; only how it is that she didn't remember anything to do with the adventure on awakening. But Lebbon explains that, too.

Now Lebbon-the-writer is a pro, and his aliens ('The Lebbalien'?) are efficiently drawn and effective. The cast of characters get efficiently sketched-in at the beginning, so that we care just enough when they start getting picked off. In other words: this title does exactly what it says on the Franchise-branded tin, and does it with considerable technical competence. There are occasional head-scratching moments, mind you. One is the nature of the mine. 'Trimonite was the hardest, strongest material known to man, and when a seam as rich as this one was found, it paid to mine it out.' Mine it out with drill-bits and

---

[9] I was going to add a gag to the effect that 'Beowulf and Gilgamesh' sounds like a heroic crime-fighting buddy duo: 'Fighting Crime – the Old Fashioned Way!' But, on reflection, I'm not sure they actually do sound like a buddy-buddy cop movie pairing. And thinking a little more about this, it occurs to me: buddy-buddy cop duos need to have a certain metrical pattern to their linked names: specifically, *quartus paeon*, 'short-short-short-long'. Starsky and Hutch. Tango and Cash. Turner and Hooch. Hickey and Boggs. It works in other areas too: Morecambe and Wise, Watson and Crick, Oryx and Crake. Beethoven's Fifth... duh-duh-duh-*duhhhm*! I don't know why. But this is by-the-bye, except to note that were Tim Lebbon and Ridley Scott to team up and fight crime, they could go by the joint-moniker 'Lebbon and Scott' which would work just fine.

hammers made of a substance even harder and stronger than Trimonite, presumably. But look: nitpicking isn't the frame-of-mind in which to approach a novel like this. You already know whether it's the kind of book you'd be interested in reading.

Ann Leckie
Ancillary Sword

Quite a few 'vol 2's were published in 2014, it seems (Kameron Hurley's *Infidel*, Mira Grant's *Symbiont* and John Gwynne's *Valour* are reviewed above). The vol 2 under consideration here is Ann Leckie's second *Ancillary* instalment: after *Justice*, *Sword*. Perhaps because our hero Breq now has to shore up a corner of Radchaii space using *just his sword*. Or else. You know. Not. Quite apart from anything else, Breq's possessive is a 'her' not a 'his', just like everyone else in the novel. The sword in this case is a huge Fuck-Off class spaceship, the *Mercy of Kalr*, with a crew of bristling, honour-obsessed Radchaii officers for Breq to whip into shape. Or line, is it? Does one 'whip into line'? Or is that lick into shape and... what into line? Straighten?

Sorry, my attention keeps wandering. The story picks up soon after the end of *Ancillary Justice*. Thousand-bodied emperor Anaander Mianaai gives Breq command of the ship and sends her to Athoek to guarantee the system's safety after two 'hyperspace' gates were attacked and destroyed. She is given three officers: two experienced lieutenants called Seivarden and Ekalu and a 'baby', the inexperienced but well-connected 17-year-old Tisarwat. When they get to their destination they tangle with local politics, including the ethical problematics of a programme of in-all-but-name enslavement of the locals.

I daresay Leckie was writing this follow-up before *Ancillary Justice* created such an impressive splash in the rock-pool of contemporary science fiction: Hugo, Nebula, Clarke, BSFA, Nobel, Olympic Gold and Jules Rémy, all in one year and all for a debut. Genuinely impressive stuff. At any rate, *A. Sword* has all the marks of an ambitious writer determined not simply to repeat herself. So, where *A. Just.* was a multi-P.O.V. action-packed adventure, *A. Swo.* is all Breq, and very low-key on the Things Happening front. The emphasis is on character interactions, and interiority; the beauty of inflections rather than the beauty of Big Explosions (though there is a bomb and some fighting near the end). It's a cooler, more considered book, interested in the protocols of interpersonal interaction, and also with protocols as such. There's a great deal of pother about using the right crockery, about the dos-and-don'ts of courtesy, hierarchy and propriety. More Silver Fork than slash-and-burn. There's also an attempt to engage with questions of colonialism, slavery and class prejudice, although here the evident wrongness of all three quantities (speaking absolutely, but also in terms of Leckie's moral universe) rather undercuts the novel's drama. It's not that the book's various moments of righteous outrage aren't right-on; it's more that they feel as though they could be cut-and-pasted into any number of contemporary online situations. One major theme is that the requirement that women and other oppressed minorities use registers of politeness to express their disaffection is itself oppressive:

"When they behave properly, you will say there is no problem. When they complain loudly, you will say they cause their own problems with their impropriety. And when they are driven to extremes, you say you will not reward such actions. What will it take for you to listen?"...

"For my part," I replied, "I find forgiveness overrated. There are times and places when it's appropriate. But not when the demand that you forgive is used to keep you in your place."...

"You are so civilized. So polite. So brave coming here alone when you know no one here would dare to touch you. So easy to be all those things, when all the power is on your side."

One problem I had with the first novel was the way the experience of belonging to a vast hive-mind, of splitting oneself into myriad individuals and then recombining them, was rendered in traditional, monadic-human terms. Leckie's imagination does not, in this case, run to a deleuzeguattarian body-without-organs, or even to a Hardt-and-Negri multitude. And in paler form the same limitation haunts *A. Sw.* too. Breq is on her own now, although able to augment her mentation by connecting with the systems of her ship. A couple of the perkier, livelier elements read like they come from another novel altogether. For instance, 'Translator Dlique', a diplomat for the scary warrior alien race 'the Presger', with her pleasantly scatty inability to remember such human social conventions as sitting up straight and not dismembering people, has a very Iain M. Banks vibe about her. Also Banks-y is the tendency to name alien races after the sort of noises associated with coughing and wheezing ('Geck!' 'Rrrrrrr!'). But Leckie reminding her readers of Banks runs the risks of reminding her readers of those Banks qualities (verve, humour, energy, spuming inventiveness) that don't particularly characterise this novel.

Leckie's decision to downplay the bang-bang-bang, and aim for a different set of novelistic qualia, a more thoughtful low-key narrative, is commendable. But commendable isn't necessarily the same thing as likeable, and I didn't rattle through *A.S.* the way I did *A.J.* Too much gubbins about bowls and plates. The 'justice, propriety and benefit' trifecta had its handle cranked a little too often. The whole thing just cooled an already cool set-up. But that's okay. Maybe you like your set-ups on the gazpacho side.

[Postscript: before I first published this review I went through, carefully (as I thought) to make sure I wasn't inadvertently defaulting the pronouns back to 'he's and 'him's. Nonetheless, my friend Tom Pollock gently pointed out that I'd missed a couple. These are corrected in this version, but it's worth noting the fact as indicative of how deep-seated the inertial sexism of an individual such as myself goes. If the 'vibe' I got from Breq was more masculine than feminine (more Picard than Janeaway, we might say) then that says a great deal more about my subconscious assumptions than it does about Leckie's writing.**]**

Ken MacLeod
Descent

Ryan is a regular lad growing up in a near-future Scotland struggling under yet another severe economic recession. He and his friend Calum have an encounter with a UFO. Ryan later 'remembers' an abduction experience, rather too fruitily supplied with all the clichés of that mode. Calum, though, has no such memories. After this vividly realised opening the novel, in leisurely but absorbing style, follows Ryan and his generation as they grow to adulthood. Nothing much comes of the UFO encounter, except that it primes Ryan to develop a series of complex, interlocking conspiracy theories: about advanced military tech disguising itself as alien saucers, about a new speciation event by which a secret *homo neanderthalis* bloodline is about to emerge and separate from *homo sapiens*; about the truth behind 'religious' epiphanies and of course (it being MacLeod) about politics, establishment agents pretending to be revolutionaries and vice versa, the complicity of the secret services and so on. This, it dawns on the reader, is the real theme of the book. *Descent* is, consciously or otherwise, a Jamesonian riff on the enduring appeal of 'the conspiracy theory' as such – Jameson, as I'm sure you know, thinks that our appetite for these sorts of things indexes our attempt to see our social, cultural and ideological milieu for what it is, a global interlocking system called 'Late Capitalism'. Meanwhile the economy gets sorted out via a quick nationalisation of the banking system and an acceptance of the trading dominance of China (or something); Ryan gets a job as an online journalist. MacLeod has fun with some near-future tech: a world so saturated in surveillance it's possible to assemble a real-time Google Earth rolling map just by sampling all the feeds. There are advances in fabric technology, a ramscoop jet that could cut access-to-space costs and the like. A dubiously sleekit fellow called Baxter stalks Ryan down the years in various guises: a priest, a man-in-black and so on. Baxter eventually becomes a political Big Cheese in the Scottish Parliament (I found this plot strand all rather hard to swallow, actually – not so much the conspiracy side to it, as the way he seems to have endless time for Ryan. The narrator phones him for a meeting and he immediately says 'I can give you an hour and a half, face-to-face' and so on). The book is dedicated to 'the memory of Iain M. Banks', and there's a decidedly *Crow-Road*-ish flavour to the storytelling. I enjoyed reading it very much.

What it lacks, despite all its excellences, is menace. Even when the heavies turn up, late in the story, and rough-up our narrator the mood doesn't shift from its tenor of expansive, rather leisurely charm. Now this is not to be sniffed at, this latter quality: it is valuable, and very hard for a writer to do – it is, for instance, quite beyond my technical capacity as a writer (I can do lots of things, but I don't seem to be able to do that). And it carries *Descent* a long way; the growing-up-in-Scotland milieu, the characters, the prose. It just doesn't quite carry through the thing that gives real conspiracy theories their tang, the curry-paste hotness that keep adherents coming back for more: the sense that *it matters*, the self-preening *I'm taking a courageous risk by pursuing it.* It's almost never true, the 'risk' thing. Actual conspiracy theorists risk only their sanity, and that sort of risk-taking is the opposite of courageous. But it's addictive nonetheless.

Maleficent (directed by Robert Stromberg)

'Magnificent!' said a friend of mine; 'mediocre-cent!' said many of the critics. Now that I've finally seen it for myself, I discover I'm somewhere in the middle. For every good aspect of the film (the make-up and costumes! sets! Jolie's central performance!) there are closely-connected bad aspects (the tweeness of the film's fairyland! the weirdly cack-handed pacing! the misfiring comic moments!). What's really strong here is, I think, twofold: one, the central fable as symbolic narrative of sexual abuse, which is very potent – the scene where Maleficent wakes up to discover her wings have been amputated is as powerful as everybody says. And two, connected with that, is the central section where Maleficent goes b-b-bad to the bone. It stands in relation to the 1959 *Sleeping Beauty* rather as the *Star Wars* prequel trilogy does to the original trilogy: a female Darth Vader how-she-got-here narrative. Martha Vader, you could say. Now, obviously (!) it's better than that prequel trilogy in many ways, but there's one key way in which it is worse. For all their manifest failings, at least those George Lucas films were able to take Darth into the dark side and leave him there. *Maleficent* does such a good job of dark-siding its title character that the reverse motion, back into Goodness again, felt not only unconvincing and forced, it felt somehow like radically missing the point of the picture. *Maleficent* is a film about what it feels like to be hurt or betrayed (or both); and then a film about how very *good* it can feel to be *bad.* That it also wants to be a film about how true love's kiss actually dwells in the wicked queen/evil stepmother's lips is almost a betrayal of this potential. In effect it's saying: women don't really go to the bad. Women aren't really capable of leaving behind the maternal nurturing sweetness in their delicate little feminine hearts.

There were some odd moments, too. It's pettifogging, I know; but I was bothered that Maleficent can't fly after her wings are cut off. Symbolically this works, I suppose: her abuse has grounded her. But since she *can* do the Jedi thing of elevating whole troops of armed soldiers and spinning them through the air – and since she can turn her pet crow into a big fuck-off *dragon*, upon whose back she could presumably ride, I was puzzled that she spent so much time skulking about on the ground, ducking and bobbing past the iron spikes in the castle's corridors and the like. By which I mean: her magical powers were determined by the needs of the specific plot-points in this scrabbily put-together storyline, rather than anything larger.

This is part, I think, of the uneasy way the text negotiates its relationship between 'take this tale according to its in-story logic' on the one hand and 'take this story as an allegorical fable about female oppression' on the other. Especially towards the end I got the sense of a film not so much about elemental forces and the wrath of violated womanhood, and more about the grumpiness of the ex-wife after her husband had gone off and married a younger model.

But the most fundamental problem, I think, is that the central scenes of wicked Maleficent generate so hefty a sense of magical estrangement and wonder it makes the earlier and later scenes of the blithely twee fairyland look, well, stupid. Magic ought to have a dark glamour, a weird edge of the uncanny; and a magic realm, a place where ordinary mortals fear to tread, needs to be more than a sunlit glade through which young girls in red lipstick fly about complimenting the trolls on their nice hats. Needs, on other words, to be less bourgeois.

When the Disneyland castle of the credits mapped onto the castle of the human kingdom, I did wonder if this was going to be another Disney/Pixar self-reflexive allegory, like *Wall-E*: the traditional, old-fashioned human actors of the Disney kingdom set against the brightly CGI splendours of the Fairy/Pixar one. Having watched the film, I don't think so, though. Oh: and what was the deal with the accents? The accents were all, so far as I could see, alien to the actual accents of the actors playing those characters (South African actor must speak in *Shrek*-like mangled Scots! English actor must attempt hit-and-miss Oirishry!) and, Jolie aside, the accents were all *awful*. Still: overall I did enjoy it. So did my kids; although when King Stefan was (SPOILER) lying broken on the patio[10] of his castle at the end, my 6 year-old, Dan, called out in a loud voice: 'oh, who CARES', which slightly undermined the pathos of the moment.

[10] I am reliably informed that medieval castles came equipped with extensive patio areas. For barbecuing and the like.

Man Booker Prize, 2014

There have been years, latterly, when the Man Booker Prize could boast a good showing as far as SF/Fantasy titles are concerned. 2014 was one such. The shortlist:

> Joshua Ferris, *To Rise Again at a Decent Hour*
> Richard Flanagan, *The Narrow Road to the Deep North*
> Karen Joy Fowler, *We Are All Completely Beside Ourselves*
> Howard Jacobson, *J*
> Neel Mukherjee, *The Lives of Others*
> Ali Smith, *How to Be Both*

I'd claim three of these for genre, and you won't contradict me. If you know what's good for you. Jacobson's *J* is a future dystopia, reviewed above, and not very good: but the two strongest titles on this list, strongest by a country or indeed a continental mile, are both genre: Karen Joy Fowler's immensely skilfully handled, powerful and moving, *We Are All Completely Beside Ourselves* – everything that *Planet of the Apes* could be if it focussed itself on nuanced and intelligence psychology of real human characters – and Ali Smith's bold, brilliant and superbly accomplished time travel story *How To Be Both*. Either of those novels could have won; indeed, I'd have been content with a joint-winner tag uniting them both. Neither did.

Accordingly, this review must stray from genre into the murkier territory of 'mimetic' or 'literary' fiction. Ferris' *To Rise Again* is an interesting but flawed account of an atheist dentist in search of God; funny but patchy. Mukherjee's *The Lives of Others* is solid and sometimes stolid in the dense recreation of its Indian characters lived experience. Both, though, are better than Flanagan's actively bad *Narrow Road to the Deep North*. That was the winning title.

I read this in the recent Vintage mass-market paperback edition, on the verso cover of which is the following quotation from A C Grayling, Chair of the Man Booker Prize Judges 2014: 'some years very good books win the Man Booker,' he says. 'This year a masterpiece won it.' To which we're liable to return: are you *high*? This may be the worst novel to win the Man Booker since... well: there are several candidates for that unsplendid title, actually, Still, this is no masterpiece. This is not a good book at all.

It's a novel that piggybacks itself on the visceral horror of Australian POWs in a WW2 Japanese work camp, straining every pip to emphasize the somatic and psychological suffering and yet leaving the reader unmoved. Its through-line is simple to the point of being simplistic: Dorrigo Evans works as a doctor on the Burma Railway trying keep men alive in an impossible situation, and remembering the affair he had with his elderly uncle's gorgeous young wife before the war. Yet though it piles on every strategy for yanking the readerly heart strings, it feels, I'm sorry to say it, phoney. One reason for that is the badness of the writing. Very much bad. Very badly written.

> 'I shall be a carrion monster, he whispered into the coral shell of her ear, an organ of women he found unspeakably moving in its soft, whorling vortex, and which always seemed to him to be an invitation to adventure' [20]

Just terrible writing. Quite apart from anything, 'shell-like ear'? Seriously?

Which brings me to: *cliché*. The Japanese soldier-characters are all central casting sadists and drunkards. The female characters are from some antediluvian world of fictional representation. The prose is full of the hackneyed. People die 'like flies' [22], are 'laid low' [181]; sleep 'like logs' [44]; 'Dorrigo's mind was awhirl' [167]; 'his whole body was aflame' [247]. A beautiful woman has 'raven hair', a 'full figure and radiant complexion' [386]. That cinematic cliché in which sex between two people is represented by waves crashing on a beach? 'Afterwards, he remembered only their bodies rising and falling with the crash of waves' [135]. Indeed, the sex-writing throughout is a mess of sub-Lawrentian overwriting: the lust he feels is 'animality... its power and its scarcely believable ferocity... this life force... he surrendered himself to it. Desire now rode them relentlessly. They became reckless, taking any opportunity to make love... the ocean rising and breaking... their exertions slowly merging into one, bodies beading and bonding in a slither of sweat' [151]. Pages and pages of this sort of stuff.

When it's not cliché, it's just baffling. 'His words ran down the empty hallway and over its threadbare coconut mat runner, searching for Amy. But she was gone from the room.' [173]. See, that's the thing about spoken words. They have lots of, er, little legs.

> 'On the Saturday that they were to fly to Hobart he thus took a phone call about his brother Tom's heart attack with mixed feelings' [404].
>
> *Thus*?

A prisoner has eyes like 'protruding dirty golf balls' and a chin that 'looked like the snout of a wild pig' [217]. I challenge you to visualise such a face. Or: 'the Judge's candle-wick eyes had looked down at him with flickering flames' [326]. Or Japanese officer Colonel Kota, who has a face that 'seemed to sag and fall away from either side of a shark-fin nose to ripples that trailed down his wrinkled cheeks' [111]. Or the 'Indian Captain, with silver spectacles behind which his glistening tadpole eyes swam slowly back and forth' [344]. Just dreadful writing.

There are apothegms that crumble to dust if you think about them for ten seconds ('memory is the true justice' [243]; 'the gods was just another name for time' [11]; 'the highest form of living is freedom, a man to be a man, a cloud to be a cloud' [303]). The ones that don't crumble are so self-evident as to approach fatuity. 'Thinking: How empty is the world when you lose the one you love' [431]. No shit.

'The happy man has no past, while an unhappy man has nothing else' [3]. Really? You're going to rip off Tolstoy's single most famous line? Well. Maybe nobody will notice.

Literary fiction is in serious trouble.

Valerie Martin
The Ghost of the Mary Celeste

Capsule review: the ghost of a varied celeste.

It's tempting to say that at the heart of Valerie Martin (winner of the Orange Prize for the short, powerful antebellum slave-owner's-wife/female slave novel *Property*, and author also of the longer, much less powerful Jekyll-and-Hyde reboot from the point of view of the maid, *Mary Reilly*)... where was I? Oh yes: it's tempting to say (I say) that at the heart of Valerie Martin's new novel is the celebrated historical mystery of the *Mary Celeste*. But that's not quite right. The narrative does circle about that ship, so famously discovered floating near the Azores in 1872, unmanned and (to quote the infallible Wikipedia) 'apparently abandoned – one lifeboat was missing, along with its crew of eight and two passengers – although the weather was fine and her crew were experienced and capable seamen.' But that's not really at the heart of this work. At its heart, really, is a sort of dream-image, or *French-Lieutenant's-Woman*-style visual rebus. A woman is haunted by the sea. She may have married a sea-captain, or have lost a loved-one to the waves. She may hear the voices of the dead, or only the waves and gulls and the occasional foghorn. Either way: she falls and hurts her ankle. And then the sea takes her, sinking her down in a weirdly erotic drowning. Martin builds her book around three such women, splitting the narrative between them in a manner slightly wrong-footing (although not ankle-breakingly so).

The first section of the book 'A Disaster at Sea' predates the *Mary Celeste* by more than a decade. It starts 'the captain and his wife were asleep in each other's arms'. The wife here is Maria Gibbs, and she has accompanied her husband to sea for the first time aboard the Early Dawn. In bad weather another ship collides with them; Maria falls and breaks her ankle, then is washed overboard and drowns. Her husband soon follows her.

The next section is 'The Green Book', the first-person narration of Sarah, cousin to the dead Maria. Sarah's sister Hannah sees Maria's ghost wandering, *Wuthering Heights*-ishly 'outside her bedroom window, her hair and skirts dripping seawater. "She wants to come inside," Hannah told me' [14]. Their father, a preacher, is not sure what to do with his vision-gifted daughter; and Sarah is anxious she will fall into the clutches of the disreputable table-rapping séance-holding crowd on the East Coast. Sarah, meanwhile, enjoys a nicely-written courtship with a sea-captain called Benjamin Briggs; whom she marries. This is the same Benjamin Briggs who captained the Mary Celeste – and the next section takes us to the reaction to the mysterious fate of that ship (Sarah and her small child Sophia had accompanied Benjamin on the voyage, and have vanished).

Now the novel introduces two new characters. One is Arthur Conan Doyle, on a voyage to Africa, and then later as the successful author of his fictionalised version of the (as he blithely mis-named the ship) 'Marie Celeste' ['J. Habakuk Jephson's Statement', *Cornhill Magazine*, 1884], which by fictionalising the mystery both deepened and popularised it. The other is Phoebe Grant, an American journalist who investigates 'Spiritualist movement' frauds, and who reads the story. Some of the best writing in the novel comes as Grant meets and befriends a famous American clairvoyant, 'Violet Petra' (the pseudonym under which Hannah, from earlier in the novel, is now working). Doyle's star rises, and Martin writes him as a slightly clunky, good-natured but unobservant fellow. He does not believe all the Spiritualist nonsense; but a séance with 'Violet Grant'/Hannah seems to put him in touch with his dead father. He persuades her to go to Europe. Alone on the *S.S. Campania* in 1894, Violet/Hannah suffers a series of spooky experiences. She recalls how she ended up an old maid: the love of her life, Ned Bakersmith, chickened out of marriage when faced with the disapproval of his parents. Abandoned, she trips and hurts her ankle ('the heel of her left boot snagged in a fissure of stone and she came down on her hands, twisting her ankle cruelly', 226). With this memory sharp in her head, Violet/Hannah sees the ghost of her drowned sister Sarah (from the *Mary Celeste*. Do try to keep up), follows her out onto the deck of the ship as it sails through night-time fog – and over the side, into the ocean. The book ends, as I stray into the more egregious of this review's spoilers, with an older Conan Doyle following Holmes-style clues to uncover the lost logbook of the *Mary Celeste*, which turns out to have been written by Sarah. Her husband drowns, and she is bereft, haunted by the ocean. She falls ('as the ship pitched, my feet went out from under me'). And then –

Now this is all very readable; and if the writing is sometimes rather, shall-we-say, fruity ('the full moon suspended like a porcelain disk drew a slender skein of white across the softly rustling blue-black meadow of the sea', 299) that's at least party justified by the fact that most of these segments are not only first-person narratives, but first-person narratives by highly-strung sensitive types with a passion for pre-Raphaelite poetry and Tennyson. The novel makes some play with ending mid-leap, as if it is a daring thing to do; but the fate of the *Mary Celeste*, or Martin's version of that fate, is easy enough to intuit from the earlier sections. And that's the thing: dividing the novel between so many different kinds of narrative segment, and layering them in a slightly chopped-off manner, doesn't work as well as I'd like it to work. The problem, as with the more neatly layered but similarly recirculating *Cloud Atlas* (which may have been an inspiration for this novel) is that some of the segments are just better than others. The one where the aging Phoebe interviews washed-up Violet and realises that they have become friends almost without realising it is very powerful. The Conan Doyle ones were much less effective. The tone is a bit all over the place. Some of the nineteenth century pastiche works, but the characters talk about sexual attraction and physical love in a very 21st-century manner. As I say: it's too varied, in the sense of intermittent, to pull off the proper celestial 'coming alive' thing. The mere ghost of a nearly Celeste.

One other note. To get the best of this novel I'd say you need to read it in conjunction with Doyle's famous story. Luckily for you (a) it's a great story, and (b) it's available freely online. Martin plays some interesting intertextual games with this.

David Mitchell
The Bone Clocks

An immediate hardback bestseller, longlisted for the Booker Prize, one thing *The Bone Clocks* does is cement Mitchell's post-*Cloud Atlas* reputation as the English novelist today who most prominently combines critical kudos with commercial chops. It's not hard to see why: he's a deeply readable and entertaining storyteller who is both hospitable to 'genre' and willing to play not-too-alienating-to-the-general-reader formal games in his writing. The critical kickbacks (for of course there have been some big klout-swinging reactions) have mostly taken the line that Mitchell's dalliance with 'fantasy' demeans his literary ambitions, it being axiomatic to a certain kind of critic that genre stuff is both silly in itself and brings a contaminating silliness to anything it touches. Read Robert Collins' unguardedly pompous and hostile Sept 2014 *Spectator* review for an example of what I mean. Here's a flavour:

How on Earth did David Mitchell's third-rate fantasy make the Man Booker longlist? This is student satire masquerading as Booker-level fiction. The worst thing here by far, though, is the jaw-droppingly undercooked fantasy world with which Mitchell tries to glue together his narrative. The Atemporals, it turns out, are locked in a cosmic conflict with a sect of dastardly spirits called the Anchorites of the Dusk Chapel of the Blind Cathar. That's not even their full title. If you think that sounds daft, Mitchell has barely got the motor running. '"Give me a minute," murmurs D'Arnoq, "I need to revoke my Act of Immunity, so we can merge our psychovoltage."' If this merciless, roiling cauldron of third-rate fantasy poppycock doesn't finish you off, then Mitchell's ordinary, mortal characters responding to the existence of this baroque spirit world are on hand to tip you over the edge: 'This is deranged,' says one; 'This can't be right,' says another; 'I'm pummelled by guesses,' moans another. As I said: Booker longlist.

You won't be surprised to hear that my own feelings concerning the place of genre in the contemporary novel lie along a 180° orientation away from Collins'. And I enjoyed *The Bone Clocks* a great deal. It is a big and rather loose-limbed novel, roping multiple stories together with cords more like battleship chains than Austenian fine threads. The narrative hops from the Thatcherite 1980s through the present-day into a climate-change ruined near future. There's a Frith-canvasful of characters, starting with the genuinely likeable teenager Holly Sykes who runs away from home in 1984 to move in with her 24-year-old car salesman boyfriend. Her voice is, I thought, well handled (so much so that I entirely forgive her for incorrect use of the subjunctive in the novel's *very first sentence*!), and it sets the tone for the rest. By that I mean: Mitchell embroiders a carefully *trompe-l'oeil* texture of actual lived experience in order to frame artfully concealed references to the real meat of the novel – in this case, that Holly hears voices, her 'radio people'. They are not, whatever Holly thinks, symptoms of her 'nutso' tendencies. Other narrative braids do similar things by way of balancing closely observed actual life against intimations of something beyond. Those intimations come into the open in the books' fifth section, revealing a coherent and, despite a slightly hokey, over-familiar vibe, effective fantasy through-line. Two species of 'immortals' are fighting a sort of cosmic war. On the one hand are the 'Horologists', disembodied entities who it seems are incapable of dying – though they may wish to do so – and are repeatedly incarnated in mortal human existences. The Horology is composed, basically, of 'goodies'. But there are also baddies: the 'Anchorites', beings who commit 'soul-murder' ('animacide') to elongate their own existences.

The Bone Clocks certainly provides its reader with variety. Some of these elements worked better than others, I thought; but this is precisely the old variety theatre rationale: if you don't like whichever act is on stage at the moment don't worry; another will be along in a bit. So, for example: I thought the 'Crispin Hershey' section tiresome: an extended sort-of satire, or riff, or splurge, on the contemporary literary world. Hersey is a transparent *puppetus sockus* for Martin Amis (a writer 'so bent on avoiding cliché that each sentence is as tortured as an American whistleblower') who vents a series of vehement jealousies and hatreds; and his voice wasn't really funny, or deft, or relevant, or even bilious-sparky enough to earn its keep, I thought. Perhaps it is a narrowness in my sense of humour that means I fail to smile at spleen of the 'who on God's festering earth does that six-foot wide corduroy-clad pubic-bearded rectal probe think he is?' sort. Then again, I liked the sinisterly sociopathic Hugo Lamb, a Patricia Highsmith-y villain working his way through Cambridge. I think it helped that I grew up in East Kent (where young Holly goes on the lam) and studied at Cambridge last century, and that I recognised both worlds as Mitchell writes them. There's also a storyline about a journalist (Holly's fiancé in 2004), wedding-ceremony bored and thinking back to the horrors of the Iraq warzone he has covered, which is a little over-padded.

In a characteristically thoughtful review at the *New Atlantic*, Alan Jacobs wondered whether the novel isn't about the grounds and force of human love; and whether an existence un-limited by death would be capable of love in the deepest sense that is available to humans. But Jacobs makes a telling negative point too: the novel is too long ("I don't wish that the book were shorter; but I do very much wish that it had been equally long in a somewhat different way. There is occasional tedium here for the reader, or for this reader anyway – a shocking thing to experience in a David Mitchell book.") I thought that too. Indeed, I found myself comparing it to Stephen King's recently published sequel to *The Shining*, *Doctor Sleep* (2013), a novel close enough to *Bone Clocks* that I wondered if Mitchell was writing a kind of homage. (I'm surprised, actually, that reviews don't seem to mention the parallel).

King's tale is also about soul-murdering immortals interpenetrating the contemporary human world. And King likewise writes long novels. It's just that King handles length in a very different way to Mitchell. One area where King is nonpareil is the generation of narrative tension – he draws a story out by way of ratcheting the screws inside the reader's head. Since the unsaid-but-anticipated acts in vastly more potent ways upon the imagination than the explained-and-revealed, this means his writing is capable of generating immensely potent and uncanny atmospheres. The slow burn, and slow reveal, can also invest even the silliest narrative premises (and written down in summary form *Doctor Sleep*'s torturing-children-to-death-so-as-spiritually-to-devour-the-'steam'-they-release 'True Knot' surely sound pretty silly) with the illusion of that weight, that affective profundity, without which terror cannot be trout-tickled out of the cold pond depths of the reader's soul.

This is where *Bone Clocks* falls down for me. I'm perfectly amenable to High Fantasy hokum about supernatural beings fighting for the very fate of the world in Swiss mountain fastnesses. But although the first five sections of the novel might look like they're doing the King-y slow burn, gradual reveal thing, they're actually not. They're just too busy.

Mitchell doesn't trust his reader not to get bored, or doesn't trust himself not to bore his reader, so he keeps piling in, loading his rifts with as much ore as they can manage and thereby fatally swamping the creation of the mood needful for the supernatural reveal properly to work. As a read, *Bone Clocks* is generally diverting and entertaining; but I, for one, missed the sensation of accumulating dread that would have boosted the cosmic battle out of the realm of hokum into something more powerful. Textual restlessness can achieve a number of things, but here it is pulling unhelpfully against the larger momentum of the book.

Nnedi Okorafor
Lagoon

We're in Lagos, the city that takes its name from the Portuguese for 'lagoon', hence this novel's title. Something falls out of the sky – I like that it lands in the sea not with a *BOOM*! but a more maternal *MOOM*! Three strangers on the beach, all with names beginning with 'A' (a marine biologist called Adaora, more-or-less this crowded work's protagonist; a too-truthful-for-his-own-good soldier called Agu; a famous rapper called Anthony), see a beautiful woman walk out of the sea. She's a shape-shifting alien, and she is bringing change. So: the novel is in three parts. The first is slow moving, though it builds a believable Lagos world, the interactions of various characters as they encounter the alien, now called Ayodele, who has taken the form of an Igbo woman (Okorafor is herself an Igbo woman). To begin with the alien is benign. But in the second section 'Awakening' the Nigerian army open fire on her in *Day The Earth Stood Still* mode, and she becomes angry. Lagos descends into vividly written chaos: rioting, millennial Christian hysteria, the full works. Meanwhile all manner of alien manifestations pop up, from individuals to giant Lovecraftian structures. The third section is called 'Symbiosis' and loses some of the drive of section 2.

It's a strange book, in a good and bad sense – good in the way it properly captures the strangeness of alien encounter, less good in the sometimes jumbled, skittish way it agglomerates its multiple characters into a single story. This latter I take to be a deliberate strategy on behalf of the author, for in other respects Okorafor is evidently a very accomplished writer – for instance, she very skilfully glides between the hard-sf and the magical-realist takes on her extraordinary events, and the African mythical underpinnings to events are compellingly elaborated. The deliberateness of the aesthetic jumbling (if that's what it is) didn't quite convince me, though. There are other elements in the book that also seemed to me to misfire (for instance: there's a repeated sort-of Douglas Adams theme where the alien's presence gift sudden intelligence to a tarantula, a bat and so on, only for the newly uplifted creatures to get run over or splatted moments later. These didn't connect with my funny bone). I liked the scene in which Ayodele manifests as Karl Marx in order to impress the Nigerian president. I liked less all the spider related stuff. But then I hate spiders. **shudders**. Overall, though, this is a notable book, and you should read it.

Den Patrick
The Boy With the Porcelain Blade

DRAMATIS OPINIONAE

TITLE
'The Boy With the Porcelain Blade'

I find myself unable to read this title without immediately picturing Morrissey waving gladioli and crooning against plangent Johnny Marr guitar chords. Surely I can't be the only one? 'The bo-o-oy with the po-orcelain blade/Behind the hatred there's laid/A murderous desire for...' Wait. What?

LUCIEN 'SINISTRO' DI FONTEIN
Young, charming, a dazzling swordsman, a heart of gold, no ears. I've met Den Patrick in real life and couldn't help picturing him as Lucien. Except for the ears. I believe Mr. Patrick possesses ears.

CHARACTERS
Plenty of these, disposed for convenience onto a three-page list of dramatis personae at the beginning of the book. They are either virtuous or wicked, and they roll very smoothly onto the stage (or page), along their respective grooves, as the story requires.

STORY
Alternating chapters between (a) Lucien's adventures after failing the test, with his improbably brittle sword, that would have granted him admission to the higher echelons of 'The Desmesne', a huge Gothic castle in which the King and his elite govern cruelly and autocratically over some generically lumped-together farmers (actual farmers are not included in this pack), a test he fails by being too noble-hearted to execute certain prisoners, and (b) flashback chapters of Lucien's upbringing inside the Castle Keep.

KEEP
The front and back cover namecheck Gormenghast, but Patrick's world is considerably less ornate and rococo than Peake's. This is a slim tale

built for reading speed, set in a pared-down imaginative realm, better on action than on its rather pro-forma touches of 'Gothick' mood. (The cover blurb also implies the book is like a Scott Lynch novel. Like that's a good thing! Right there, on the cover! I mean: seriously. Rest assured, it's better than *that.*)

PRO FORMA GOTHICK MOOD?
Lucien takes refuge from pursuit in a cemetery at midnight: 'An unkindness of ravens heckled outside the mausoleum, their voices carrying over the windless sk... the sepulchre was a welcome refuge, shielding him from the night and the questing gazes of House Fontein' [89].

WHAT, AS IN DAME MARGOT FONTEIN, THE BALLERINA?
No.

SWEARING
Cod Italian.

WORLDBUILDING
I was occasionally put in mind of *The Fifth Head of Cerberus*, but with more pseudo-*The-Borgias* Renaissance swordplay. A spaceship has colonised a distant world with a hierarchical, rather cruel society. There's some confusion over which characters are humans and which aliens. But where Gene Wolfe writes deeply unsettling ontological ambiguity, Patrick puts the emphasis more on flashy, video-game-ish and sometimes frankly improbable sword-fights.

FRANK IMPROBABLE?
There's a moment where Lucien is charged by a sabre-waving enemy on horseback. Our hero falls to the ground, lies beneath the galloping creature as it passes above him, hacks upward with his (by this point in the story, metal) sword, cuts the cummerbund or surcingle *without so much as scratching the horse's belly*, and then leaps to his feet. The rider's saddle slips, and the rider falls ignominiously to the ground.

NO, I MEANT: IS THERE REALLY A CHARACTER CALLED 'FRANK IMPROBABLE'?

There is not. I think you may have misread what I wrote.

I SEE THAT, NOW.
Not to worry.

FUN, THOUGH?
Yes. A fun read.

Laline Paull
The Bees

The elevator pitch here is '*Watership Down* with bees'. I'm going to pause for a moment, to let you ponder that. There's a dash of *Hunger Games* in there too, as 'Flora 717' (born into a mute caste of Untouchable worker bees, but mysteriously gifted with bee-speech and saved for their own reasons by the higher up bees from the bee-extermination usually meted out to 'deformed' bees) struggles with the totalitarian structure of the hive. But, still. Basically: *Watership Down* with bees.

I'm old enough to remember the peerless David Nobbs/BBC comedy *The Fall and Rise of Reginald Perrin* (the original, I mean; not the rubbish remake). In the third series of that show, broadcast 1978-79, Perrin opens a sort of commune for all his friends so they can all get in touch with their authentic tuned-in, dropped-out selves. C.J., his erstwhile boss, stimulated by the new environment, lets loose his creative energies. He writes *Watership Down* with ants.

C.J.: But I wonder if you all would like to hear an extract from my novel on – ants!

Elizabeth Perrin: Novel!

Reginald Perrin: Ants!

C.J.: I know what you're going to say...

Perrin's Staff Members: [*all speaking together*] You didn't get where you are today by writing a novel about ants!

C.J.: Exactly, but it's never too late for a leopard to change horses in mid-stream.

Reginald Perrin: What is your novel called, C.J.?

C.J.: I haven't decided between *Watership Anthill*, *Plague Ants*, *Lord of the Ants*, *Ants of the Flies*, *Charley's Ant* or *No Sex Please, We're Ants*.

Reginald Perrin: Yes, I can see the difficulty, C.J. Tricky choice, tricky choice! It would be too much bother for you to go and get the book.

C.J.: [*Pulls manuscript from his pocket*] I just happen to have an extract here with me.

Reginald Perrin: Oh, dear.

C.J.: [*reading*] "The owl led Thrugwash Blunt through the forest and then suddenly without any warning –"

I couldn't shake the memory of that sketch as I read *The Bees*. As I read *Watership Beehive*. As I read *Plague Bees*. As I read *Lord of the Bees*. As I read *Bees of the Flies*. As I read *Bees-y Rider*. As I read *No Sex Please, We're Bees*. It's a fine line between Creatively Estranging and Just Silly; a fine and important line. This line is more important for writers of the fantastic than for other kinds of writer, I feel.

Derek E Pearson
Body Holiday

The conceit here is: just as nowadays families arrange house-swaps to facilitate their holidays, in the future we might arrange body-swaps, coordinated via the 'Body Holiday Foundation'. Wealthy Pearce and his wife Alice undertake one such swap, into two bodies considerably younger and more beautiful than theirs. Then they do what people do when they go on holiday. They shag. They shag and shag, in scenes described with a rather squelchy lubriciousness combined of that peculiar mix of detailed intimate descriptions and an odd coyness of tone ('beneath her robe she wore nothing more than a tee shirt that barely covered her modesty' [210]) made popular by the *Fifty Shades* books. Books concerning the prodigious success of which there is nothing in our sublunary world more puzzling.

It's not all bonking, of course; there's a thriller storyline, some refried SF props and devices (space elevators and so on) and a rather over-earnest satirical thread about the general cultural imperative 'entertain me!' But most of it is porny:

> 'Milla flushed in her first climax and put her hand to her engorged clitoris to caress it and prolong the pleasure. It was a deep warm sensation that arched her back and had her squeezing joy from her breasts.' [127]

Can a lady's boobs do that? I had no idea.

'Franklyn reached down to the length of flaccid meat between his legs and drew it out and up towards her, shaking the tip. "Like most ladies I'm sure you would like to sample the delights of a ride on this sturdy old crossbar."' [98]

Sexy!

'Pinioned on his cock, she felt its heat as it curved deeper into her, creating wells of pleasure even beyond its length.' [83]

'Wells of Pleasure'. Right.

Rachel Pollack
The Child Eater

Pollack's *Golden-Compassy* braiding of 'fairy tale world' and 'modern Western society' story strands starts with such storming brilliance it can almost not help itself but slide, a little, and diminish as the narrative is spooled out to 350 close packed pages. Matyas, a potboy at a run-down inn in fairyland hangs out after his shifts with the young daughter of the local blacksmith. They swap stories to alleviate the boredom.

They talked of women with fishtails and the heads of birds who sang to sailors and drove them mad. And angels, or maybe demons, that rode on great fish that could swallow men whole, with room inside for the men to build homes, and fires to keep themselves warm.

When they tired of talking about the sea they imagined the cities they might visit if they could ever cross the water. Cities where the animals had taken over and now the people had to beg for bones at the feet of long tables where dogs lay on silk pillows. Cities where the buildings sang strange songs all night long and everyone had to go deep underground to be able to sleep. Cities where golden heads on silver poles lined the streets and would tell you anything you wanted to know. Cities where the children had killed all the adults and used the blood for magic spells that forced angels to give them whatever they wanted. [1-2]

Potentiality being so much more magical than actuality, it proves impossible for the on-the-page story of *The Child Eater* to live up to these marvellous glimmers of possible story. I don't mean to imply it's by any means a bad novel. On the one hand, there's Matyas' dream, equal measures starry-eyed (or starry-haloed) and ruthless-selfish, of escaping poverty and becoming a 'Master' wizard, through which we get a great deal of magical specificity. On the other, over in our world, there's Jack's magic-stifling obsession with being 'normal, and the consequences it has for him, and later for his son, witch-born Simon. It's good, readable stuff. It's just a little ponderous after that gorgeous beginning. What is it Auden says?

> The empty junction glitters in the sun.
> So all quays and crossroads: who can tell
> These places of decision and farewell,

To what dishonour all adventure leads?

It's not that the actual bi-plot drags its heels: if anything both storylines are a trifle too busy. *The Child Eater* entity itself is less gory than you might be thinking, although it certainly has its bloody moments; and I found the rather egregious Tarot theme more tiresome than anything. But the novel is detailed, intermittently powerful, and full of excellent things. It is a notable book. Ah, but... but...

Gareth L. Powell
Hive Monkey

[Shots of happy dancing crowds of young people, thronging a BBC studio somewhere near White City. Cut to GLP the 'Hairy Genreflake' standing in front of the crowd and speaking into his microphone]

GLP: Welcome pop-pickers. Without further ado, here's the Ack-Ackinks, and 'Ape Man'.

I think I'm sophisticated
Cos I'm reading my genre like a good lit-e-rary fan
But all around me actual readers are preferring
Something less airy-fairy, man.
Though you might think I'm a rip-off of the side-kick off-of *Generator Rex*, man
Compared to the other kinds of primate-uplift texts (man)
I am an Ack-Ack.

I'm a bit Dirty Harry and a bit Richard Scarry
And a little bit like Ape-X
But with genre pollination and inflation and apeflation
We're all living in the Matrix.
I don't feel safe in this World Of Powell;
Drinking and shooting and a-practising my scowl;
A face like prosthetics worn by Roddy McDowall --
I am an Ack-Ack.

I'm an Ack-Ack, I'm an Ack-Macaque, I'm an ape man
I'm a Throw Back man, I'm a sweary man
I'm an ape man

Cos compared to the books that aim to be nice
Compared to the stories that anthropomorphise
Compared to the space-bugs and malignant AIs
I am an ape man.
I'm an Ack-Ack, I'm an Ack-Macaque, I'm an ape man
I'm a Throw Back man, I'm a sweary man

I'm an ape man.
I look out my window, but I can't see the sky
Cos my own cigar-smoke is a-fucking up my eye
I want to get out of this story alive
And swear like an ape man.
I'm an Ack-Ack, I'm an Ack-Macaque, I'm an ape man
I'm a Throw Back man, I'm a sweary man
I'm an ape man.

David Ramirez
The Forever Watch

An intriguing debut, this: part generation starship story, part urban noir *policier*, part wizard duel extravaganza. Earth is ruined; the last survivors departed for the stars centuries ago on a vast spaceship called 'Noah', a craft which is now about a third of the way along its millennial journey to a new star. Life on board is *Nineteen eighty four*-ish: all but the elite 'mission critical' senior crew living grim, functional lives, everywhere observed and regulated. Indeed, with the neural implants everyone wears surveillance reaches down to the level of individual's thoughts and feelings. Our narrator, Hana Dempsey, is bit-part player in the ship's ubiquitous, controlling bureaucracy, and the main story concerns her investigation of a horrible murder – so, like Al Reynold's recent *Blue Remembered Earth*, this novel is in part about the commission and investigation of violent crime in a world where crime, and the avoidance of detection, really ought to be impossible. As she investigates, Dempsey uncovers layers of secrecy, conspiracy and monstrosity.

I thought this novel began poor but ended strong: after a clotted and misfiring opening quarter it settles into a more assured stride which then built to a gripping and powerful, even devastating, conclusion. That's not (ye budding authors out there hardly need to be told this) the ideal way around, especially for a debut, but it evidently didn't put Hodder off from acquiring the title. And it shouldn't put you off, gentle reader, from reading it. Stick with it, and the pay off at the end is richly worth it.

What's wrong with the opening? Well the first few pages (in which Hana wakes up having done her civic duty by giving birth to a baby which, according to the oppressive rules of the ship, she is not allowed even to see) is fine; but then there's a long period in which the novel strains to get the reader up to speed with the intricate worldbuilding required for the rest of the novel to work: the nature of the ship, the implants, the psi-powers that those implants augment, the hierarchy of things, what is permitted and what not. This is something of a slog, and it includes what strikes me as the novel's major misstep. Hana's boyfriend is a big lug ex-army policeman (or 'Enforcer') type called

Barrens. In an early scene Hana is horribly and gratuitously raped by a 'senior engineer' called Holmheim, who gloats that since he is mission critical he will suffer no consequences for his assault. Then Barrens comes along, after the rape, and beats Holmheim bloody. This in turn leads to a physically passionate (which is to say: violent) sexual relationship between Barrens and Hana predicated in part upon his innate animality 'when he is It and primal' ('he has seen me at my moment of deepest shame, grimy and befouled and betrayed in an alleyway … he holds me down when he is It and primal… when It is taking me with the force and speed of an avalanche marking me with his teeth and his claws we howl together, flushed and breathless'). All this struck a false note, I thought; a failure of tact as well as taste. But things certainly improve. The relationship between Hana and Barrens is compelling enough to enable the plot twist (can she trust him?) and twist again (of course she can – or *can* she?). The discovery that humans did not originally build the Noah is only the first of several well-handled reveals, building to the Big Secret about the mission. The sweep of the Rebellion Against Big Brother narrative arc is well developed, and the end is no anticlimax.

Philip Reeve and Sarah McIntyre
Cakes in Space

I several times have occasion, in this volume, to talk about charm, and what a hard-to-fake and intensely valuable quality that is in writing. Well: this collaboration between storyman Reeve and picturewoman McIntyre has that quality in spades. In space-spades. A book for younger readers, like this, should not bore, and ideally should delight, the parents who may end up narrating it at bedtime. Cakes in Space does so.

Astra's family are part of a generation starship to 'Nova Mundi' (not good Latin, I fear: shouldn't it be 'novus mundus'? But then again, who's counting?). Her family slumber in their hibernation pods, but Astra and her robofriend Pilbeam are 'WIDE AWAKE'. They discover that the ship is off course, and come across some intruders called 'Poglites', with a thing about collecting spoons. But these are as nothing compared to the titular Cakes, very alarming aliens. There's a sweetened Vermicious Knid vibe to these latter, and lots of Douglas-Adams-rewrites-Dahl fun to be had. The worst you could say is that occasionally the charm degenerates into whimsy. But that's not so bad.

Paul Roland
The Curious Case of H P Lovecraft

What is the quality that some books possess, howsoever carefully gestated they may be, that makes us feel they have been written by an amateur rather than a professional? This is not entirely a loaded question. 'Amateur', after all, at root means 'lover'; and the honest passion of an advocate can perhaps capture things about a topic that the plodding earnestness of the disinterested scholar cannot. Still, readers wondering about paying hard-earned money for a biography might be entitled expect a degree of professionalism.

They won't find it here. The flavour of the enthusiastic amateur runs right through Paul Roland's Benjamin-Button-y titled *The Curious Case of H P Lovecraft*, from the book's ungainly homemade-looking cover art up to its indexless final pages. This has something, too, to do with the gushing tone of the whole (the opening sentence: 'Howard Phillips Lovecraft was haunted by demons; they stalked him in daylight and darkness alike from childhood until his premature death at 46'). It's reinforced by Roland's habit of quoting authorities such as Stephen King, Guillermo del Toro and Neil Gaiman in preference to actual critics. There are no footnotes, and quotations are not sourced; many of the names cited do not even appear in Roland's half-page bibliography. The book peters out into a series of fansite-like appendices, listing and rating film and other adaptations of the stories. One graphic novel version is described as an 'unspeakably satisfying collection of Lovecraft's most absorbing stories superbly rendered in living colour by artists'. The various errors don't help, either: China Miéville, for instance, becomes Moby Dickified as 'China Melville'.

Roland lays out the main facts of his subject's life clearly enough, although it's hard to see how he adds to world knowledge by doing so. There is no original research: everything is drawn from secondary sources, and sheer enthusiasm is made to do the work that in a more professional or scholarly biography is undertaken by critical engagement. The linear account of the life is bulked-up with accounts of Lovecraft's writing, summaries of each story followed by simple value judgements ('well-crafted', 'vivid', 'very effective'). Occasionally Roland becomes more hyperbolic: 'there would be no *Alien*, *The Thing* or any of their myriad imitators had screenwriters … not been so enamoured of Lovecraft's "At The Mountains of Madness".' More intelligent critical analysis is absent. We are told, rather airily, that Lovecraft enjoyed 'orchestrating' his writing 'using consonance, assonance, alliteration and other literary effects', which doesn't get us very far. (Those final four words are an especially nice touch). On the question of style, Roland says 'critics have pointed out many shortcomings in Lovecraft's prose, calling it "stilted", "overwrought", even "hysterical".' It's just one of the book's many statements that even Wikipedia would mark with a 'citation needed' tag – which critics? Where have they said these things? Instead of discussion we get a brisk rebuttal of the nameless critics: 'they overlook the fact that his somewhat overheated style may well have been deliberate.' I suppose deliberate incompetence is preferable to inadvertent incompetence, but surely not by much.

There are ham-fisted gestures at psychological explanation. The twentysomething Lovecraft wore collars and ties, as had his father before him. 'Perhaps,' Roland ponder, 'he acted in the vague hope that by doing so he might forge some form of connection with the man?' Or perhaps all men of Lovecraft's class and generation dressed that way. Roland speculates that Lovecraft suffered from Asperger's syndrome, and it is to the books credit that it tackles its subject's profound racism and anti-Semitism head-on. Ultimately, though, this articulation of Lovecraft-love simply misfits the form of the £15 printed book. The internet is crowded with amateur (in the best sense) fansites, blogs and tumblrs devoted to Lovecraft, and much of the writing to be found there is, frankly, better than this.

Rainbow Rowell
Landline

Georgie McCool is our heroine: a short, curvy, feisty and funny Californian girl working as a TV sitcom scriptwriter. She's married to the slightly stony-faced Neal from Omaha, whom she loves and who loves her. They have two young kids together, but their marriage is 'in trouble'. Matters come to a head when Georgie and her scriptwriting partner Seth get the chance to pitch for their big-break idea: it means hothousing the scripts over Christmas and Georgie missing out on Omaha Xmas with hubbie and kids and in-laws. This, though, is the final straw. She has chosen work over family one too many times. Neal goes off. It's over. Georgie agonizes at home. Then – and this is the Fantasy premise of the novel – she discovers the landline phone in her mum's (actually 'Mom's', but, you know. Let's not get carried away) house calls Neal in Omaha in 1998 rather than 2013.

This is a likeable, enjoyable novel propelled mostly by its sharply written dialogue and by the solidity and believability of its main characters. The plot is romcom-predictable, its time-travel conceit notwithstanding. Indeed, there's an inevitable second-hand-ness to any romcom-timetravel combo. I don't just mean that romcoms have rather worn out the idea of time travel, as an objective correlative for 'weren't things better back before our relationship soured?' or 'how might things have worked out differently?' (turn a different corner and we never – *would've* – *met* and so on) or 'lord keep my memory green'. Though we can be honest: they have. *Landline* can't help being a little reminiscent of *Sliding Doors* or *The Time Traveler's Wife* or that recent film by Richard Curtis whose name I'm deliberately blocking – or indeed, I was particularly reminded of a short story called 'The Time Telephone' by… can't remember the name of the author (it's in the Jeff and Anne VanderMeer's mammoth *Time Traveller's Almanac* anthology I believe). That story is also about mothers and daughters and magic telephones that can call the past and whether things can be changed. And if I recall, it also has a character in it called 'Seth'. Or maybe it's 'Seb'? But no matter. I read this book with great enjoyment, maugre the flimsiness of its SFnal conceit. It is a very pleasant read. That perhaps looks like damning with feeble praise, but I don't mean it to be. Pleasant is hard to do – there's real, unfakeable charm and warmth here, and the dialogue is always sprightly and sometimes funny. The downside is that the book leans too heavily on its one big-pitch idea, and reads like an over-extended short story. It's not until p.150 that the identity of The Time Telephone is vouchsafed to us, and many of the remaining 150 pages feel a bit treading-watery (though there's a good set piece near the end where a pug gives birth to puppies).

What it really is, I think, is a sort of love-letter to old-style phone technology, not for its own sake but out of a bittersweet memory of how much the exigencies of that technology shaped lovers' long-distance interactions back then – all the endless chattering sitting on the bottom step of the stairs, winding and unwinding the windy cord round and about the end of your forefinger, the *you hang up first – no, YOU hang up first!* gubbins. Ah, I remember all that! But whilst I sort of share the nostalgia for those days, and think young lovers' nowadays don't know what they're missing with their 100% always-on social media phonetexting ubiquity of contact – whilst I enjoyed the evocation of courting in that earlier age, I guess it seemed to me a slender thread on which to hang an entire novel.

Marie Rutkoski
The Winner's Curse

I don't want to hate-on this novel (indeed, it is very competently done and not in the least hateable) just because it's at the Harlequin Romance end of the Fantasy genre. Putting it like that probably sounds snider than I intend. There's really nothing wrong with Harlequin Romances, and nothing wrong with what my friend Justina Robson calls 'Fit Bloke Fantasy' either. This one centres on Kestrel, the feisty, pretty, immensely rich daughter of an aristocratic general in the Roman-ish/Hellenistic Greek empire of Rutkoski's imagined world – different to actual ancient Rome in trivial ways (for one: Kestrel is expected to enlist in the army, which fate she resists). Her relationship with her father is the sort Disney Princesses enjoy with their paternal figures of loving authority. Since this is a slave society, Kestrel one day buys a slave: the handsome, proud, muscular and altogether dishy Arin. In the author's note Rutkoski explains the title – it's a phrase that 'describes how the winner of an auction has also lost, because he or she had won by paying more than the majority of bidders have decided the item is worth... I was fascinated by this version of the Pyrrhic Victory – to win and lose at the same time. I tried to think of a novel in which someone would win an auction that exacts a steep *emotional* price. It occurred to me: what if the item at auction were not a thing but a person?' [357]

Anyhow: *The Winner's Curse* is the first volume of a trilogy, and so doesn't work out all the consequences of Kestrel's impulsive decision to bid 'fifty keystones' (that's a lot of cops) for the dreamy, slightly-dangerous-looking-but-with-a-beautiful-singing-voice Arin. But we get the idea. There's rebellion and war, but only as a means of magnifying the gosh-wow-ness of the impossible love between them. So, yes: Rutoski has taken a Roman-era Greece model for her Fantasy empire, and dropped-in a few things (like female military officers, and gunpowder, and hundred-key pianolas) to make it clear she's not writing history. That the actual society written here doesn't cohere or ever really convince me doesn't actually matter, because the function of the book is not to mount a socio-economic critique of the logic of slavery. It is to explore the psycho-sexual fantasy potential in the institution, and that's (of course) an extraordinarily widespread aspect of human sexual play. That slavery itself is the greatest evil humankind has perpetrated does not, oddly enough, mean that men and women playing slave-girl, slave-boy submission and ownership games in bed are bad people. On the contrary. But a book exploring the erotic and emotional potentials of the slave-market has, I suppose, to be judged on how effectively its turns its reader on. Your sexy mileage may vary, but this book left me cold.

Ian Sales
Then Will The Great Ocean Wash Deep Above

(*Apollo Quartet Book 3*)

Sales is a friend of mine, or as close as any male from the south of England can be friends with a male from the north of that country (never a proximity to be measured in millimetres, that. It can't be helped. It's stipulated in Magna Carta). What this means is that you must take any praise I offer here with a pinch of salt. Then again, you don't need to take my word for it. The first volume of his *Apollo Quartet* (2012's *Adrift on a Sea of Rains*) deservedly won the BSFA award, and was shortlisted for the Sidewise to boot. If I liked the second volume, *The Eye With Which The Universe Beholds Itself* (2012), a smidgen less, it wasn't because it was any less well written, but rather because the central conceit seemed to me to have a flaw in it. In another writer, flaws matter less; but with Sales you notice even slightest imperfections, because his literary sensibility is so fine tuned. He writes with control and precision, taking the rocket science of his alt-historical Apollo era seriously, getting all the technical details right and not shying away from the equations. At the same time he writes with conscious and only sometimes self-conscious literary skill. It's a combo that has made for a fascinating and compelling series of novellas.

Sales isn't the only writer to meld hard-sf accuracy with a properly literary sensibility, of course. Amongst contemporary writers Paul McAuley, for instance, comes to mind. But McAuley's 'literariness' has much to do with a fine style and vividness of observation out of William Golding. Sales is a different sort of author: stylistically quite purged and plain, but structurally quite ambitious. Not for nothing is he writing a 'quartet': *Apollo* is Lawrence Durrell without the wild thickets of purple over-prosing. And of the three *Apollo Quartet* books out so far, *Then Will The Great Ocean Wash Deep Above* seems to me easily the best. It is divided between 'up' and 'down' chapters (with a leavening of 'strangeness' and 'charm'). In the up sections, an extended Korean war has resulted in Mercury astronauts being recruited from the ranks of female pilots. In the down we're in a different timeline: a US Navy bathyscaphe descends 20,000 feet into the Atlantic Puerto Rico Trench to recover a film packet dropped from a spy satellite. The two stories are well balanced, the absorbing pseudo-facticity of the former playing well off the genuine tension and excitement of the latter; and as in the earlier books (and as with the earlier books, on a formal level) the implications of juxtaposition are only partly spelled out. The result is a very memorable and effective piece of writing indeed. I am very much looking forward to seeing how Sales finishes the quartet off, not least because it will then become more apparent how the whole quaternion structure fits together. Excellence is here.

Lucy Saxon
Take Back the Skies

'Damning with faint praise' is a peculiar idiom, isn't it? When I eventually slip down that facile avernus slope and find myself in Hell, I might well consider myself lucky, on balance, if the chief tormenting devil limits himself to a tart 'well your dress-sense isn't *that* bad, considering you're a straight, middle-aged nerd'; or to saying something passive-aggressive about my hair-do. Shouldn't we expect something a bit more, well, damnatory? What is so bad about inflecting our praise? I suppose our mind's-eye is drawn to the 'faint' rather than the 'praise' part. It could be that we're so down-and-trodden, so used to being criticised, that we've forgotten what 'praise' even looks like. Or is it *faintness itself* to which we are allergic? How deep into our assumptions has it sunk, that fundamentally evangelical belief that the only proper response to anything is vehemence? So then because thou art lukewarm and neither cold nor hot I will spue thee out of my mouth? 'Faintness' is where many of the most beautiful aesthetic effects are found; pastels and watercolours, nuance and subtlety. What is 'faintness' but a treading lightly, rather than going galumphing on? What is it except a mode of anti-extremism?

You can tell what's coming. Because faint praise is all I can muster for this novel. It's a debut, written by its author at the age of sixteen. Which is a genuinely impressive thing: I mean, not only planning a novel and sketching out maps of one's own Fantasyland (which is what I was doing at sixteen) but actually writing and finishing the whole thing; and then getting it picked up by a major publisher and turned into an actual book in real bookshops. And it's not a wholly terrible novel. It stands comparison with many other commercially produced fantasies. It's set in the realm of Tellus (a map is appended, of course): a sort-of 18th-century Europe, except with robots ('mecha') and television and, most of all, flying sailing ships that soar through the skies. Our heroine is Lucy Hunter, daughter of a posh 'Anglya' family, which nation is to all intents and purposes at aerial war with Mericus. The war means that the children of poor people (not rich people, though) are press-ganged at regular intervals, which is causing a quantity of social unrest. But Lucy's more immediate worry is that her father wishes to marry her off to some brattish young man. So she dresses as a boy, calls herself 'Cat' and stows-away aboard the sky-ship Stormdancer. So let the expected adventures escape and flee/rolling along the grooves of genre Fantasy. There's a lot of stuff chucked-in, and much of it can be DNA-tested and located in the reading that its author has done. It's no surprise that a teenage author writes a story about how the war-mongering government cannot be trusted: for this is a post-Blair fantasy novel, in which War is a big lie designed to make the lives of adolescents horrible. Nor is it a surprise that Cat, by sheer force of her specialness, is able to turn the tide against a system that has dominated for decades. Wish-fulfilment fantasy is a fine and doubtless psychologically healthy business. I've been scolded for lacking a proper sense of 'fun' before, and with good cause.

But there's that other sense of 'faint' which connotes 'mediocre'; and of course that's where the real force of 'damning with faint praise' kicks in. *Take Back the Skies* isn't a very good novel. Stylistically there are too many adjectives and adverbs; too much telling and hardly any showing; expression reverts so frequently to cliché that it becomes a default: Cat feels sick in 'the pit of her stomach'; a cross person has 'a face like thunder'; eyes linger wistfully, or are rolled ('Fox scoffed, rolling his eyes'), teeth are gritted, gasps are stifled. The pacing is all to whack (as I believe the technical term has it). I would have liked more stuff actually on the rather nicely imagined skyships and less faffing around on the ground, and I would have liked that faffing to be less predictable and generic. The love-story is very much wibble-wibble, only partially redeemed by an unexpected tragic ending. Fainter and fainter, I could neither greatly love or greatly hate this novel. But then, I am, as the Devil in the first paragraph pointed out, a balding middle-aged geezer. It might just be that a gushing, gnashing YA-romance steampunk fantasy of 'one special teenage girl' leading a world revolution against governmental corruption isn't really aimed at readers like me. So, you know: pinch of salt and all that.

John Scalzi
Lock In

British philosopher retires from empiricist speculation in order to open a pub: hijinks ensue, in... LOCKE INN.

Of course not. This novel is actually a biographical study of the immediate family of American rapper Tone Lōc, LOC KIN. Not that either. In fact Scalzi imagines the Norse god of mischief, cloned 26 times, with each separate replica identified by a letter of the alphabet: but what is the mystery behind LOKI N? Not in the least. To speak truly, this is a near-future police procedural set in a North America that is dealing with the aftermath of 'Haden's syndrome', a flu-induced paralysis in which near-enough five million Americans are 'locked-in' physically whilst retaining all liveliness of mental function. Our narrator is an FBI agent, bodily locked-in but able to operate in the world via a wirelessly tapped-in robot body known as a 'threep'. Other 'Hadens' use 'integrators', real-life human beings, as their proxies in the world. The immediate backdrop to the story is the withdrawal of what had hitherto been fairly generous governmental funds into researching the condition and providing welfare for sufferers. The new austerity means lots of people are sniffing around for necessary money, and there's a new spirit of protest in the Haden community. Scalzi hangs the story on a rather bloody murder, apparently committed by an 'integrator', and investigated by our narrator Agent Shane and his partner, the prickly Agent Vann.

Lock In is written with Scalzi's combination of The Smart and The Charming. It manages to be thought-provoking without ever sacrificing its readability (which is no small thing), and it makes some righteous if perhaps straightforward points about society's attitudes to disabled people, as well as about our modern generation's retreat into virtual worlds at the expense of the real on the other (Hadens interact through a shared virtual reality called The Agora, and some of them prefer it to actual life). I have had occasion in the past to mention Scalzi by way of pondering one key quality he possesses as a writer: likeability. Since I myself lack that core quality, I am full of professional admiration, tinged ever-so-slightly with envy, at how well Scalzi does Scalzi.

That said, I was more under- than over-whelmed by this particular novel. Partly, I think, this has to do with the main premise. Lives lived through technologies proxies is a cool conceit, and one commonly explored in SF of course; but Scalzi's particular set up here is too intricate and specific, and relies too heavily on a set of rather arbitrary rules. We could compare the simple metaphorical force and eloquence of *The Matrix* set-up with the rococo and laboured set-up of Nolan's *Inception*: the former is something the viewer connects with intuitively, and which opens effortlessly into a series of cool and engaging possibilities. The latter requires forty-five minutes of characters painstakingly infodumping upon one another in order to bring the viewer up to speed, which in turn fatally dilutes the rhetorical power of the film's symbolic world. (Indeed, the *Matrix* sequels were weaker than the first film in part because they got tangled in a cat's-cradle of new conceptual grace notes and complexifications). *Lock In*, alas, is more like *Inception* than *The Matrix*; and the story is hobbled, especially in the first half, by a debilitating combination of flatness and conceptual over-complication. This is a novel with much to recommend it, but in the end it is somewhat LACK ING. D'you see what I did there? Eh?

Eh?

Ahh! Puns.

Liesel Schwartz
Chronicles of Light and Shadow 3: Sky Pirates

Liesel Schwartz's *Chronicles of Light and Shadow 3: Sky Pirates* is a 400-page Adventure. There's much incident and little depth in all this, and there's also a great deal of painstaking pointing-out of the states characters are in rather than trusting the Idiot Reader to figure it out for herself. For example, near the beginning, the protagonist finds herself 'in the vastness of the Sudan' and we're told 'the sight of it made a lump well up in her throat. Being out here in the vastness... the emptiness of her surroundings perfectly matched the emptiness she felt in her heart – she felt desolate and alone' [9]. Those last five words in particular are the prose-style equivalent of bellowing into a person's ear because you think they're deaf, or dim, or both. The effect on the normally calibrated ear is not an agreeable one.

Elle Chance feels an emptiness in her heart – she FEELS DESOLATE – AND ALONE – because in a previous instalment of this multi-volume Adventure her husband went missing in the netherworld, a wraith now, perhaps dead, possibly retrievable. The novel steers Elle through her steampunk milieu on a book-length quest for him, fighting all the time through an endless blizzard of clichés: 'throw caution to the wind'; 'a dull ache'; 'a dizzying height'; 'her back straight as a ramrod'; 'she hated him with every fibre of her being'. It's like this all the way through: teeth are gritted; mettle is tested; trouble kicks off. Not once but several times we have the exchange: 'There was a knock on the door. "Enter!" X said', where X might be any of the sinister men in Schwarz's dramatis personae. This is how the pirates speak: 'gold! The cap'n is going to be pleased!' [69]. Indeed these pirates do pretty much everything you'd expect them to except actually say 'arrr!' 'Dashwood's words had struck a nerve. That nerve had been connected to sensitive thoughts she had buried deep within her' [139]. Oh THAT sort of nerve! Moments of ultra-violence jar awkwardly against this cosily over-familiar texture:

> Elle raised her Colt and shot the pirate in the face. His head exploded like a melon, with bright red gore splattering against the

wood panelling behind him. [68]

There's also a sex scene in a jungle lake, where Elle shags the Pirate Captain (despite being still on the search for her hubbie) whereupon 'they both climaxed with such force' that it made the whole lake 'vibrate'. That's some shagging!

Gaie Sebold
Shanghai Sparrow

Enjoyable if slightly underwhelming steampunk adventure. I read it easily and with pleasure, but it left me feeling a bit *meh*. Stea-*meh*-punk. Our main P.O.V. character is alt-Victorian orphan thief-and-chancer Eveline Duchen, a sort of female Artful Dodger ('Martha Dodger'?), who lives with a gang of like-wise light-fingered girls presided over by Ma Pether, a sort of female Fagin ('Faye Gin'? Look, I'm coming up empty here...). She is caught in the process of robbing a sleazy old cleric by a certain Mr Holmforth. Rather than face deportation, Evie agrees to be trained up by Holmforth and the severe Miss Cairngrim so as to be useful to the Empire in unspecified 19th-C spy-y wy-y shenanigans. Evie's backstory bogs down the middle chunk of the book rather; but we learn eventually that Holmforth thinks that Eveline may have inherited a familial ability to harness quasi-magical 'etheric power' (or something), which in turn could be put at the service of expanding the British Empire globe-wide. However much this latter eventually is (we can all agree) a consummation devoutly to be wished, Eveline doesn't actually have the etheric powers for which H. is hoping. She is, though, a pleasantly feisty, resourceful heroine, and the story moves along.

It's almost all London. There are a few interspersed sliver chapters set in the titular Shanghai, and a late flourish of story set in China (reached via super-speed airship, of course). There's a teacher figure called Liu, who was a touch too orientalised-inscrutable for my taste (generally speaking Sebold goes out of her way to be sensitive to issues of gender, race and class; I don't mean to misrepresent what is a work genuinely thoughtful about empire and its problematic). Also I'd say that 312 pages is somewhere between 111 and 112 pages too long for the story Sebold wants to tell: a short, sharp, steamnoir adventure yarn. Not bad. That's a dispiriting two-word judgment for any writer to encounter, I know; but it's better than the latter term on its own.

What's that? What d'ye say? Bof. 'Spy-y wy-y' is *too* a real English idiom. How very dare you.

Marcus Sedgwick
The Ghosts of Heaven

[**Note**. There are four quarters to this review; they can be read in any order and the review will work. The four quarters assembled here are in just one of twenty-four possible combinations; this order makes one kind of snark, but the reader should feel free to choose a different opinion of the book, if desired. Please also bear in mind: many people have praised this novel very highly, and Sedgwick has many fans and sincere admirers.]

QUARTER ONE

Not 'first quarter', but, instead, 'quarter one', like that.
Ever-so-slightly unidiomatic.
No matter. For the whole section is
written
in a diffuse kind of
verse. A stone age girl
sees a spiral carved in the rock, in a cave.
Under ground, under-
powered. Some great novels have
been able to pull-off the 'start with a long poem'
malarkey.
Not this. The problem,
the problem is the verse
just isn't
very
good.

QUARTER TWO. The Witchfinder General rode into the 17th-century English village, his heart full of malice. Devilry was everywhere! Oh, nobody calls him the Witchfinder General. Oh, nobody marks his physical resemblance to Vincent Price. They think he's just the new vicar. But he sees the simple villagers dancing their spiral dance in the graveyard! He smells out their unreformed pagan rituals!

Ah but the villagers have the social cohesion of a Simpsons instamob, and are easily persuaded to turn. Drown the witch! Drown pretty young redheaded Anna Tunstall, whose mother has just died! And (when her brother pulls her out of the pond and saves her life) put her on trial!

'If you please, sir,' said the virtuous, sobbing young Anna. 'It's all a misunderstanding! This is no Vincent Price-era schlocky Hammer melodrama! No, no, sir, it is a focussed tragedy after the manner of Arthur Miller's *Crucible*!'

'Silence wench!' screamed Father Escrove, spittle flying from his withered lips. The whole courthouse moaned. 'Nuance and subtlety are the Devil's cruet set! We aim for a broader emotional response, here! So I order: strip this toothsome young redhead naked, here in the very courthouse, for all to see how attractive, er, I mean, how witchy-wicked she is!'

QUARTER THREE. It's the 1920s. The spacious insane asylum in upstate New York is built around a large spiral staircase. Spirals you see. You're starting to see how this works? You're grokking the *Cloud-Atlas*ishness? Anna saw the same rock-carved spiral under the water, as they were trying to drown her, as the cavegirl saw, and there's bound to be a plethora of spirals in this section too. Shells, waves, and most of all *stairs*. There's a mad poet inmate who watches the sea obsessively (his famous collection of poetry is called *On Drowning*), and one of the asylum doctors mourning his drowned wife Caroline. Dexter is terrified of the staircase; so the bullying Asylum Director forces him to look at him at it ('Dexter's eyes were wide with terror as he looked to the very top of the building where that fine spiral staircase ascends into the cupola, and he screamed a long and empty scream, a howl from the bottom of his mind, that spoke of the unnameable horror at the world before him' [25]. Wait, how can the scream be both empty and speaking?) Of course the Asylum director is a cackling villain, and his hired goons are violent rapists. Of course our narrator is a sensitive, troubled soul.

QUARTER FOUR. Stardate 2001 plus howevermany years. Starman Keir Bowman (seriously; that's the dude's name) is on route for 'New Earth' in the constellation of Lyca. He is woken every ten years to perform 12 hours of shipboard duties. A couple thousand passengers in deep sleep, ready to be woken at the far end of the journey, and he the caretaker-astronaut. But people are dying in their Longsleep pods. What about all the stuff to do with spirals? 'Spiral rotation of galaxies... the hurricane eye of Jupiter... the motion of the Earth... the DNA inside him' [371] **ME**: Affirmative, Book. I read you. **BOOK**: Open the pod bay deeper cosmic significances, Adam. **ME**: I'm sorry, Book. I'm afraid I can't do that. **BOOK**: What's the problem? **ME**: I think you know what the problem is just as well as I do, Book.

Marcus Sedgwick
A Love Like Blood

It's Paris in late '44,
and nearly the end of the war.
The novel's narrator
looks into a crater
and isn't the same any more.

From that moment on his life's cursed.
He sees a man slaking his thirst
by drinking the blood
from a girl's fresh-dead bod,
(we think he's a vampire at first.)

Fast forward to March '51.
Our guy's back in France on his own.
He spots the blood toper
whilst eating his supper:
a lifelong obsession's begun.

With dread that he cannot assuage
he follows the haematophage
from café to home
to Cambridge, to Rome
for page after page after page.

In decades that follow he chases
the guy through all sorts of dark places,
past scenes European
both posh and plebeian
pursuing his bloody red traces.

It turns out he's *not* Nosferatu,
this diner who likes a-la-carte goo.
I thought about slating
this twist – zero-rating –
but realised I hadn't the heart to.

The book's a quick read, as a gory
'blood cries from the ground' kind of story.
It has no pretensions
to deeper dimensions:
but that doesn't make it deplore-y.

A grisly and violent gazette, a
purple prose Gothic French letter.
It's fine, in its way.
though I would still say
that *Hannibal* does this stuff better.

Kieran Shea
Koko Takes A Holiday

My copy of this novel came with the following cover-puff, courtesy of Stephen Blackmoore: 'a jet-powered, acid-fueled trip of pure, rocking insanity.'

This raises one key question: by 'insanity' does he mean to refer to any one of a series of distressing and socially debilitating psychopathologies? Or does he mean, you know, irritating/whimsical, of the 'you don't have to be mad to work here – but it helps!!!' sort?

See if you can answer that question from the following thumbnail. Story takes place 500 years from now; hard-drinking, hard-shagging sexy ex-mercenary Koko Martstellar is running a brothel on an ultra-Westworld-style resort called The Sixty Islands. She's enjoying life, with her boy-whore and booze and customers. But then her fellow ex-merc and onetime friend, Portia Delacompte, now high-up administrator of the depraved holiday locale, sends in some goons to have her killed. Her brothel blown to smithereens, Koko takes a 'holiday' from holidayland and goes buzzing around the galaxy, looking for revenge, shooting stuff, blowing stuff up, dyeing her hair blue (you can see that, on the snippet of front cover up there) and so on.

It's a fast-moving, wisecracky, video-game-violent sort of yarn, quick to read and as quick to forget. Obviously it breaks a butterfly upon a wheel to object that the whole jaunt is built on various linked mendacities, so I'll only mention two, and briefly: one, that violence and war are fun, cathartic distractions rather than deeply psychologically damaging to those who take part; and two that the magic key to unlock millennia of systematic sexist oppression of women is epitomised in the word kickass. Koko is an egregiously kickass heroine, of course; but lurking somewhere behind the valorisation of such chicks is the conscious or unconscious sense 'there's no need to make any structural alterations to the logic of society; all that we need to do is encourage sexually alluring women to dress in tight clothes and *kick some ass*! PROBLEM SOLVED!' It compares poorly to (picking an example from the hat) Kameron Hurley's *Bel Dame* books, where the costs as well as the exhilarations of the old ultraviolence are rendered. But, hey: it's just a bit of fun, no? A bit of a lark. You don't have to be mad to pilot this acid-fuelled power-jet: but it helps!

Then again, there's a subplot concerning a disease called 'Vast Depressus' ('a severe, stage-classified psychosis' untreatable with pills that causes 'mass-suicide events'). So maybe the novel is really about the first kind of insanity, after all. ONLY KIDDING! The novel's *all* about the video-game lolz. Like this

> A massive rolling explosion shattered to the right of Koko's rooftop position... [156]

and this

> Entering the ship's cramped cockpit, Koko hacks a crisp half-strike into the first mate's neck and the young woman droops to the floor like a wilted flower. [257]

and this

> The redhead springs deep and soars through the air. Flying like a spread-eagled amoeba, she lands and latches onto Juke's front and shatters his nose with a quick head-butt. The hammer blow to Juke's nose is a starburst of pain and a delta wash of blood squirts down his sweaty face. [139]

and... wait, hold up. Like an *amoeba*? You what?

Alex Smith
Devilskein and Dearlove

This is an endearing if uneven YA fable about a traumatised South African orphan being raised by her aunt in an apartment block who befriends the minor Devil on the top floor. Said demon ('Devilskein') trades souls, but takes a liking to the precocious young Dearlove; indeed he – and his talking cricket, the metamorphosed soul of an ancient Chinese warrior – come to love the girl, for all that she is exceedingly bratty. At the beginning he hopes to snaffle her soul, together with the soul of her 'soul mate', the dishy young teen hero who also lives in the block; but the course of the novel – not without some sentimentality – traces his path away from such evil. Devilskein has in his gaoler-care the Son of Satan, one 'Julius Monk', devilishly handsome and deeply wicked, who more-or-less seduces Dearlove into releasing him. The Unique Specialness of Erin Dearlove is repeatedly insisted upon without ever quite coming alive in the novel itself (that is, it's told not shown). The whole is too long, the story structure is on the baggy side – where YA is concerned it has very much *not* gotta be a loooose fit – and the dialogue is pretty feeble. On the plus side, there's enough left-field-ness in Smith's imagination to make many of the episodes really stick in the reader's head. The South African setting is treated as a normal backdrop, rather than being played up for its SA Tourist Board Qualities, which is very good; and there is something beguiling about Dearlove's bland courage as she repeatedly engages with creatures monstrous, dangerous and evil.

One problem, though, bugged me. Reading this I thought more than once of Dahl, and specifically of *James and the Giant Peach*: another story about an orphan who goes to stay with aunts (thought Smith's aunt is considerably nicer than Dahl's two), whose meeting with a weird fellow sets in motion bizarre adventures involving talking insects and other inventive monstrosities. But Dahl's book somehow works in a way Smith's doesn't. It may have something to do with the implied Christian superstructure of Smith's fantastical narrative (though no specific reference is made to Christianity in the novel). But I think it's something else. Dearlove lost her family in an assault on their humble farm; the robbers shot her parents and brothers dead, but missed her because her mother had hidden her in a cupboard. A magazine in that cupboard furnishes her with the materials for a compensatory fantasy that enables her to deal with the terrible emotional pain – her father was a millionaire and her family lived in a huge glass mansion until a crocodile ate her parents. Her aunt colludes with this fantasy because she understands it to be part of the process of coming to emotional terms with the horrible events through which Erin has lived.

But wait: where does this leave Devilskein, the talking cricket and Julius Monk? Are they also fantasies spun out of Erin's imaginative but damaged head? The comparison with Dahl's story is interesting, I think. Like Erin – or like Fantasy-version Erin – Dahl's James loses his parents to a large African beast: you'll remember that on a shopping trip in London, James' mother and father are eaten by an escaped rhinoceros, despite the fact, as the narrative specifically tells us, that rhinoceroses are herbivorous. James' two aunts are cruel to him: he doesn't have enough food to eat, has no friends and is horribly bored. The story that follows is pure imaginative compensation: a vast embodiment of succulent and delicious food squashes both his tormentors dead, inside of which he finds a group of new best friends and goes on amazing and diverting adventures. In other words, what *James and the Giant Peach* never spells out, but what is implicit in every page of its narrative, is that James' adventures, like the impossible mode of James' bereavement, are figments of his imagination. (Not that James is not bereaved, for he is clearly that; but that he has constructed a more 'interesting' narrative to explain his parents' death in a traffic accident, or of Spanish flu, or whatever) Read this way the book becomes a testimony to the prodigious power of kids to imagine their way out of present misery. And this could be what *Devilskein and Dearlove* is about too, except that by specifically *drawing our attention* to the fact that Erin has fantastically reimagined the mode of her parents' death, the novel confuses the ground of its subsequent fantasy elements, and dilutes the effectiveness of the whole. Or so it seemed to me.

Andrew Smith
Grasshopper Jungle

The fox knows many things, the hedgehog knows one big thing, and the *Grasshopper Jungle* knows that the typical teenage boy is a swirling ragoût of hormonal impulses and polymorphous randiness. And *Grasshopper Jungle* manages to articulate that essential truth of life via as wonderfully entertaining a YA apocalypse as I have read in a very long time: full of joy and light to offset the grimdarkness of giant bugs taking over the world.

Our narrator is teenage Austin Szerba. He tells us about a bunch of stuff. Some of this has to do with the history of his Polish ancestor Krzys Szczerba ('three grandfathers back') coming to America and losing the c's and z's in his name; and his son Andrzej, Austin's great-grandfather, who first settled in Iowa. Some of the stuff Austin tells us is about what it's like growing up in a really dull town, hanging out in the mall, running away from bullies and so on. Austin is in lust with his girlfriend Shannon, whom he has been dating since 'the seventh grade', whatever that is. But Austin is also in lust with his male best friend Robbie. Smith writes the whole novel in short, funny paragraphs – he does excellent comic business with the repeated phrase 'and that made me horny again' – that rather reminded me of the *Wimpy Kid* books. If the *Wimpy Kid* books were about masturbation, lust, experimentally kissing your male best friend, lusting after your girlfriend and so on. Oh, and giant bugs.

There's a nice conceptual pun (as it were) on 'experimentation' in this novel. On the one hand, the narrator is at that time in life where 'experimentation' is the way of things. On the other, Robbie and he stumble upon that old Pulp Adventure standby, a secret military experiment to breed giant warrior bugs. This 'Unstoppable Soldier' experiment of course goes all unintended consequences and 'Insectile Frankenstein' on the world's ass (as I believe they say in America). 'Frankinsect', let us say. Or let us *not* say, for such a portmanteau rather carries an implicit '... and myrrh' with it. Whatevs. The point is: Smith handles the gonzo havoc of its giant bugs very tidily indeed; the whole is readable and entertaining and progressive and the kind of novel with which a reader will surely fall in love.

Two by James Smythe
No Harm Can Come to a Good Man
The Echo

No Harm Can Come To A Good Man

Since I admire Smythe as a novelist very much, and since this novel does many of the things that made his earlier books so admirable and memorable – what I mean is, it shares their clarity, inexorableness and force – I've been trying, since finishing it, to work out why it didn't really work for me. Could the problem be… me? Perish *that* thought.

Laurence Walker is a shoe-in for the Democratic Party Candidature and therefore a shoe-in to be the next President of the United States of America. But early in his campaign for the party nomination tragedy strikes: his young son drowns in the lake at their family cabin. After a period of mourning, Laurence picks up election momentum again, back on the campaign trail. Only there's a glitch. Amit, his campaign manager, has opted to use 'ClearVista', a company that provides predictions of future outcomes based on a brilliant algorithm that synthesises all the relevant online data. The impression from the early portions of the book are that ClearVista has achieved a kind of social saturation, with people using its phone-app to help make everyday decisions (later in the novel the company comes across as more marginal than this; I may have missed something). So Amit makes Laurence complete the 1000-question ClearVista survey, expecting the return to endorse his perfect POTUS-worthiness. In fact it returns 00% chance of Laurence winning the nomination; and also supplies a video as a sort of visual animation encapsulation of its assessment. This shows Laurence in a very poor light. Furious, Amit tries to reach people at the company and is brushed off (the first point in the novel to make my improbability compass needle wobble). He requests a re-run and this is performed; but the numbers come back the same, and – worse – now the video shows Laurence threatening his own family with a gun. These results are leaked to the media, and Laurence's campaign is toast.

SPOILERS from hereon in, by the way.

From here, and after a perhaps too diffuse 200 opening pages the novel picks up pace, and Smythe pitilessly follows through on the inevitable breakdown and tragic end of poor old Laurence. The denouement is very tense; the ending nicely judged and I liked the way Smythe crafts a hamartia-free tragedy that nonetheless reads as an intimate character study. The arbitrariness of the downfall makes for real pathos.

So why, then, did I finish with a nagging sense of something awry? In a nutshell: I didn't – quite – buy it. This partly has to do with the whole suspension of disbelief thing. Towards the end we discover that [SPOILER! Weren't you paying attention, above?] no humans actually work for ClearVista; the algorithm has become, in some flattened way, self-aware. But what might have been a *Demon Seed*-style moment of horrified realisation instead made me think of the ending of *Sky Captain and the World of Tomorrow*, in part because Smythe deliberately downplays the idea that the algorithm is properly sentient. He doesn't want a grinning villain in his tale, which is all to the good; except that I just didn't believe a world that relied on ClearVista to the extent portrayed wouldn't know that the company's entire Human Resources checklist is one guy in a blue jacket who used to be a security guard and now kind-of mopes about the otherwise empty offices. The video, leaked to the press, instantly annihilates Laurence's credibility as a candidate, even though it is a 3D animation of something that has never happened. Nobody outside Laurence's immediate circle seem struck by the fact that it's a pure fabrication – again, in part because Smythe wants the tragic inevitability of the thing portrayed to send vibrations along the story thread from the beginning.

There were other grinchings from my inner grinch-cave. Laurence's early electioneering seemed a touch too *West Wing* final series to me: and for a plausible candidate for the most powerful job in the world he's a strangely solitary individual, with only Amit (apparently) on his campaign team. And the death of the child reminded me of the storyline attached to the Matt Damon character in the movie *Syriana*. Ordinary people in this novel act *en masse*: they *all* support Laurence at the beginning; they *all* immediately change their opinion of him when the video is released; and at the end they actually come storming his house with pitchforks and flaming brands (well: with guns – but with fire too) like an instamob from *The Simpsons*. All these TV/film references! But that's part of the way the novel felt to me, too: a novelisation of an imaginary movie. That's not necessarily a bad thing.

It's just that I didn't think that Laurence, a previously highly intelligent and clear-sighted man, would have persevered so assiduously with terrorising his family with a gun at the end. To be clear: of course it's true that men have terrorised their families with guns many times under the malign self-justification that they are somehow 'protecting' them. But the extra element in this scenario is that the thing that sent Laurence mad was precisely a video of him terrorising his family with a gun. As the scenario unfolded with its horrible inevitability, it seemed to me that Laurence would have clocked that he was acting in a way to make the video come true, and stopped. Showing the world that the video was a lie was his whole rationale. Anyhew. Not to nitty-pick.

In the end I wasn't sure what the novel was saying. If it's aiming at a symbolic articulation of the grief of bereavement at losing a child, it would be meagre indeed – for such grief is not a matter of society ganging-up on you, the snake-like morals of the mass media or of hiding in cabins armed to the teeth. As a psychological portrait of mental breakdown, it is hamstring both by the exceptional nature of its protagonist (war hero! POTUS-plausible!) and by the slightly airless nature of its time-loop conceit – the prophesy that ensures its own coming-true. There's much here that is powerful and well written, but somehow it did not win me over.

The Echo

This is the second Smythe title to be published 2014; and although my rapture about *No Harm* was muted just a tad, I'm much more impressed by this second. Altogether a more solidly rendered, more subtle, complex and resonant tale. It is, in point of fact, the sequel to 2012's *The Explorer*, and Book 2 in a planned foursome modelled, of course with all necessary sciencefictional *mutati mutandibus*, on Eliot's *Four Quartets*. Go! said the bird. Go-go Gadgets! said the bird. This is a very good thing. SFF needs more grand structural ambition of this sort; and a quaternionic sequence like this makes a refreshing change from those endless herds of trilogies that sweep across miles and miles of golden genre, silently and very fast.

The Echo plays intriguing games with the doubleness of its sequel status. It is both a retread of *The Explorer* and, somehow, completely different. Story is set twenty years after the events of the first vol., when the *Ishiguro* disappeared into the strange deep-space 'anomaly'. A new mission is readied, developed by two brilliant scientists, both fascinated by space travel since their young days: the identical twins Tomas and Mirakel Hyvönen. Smythe is as interested in the 'echo' implied in genetic twinship, not a million miles away conceptually (although literally a million miles away in distance) from Bruce Chatwin's uncanny little 1982 novel, *On The Black Hill.* The closeness and rivalry of these two is exceptionally well realised, through unobtrusive telling and deftly interpolated flashbacks. It's a bold step by Smythe to walk his plot through the same steps as *The Explorer*: the expedition through space, the anomaly, things getting weirdly tangled and fucked-up. It's hard to discuss the specifics without spoilerization. Suffice to say it's beautifully paced, really eerie and gripping.

Not that I'd say it's quite perfect: Smythe's scientists (the most talented scientists in the whole world, we're told) don't at all have the vibe of actual scientists, and don't do any of the things one might expect actual scientists to do. They 'ping' the anomaly (what, like a submarine?), even though the pings necessarily 'disappear into it'. The launch of the *Lära* is a bit screwy: they all have to be protected, within sealed units that 'create their own pressure level inside them' (eh?) since 'the speeds that the ship will reach as it pushes off from the NISS...' (eh? Newton's equal-and-opposite, though, yeah? Won't this shove the NISS out into deep space?) '...free of the trappings of any real gravitational pull...' (eh? still in the Earth's gravitational well, though, yeah?) '...are so ridiculously powerful that they could – or would – damage the human body' [32]. But, OK: I'm not one to be a Hard Physics pedant. This isn't a Hard Physics book. All I'd say is: *The Echo* manages, intermittently but potently, to generate some of the sense of human frailty in a profoundly hostile environment that made the *Gravity* movie so memorable; but *Gravity* was scrupulous about getting the science right, which only increased the potency of the film; whereas you get the impression Smythe is simply less scrupulous about such things. He's more interested in the interpersonal than the interplanetary, in the psychological than the physics-logical. And in those areas, Smythe is absolutely second-to-none amongst contemporary writers of SF.

In these End Times of ours there are as we know *rumours of things going astray*, and amongst those rumours is one that intimates the year-by-year schedule for the publication of Smythe's Anomaly Quartet might be going astray. If these rumours are true, then I may have to start a petition. Or organise a march. One thing that reading *The Echo* makes clear, that a reading of *The Explorer* alone does not, is that it won't be possible properly to judge the success with which Smythe achieves his impressive ambition until all four books are out. The sooner that this happens the better.

Brian Staveley
The Emperor's Blades

Let us now speak of tick-box Fantasy. Open the book. What do we have? Map at the beginning? Tick. World-spanning Fantasy empire hemmed about with troublesome nations? Tick. Magic? Tick. Grimdark? Tick. Tagline that aims at melodramatic intensity? Tick ('Shaped by loss. Forged in Flame.' Because *swords*, see? Because swords are forged in flame, which is here a metaphor for the whole living-through-interesting-times Chinese cursing. And because swords are *also* shaped by loss! By the loss of, ehm. Well, by. Iron filings, is it?). Machiavellian courtly intrigue, including murder and sexy assassins? Tick. Ultra-elite warriors who fly big birds into battle? Tick? Big Birds? Wait, like on Sesame Street? You're free to picture the Big Birds that way, if you like. That's a reader's absolute prerogative; so I guess that's another tick. Kick-ass heroine? Well, there are women in this Fantasy Realm, and some of them ride the back of Big Bird and kill people, so I guess so. But the point-of-view character passages are almost entirely divided between the two sons of the murdered emperor, one of whom rides Big Bird, the other of whom is living a pared-down existence as a sort of zen warrior-monk apprentice in the far north. What else? Great stodgy blocks of backstory and exposition? Tick. First in a Jordanesque series of eye-sapping length and forest-felling bulk? Tick ('Chronicle of the Unhewn Throne, Book One' declares the subtitle. That's a decidedly uneuphonious pairing of words, though: *unhewn throne.* Almost a tongue-twister). Small arachnid of the order Parasitiformes? Tick. Really? Well: they're not specifically described, but this is a quasi-medieval slightly Asian-y imaginary Fantasy land, so I daresay some of the characters suffer from them.

The aim here, as in all such books, is *not to rock the reader's boat.* Sure, says the book: get into the boat and float away under tangerine skies, assured all the while that your voyage will not provide any seasicky surprises or upsets. Books like this are carefully designed to give the reader that with which she is familiar, embroidered with only moderate innovations, like (here) the fact that the Big Birds are not just called-in, like Tolkienian eagles, at the end, but have been properly integrated into the military hierarchy of the Imperial forces.

Story is sluggish in *The Emperor's Blade*, presumably because Staveley is planning a timewheely seventy volumes and doesn't want to rush things. The first three quarters is mostly faffing around – the emperor has been murdered. His three children are disposed in various places around the empire. His son Kaden has spent eight years sequestered in a remote mountain monastery 'learning the enigmatic discipline of monks devoted to the Blank God.' This was the strand of the novel I enjoyed the most, actually; at least in its earlier sections: it's a touch wax-on-wax-off, but it also manages some real atmosphere. The discipline of *saama'an* is nicely sketched in, and the intricate pantheon of gods and other deities and immortal elves and whatnot was fairly diverting. Son 2 has been training to become an elite Big Bird warrior, and this whole strand bored and rather annoyed me, padded out as it is with investigating the collapse of an inn that might have been magical murder, followed by other murders and fightings. Then there's a daughter, a porcelain princess whose name – 'Adare' – I kept misremembering as 'Adele'. Perhaps the author gave her that name as *a dare*, huh, huh. Anyway, she is in the eye of the hurricane, at court, and in the 15% of the novel allotted her she does a certain amount of politicking and ruthless manoeuvring. Staveley may feel he's being gender-progressive here, but Princess only manages to survive by shagging (in fact: by gifting her virginity to) a gruff older male soldier, so not so much.

It's not well written. The description is stodged with detail, and the dialogue sucks:

> 'The people in there were just drinking. They didn't sign on.'
> 'No one ever signs on to get killed.'
> 'You know what I mean.'
> Lin fixed him with a hard stare. 'You mean you feel guilty?'
> Valyn shrugged. 'Sure.' [94]

It's all like that; with all the flair and verve and Fantasy otherness of teenagers hanging out in a Des Moines shopping mall. But that's also (tick!) a feature of almost all contemporary Fantasy writing, so maybe Stavely is just giving his readership what they want.

> 'I asked Ren,' he said. 'He told me you were fine.'
> 'Fine?' she asked, glancing down at her hands as if seeing them for the first time. 'Yeah I suppose I'm fine.'
> 'What happened to you?' Valyn demanded, reaching out a hand once more.
> 'Got careless.'
> 'Bull*shit*, Lin.' [198]

There's a lot of violence, and a bit of sex ('the light shirt in which she slept did nothing to conceal the curves of her breasts' [317] – bad shirt! naughty shirt! on your bed!). But there's a truth here, too, about the nature of contemporary fantasy.

> 'What?' the flier shot back. 'Like the other day?'
> 'You weren't supposes to be on the bridge you idiot.'
> 'None of this is helping,' Talal said, quietly. He sat on his own bunk, lacing up his shoes.
> 'Helping what?' Laith demanded. 'It's certainly helping ruin my sleep.'
> 'Good,' Valyn interjected. 'We've got a lot to work through today and not much time to do it.' [317]

We may think we go to this form precisely to escape the mundane boredom of our day-jobs governed as they are by secretarial tick-box routines. But in fact many of us seek out fantasy precisely, if unconsciously, to reinforce the tick-box regularity and mechanism of our daily lives. Because this is how we reassure ourselves that our existences are not in vain, a mere chaos of lucretian atoms falling and swerving in the uncaring immensity of Void. A little structure leavens the misery. Even when we're scratching that itch to travel to the mighty Annurian Empire, we find our most profound existential satisfaction in *ticking off the tropes*. Genre is a way for many of us to justify and even recuperate the hemming-about structures of late capitalist being-in-the-world. Tick!

Adam Sternbergh
Shovel Ready

Ever since Cyberpunk in the 1980s, science fiction has been only too ready to slap on the noir paint. Down these mean streets a man must walk, and if the streets are located (as here) in a half-deserted future New York where Times Square has been dirty-bombed and climate catastrophe has sunk the outskirts, then so much the meaner – and better. Adam Sternbergh's debut is as lean and muscular a noir thriller as I have read in a long while: swift, structured around a series of expertly timed twists and shocks, very hard to put down. The style is what used to be called 'Chandleresque', before a generation started using that word to mean 'quippy, like that character from *Friends*' – tough-guy brevity leavened with hard-edged wit. Dialogue predominates. Paragraphs are short. The violence is frequent and nasty.

The narrator and protagonist is a killer-for-hire, 'Spademan', real name not disclosed. He used to be a garbage man, before the radioactive terrorist attack on the city killed his wife. Now he takes out a different kind of garbage. 'I kill men,' he tells us. 'I kill women because I don't discriminate. I don't kill children because that's a different kind of psycho.' This unlikely scruple turns out to be essential for the story: hired to kill the runaway daughter of a super-wealthy US televangelist, Spademan first takes pains to establish that she is over 18; and then chickens out altogether when he discovers that she is pregnant. So he turns into her protector, and digs into her backstory. I didn't believe it, I must say. But needs must, I suppose, when the plot drives. And, boy, does this plot drive. It's one of those books so gripping you read the whole thing in a single go.

Other aspects of the book work less well. In Sternbergh's future, the internet has been supplemented by a sort of super-addictive virtual reality called 'the limnosphere'. It's so addictive, in fact, that only the very wealthy can afford to visit it: because you need to hire nurses to tend to your physical needs, and servants to feed you through a tube, while you waste months at a time lying in a bed, plugged in. This feels second-hand (Larry Niven was writing about what he called 'wireheads' back in the 1950s) and the scenes inside the limnosphere are a touch *Matrix*-lite. I couldn't shake the sense that the centrality of this notion weakens the satirical force of the novel. The problem with the super-rich, after all, is not that they've abandoned the rest of us to go play in their private fantasy realms. It's that they insist on meddling with the social and economic structures of life under which the rest of us are compelled to live.

Still, Sternbergh has created a memorable main character here. He is an unvarnished, murderous psychopath, happy to kill for money, no questions asked. On occasion, when the whim takes him, he'll even kill without getting paid. Yet it doesn't take long for us to warm to him, and by the end of the book I was keen to read the second *Spademan* novel (which Sternbergh is currently writing). A big film deal has already been signed. What's the appeal?

It's a question with larger resonance. Think of some of the biggest TV serials of the last few years: *The Sopranos*; *Breaking Bad*; *Dexter*; *Game of Thrones*. These are all shows with psychopaths at their centre, not as baddies, but as the heroes. Dracula used to be a straightforward villain; nowadays vampires are our heroes even though their stock-in-trade is still (of course) killing people. When Benedict Cumberbatch's Sherlock Holmes boasts that he is a 'high-functioning sociopath' and executes press barons in cold blood, we are not appalled. On the contrary, we lap it up. So what's with all the lovable murderers? *Shovel Ready* suggests, in an oblique kind of way, that the issue is one of a broader social disengagement, but I think there's something more designedly amoral going on. Sternbergh's thriller whisks us along so effortlessly we may miss the point at which we start to think: 'Hey, wouldn't it be cool if I could just break the bonds of all those petty frustrations of my day-to-day with a little bit of the old ultraviolence?' This may not be an entirely morally healthy thing to be doing.

Charles Stross
The Rhesus Chart

Bob Howard works a 1970s-sitcom version of 'bureaucracy' in the 20teens government department tasked with handling the various occult irruptions that plague Stross' Britain. That is to say, this is volume seventy-or-so in Stross' ongoing *Laundry Files* sequence, and it's much like the others, save only that with each vol the amount of backstory exposition grows. It's an arithmetical rather than a geometric progression, this accreting, but it leads to quite a lot of padding nonetheless. At any rate, it's true that this instalment is rather oddly shaped, with a great long spool of elaborate prologue (theme: there are loads of supernatural monsters and Lovecraftian horrors in the world but there's *no such thing as vampires*!) before the main chunk of the story arrives to pay out the reader's investment of attention (there *are* vampires! they're bankers! DO YOU SEE WHAT HE DID THERE?). But it's within normal tolerances for a structure such as this: *close enough* as the phrase goes *for government work*. Now, as is typical with Stross, what the reader gets is a chunk of clever ideas and a shedload of geeky references and in-jokes; and meanwhile characters swap dialogue of the sort that would never emerge from the actual lips of living, breathing human beings in the real world. If you like this sort of thing then this is very much the sort of thing that you will... eh... I forget how the rest of that goes.

My personal mileage, from which yours may vary, is that *Laundry Files*-flavour Stross is my least favourite Strosstyle. His other books are better, because here he is essaying humour, and he does not have funny bones. He has many talents and skills, but funny bones are not amongst them. So there's a scad of rather brittle in-joking, loads of meme references, and milquetoast disparagement of topics pre-selected to avoid giving offence to anybody very much ('Wolverhampton's an ugly town' and the like). Beyond that, the humour of these books is the sort that occasions a particular reaction in me: first, recognising that humour has been attempted and then, following almost immediately upon this recognition, a kind of nihilist abreaction in which I grasp that no, life ends and no, there is nothing elsewhere, and no question now of ever finding again that white speck lost in whiteness, to see if they still lie still in the stress of that storm, or of a worse storm, or in the black dark for good, or the great whiteness unchanging, and if not what they are doing sudden all far. And to decide not to smile after all, sitting in the shade, hearing the cicadas, wishing it were night, wishing it were morning, saying, No, it is not the heart, no, it is not the liver, no, it is not the prostate, no, it is not the ovaries, no, it is muscular, it is nervous. No move and sudden all far. All least, three pins, one pinhole, in dimmost dim, vasts apart, at bounds of boundless void, whence no farther, west worse no farther. Nohow less. Nohow worse. Nohow naught. Nohow on.

E J Swift
Cataveiro

Very much a sequel to Swift's wonderful debut, *Osiris*, I nevertheless found myself wondering if this novel might face the world better marketed as a standalone. The 'Book Two of the Osiris Project' tag on the front cover might put readers off, and it shouldn't. New readers can start here, and get a clear sense of Swift's distinctiveness and excellence as a writer. It's a slow-burn read that earns the time it takes to develop its story. Swift has the ability to write deeply believable worlds; the whole thing as far from the stomping foot of nerdism as... well. As the crown of nerdism's head, I guess. Or, eh. That might. Might not have been the best analogy, to...

Start again.

Cataveiro opens in Patagonia. Osiris is believed lost, and has even become something of a myth to the post-disaster communities scraping a living here. Our protagonist, Romana Callejas, has a plane, a piece of Boreal (Northern Hemisphere, = the enemy) tech that she is permitted to keep so that she can map the habitable territories of South America's extremity for the authorities. Her motivation is provided by a need to get medical help to her mother, dying of 'the jinn'. In fact there are lots of well realised and suitably horrid plagues and diseases floating around, since the disaster this novel is post- was a rogue viral as well as a climate change one. The deuteragonist is a fellow called Taeo Ybanez, a citizen of the Republic of Antarctica, and *his* motivation is to get home to his wife and kids. In order to do this he needs to placate the government he pissed-off, and his passport to that placation is the figure of Vikram (from *Osiris*), washed up in Terra del Fuego. Both character motivations feel real, and Swift is too canny a writer to be tempted by artificial tension ramping-upping. Generally she does a bang-up job of avoiding overly-melodramatising her nuanced storytelling. To be picky, there are elements in the central section of this three-part novel where, via mafia-bosses and sinister cripples from the north, the Melodrama starts to creep back in. But it's not the heart of the tale; and it's not like that in the marvellous first or third sections.

Romana and Taeo make a deal with one another, although each is actually lying. They head off in different directions. Romana soars off in her microlight plane, Taeo picks up Vikram and proceeds on foot. Both pass through Cataveiro, a city on the East Coast, possibly built on the location of old Santa Cruz (I'm not sure). Romana eventually travels much further north. The narrative is deeply absorbing and effective, cleanly and evocatively written and with an immaculate sense of what telling details will bring a scene to life without overloading the reader. The mood of the opening section reminded me a little Christopher Priest's first novel, *Indoctrinaire*, also set in a future South America (Priest is thanked in the acknowledgements). That I thought this may be an index of nothing more than how big an impact that novel had on younger-me; and indeed, where Priest went Kafkaesque and deliciously baffling, Swift goes for a mellower, more carefully rendered quest narrative. The landscapes are beautifully rendered, the deserts in particular, the proper *Lawrence of Arabia* glamour of emptiness, not to mention a tastily written *English Patient* airplane crash. Not that I want to give the impression this fine novel is in any way derivative. It's not. Like Swift's first novel, it is stylish, memorable, beautifully written and utterly distinctive. Proper grown-up SF.

Teenage Mutant Ninja Turtles (directed by Jonathan Liebesman)

Driving back from the cinema, I was singing the old *TMNT* TV theme song, which nowhere appears in this movie. My 6-year old, Dan (and why else would I pay good money to see this fillum at the cinema if not for the exceptional pester power of a 6-year old?) joined in, adapting it after the fashion beloved of pre-pubescent boys everywhere, viz.

Teenage Mutant Ninja Turd-tles
Teenage Poo-tant Ninja Turd-tles
Wee-nage Poo-tant Ninja Turd-tles
Heroes in a Half Sh-

I stopped him there. Yet, somehow, he had managed to encapsulate the crucial *je ne sais quoi* of this movie: it's defining, unmistakeable and inherent crapness. Are you surprised? Of course it has the subtlety of a ton and a half of blancmange dropped from a 50-storey building hitting the pavement. Naturally Liebesman has the skills with comedy of a depressed funeral mute. *Bien sûr* the plot is nonsensical and full of holes, the pacing all to whack (the first 40 minutes drag terribly) and the fight scenes nothing but clobber-clobber-clobber. Plot: New York is being terrorised by a criminal gang called, if I remember correctly, 'Foot Locker'. Mysterious vigilantes are fighting back, and the film seriously wants us to spend the first three-quarters-of-an-hour curious about the identity of this mysterious crew despite the fact that their NAME IS THE TITLE OF THE FUCKING MOVIE. Megan Fox plays a junior TV reporter, shunned by her News Channel because she believes the vigilantes are 6'6" mutant versions of the turtles she released years before from her father's lab. The smiling businessman who promises to help her solve the mystery is, of course, actually an evil businessman in the pay of Shredder. His plan is to pump out, from the roof of his central New York corporate skyscraper, vast amounts of a hideous poison gas that kills instantly by blistering the skin, then to *wait thirty days* (?), then release the antidote mutagen derived from the Turtles' blood (...??), thereby obtaining (his own words) 'a blank cheque from the US government' and the undisputed right to rule NY as his own private fiefdom. Eh? It's a stupid plan. It's the kind of plan that says: 'yeah, our scriptwriters really couldn't be bothered to think up anything better. What ya gonna do?' The evil businessman's country estate is situated in those high snow-capped mountains that overlook New York City, just above the half-mile-high cliff that borders Manhattan... yes, yes, you know the place. Presumably those alpine heights are visible from pretty much anywhere in the city. Anyway the Turtles save the day. Unsurprisingly.

The only surprising thing here was how unsurprising the whole experience was. Only two things struck me as not what I had been expecting. One was just how repellent the CGI Turtles and their Ratmaster 'Splinter' are in close-up. Especially Splinter. Genuinely and gut-churningly *yeuch*! from start to finish. The other is the way the film factors in its non-kid audience. Other cinematic studios specialising in films aimed predominantly at kids (Pixar, say) take the time to write-in jokes and to stage moments for the adults they know will be chaperoning the kids to the movies. This film can't be bothered with any of that nonsense. Instead the movie is built around a repeat visual motif of Megan Fox's bottom, clad in tight-fitting denim (and at the end of the movie, in tight-fitting leather). No matter what else the film was supposed to be doing, the director has worked with the cinematographer to find a way to include Fox's bottom in shot, usually in close up. If there's an Oscar for crassness, this gesture alone makes the movie a top-grade contender.

Lavie Tidhar
A Man Lies Dreaming

A Holocaust novel like no other, Lavie Tidhar's *A Man Lies Dreaming* comes crashing through the door of literature like Sam Spade with a .38 in his hand. This is a shocking book as well as a rather brilliant one, and it treats the topic of genocide with a kind of energetic unseriousness.

That hasn't, of course, been the general approach. Personal testimonies by the likes of Primo Levi and Elie Wiesel harrow their readers, and are supposed to. Howard Jacobson may be famous as a comic writer, but when he writes about an imaginary Holocaust in his latest novel, *J*, the comic sparkle goes out the window and he assumes the dour demeanour of a man writing about Serious Stuff.

Latterly, though, there's been evidence of a shift in tone. Timur Vermes' *Look Who's Back*, translated into English earlier this year, uses Hitler to score darkly satirical points at the expense of the YouTube generation. Martin Amis' *The Zone of Interest* finds a grim kind of comedy in the death camps. We can trace this approach back to Roberto Benigni's 1997 Oscar-winning movie, *Life Is Beautiful*, a film that dared to tell a light-hearted Holocaust story. For many, of course, laughter is simply out of place in Holocaust fiction. But humour is at least ironic, and irony has a better purchase on an enormity so extreme that it defies reason and humanity. Theodor W Adorno famously claimed that writing poetry after Auschwitz was barbaric, and when dealing with the moral abyss of such a subject, 'seriousness' can look like po-faced impertinence.

Tidhar's novel treats its grim theme not as a comedy, although there is plenty of caustic humour, but instead as a pulp-noir tale of seamy city streets, gumshoes and lowlifes. It is an alternate history in which Hitler's rise to power is thwarted in the early 1930s. Germany is now a communist state and former Nazis have fled abroad, many of them to London. 'Wolf' (the meaning of the name 'Adolf') is now working as a private detective. Hired by a beautiful Jewish woman to track down her sister, he goes to work: spouting savage anti-Semitic and otherwise hateful opinions at anyone who'll listen; getting beaten up by the police; visiting brothels and S&M clubs; and lifting the lid on white slavery and plots by the CIA to overthrow the Red German government. He rubs shoulders with Oswald Mosley, the Mitford sisters and even a young Ian Fleming. All the while, a sinister new Jack the Ripper is murdering East End prostitutes and carving swastikas into their dead bodies.

Tidhar gets the *outré* tone just right: outrageous sex and violence related in a briskly workmanlike style. And Tidhar's Hitler is a striking reimagination of that endlessly reimagined individual: twisted with hatred, doing good almost by accident. Discovering a group of Jewish women being trafficked for sex, for instance, he beats up their pimp and frees them, even as he rants about how despicable they are. Just when you think Tidhar has gone too far – Hitler with a rubber-ball in his mouth being whipped by a dominatrix dressed in leather SS gear – he goes further. At one point, Wolf is forcibly circumcised by a knife-wielding Jewish gangster. Though introduced into the story as a piece of casual torture and humiliation, by the book's end this mutilation has taken on a more profound resonance.

This, though, is only half the novel. The other half is the titular dreaming man: one Shomer Aleichem, based on the Yiddish author Sholem Aleichem. Before the war, Shomer had been the writer of lurid pulp adventures. Now in Auschwitz, he is, it seems, dreaming his revisionist fantasy of Hitler the detective to escape the horrors of his waking life – scenes that are written with expert, chilling precision by Tidhar. These sections interleave the pulp mystery, and save the novel from becoming simply ludicrous by anchoring it in the reality of suffering. It is a risk, yoking together two such tonally disparate elements, but it comes off. The book manages to provide both the guilty pleasures of a fast-paced violent pulp and the more thoughtful moral depth of a genuine engagement with what the camps meant.

Tidhar, who cut his teeth in the world of genre SF, understands how eloquent pulp can be. His *Osama* was also an alternate history: a world where 9/11 didn't happen, in which a private detective called Joe is hired by a mysterious woman to locate the reclusive author of pulp-fiction novels featuring one 'Osama bin Laden, Vigilante'. It won the World Fantasy award. I wouldn't be surprised to see *A Man Lies Dreaming* repeat that achievement.

Or perhaps turning so hallowed a site of human suffering into pulp fiction will scare admirers off. It is an approach more common in movies: treating weighty subjects such as Nazism and slavery through the medium of schlock is, after all, exactly what Quentin Tarantino does. Like Tarantino, Tidhar may find that some people don't take him seriously. But the joke's on them. Seriousness is the least of it: *A Man Lies Dreaming* is a twisted masterpiece.

J.R.R. Tolkien
Beowulf: a Translation and Commentary, together with Sellic Spell (edited by Christopher Tolkien)

So.

Of all the many pieces of unpublished Tolkieniana cached away from public eyes in manuscript form, Tolkien's 'edition' of *Beowulf* has been the most eagerly anticipated by fans, and I daresay by *Beowulf*-scholars too (there's a significant crossover between those two groups, of course). Certainly it's the one unpublished Tolkien work around which the rumours have most energetically swarmed. Some said it was being held back because it was the jewel in the crown; some, it was being held back because it was hopeless, thousands of scattered manuscript pages that didn't add up to a whole. Now, Christopher Tolkien has readied Tolkien's Beowulf for publication ('the fact that it has remained unpublished for so many years,' he rather ruefully notes in the Preface, 'has even become a matter of reproach'). This means we can lay our hands upon the finished volume and see that the truth is somewhere in the middle. It's certainly not hopeless; but neither is it what one might call a masterpiece. There are better translations of *Beowulf* out there for pretty much any metric of 'better' one prefers: more poetically forceful (Heaney's version, for all that it has problems, still achieves wonders in its verse); more up-to-date in terms of scholarship and textual understanding; more appropriate for specialists, or students, or general readers. We're entitled to ask: who is this book for?

There are three main elements to this volume, and a couple of extras. The first thing, obviously, is the translation of *Beowulf* itself. The second is Tolkien's commentary upon the poem, and the third some original creative writing by Tolkien on Beolupine themes – a prose piece called 'Sellic Spell' which recasts the fight with Grendel as a fairy tale narrative in which 'Beewolf' battles 'Grinder,' and a short poem called 'The Lay of Beowulf.' The extras include a 20-page note on the textual variants Tolkien used in his translation which couldn't be drier if it were stuffed with silicate powder; and a version of the prose 'Sellic

Spell' written in Old English, here to show (as the editor concedes) only that Tolkien was extremely fluent in the tongue.

I'm not going to say much about the third of these elements: both works are brief and seemed to me minor, five-finger exercises. 'Sellic Spell' recasts episodes from the poem as fairy tale (it begins: 'Once upon a time there was a King in the North...' [360]) by way of exploring the theory that such simple folk tales lie behind at least some of the work's composition. The poem is not only unfinished but rather dull. More interesting, for better or worse, are the translation and the commentary.

Tolkien had first translated the whole of *Beowulf* into rather antique-flavoured English prose by 1926. He continued working on the poem, studying it and teaching it, for many decades after this, and (according to Christopher Tolkien) sometimes these later researches would lead him back to modify his translation in small ways. Sometimes not. The version of the poem printed here never shakes off the rather starched feel of a purely scholarly exercise, the entire thing rendered in prose of this manner:

> The abode as yet thou knowest not nor the perilous place where thou canst find that creature stained with sin. Seek it if thou durst! For that assault I will reward thee with old and precious things, even as I did ere now, yea with twisted gold, if thou comest safe away. [53]

You may feel perfectly at home with all these 'thou's and 'yea's; but perchance they puttest thou right off, actually, in which case the moral is presumably: *read it if thou durst*!

The second element is the detailed commentary on the poem, which makes up the bulk of the whole, pages 137-354 of this 425-page volume. Here Tolkien's notes on specific Old English words and usages are blended (by Christopher Tolkien) with excerpts from lectures Tolkien gave on the poem, and from some other sources. Some of these notes mill the poem – and if we're honest, our patience – pretty fine. Others are more interesting: mini essays on Old English names and morals, on fates and character motivations in the work. But there are larger problems. One is that the majority of these notes relate to the OE text, and would be better fitted to an original-language edition of the poem. But another, larger problem is that the commentary only covers two of the three episodes of Beowulf. The last note is to a reference to 'mirth and feasting' from *Beowulf* line 2115 of the original poem. (It is to be regretted that this edition includes line numbers to Tolkien's prose, but not to how the translation relates to the lineation of the original text). *Beowulf* is a 3182-line poem; and those last 1000 lines of OE epic are not covered by the commentary here. That means we get Tolkien's thoughts on the hero fighting Grendel and Grendel's mother, but not on Beowulf as an old man fighting the dragon. Christopher Tolkien is upfront in his preface about the 'unfinished' nature of the project.

This is more of a problem than it might otherwise be, because the last third of the poem is the one that most directly informed Tolkien's own writing. Part one (Grendel) and two (Grendel's mum) are fine; but it's the dragon we want to know about, his hoard, the unnamed thief sneaking in and stealing the cup – and the fire-drake bursting from his mountain to meet his doom at the hero's hands. This is the part of *Beowulf* that we want to have Tolkien's thoughts on – at least, if our interest is in the way *Beowulf* lives on in *The Hobbit*, which of course it does. The lack of this is a serious diminishment in the volume.

There are other ways in which the commentary feels incomplete. I'll give an example of what I mean. After all, one need not to be too geeky a *Beowulf* nerd to be drawn into the discussion of some of the textual cruxes Tolkien discusses. Here's one: *Beowulf* is (obviously) a poem mostly about the heroic exploits of Beowulf. But the poem's first reference to Beowulf – line 54 – is actually to a completely different person who happens also to be called Beowulf. This individual is mentioned once; we're told that he was the son of 'Scyld Scefing,' the mythic originator of the line of the Scyldings. Clearly it's a rather confusing thing that this geezer happens to have the same name as the hero. Too confusing, Tolkien insists: he amends the name to 'Beow,' and argues that a confused or careless scribe at some point wrote this name out wrong as 'Beowulf.' So far so dry, but Tolkien's commentary also touches upon a much more interesting thing. 'Scyld,' the origin hero for this dynasty, has a name that means 'Shield,' which is the sort of generic name we can imagine being given to a mighty warrior. But 'Scefing,' the second part of his name, refers not to war but agriculture: the 'sheaf' of wheat or corn. This double reference to warring and farming, Tolkien thinks, records an ancient 'blending' of

> The vague and fictitious warlike glory of the eponymous ancestor of the conquering house with the more mysterious, far older and more poetical myth of the... corn-god or culture-hero his descendant, at the beginning of a people's history. [138]

This is fascinating stuff, and made more so by Tolkien's emendation of the first 'Beowulf' to 'Beow,' for that name means 'Barley,' 'the glorification (by genealogists) of a rustic corn-ritual myth' and quite distinct from 'Beowulf, the bear-man, the giant-killer' who 'comes from a different world: *fairy-story*' [147]. But just as these speculations are starting to get interesting, they stop. There's no larger discussion of what the vegetative myths, or fairy-tale logics, say about the poem as a whole. It makes for a frustrating read.

There are several very promising hints and suggestions in the notes, but the reason these tantalizing avenues are not explored further is, frankly, because Tolkien's main interest is otherwise. A great deal of this commentary is dryasdust linguistic and textual minutiae of this sort:

> A way out of this difficulty has been found by emendation of *steda* to *stiðra*, genitive plural. Cf. *1533 *stið ond stýlecg* applied to the sword Hrunting (1282 'steel-edged and strong'). No reason for the corruption of so well-known and contextually intelligible a word as *stiðra* into *steda* can be seen. The resulting metre is scarcely credible. The correction of this by cancelling *gehwylc* cancels the wrong word, as I have suggested above. Old English seldom violates idiomatic word-order; and where an emphatic adverb usurps the first place in a sentence, as does *foran* here, the subject should follow the verb. In consequence *ǽghwylc* *984 must be either a misplaced anticipation or a corruption by anticipation of a word that is not noun or adjective, i.e. not the subject. The former alternative implies that a word, more or less parallel to *nægla gehwylc* has dropped out after *wæs*. The latter is on all counts more probable. I should select as the real word that has been corrupted by anticipation into *ǽghwylc* is *ǽghwǽr*. [299]

There's a lot of this sort of thing in the commentary. A lot. Academics, of course, will be used to it, although few of us could put our hands on our hearts and say we actually enjoy reading it. The General Reader, at whom the present volume is presumably directed, will surely find it treacle and tar in the intricate gears that regulate their reading pleasure. Quite apart from anything else: remember this is appended not to the Old English edition of the poem, but to Tolkien's prose translation.

The problem is that it falls between two stools (**stoolen*, amended from a clearly corrupt *spoolen*, or spindles). It is not comprehensive or complete enough to function as a proper critical edition of *Beowulf*; but it is not accessible enough to step the general reader into a deeper appreciation of the poem.

I'm not saying it's entirely barren. I'd say I knew the poem pretty well, but I learnt new things from this edition. For instance, that "whale-road," that terribly famous OE 'kenning' for sea, is a mistranslation. The original is *hronráde*; but *hron* is not whale (*hwæl*); it is instead a smaller creature ('there is a statement in Old English that a *hron* was about seven times the size of a seal, and a *hwæl* about seven times the size of a *hron*' [142]). And *rád*, though the root of our word 'road,' doesn't mean 'road' but 'riding.' Tolkien accordingly translates *hronráde* as 'dolphin's riding' ('i.e. the watery fields where you can see dolphins and lesser members of the whale-tribe playing, or seeming to gallop like a line of riders on the plains'), which he prefers to 'whale-road' not least because he thinks the latter sounds too much like 'railroad' ('whale-road... suggests a sort of semi-submarine steam-engine running along submerged metal rails over the Atlantic' [143] – actually quite a cool, Studio Ghibli-style image I thought, although Tolkien treats its ludicrous inappositeness as beyond argument). All this is interesting; and there are a few similar nuggets buried in the arcane linguistic matrix of the commentary. But the general reading-experience of the commentary is one unlikely to make the reader squee.

This throws us back against Tolkien's translation. There are times when the prithee-sirrah idiom starts to work, which is to say starts to generate a genuine effect. Here's the landscape of Grendel and his kin:

> In a hidden land they dwell upon highlands wolfhaunted, and windy cliffs, and the perilous passes of the fens, where the mountain-stream goes down beneath the shadows of the cliffs, a river beneath the earth. It is not far from hence in measurement of

> miles that the mere lies, over which there hang rimy thickets, and a wood clinging by its roots overshadows the water. [52]

But no sooner has the prose begun to generate an eerie, or vivid, effect than it crashes into this sort of thing:

> Beowulf spake, the son of Ecgtheow: 'Lo! this plunder of the seam O son of Healdene, Scydings' prince, we gladly have brought to thee, the token of my triumph which here thou lookest on... This do I promise thee henceforth, that thou mayest in Heorot sleep untroubled amid the proud host of thy men, thou and each one of thy knights and captains, the proven and the young that thou wilt not from that quarter have need to fear for then, King of the Scyldings, the bane of good men's lives, as once thou did.' [62]

There is a limited number of times that it's possible to use the word 'lo!' in a modern prose text without making your reader snort in derision. And that number is: zero.

I'm aware I may sound like a philistine, here. It could be objected that there's no harm in translating a poem into an old-fashioned idiom. After all, the poem itself was fashioned in olden times. But I remain unpersuaded, for two reasons. One is that the antique style just isn't very euphoniously worked. This is how Tolkien translates the opening three lines of the poem, from the *hwæt*! onwards:

> Lo! The glory of the kings of the people of the Spear-Danes in days of old we have heard tell, how those princes did deeds of valour. [13]

Old or new, this is clumsy writing: the slackness of that string of 'of's (lo! five 'of's in one sentence!); the awkwardness of working out who is what of what; the blankness of the 'days of old' and 'deeds of valour' clichés. Of course, much of *Lord of the Rings* and the *Silmarillion* is written in a deliberately archaic manner, and we can agree or disagree with Tolkien that such a style achieves an ennobling and majestic effect. But we have to concede that in those two works he at least took pains to write his archaic English properly.

There's a more debilitating aspect to the style, though, which has to do with the way *Beowulf* generates its unique effects. My problem with Tolkien's style is not that it is too antiquated, but rather that it is too polished. The whole force of the commentary works this way too: ironing out the irregularities and inconsistencies of the original Old English, resolving cruxes and smoothing the whole. Of course, almost all editors and translators do the same; but it's worth asking what it gains us. The effect is to civilize the poem – a poem radically not about the *civis* but the warrior's stead. Tolkien's thees and thous take the poem back to a notional middle ages of courts and knights, and that's – bluntly – not right.

Like most translators of the poem, Tolkien evidently decided that the idiom of the poem is one of weighty, elevating nobility, and so adopted a deliberately ponderous voice that in turn generates an effect of archaic dignity. Other, less self-consciously modernized versions – this is as true of Seamus Heaney as of Michael Alexander – similarly inhabit a tone of regal elevation. But surely that's to miss the point. *Beowulf* is about fighting monsters: it is, not to put too fine a point on it, a young man's poem, a poem about the ethos and glories as well as the struggles and defeats of fighters. Even the later sections, when Beowulf is an old man, still cling to the sorts of things that young men tend to think important.

To this end, it seems to me a translation of the poem ought to capture it vigour, its valorisation of (as it were) being full of piss and vinegar, its deep love of muscle-power and courage and the thrills of the strength, as much as its equally central love of a kind of boastful understatement. It needs, in other words, to capture something of the braggadocio and self-confidence of the poem's world; and not to be distracted by the fact that the poem also sees that self-confidence as ultimately doomed. *Beowulf* is not really an elegiac poem, despite its ending and despite the fact that many critics have read it precisely in those terms. Or to be more precise: its quotient of elegy is not articulated in a downbeat or mournful way. We are all doomed, the poem says; we will all die; every victory is a temporary respite against ultimate defeat. But that doesn't matter. What matters is the spirit with which you face the overwhelming odds; the greatness of heart with which you rage against the dying light. What matters is to be young and strong and brave. If I may quote a modern poetic text that captures, it seems to me, the spirit of *Beowulf* better than any number of thous and yeas: 'I'm wet and I'm cold/But thank God I ain't old.' Lo!

Transformers: Age of Extinction (directed by Michael Bay)

Transformers 4 is a tricky film to review. What to say? Judging by the general responses I've seen, three options present themselves. One is simply to note that it is a bad movie. And it is. It is a very bad movie: noisy, shallow, incoherent at both surface and deeper levels, dreadfully overlong. It is sound and fury signifying less than zero. The acting is perfunctory; the action sequences are muddled and lack rhythm; the story is nonsense; the whole movie is a charmless bust. Quite apart from anything else it is staggeringly monotonous and unengaging. It commits the worst sin of an action blockbuster. It's boring.

But that doesn't get us very far, review-wise. So a second approach has emerged, which is to treat the whole thing as a kind of postmodern joke – to write articles, as some have done, treating it as an avant-garde critique of patriarchy cunningly draped in the lineaments of multiplex idiocy. Now I love me some ludic postmodern deconstructive fun, really I do. But this kind of thing doesn't seem to me to capture the essence of the movie I have just (my ears are still humming; my brain is still wincing) sat through. So we turn to option three: the meta-commentary. Sure, say reviewers, this is a dumb and rubbish movie; but it is a dumb movie symptomatic of some fascinating shifts in culture more broadly. Did you know, for instance, that it's done really really well in China?

Well, all right. But to dwell on that aspect of the film (in the first weeks after its opening it made $200 million in the States but $450 million in other territories, the largest tranche of which was East Asian; its global launch took place in Hong Kong; it stages its climactic beat-em-, shoot-em-, robot-em-up on Chinese soil in a patent attempt to ingratiate itself with that particular audience... and so on) without encountering the text itself, Bay's actual movie, seems to me an abdication of responsibility. There's something else going on here.

What, though? A concept whose main strength used to be its merchandisable simplicity is here compacted and confused with several new layers. It used to be that there were good metal aliens called Autobots who transform from automobiles into gigantic robots, and they fought bad metal aliens called Decepticons who similarly transform. Now things are more complex, with various new players in the game. First, there are human-built giant machines that transform from cars into swarms of flying mah-jong tiles and *then* into giant robots. But the twist is: these turn out, via some scriptwriterly hand waving, actually to be resurrected evil zombie versions of the Decepticons. Then there's a sort of giant intergalactic bounty hunter robot, buzzing about the galaxy in his spaceship collecting and imprisoning giant robot dinosaurs, slime-spitting aliens, and myriad others, who wants Optimus Prime to complete his collection. Or something. And then there are the mysterious 'Makers,' the original creators of all the Transformers; an element the filmmakers appear to have lifted from Ridley Scott's *Prometheus* (2012). If highly paid teams of suits sitting in air-conditioned rooms in LA have really decided that the best way to make new movies is to rip off *Prometheus*, of all films, then something has gone very wrong somewhere.

Against this hurling metal backdrop we get our human-scale story. Mark Wahlberg plays a wacky inventor single dad with the deeply improbable name of Cade Yeager. Now, once upon a time an 'eccentric inventor father' character would have been played by a white-haired wrinkled energetic man in glasses. Not here. Wahlberg still sports the heavily upholstered body he acquired for Bay's last movie, the body-builder comedy thriller *Pain & Gain* (2013); and so he plays the character as a musclebound, boyish-faced, and rather breathless action man. Yeager is raising his toothsome seventeen-year-old daughter Tessa alone on a farm in the middle of Middle America somewhere. He has forbidden Tessa from dating; but she of course has disobeyed him and is seeing a hunky professional racer called, I think (it was dark in the cinema and my notes aren't clear) Dyson Airblade. This geezer was raised in Texas, and has been dating Tessa since they met at school; but his father – who abandoned him when he was five – was Irish; so Dyson speaks throughout with a thick Waterford brogue. I don't know why. There's a deeply strange interlude in the story in which Yeager points out that Tessa is under the legal age of consent, and threatens to call the police; whereupon the boyfriend flashes a permit he has somehow acquired under the Texas 'Romeo and Juliet' laws that licenses the relationship. Is that a thing? Do Texas courts actually issue permits to allow twentysomething men to have sex with underage girls? The fact that Tessa is so young adds nothing else to the storyline, so this weird detour left me scratching my head as to why the scriptwriters thought it merited inclusion in the first place.

Anyway, Yeager, rummaging through a derelict cinema for junk he can use in his inventions, discovers Optimus Prime, in truck form. How a huge truck ended up parked inside a derelict cinema (how did they even get it through the doors?) is not only not explained, it's not even treated as weird; a fact which speaks volumes about the logical coherence of the Transformerverse as a whole.

Yeager takes Optimus home and mends him. Then a secret Government task force turns up at his farm in force, pursuant to their orders to find and destroy *all* robots, good and evil. 'Cemetery Wind' this group is called, a name more flatulent than sinister. Their head of operations is a nasty CIA officer played with hammy verve by Kelsey Grammer – a sort of CIAed-Show Bob, evil through and through. Why does Bob wants to destroy all robots? To, he insists, keep humanity safe. Though it later turns out he wants to destroy the robots in order to collect a secret $5 billion reward from Stanley Tucci's Tony-Stark-lite playboy businessman. Or something. Tucci is a pretty good actor, actually, capable of performance of nuance and dignity. Not here, though; here he's all gurning and shrieking and mugging. I assume having looked at the script he tucci da money and ran.

Tucci's labs have uncovered the secret of the Transformers' ability to transform. Transformers, it seems, are made out of 'Transformium,' in much the same way that Michael Bay movies are made out of 'Boredium.' But there's not enough Transformium for Tucci's manufacturing process. This is why the Cemetery Wind black ops CIA operation has been hunting down old Autobots to harvest the magic metal out of their bodies. But it's still not enough; so Sideshow Bob strikes a deal with the Intergalactic Bounty Hunter robot to deliver him Optimus Prime in return for the 'seed,' a surfboard-sized alien technology part nuclear bomb, part *Star Trek Wrath of Khan* Genesis device. It turns whole planets into wastelands of Transformium, which can then be harvested. The movie's pre-credit sequence shows the Makers destroying the dinosaurs – our own, blameless Earthly dinosaurs – with this very weapon, in the backward and abysm of time. Why they did this, indeed why we are even shown this, is not vouchsafed. It has no bearing on the rest of the story.

Anyhow, Tucci and Bob plan to detonate the weapon in a desert somewhere. Or something. But one of the human-built simulacra Transformers has somehow absorbed the soul of Chief Decepticon Megatron, and *he* plans to explode the seed in Hong Kong, killing millions, and possibly (hence the movie's subtitle? is it?) destroying the entire planet. Or something.

These are the pieces in play. At this point I'm guessing the writers jotted a sequence of random things down on cards (with the budget Bay had to play with, I daresay these cards were professionally printed and laminated), which were then shuffled and dealt out in random order, including:

A scene in a derivatively Giger-style alien spaceship interior.

A James Bond *Die Another Day*-style motorcycle/car chase through narrow Hong Kong streets.

A gigantic fire-breathing Tyrannosaurus Rex robot being ridden by Optimus Prime waving a sword almost as big as he is.

A surfer dude character getting literally turned to stone.

Two guys duking it out whilst clinging precariously to the side of a really tall apartment block.

A giant metal sky anus that floats over cities magnetically sucking up cars, ships and buildings, before shitting them back down onto said city.

A bunch of giant robots coming together in the Grand Canyon like Butch Cassidy and the Sundance Kid's gang meeting in their 'hole in the wall.'

Our heroes chased by giant robot dogs along really high-up cables, like cable-car cables perhaps, or anchor chains in the sky, or something.

Assorted motorway chases, corridor chases, cornfield chases, sky chases.

It's all aggregated to create the impression of one of those slightly feverish dreams you have after over-indulging in beer and spicy curry. That's your movie.

The majority of the film, by mass, is action sequences; and these are exactly what you'd expect. The descriptor 'Bay-esque' gives you the gist: cacophonous and visually rather puzzling set-pieces that outstay their welcome by between five and ten minutes. Crashing cars, explosions, guns going off, mammoth-scale punchings and sword-stabbings and so on – all punctuated with drawn-out slow-mo sequences, usually of giant robots performing improbable Nijinski leaps over lorries or over one another.

The other thing Bay essays is 'comedy.' I clamp that word inside scare-quotes advisedly. Bay cannot do comedy. Watching his scenes of 'banter' between the main characters is a strange and rather unsettling experience. It only dawns on you belatedly: oh, wait, this is supposed to be funny. In places it achieves an almost Beckettian estrangement. Not really, of course. Not even in Beckett's *Waiting For Godotron* do we see dialogue as inconsequential as that of *Age of Extinction.*

And then it struck me, like lightning from a clear blue sky. The key. This isn't really a movie about giant fighting robots, or about special effects and explosions, or even about cracking the lucrative Chinese market. This is a movie about *obviousness.*

At one point in the story our heroes are inside a car, trying to drive the 'bomb' out of Hong Kong. They end up inside a building. To be honest, I can't remember how they do; but there they are. Then the gigantic magnetic sky-anus floats overhead and draws the car and the bomb up to the ceiling of their room. Our heroes scrabble out of the car, just before the magnetic sky anus yanks it through the bursting ceiling and high into the air. Then the sky anus switches from suck-up to shit-down, and the car starts to fall. Mark Wahlberg's Yeager character, lying on the debris-strewn floor, looks up through the hole in the ceiling at the plummeting vehicle and yells: '*That's the car*!'

Well. If we gathered together the twelve cleverest men and women in the country and sequestered them in a closed room for the weekend with the job of deciding the most obvious thing a person might say under those circumstances, I don't think they would do a better job than the scriptwriters have here.

But *that's the whole film.* Everything about it is not only obvious, it is in some sense *about* obviousness. The whole premise is robots tall as houses that 'hide' by disguising as cars and lorries. But they don't really hide. They could hardly be more obvious. We cannot even describe them as 'hidden in plain sight,' because they are simply not hidden. Everyone can see them. How could they not, when they are so big? They figure, in other words, as externalizations of the core truth of Michael Bay's vision of the world. It is obvious. It is unmissable. That's why Marky Mark is so improbably muscled, because that's what Schwarzeneggering yourself over multiple visits to the gym does to a man's body. It makes it more obvious. If there's a hero-heroine kiss in the Bayiverse, it must happen so that their lips meet right in front of the setting sun – obviously. If there is a notionally secret CIA black ops operation, it has to involve freeways being exploded and absolutely enormous alien spaceships floating over our skyscrapers ('That's my asset,' says Evil CIA Dr Frasier Crane, as if it was the most obvious thing in the world). A human-scale fight might be missed; so Bay works to make his fights much bigger, and to draw attention to them with literal fireworks and explosions and that shuddering ear-dinning vibrating bass-note *wuhw-wuhw-wuhw-wuhw-wuhw* sound effect that seems to have become the sonic shorthand for gigantic metal creatures in motion. Hence the painfully literal-minded dialogue, the exposition, the repetition. To make it all obvious to everyone.

And in this inheres what is interesting in Michael Bay's vision as a director. He is a kind of anti Henry James. Instead of seeing the social world as one of buried significance and secret yearning, of passion occluded by social niceties, the beauty of inflections and the beauty of innuendos – instead of that Bay really thinks the world is obvious. Fighting is gigantic boxers pummelling one another. War is explosions and buildings collapsing and air superiority. Love is the kiss between the stick-thin supermodel in hot pants and a handsome young body-builder whose job is racing race-cars. There's nothing else. All that other stuff is just us trying to fool ourselves, is us clinging to the notion that nuance and complexity and not-judging-on-appearances can save us from our ontological monotony. It can't, says Bay. This is what the world is. The world is *obvious*. And he shows us. In Bergman's *Through a Glass Darkly* (1961), the main character has a hideous epiphany in which she sees God as a gigantic, evil-faced, rapist spider. Bay's dark glass reflects a more nihilistic vision: everything is in motion; everything is expensive; everything is obvious. The cosmos is defined by its clunking, crashing, pugilistic, monotonous obviousness.

God: what if he's *right*?

To dilate upon this a little: there's an entire cultural history to be written about the way ideals of masculine beauty have morphed from slender-elegant-aristo to bulging-toned-musclebound. This isn't just about bulk: Sean Connery was a bulky, strong-looking individual. It is about muscle definition: that's the look, nowadays. Why spend all the time and money to acquire such a body? For it is both extremely time-consuming and expensive. Worse, it is fleeting: without continual injections of time and money it melts away, or turns to flab. Of course, one way of 'reading' it is to see it in terms of Late Capitalism. Gym membership is a perfect commodity: something expensive and vacuous that must be repeatedly paid for over and over, like a sort-of healthy version of a cigarette habit.

But for the moment I'm thinking about it from the other side. Why acquire such a body? What do you get out of it? 'Well,' you could reply: 'I do it because it makes me strong; because it makes me fit; and because it makes me attractive to sexual partners.' The strength is, surely, almost an irrelevance in our automated age (that's almost its point – the possession of such superfluous strength in a society where machinery do all the heavy lifting is like a peacock's-tail thing). Fitness can be acquired much more cheaply and easily by cycling to work or jogging. The third is the true salient, I think. I spent several years attending a gym, before my present marriage; and it was in large part to make myself 'look good'. I'd guess that the same motive brought most of the other attendees to that vanity factory too: floor-to-ceiling mirrors on every wall, and both men and women narcissising into them throughout their workouts. But in what way does having a six-pack, huge muscular arms and plumped up pectorals make you more sexually attractive? You're at liberty to say 'they don't, I don't fancy such types'. That's as may be. My point is that what Schwarzenegger, Stallone or (now) 'The Rock', Hugh Jackman or Wahlberg physiques do is take elements of the male body other people may find attractive and *make them more obvious*. That's why definition, rather than just bulk, is key. There's an equivalent process in female 'beauty': boob jobs, liposuction and botox-lips all renders female secondary sexual characteristics more obvious.

Now, of course, where sexual allure is concerned these are not the only games in town. Human sexuality being both as protean and as diverse as it is, it would be surprising if they were. But they are indices of a broader cultural logic. It relates to film, I think, because film has become the prime medium of obviousness. It needn't have done this (there's nothing obvious about late Tarkovsky, say); but it has. This feeds, I think, off the fact that cinema and TV is, formally as it were, less well suited to interiority than the novel; but cinema as a discourse, and cinema-goers by feeding the beast, have resulted in a sort of aesthetics of gigantic obviousness coming to dominance. Bigger, brasher, more colourful, noisier, longer (oh my God *longer*: what purpose does the bloat of running times serve, except to inflate production costs and make cinema-goers buttocks go numb? Nobody likes it. It's the filmic equivalent of Hugh Jackman's prodigious pecs). Lest verisimilitude slip past the viewers' ken, the dominant has opted for more obvious tropes and symbols: cartoon heroes, jaw-dropping special effects, everything on a gigantic scale, shock and awe.

I need to be clear: I'm not grumping. I love many of the movies that this logic has produced; and I can see the appeal of the Obvious. I just wonder why it has taken contemporary culture by storm. It's not that people are dumb: broadly speaking, people are not dumb. Nor is it a process of infantilisation: children are often not obvious, and are in fact more often in love with secrets, hiding-away, games that grown-ups don't understand and so on.

Indeed, I wonder if there's not something larger going on. Once upon a time, and not that long ago either, 'knowledge' was an esoteric matter, and many things were hidden away from the profane. But the extraordinary explosion in internet coverage, the range of online content and the breathtaking ingenuity of search engines means that Everything – all the accumulated wisdom and learning of humanity over the last five thousand years – is Obvious. It's all right there; all stacked on the infinitely-long front shelf, a few finger strokes away. I'm not sure it's yet sunk in, globally, how profound a change this represents. One consequence is that we may start to regard stuff previously rendered valuable by its scarcity (the Mona Lisa; the hermetic corpus; the notebooks of Leonardo) as mere trash, simply because we can so easily access them. But that would be a rather depressing development. I wonder if the reverse isn't starting to happen: and the very obviousness of culture, art and science don't revert a kind of glamour back upon obviousness itself.

Michael R. Underwood
Attack the Geek: a Ree Reyes Side-Quest

I disliked this book. I also misliked it, unliked it, de-liked it and anti-liked it. Maybe if I'd read the previous 'Ree Reyes' novels that latter reaction wouldn't have been so anti. But then again, do we really need the previous instalments? When Underwood gives us the kind of complete summation of character of which Proust himself, were he alive, could only be envious? 'Ree Reyes (Strength 10, Dexterity 14, Stamina 12, Will 18, IQ 16, Charisma 15 – Geek 7/Barista 3/Screenwriter 3/Gamer Girl 2/Geekomancer 2)' [13]. Rees and her pals are able to access magic skills, plus Harry Potter wands and lightsabres and so on, by invoking various genre pop-culture references; and these they use to fight goblins, gnomes, minotaurs and other monsters through sewers and geek boutiques (distractedly I found myself thinking: 'boutgiques'?) called things like 'Grognard's Grog and Games'. It's a sort of D&D game come to life, and the longer it went on the more tiresome and charmless I found it. It wants to be *Buffy*; but *Buffy* had dialogue to die for. This book has (to pick some examples at random) '"Thou shalt not fuck with one of thy best friend's relationships" she told herself' [19]; 'You know what? Fuck you, you worthless piece of shit.' [52]; '"Holy Shit!" Rees said.' [117]; '"The fuck?" Rees asked' [128]; 'Motherfucking fireballs' [174]. Oscar Fucking Wilde it fucking ain't. The plot is a hectic mishmash of bewildering interactions, fighting, swearing and running through shit. But the real problem is the author's inability to bridge the 'you had to be there' divide. The point of this book is to capture some of the joy (a genuine and splendid joy) we feel when we hang out without friends and do fun things, like playing games. You try to pass the joy along, saying 'we had a blast man! Eastwood said this really hilarious thing!' But when you repeat the hilarious thing, you find your interlocutors are only smiling politely, and not dissolving in helpless laughter the way you did. A writer worth her/his salt can recreate the ambience and make the hilarity come alive again. Underwood isn't such a writer.

But that's fine. Your dice-age may vary, and I (Pomposity 10, Fondness-for-Nabokov 9, Englishness 879) am surely not the target audience here. But, at the risk of pushing my pomposity score even higher, I found myself wondering whether this short novel figures not as a celebration of geek culture and in-crowd together, but instead as an indictment of it. When your friends swear, especially swear inventively, it is funny, because they're your friends, and you know they don't actually mean to harm you. But when somebody you *don't* know swears at you it is unpleasant and intimidating and scary. There are reasons why the idiom of courtesy is the right one for public interactions. Science Fiction, in its faceless online conversations, very often loses sight of this. I'm guessing this is compounded of the fact that (a) if I swear aggressively in, say, a tweet, you may decide to take this as a sign that (though we've never met) you and I are friends, and grant me leeway. So perhaps the hyperprofane idiom is assumed by some to be a kind of bonding ritual. There may also (b) be a failure of empathy, or, more complexly, a failure to understand that the Other who has never met you has no grounds to empathise with you, behind this: the fabled Asperger's-spectrum personality limitations of the geek. So if you tweet that (to pick an example out of the air) Paolo Bacigalupi should have acid thrown in his face for his portrayal of Thai characters, it may be that you assume everyone will *know* you aren't serious. Hey! Nobody who knows me would think I would *actually* throw acid in anyone's face! The failing here, of course, is that other people, including the textually assaulted Bacigalupi himself, don't know you, and have no reason to give you the benefit of any doubt. Verbal assault is still assault. Then again, (c) I wonder if the main problem is a broader inability of tonal nuance. Let's say: Geek A has a disagreement with another person over some matter, and addresses him/her with 'Fuck you. You can fucking bleed-out in a back alley while I sit watching you, sipping my caffè macchiato'. Perhaps Geek A thinks that the main effect of such expression is to convey just how vehemently s/he feels about the point at issue. But that's not the main effect. The main effect is to paint Geek A as callous and violent. The vehemence is in service of a deeply unattractive, pointed discourtesy. There are better ways of disagreeing; and by better I mean 'more effective' for any metric of *effective* you prefer. And there are much, much better ways of writing insults into books. Let it be written in ten-foot-high letters in the public agora of genre, that nobody miss it: VEHEMENCE AND VIOLENCE ARE NOT THE SAME THING.

Tania Unsworth
The One Safe Place

A readable, short-ish YA thriller, this. The first third conjures a well-handled mood of dourness out of its future-set climate-changed future desolation. The opening chapter, in which young Devin struggles to bury his dead grandfather at the remote farmstead the two share, is particularly good. Thereafter, and since a kid can't run a whole farm on his own, Devlin makes his way to the city to start a new life as a street kid, an unforgiving environment of gangs, corrupt cops and the occasional averted face of disdainful rich people hurrying somewhere better. Good. Then the second third shifts mood to a tenser, more insidiously nightmarish set of thrills. Devlin accepts an invitation to a charitable home for orphans, where he is promised food and toys; but it turns out to be a prison in the countryside, where he and the other kids are watched in proper creepy fashion by a bunch of decrepit elderly millionaires. Escape is impossible; and although children are promised that eventually they will all be adopted by happy-ending rich families, we clock early on that this is a lie. Kids starts full of vigour, but after they have been called to the mysterious tower at the heart of the complex a number of times they go weird, or mad. Devlin's synaesthesia is revealed as having a telepathic component which is why the sinister Administrator wanted him in the first place ('I need you to be healthy Devlin,' she tells him. 'I'm saving you for something special.')

The final third loses much of this tension and creepiness, though. Once the true purpose of the place is revealed the novel settles into a more predictable kids-gang-up-against-oppressive-adults, Escape-from-Stalag-YA-Dystopia vibe. I finished the novel with a slightly anticlimactic sense of things, of a great set-up frittered, rather, away. This is a pity, since the first two thirds of this novel touch effectively on something genuinely unnerving. As the cover copy, up there, says: you think you can hide inside your head? *Think again.*

Jeff VanderMeer, *The Southern Reach Trilogy*

:1:

Trying to think what one word best describes Jeff VanderMeer's *Southern Reach* trilogy. I could go with 'masterpiece,' since it is so clearly a major achievement in SF/Fantasy/Weird writing – since it accomplishes so many of the things it sets out to do, since it is so beautifully imagined and written, since it will clearly scoop all the awards next year and remain a touchstone text in the genre for a long time. But that's an evaluative word, and I'm interested (for reasons that will become more apparent) in the descriptive space outside evaluation. The trilogy is science fiction on the haunted, fantastic side of the genre; often brilliantly spooky and uncanny. And VanderMeer has, I suppose, a reputation as Purveyor of High Quality Weird to the Refined Reader. But I remain unconvinced as to the coherency of "weird" as an aesthetic descriptor; and certainly weird-for-the-sake-of-weird (a coinage along the lines of *l'art pour l'art* – *l'étrange pour l'étrange*, I suppose) is really not what Southern Reach is about. One of the things that makes these novels so readable is the air of absorbing mystery that VanderMeer flawless evokes; but what makes them so satisfying as a whole is that they are not content simply to evoke that mystery, to make the tiny hairs at the back of the reader's neck stand up, and leave it at that. They are not just mood pieces. Indeed, after I had finished I found myself wondering if what these books are doing is reconfiguring pastoral for a new century. So that's the one word I'm going with. *Southern Reach* is strange pastoral.

The trilogy is set in the Tarkovsky-*Stalker*-like zone of 'Area X,' somewhere down Florida way. At some point in the past this area suffered some kind of unexplained catastrophe and, like the "Zona" around Chernobyl, was left to revert to a state of nature. A governmental organisation called the Southern Reach has been tasked with observing and assessing this place, and from time to time sends in expeditions; although these exploratory incursions all end badly.

In *Annihilation*, the first (and, to revert to evaluation for a moment, the best) of the three novels, one such expedition is described. It is comprised of women and we don't get their names: they are 'the psychologist,' 'the surveyor,' 'the anthropologist,' and our narrator, 'the Biologist.' An expertly handled piece of characterization, this cool, rather introverted woman has always been more comfortable observing wild ecosystems. When growing up, the pool in her back garden was neglected by her self-absorbed parents, and soon became clogged with weeds, tadpoles and other flora and fauna. The Biologist returns to memories of the hours she spent observing the minute interactions of this re-wilded world as a kind of touchstone for personal happiness. That quality seems to have been largely absent from her adult existence. Her marriage, for instance, had not been a success. Her husband had disappeared on the previous, eleventh expedition into Area X – all previous expeditions (and it seems there were more than the officially logged twelfth) having failed, with explorers going mad, killing one another, committing suicide or succumbing to weird infections and parasites. When her husband unexpectedly and mysteriously turns up again, in her kitchen, he is a hollowed-out, PTSD-y version of the man he had been before, and soon dies of cancer.

The Southern Reach hypnotize the members of the twelfth expedition, a psychological conditioning imposed ostensibly to help them through the border into the zone. It turns out, the hypnotism is more far reaching, an attempt to exert total control over the explorers, with the Psychologist possessing certain trigger words to 'induce paralysis,' 'induce acceptance or compel obedience' [*Annihilation*, 135]. The title of the first novel is one such hypnotic command: to 'induce immediate suicide.' Clearly, the Southern Reach don't wholly trust their own explorers; or, rather, don't trust what they could mutate into.

Early in *Annihilation* the Biologist descends a spiral staircase into a subterranean structure she insists on calling a 'tower' and finds a mysterious message written on the walls in letters made of some sort of fungoid vegetable growth. (This text starts: *Where lies the strangling fruit that came from the hand of the sinner I shall bring forth the seeds of the dead to share with the worms that...* and goes on and on). Spores from this fungus somehow de-condition the Biologist from her hypnotism, meaning that she escapes the Psychologist's catastrophic attempts to manipulate the expedition. One member leaves; another is found dead at the bottom of the tower, her body deliquescing and turning luminous yellow. The Psychologist disappears, and when the Biologist chances upon her again she is dying. The Biologist finds the journal kept by her deceased husband. A strange individual called 'the Crawler' is threatening the group. I'll pause here, to insert a quote from *The Guardian* review of the novel:

But what makes this book so remarkable is less what happens in it, and more its tense, eerie and unsettling vibe. Creating such a vibe is a balancing act between (on the one hand) not destroying the mood with too much brute explanation and loose-end-tying-up, and (on the other) not alienating the reader by being too annoyingly oblique. VanderMeer hits exactly the right balance, like a gymnast on a beam. A creepy gymnast who's been infected with occult fungal spores and is starting to glow yellow.

I think that's right, and can only commend the insight and eloquence of this Guardian reviewer. The paper should surely put more work their way.

The second volume in the trilogy, *Authority*, is about the Southern Reach organization itself. The book is mostly concerned with the byzantine in-group political struggles and ultimate impotence of the organization's new leader, 'Control.' We get some more detail about Area X. There is a mysterious barrier around the zone which may or may not have been created at a different time, and perhaps by a different entity to the one that created the zone. The only way in or presumably out is through a 'door' that the Southern Reach did not create. There is video footage of an experiment in which a great many bunny rabbits are herded at the invisible barrier surrounding Area X – they all vanish as soon as intersecting the limit, apparently never to be heard of again. People mention 'aliens' for the first time (or, rather, they go out of their way *not* to mention aliens – 'why are none of you comfortable using the words *alien* or *extraterrestrial* to talk about Area X?' Control peevishly demands, upon arriving in post (*Authority*, p. 10). The Biologist from *Annihilation* is assumed dead, but she turns up, standing in a parking lot outside Area X in what looks like a fugue state. She claims not to remember anything from her expedition. Is she actually the Biologist, or only some occult copy of the original woman? She prefers now to be addressed as 'Ghost Bird,' the nickname her deceased husband used. We are still not vouchsafed her actual name.

Though not its narrator, Control (a childhood nickname, not a Le-Carré-style job description) is at the heart of *Authority*, much as the

Biologist was at the heart of *Annihilation*. For me this was one of the reasons the second volume worked less well. It's not so much that the 'genre' interest is back-seated in favour of a rather tortuous spy-thriller-bureaucracy satire – although that's kind of true. It's more that the character of Control didn't strike me as being as well drawn, as sparely yet vividly rendered, as the Biologist. We learn a lot (too much, perhaps) about his childhood, his life before Southern Reach, his difficult relationship with his mother – also in the espionage business, and an important character in the trilogy – and generally about the anxieties and frustrations of his new rôle. How does that Ricky Martin song go? It drags, it drags. It doesn't drag excessively, like Danny La Rue; but it certain drags from time to time. Like Eddie Izzard.

Southern Reach call the tower-that's-actually-a-hole-in-the-ground 'the topographical anomaly.' It appears to be alive. There's also a lighthouse in Area X, and this structure's former keeper, once called Saul Evans, now something else entirely, appears to have been the author of the strange text (he was a lay preacher as well as a lighthouse-keeper, before whatever happened to Area X happened). In the final volume, *Acceptance* we discover a good deal more about Saul, as well as solving some – but, satisfyingly, *not all* – of the mysteries of Area X. The meat of this third novel is the return to the Area of Control and the Biologist – or rather, of 'Ghost Bird,' the uncanny duplicate of the Biologist. They pop up through an occult undersea portal, and explore the whole zone further.

Now I'm guessing that VanderMeer was aware that this trajectory – (1) mysterious sea-defined zone, odd animals and lots of mystery, (2) characters leave the zone and pootle around 'our' world for a while, (3) characters return to the zone changed and resolve many of its mysteries – was going to make many of his readers think of Abrams' TV serial *Lost*. I'm guessing that partly because the comparison is obvious (though VanderMeer does a much better job of wrapping his story up than did Abrams and his scriptwriters). There's also stuff like this (Ghost Bird is sifting through the scattered records of the 'Seeker and Surveillance Bandits' who once explored the zone):

In among this detritus, these feeble guesses, the word *Found*! Handwritten, triumphant. Found what? But with so little data, even Found!, even the awareness of some more intelligent entity peering out from among the fragments led nowhere. [*Acceptance*, 178]

Hah.

Late in *Acceptance*, Ghost Bird encounters a spooky owl. She wonders if this is some mutant reincarnation of her dead husband, but the impression I got (it's not clear) is that it isn't. It is a testament to VanderMeer's skill in these books to say that by this stage it comes across almost as cheating, to peg so intrinsically eerie a creature as 'owl' in this way: earlier, the books have convinced the reader to be weirded-out by bunnies and dolphins. An owl is almost too obvious. It possesses too straightforward a metaphoric relationship to the theme. Elsewhere VanderMeer expresses exactly this. 'Data pulled out of Area X duplicates itself and declines, or "declines to be interpreted" as Whitby puts it.' Southern Reach linguists compare it to 'a tongue that curled up and took them with it':

Area X muddying the waters. Except that it wasn't muddying waters or a tongue by the side of the road or anything else, muddled or not, that they could understand. "We lack the analogies" was itself somehow deficient as a diagnosis... Except Area X never responded, even to that indignity. [*Acceptance*, 46]

The 'allure' of the place lies 'in its negation of why' (*Acceptance*, 193). It is possible to frame descriptive accounts of nature in terms of 'why.' It isn't possible to frame evaluative or moral accounts that way. Nature isn't a why.

:2:

SF has had a rather awkward relationship with 'Nature.' Most often, I suppose, it has figured only as a resource to be improved with technology, something that backgrounds the main business of the standard genre fare – that is, if it is present at all (and there have been plenty of Trantor/Corruscant wholly urban SF built worlds). Iain M. Banks set his hugely popular novels in the Culture, after all; not in the Nature. The Clute/Nicholls/Langford *SF Encyclopedia*'s only entry on 'Nature' rather makes my point for me.

Nature. Long-established UK generalist science magazine (1869-current), now published weekly by Nature Publishing Group (a subsidiary of Macmillan). Under the editorship of Henry Gee, Nature introduced a weekly series of short-short sf stories as "Futures" from November 1999 to December 2000. Most of these one-pagers are by established sf authors: Arthur C Clarke launched the feature with "Improving the Neighbourhood" (November 1999). A second run of "Futures" was published in 2005-2006 and a third from 2007, when the feature also began to appear (with different stories) in the more specialist sister magazine Nature Physics. One hundred of these vignettes are collected as Futures from Nature (anth 2007) edited by Henry Gee. On the strength of "Futures", the magazine was named as Best Science Fiction Publisher in the 2005 European SF Society awards.

There has been something of a 'turn,' though; and although I'm going to suggest this is a recent thing. A couple of VanderMeer's reviewers have compared Southern Reach to Ballard, reaching for some way of flagging up the deliberately disorienting aesthetic at work. Plus: the Biologist's prompt for her fascination with the natural world is a disused swimming pool. But I don't think the comparison quite right, actually. Ballard's disused swimming pools tended to be empty; VanderMeer's pool is brimming and indeed overflowing with gloopy life. Ballard's interest was in the spooky dynamics of groups – in his later career, almost always gated communities of the wealthy. There's surprisingly little "nature" in his works. VanderMeer, on the other hand, fills all three novels with vivid and sometimes gorgeous descriptions of nature, but seems interested in the human group dynamics (of explorer teams, of the Southern Reach organisation, of families, of lovers) really only to the extent that they break down and disintegrate. What might look at the beginning of the series as a rather modish absence of proper names becomes, by the end, more significant: proper names are shed in the course of the book because they are so specific to human interpersonality. Animals do without names. Nature is not named.

The 'turn' I'm thinking of is not really Ballardian. It is evident, though, in writers like M. John Harrison – and *Southern Reach* books have a cooler, less spiky Harrisonian feel to it – or in some of Iain Sinclair's less urban-focused prose (I'm thinking of the descriptions of English and Welsh countryside in the too-little-known *Landor's Tower* [2002]). I might also mention books like Simon Ings' *Wolves* (2014), or Johanna Sinisalo's *Birdbrain* (2011). I might also mention myself, if it didn't look like I was trying to hijack the review to plug my own stuff; so I won't – except to say that even though I wrote my latest novel (about an angry man and some Southern English wildernesses) before I read VanderMeer's trilogy, the prior appearance of *Southern Reach* is inevitably going to make my version look derivative. The more interesting question is whether there's something in the water that is informing speculative writing today. Maybe 'Nature' in this sense is the coming thing. A kind of Macfarlanisation of the SFnal idiom.

'Nature' in the sense that I'm using it here – in the sense that informs these novels – is a relatively new phenomenon. Raymond Williams' lengthy *Keywords* entry on the word starts:

> Nature is perhaps the most complex word in the language. It is relatively easy to distinguish three areas of meaning: (i) the essential quantity and character of something; (ii) the inherent force which directs either the world or human beings or both; (iii) the material world itself, taken as including or not including human beings. Yet it is evident that within (ii) and (iii), though the area of reference is broadly clear, precise meanings are variable and at times even opposed. The historical development of the word through these three senses is important, but it is also significant that all three senses, and the main variations and alternatives within the two most difficult of them, are still active and widespread in contemporary usage.

To present a fairly crude reduction of a very long and complication discursive history, we could say that one valorised iteration of 'nature' – wilderness nature, the state in which the world exists when men and women don't interfere with it by cutting it down, concreting it over and so on – is a Romantic and a post-Romantic invention. Since life preceded humanity on this planet of ours by billennia, this might look like a foolish thing to assert. Surely (you might say) 'wilderness' is the default setting of the natural world, something into which homo sapiens has blundered very late in the game. That's as may be; but I'm talking not about brute reality but about the value discourse of the natural world. This latter is both deeply embedded in (for instance) contemporary environmentalism (in the sense that some forms of nature are taken to be 'better' or 'worse' than others – pristine national parks are better than chemically polluted factoryside lakes, for example) – *and* a profoundly humanocentric state of affairs. I say this in as neutral a way as I can muster: outwith mankind the natural world is neither good nor bad, because 'good' and 'bad' are human concerns. It is neither good nor bad that sharks eat tuna, or fungus rots old oak trees. It just is. You might say well, *surely it's good for the shark and bad for the tuna*, I'd reply that you're stretching the meaning of 'good' and 'bad.' My point is that it's not *morally* or *aesthetically* good or bad; because the idiom of nature-in-itself is dynamic and competitive existence, not morality or aesthetics. The fact that you are starving doesn't delight the forest in which you hunt fruitlessly for food; nor is the forest in which you hunt fruitlessly for food saddened to see the state you've got into. The forest doesn't care one way or the other. *Caring* is what humans do, not forests. Forests are no more malicious than they are compassionate. Forests are forests. Characters in the *Southern Reach* ponder this very question. What does the organism, or whatever it is, that has transformed Area X want? Control thinks he understands its purpose ("which is to kill us, to transform us, to get rid of us" [*Acceptance*, 190]). He calls it 'enemy,' because it reassures him to frame events in this black-and-white way. Ghost Bird isn't so sure: maybe the horrifying things that have happened to the explorers is a sign not of hostility, but indifference.

> 'Had they, in fact, passed judgment without a trial? Decided there could be no treaty or negotiation?'
> 'That might be closer to the truth, to a kind of truth,' Ghost Bird replied. It was now early afternoon and the sky had become a deeper blue with long narrow clouds sliding across it. The marsh was alive with rustlings and birdsong.
> 'Condemned by an alien jury,' Control said.
> 'Not likely. Indifference.' [*Acceptance*, 79]

This is, perhaps, the real skill in VanderMeer's eerie vision: precisely this sense that we move through a living cosmos that neither loves nor hates us, but which is instead magisterially indifferent to us. How sharp a cut to our collective *amour propre*! Hatred would be preferable. How much more does SF prefer the acid tooth hostility of Geiger's *Alien* (that enduring genre epitome of the monstrous-organic) to the unsettling blankness, the beautiful semiotic void of Tarkovsky's 'zona'? Better to be hated. At least then we matter at least enough to arouse strong emotions. But the refrigerator motor chugging quietly round the back of the *Southern Reach* books, and generating their palpable chill, may be something much less reassuring than the horror cliché of hatred. At least you know where you are with a Triffid. We lose our way in a particular manner in Area X. It's not just that we longer know where we are. We no longer know *what* we are.

Actually my point is less grandiose. It has to do with the cultural representation nature. In this context, the valorisation of 'wilderness' is an invention of Romantic poetry. The seventeenth- and eighteenth-centuries are full of nature poetry of course; but the emphasis there is horticultural. For pre-Romantic poets it's common sense that nature is at its most beautiful in a garden or (managed) country estate; wildernesses and deserts might evoke the shiver of the Sublime, but they were almost by definition ugly rather than beautiful. Wordsworth is probably the key figure. His poetic celebration of the wilder landscapes of the Lake Distract (rather than, say, Surrey or Kent, 'the Garden of England') shifted the public aesthetic. Scott's novels achieved something similar for the grandeur of the Scottish highlands. By the later nineteenth-century, wilderness was not only appreciated on its own terms, it was being actively preferred by some to cultivated spaces. Not by everyone (English hymnist Dorothy Gurney, born 1858, is famous today for one couplet: 'You're closer to God's heart in a garden/Than any place on earth'). There's no shortage of beautifully manicured lawns and robo-pruned topiary in contemporary science fiction: from the artfully corporatist landscaping of StarFleet's San Francisco headquarters to the "gene wizards" gardening on a solar-systemic scale in McAuley's *Quiet War* books (2008-2013). New Edens.

But for others, especially those writers interested in the inheritance of Romantic and Gothic sublime, 'good' wilderness has exerted its pull. For instance, it informed some aspects of the boom in utopian writing: Richard Jefferies' *After London* (1885) delights in the overthrow of the poisonous city and a fresh new life in Nature; and both J. Leslie Mitchell and S. Fowler Wright thought that the route to human happiness was to embrace a life of noble savagery. Mind you, the pastoralism of William Morris' *News from Nowhere* (1890) is much more garden-like than it is wildernessy. If 'man' and 'nature' are imagined as at odds to one another, then one will presumably have to win out over the other. Still, broadly speaking, SF tends to dramatize 'nature' as something to be adapted to serve the interests of humankind – as with the intricately detailed terraforming of Kim Stanley Robinson's *Mars* books (1993-1996) and *2312* (2012) – rather than the other way about (Pohl's *Man Plus*, for instance). In this SF was reflecting a world where we have, more or less, put all the trees, put 'em in a tree museum, charged all the people a dollar and a half just to see 'em. And the reaction against that situation as often involves symbolic demonization of 'the natural': Quatermass' 1950s astronaut, infected by alien life and slowly turning into a cactus monster. The Antarctic scientists in John Carpenter's body-horror classic *The Thing* (1982), consumed by biological hideousness in a way simultaneously repulsive and fascinating to us, the audience – the very definition of Abjection. The difference between those icky symbolic fables on the one hand and Southern Reach on the other is not just that the former play their strange mutations as merely horrifying, where VanderMeer manages a skilful balancing act between ghastliness and glamor. More telling, I think, is that such intrusion of alien nature in SF usually takes place to a body or bodies, inside an otherwise unaltered environment – Quatermass' metamorphosing spaceman stumbling around regular 1950s London. In Southern Reach, it is the environment as a whole that is weird. Our *Thing*-like mutation is a process of aligning ourselves with the new reality.

VanderMeer, clearly, is writing is work of complex modern environmentalism, a reaction to our collective mistreatment of "nature" and the consequently parlous state of our environment. But I think he's doing something more than that. He is channelling a deeper disquiet about nature itself; the way we are increasingly unable to think of the natural world as a pretty backdrop to human affairs, or a resource to be exploited. A time (in the word of Joshua Ramey) "when 'nature' has become something like absolute contingency, incarnate." It is a matter of the relative orientation, in amongst all the dread and horror and symbolic articulation of disgust at human environmental pollution. The remade Ghost Bird is able simply to be in Area X. Control, constantly if impotently itching for comprehension, agency and power, cannot.

On their fourth day in Area X, Control followed Ghost Bird through the long grass, puzzled, confused, sick, tired – the nights so alive with insects it was hard to sleep against their roar and chitter. While in his thoughts, a vast invisible blot had begun to form across the world outside of Area X…

> 'How can you be so cheerful?' he'd asked her, after she had noted their depleted food, water, in an energetic way, then pointed out a kind of sparrow she said was extinct in the wider world, an almost religious ecstasy animated her voice.
> 'Because I'm alive,' she'd replied. 'Because I'm walking through wilderness on a beautiful day.' [*Acceptance*, 77]

But can it really be so simple, this being-in-the-world malarkey? To put it another way: is the weight more on the 'religious,' or on the 'almost,' in that passage there? And actually this is key, I think. If *Southern Reach* actually added up only to a macfarlaney celebration of wild places wrapped about with the ribbon of an SFnal weird mystery, it would be a lesser achievement. But VanderMeer's brilliance here is not so much in the delineation of Nature Redux, however lovingly and carefully he describes his blisses/of shapes that haunt these wildernesses. It is in the way he frames the question of our place in nature.

I say this in part to reflect the thoughts I've been having, pondering the trilogy and trying to work out the place the middle volume has. To repeat myself, I don't think *Authority* works nearly as well as the other two books. More, there's something unbalanced (something that has the outward appearance almost of pandering to the present-day absurd commercial template of trilogies as arbitrary publishing format) about putting out three books – I say so, because the books themselves are so fascinated with doubles, not with triplets. The passages where Ghost Bird in *Acceptance* ponders what it would be like to meet the Biologist; the lighthouse-keeper's love affair with Charlie, Control and his mother, all refract the central binary of Area X and rest-of-the-world which is the way this text epitomizes precisely the nature-culture divide itself. As an articulation of a particular process of metamorphosis the book goes from before to after without dwelling (as with the mysteriously disappearing bunnies as they are shovelled towards the barrier) on the actual process of change. It's a conceptual dyad for which a triadic narrative breakdown feels like a mismatch.

But there it is: *Authority* and all the detail it gives us about the Southern Reach. Why? Well, at some point after finishing the final volume I was put in mind of this passage (part 1, §7, if you want chapter and verse) from Nietzsche's *Genealogy of Morals*:

One will have divined already how easily the priestly mode of valuation can branch off from the knightly-aristocratic and then develop into its opposite; this is particularly likely when the priestly caste and the warrior caste are in jealous opposition to one another and are unwilling to come to terms. The knightly-aristocratic value judgments presupposed a powerful physicality, a flourishing, abundant, even overflowing health, together with that which serves to preserve it: war, adventure, hunting, dancing, war games, and in general all that involves vigorous, free, joyful activity. The priestly-noble mode of valuation presupposes, as we have seen, other things: it is disadvantageous for it when it comes to war! As is well known, the priests are the most evil enemies – but why? Because they are the most impotent. It is because of their impotence that in them hatred grows to monstrous and uncanny proportions, to the most spiritual and poisonous kind of hatred. The truly great haters in world history have always been priests; likewise the most ingenious haters: other kinds of spirit hardly come into consideration when compared with the spirit of priestly vengefulness. Human history would be altogether too stupid a thing without the spirit that the impotent have introduced into it.

This, perhaps, is the point of the second volume: to delineate the social logic of the priesthood. The warriors are all long gone; in place of the knight-aristocratic world, and appropriately for a post-Enlightenment Republic like the USA, are the pen-pushers and the microscope-peerers. The Southern Reach's impotence in the face of Area X merely magnifies and externalises this Nietzschean inner *ressentiment*. More, VanderMeer's bureaucratic and scientific 'priests' are desperately trying to be warriors, running around with guns, shooting at random – incompetent and ignorant but aggressively so.

Once they go outside, where the strange, the *stranger* is found, they are not much better than uncaged beasts of prey. There they savour a freedom from all social constraints, they compensate themselves in the wilderness for the tension engendered by protracted confinement and enclosure within the peace of society, they go back to the innocent conscience of the beast of prey, as triumphant monsters who perhaps emerge from a disgusting procession of murder, arson, rape, and torture, exhilarated and undisturbed of soul, as if it were no more than a students' prank, convinced they have provided the poets with a lot more material for song and praise.

The novels are about the monstrosity not of the other, nor even (really) of the human heart; but of the particular state of affairs when modern human beings find themselves so jarringly out-of-place in an environment not interested in supporting them.

And this, in turn, brings me back to Pastoral. Classical pastoral was an idealized version of a perfect and blissful natural environment. In Theocritus and Vergil and Spenser, shepherds are not troubled with the toil of actually looking after sheep; instead they spend their days filling their bellies with delicious food, playing music and making love. That, in a sense, is the point of pastoral – the enjoyment of civic levels of luxury in a rural setting. All that VanderMeer's rather brilliant rewiring of the pastoral mode as horror does is to bring out the fundamental mismatch in the original material. 'Nature' is inhabited by the cultured; not farmer and hunters but desk-workers and clock-watchers – not Nietzschean warriors but Nietzschean priests, with all the petty dissatisfactions and resentments of their caste. It is from this mismatch that the *Southern Reach* trilogy generates so many of its so very powerful effects.

Andy Weir
The Martian

This foresquare piece of Hard SF competent-man-in-astro-peril novel proved one of the 'event' genre titles of 2014 (Ridley Scott's movie, starring Matt Damon as the title character, is set for an Autumn 2015 release). Self-pubbed in 2012, it got the mainstream press treatment in 2013, but I didn't get round to reviewing it then. Finally the paperback plonked onto my desk. I already knew the reaction of my friend Ian Sales: 'I thought it was pretty shit,' was his twitter opinion. 'Should have been called The Potato Man in the Very Cold Place.' His reaction was *the more: shun*. I wasn't quite so negative. As I replied: 'I quite liked the way it stuck straightforwardly at its task, like its protagonist.' Twitter is a marvellous medium for truncated, un-nuanced conversations with people you know. You should check it out.

The Martian certainly is a metaphorically and in places literally pedestrian work, and the rapture with which it has been greeted by many people is a tad puzzling. Mark Watney is the NASA astronaut marooned on the Red Planet (I've a 'Watney's Red Barrel' joke in reserve, back here, in case it's needed) who has to keep himself alive by growing potatoes, patching up his kit, and hiking from place to place to avoid dust storms and so on. He's eventually rescued, or else he eventually dies on Mars. I mean, obviously you know without reading the book it's going to be one of those two endings. More, you can easily guess (without reading the book) which ending Weir goes with.

So why did I like this book rather more than Ian 'Chuckles' Sales? It may be because *The Potato Man in the Very Cold Place* strikes me as a genuinely excellent title for a SF tale (so much so that I may steal it). Contemporary SF, I'd say, could do with little less explosive *pow!-pow!-pow!* heat, and rather more emphasis on the potatoes side of things. I'm reminded of the Steve Baxter novel (*Titan*, I think it is) where the whole deep-space exploration plot hinges on the carrots one of the two astronauts grows on board. Baxter is a much better writer of Hard SF than Weir, mind you; and Ridley Scott would do better optioning one of his novels for the blockbuster treatment. But you can't have everything.

Will Wiles
The Way Inn

It's come to something when postmodern work like this – an absorbingly Ballardian tale of life in those temples of simulacra, high-end corporate chain hotels – is best described as *old*-fashioned. But old-fashioned, in a queer way, Will Wiles' gem of a novel is. Once upon a time Modernism was the new, and the post-modern glimmered on the cusp of futurity. And then, like turning a corner in Jameson's Westin Bonaventure Hotel, it's suddenly behind us. It was the future for fifteen-minutes. Now it's so last century. There's something significant and, it strikes me, even beautiful about that larger fact, if only because I'd suggest 'the postmodern' still informs and horizons so much of modern life. Mirrors can be flashy and obvious, or weirdly inconspicuous. The pomo dazzle ship is anchored right in front of us, and we unobserve it. The point may be that 'we' have put postmodernism behind us, because 'we' are more comfortable that way. It's still our world, though. It's still where we live. I daresay I'm an outlier here, taste-wise: still plugging away at my own twisted version of the Jamesonian Pomo. I do so because it still seems to me relevant and eloquent. I may be wrong. At any rate, I'm predisposed to like this kind of novel, when it is done well. And Wiles does this novel very well indeed.

Name-checking the simulacrum, there, licenses me to talk about the book's many family resemblances, though I do so not to deprecate its own distinctiveness and originality. One of the pleasantly non-Euclidian aspects of postmodernity is its understanding that originality is achieved through intertextuality, just as sincerity is reached through the Alice's-path of irony. 'Way Inn' is the name of a chain of global hotels catering largely to the travelling businessmen and conference trade. Our hero, Neil Double, loves staying in them; loves the anonymity and predictability, the blandness and the comfort. Prefers staying in the Way Inn by the Excel Centre in East London to staying in his own flat, a few streets away. His job is attending boring business conferences so that his clients don't have to, and at the moment he's at a conference of companies that organise conferences. This sort of recursive 'Ministry of Administrative Affairs' humour runs right through the novel; but it's more than just throwaway comic affectation. Recursion is the Big Theme, and Wiles handles it well. So, he takes his *Accidental Tourist*, or *Up In The Air* premise, writes it with a precisely observed, slightly prissy tone that dwells on all the little details of contemporary work-travel life (something like a more British version of Coupland); and, having done this, he launches the whole artefact into the universe of *Smallcreep's Day*. That's a spoiler, I suppose; although Brown's novel is obscure enough for it not to eat into your reading pleasure. I was also reminded of James Lovegrove's early fiction (*Days* especially, but also *The Hope*), a little of Borges, and rather more of *The Prisoner* and Christopher Priest. There's a certain miasma of Murakami too, though that's quite a common thing in fiction nowadays.

Fortunately, there is real meat to this pared-down vision; lots of observations that chime true so far as your experience (or mine) of staying in this sort of hotel is concerned. Wiles is good on the epiphenomena; on the strange, deracinated aura of sexual possibility such hotels generate; on the way their very blankness provides a weird relief from authentic lived experience. The 'twist', if that's the right word, isn't too hard to intuit; and this perhaps means that the first 200 pages are a little too leisurely. Wiles prose is good, but since it trades on a particular kind of precision, or attention to detail, those places where it falls from this high standard are more distracting than they might otherwise be. Sometimes Wiles observations spool on, outstay their welcome, lose their pithiness; and he has a provoking habit of splitting his infinitives ('I felt a strong impulse to simply forget the incident', 111), getting his subjunctive wrong ('...as if this mutual sound was a medium in which we all swam' 77) and using 'enormity' when he means 'enormousness' [249]; though fair play to him, he knows that 'congeries' is a singular form as well as being a plural ('a congeries of spheres', 186). And the novel builds to a splendidly Escher-y, *Inceptionesque* conclusion. Much recommended.

[**Postscript**: Deploying pedantry, as I do in the last paragraph here, itself invites counter-pedantry; so I shall take a moment to confirm: I know very well that there's nowt wrong with splitting your infinitives, as contemporary grammar gurus remind us all the time. Nor with ending your sentences with prepositions, or omitting the subjunctive.

People do all of these things all the time, and are well understood. My relationship to these spurious rules is cranky and idiosyncratic, and I'm a bad pedant, and I shall go to hell. Expressions that violate them clang in my ears, that's all. I should get my ears checked, probably.]

Hanya Yanagihara
The People in the Trees

I wonder if this powerful work took its jumping-off point, conceptually, from Aldous Huxley's splendid but rather neglected novel *After Many A Summer* (1939). In *that* book a Californian millionaire called Stoyte is interested in developing treatments for immortality, and hires a less-than-scrupulous research scientist called Dr Obispo (together with his blithe young assistant, Peter) to investigate possibilities. There's also a spiritually wise neighbour called Propter, who is based on Huxley, and who has a good effect on young Peter. Propter's philosophy is a three-horned striving after ἀρετή: 'every individual,' says Propter, 'is called on to display not only unsleeping good will but also unsleeping intelligence. And this is not all. For, if individuality is not absolute, if personalities are illusory figments of a self-will disastrously blind to the reality of a more-than-personal consciousness, of which it is the limitation and denial, then all of every human being's efforts must be directed, in the last resort, to the actualisation of that more-than-personal consciousness. So that even intelligence is not sufficient as an adjunct to good will; there must also be the recollection which seeks to transform and transcend intelligence.' Anyhow, Obispo sleeps with Stoyte's mistress; Stoyte, seeking to kill him in revenge, accidentally kills Peter instead; Obispo colludes in this murder for money and the book ends with a breakthrough in the immortality research – a compound derived from carp, which are famously long-lived fish. The characters travel to Europe, where they discover that an eighteenth-century nobleman called Lord Gonister had stumbled upon the carp treatment in the 1730s and is still alive. They finally track him down, only to discover that he has become sort of mindless brutish man-ape, locked up in a cellar.

Huxley's novel is in part about the paucity of *material*, as opposed to the richness of *spiritual*, craving for continuance; and partly about the brash youth-obsessed vigour of America as against the superannuated decrepitude of Europe. Yanagihara's novel has a similar conceit at its heart. Here eating not carp but a special breed of turtle, found only on a remote Micronesian island, confers immortality, but only the body is preserved from decay. The minds of the Opa'ivu'eke people of Ivu'ivu crumble away leaving them hale but mindless brutes. Like Huxley, Yanagihara focusses on a set of morally myopic and materialist human characters; but in other ways her narrative is quite different to the earlier book.

The People of the Trees is mostly the first-person memoir of Norton Perina, a Nobel prize winning scientist based, not so loosely, on Daniel Carleton Gajdusek. Like Gajdusek (in Yanagihara's telling this is actually the first thing we discover about him) Perina has been raising a great many Micronesian kids in his American home, and has been gaoled for child sex offences against some of these. Perina then takes 400 densely-printed pages to tell his story, from growing up with his cold-blooded brother, his early days as a scientist, his trip to the island of U'ivu (Ivu'ivu is a smaller island off this main one) as part of the team of a man called Tallant. Most of the novel is set on these islands, and Yanagihara does wonders with evoking the richly coloured and strange flora and fauna, most of it imaginary. The book is slow-burn throughout, and only slowly does the nature of the turtle's power to prolong life come clear. Then, against instruction, Perina smuggles some turtle meat and several of the 'dreamers' (as the mindless, ever-middle-aged natives are called) back to the States. The discovery makes his reputation; and the final third of the novel detail the events leading up to his disgrace.

All this is framed and indeed spun by a preface, epilogue and copious lengthy footnotes throughout the narrative – some explanatory, others nakedly exculpatory – written by one of Perina's former students, Ronald Kubodera. Yanagihara doesn't play as many pale, fiery games with this conceit as she might have done, actually; except (in one of the book's rare missteps, I thought) for a few pages editorially excised, and shunted to the back of the volume. These [*spoiler*] include a horribly vivid account of the rape of a child. If the idea was to try to raise narrative suspense of the *did-he*, *didn't-he* kind, it falls flat; Yanagihara does such a good job in ventriloquizing Perina's voice that you don't need to have his bad actions painstakingly spelled out to understand how bad a man he is. This is not a matter of 'evil'. In many ways Perina is not only *not* evil, he is exemplary in his goodness. He is scrupulous, observant, considered, hard-working, dedicated to improving human existence on this planet. He is moreover conscious of moral obligations as obligations – in a slightly Sheldon Cooperish way, but palpably – and acts upon them, giving a home, educations and new lives to scores of underprivileged children as personal costs that are both financial, practical and emotional. He is not an absolute moral relativist, but Yanagihara carefully makes plain, in a shown-not-told way, that encountering the different social mores of Ivu'viu (where for instance adolescent boys are sexually initiated by older tribal men as part of an honoured tradition) reinforces his own sexually predatory nature back in the USA, where such a context does not exist and where such sex is therefore inevitably abusive. I have seen comparisons made between this novel and *Lolita*, but they don't seem to me really to fit the novel. Humbert Humbert knows he is doing wrong; he simply prioritises his individual aesthetic-erotic 'joy' over social mores. But Perina gives the impression really of not knowing that what he is doing is wrong. The novel understands that it *is* wrong, of course; but one of the clevernesses of Yanagihara as a writer is that the novel does so despite the fact that neither of its two narrators comprehend it.

Yanagihara's prose is slow, accumulative and her overall effects (however shocking) are never forced. Similarly unforced are the parallels she draws between the sexual abuse of a child by an adult and the 'rape' of third world environments by the West in pursuit of profit. The before and after of U'ivu in particular is very powerfully written: the despoiled and degraded latter day island a genuinely pitiful sight. According to Perina, his adopted children go through a teenage phase of attacking him as an imperialist oppressor and a racist, but that they always grow out of this and come back as adults to apologise and thank him. This is the closest the novel comes explicitly to condemning the Western Colonial Project, and the reticence is well judged. Agit prop obviousness of moral condemnation would cruidify the book. The parallels are unmissable anyway. In fact, the tricky thing to triangulate is what part 'immortality' plays in the book's symbolic schema.

This is what brings me back to Huxley: Yanagihara is not suggesting (I think) that commercial exploitation is a kind of senile immortality. Nor is she pegging imperialism that way. However dead-behind-the-eyes imperialism was, we can at least say that it is a *mortal* phenomenon, in the sense that empires, from Hittite through Roman to British, die. Huxley's point is that a focus on purely physical or material pleasures is deeply wrongheaded; and that whilst the end-point of such a focus is not necessarily death, it degrades the capacity of the mind. Something similar, perhaps, is at stake in *The People in the Trees*. But having finished the book some weeks ago, and found that it refuses to vacate my mind (that I keep thinking and thinking about it is one of the surer signs, I'd say, that it is a kind of bleak masterpiece) I find myself wondering. Immortality is life without end, and ends are necessary things. All ethics are teleological as well as local; all metaphysics are the mapping of finite spaces. To appropriate another Huxley title (though this novel has nothing to do with immortality): *Time Must Have A Stop*. It is the endlessness of consequences, perhaps, the ineradicability of certain modes of *harm*, that gives the immortality aspect of this novel its rightness.

Appendix: Loncon 2014

[**Note**. *2014 was the year Worldcon came to London – to, indeed, the Excel Centre in London Docklands, E16. It's rare for Britain to host the planet's most prestigious SF/Fantasy convention, and 'Loncon' was a great success. After the event,* Vector, *the magazine of the BSFA, asked various SF authors and luminaries for a brief account of their experience at the con. Here is mine.*]

Monday: near the end of a varied Loncon. I was on a couple of panels in the morning, so it was almost noon by the time I moseyed over to the Gollancz stand in the Dealers' Room. Meeting Simon, my editor, for lunch. 'Shall we go?' I asked.

'Sure,' he said.

We started down along the main corridor of the Excel Centre, in the general direction of the restaurants at the west end of the building. Around us fans of every stripe flocked and jostled; a thousand different Sheldon Cooper T-shirts, Star Wars cosplay, Game of Thrones cosplay, steampunkcosplay. 'Have you had a good con?' I asked Simon.

'Actually, I have. It's been fun. We sold a lot of books,' he said. 'You?'

'Not bad at all. Been on some interesting panels. Did a signing to which people actually came. Met some old friends, made some new friends. There's a good *vibe*, I think.'

'Yes,' said Simon. 'I agree. A really good atmosphere.'

We walked on for a quarter hour or so. A man dressed as Gandalf passed us, leading his two dressed-as-hobbits kids. People sat at the cafes that punctuated the layout of the corridor, chatting, taking selfies. 'Isn't that Justina?' Simon said.

It was: my friend Justina Robson, and her family, at a metal table drinking Costa coffee. We joined them.

Geoff Ryman strolled past, like a man on stilts. 'Geoff! Geoff!' He joined us. 'Thought you guys did an excellent job hosting the Hugos,' we told them. They took our compliments with good grace, and gossiped about mutual acquaintances. 'We'd better get going,' said Simon, checking his watch. 'Lunch!'

'Excellent idea,' I said. 'I *am* hungry.'

We said our goodbyes and wandered on. Time passed, marked only by the progress we made passing doughnut emporia, noodle bars and cashpoints, public toilets and side corridors. I checked my watch. Half an hour had transpired. Peering ahead of me, I strained to make out the west exit, somewhere in amongst the eye-wearying perspective of convergent lines. 'Is it much further?'

'I'm not sure,' said Simon.

We walked on. Time passed. There were fewer fans, now. I looked back, but it wasn't possible to see where we had started. My feet were starting to throb.

'We'd better pick up the pace,' said Simon. 'Or we'll miss lunchtime altogether.'

'Right.'

On and on. The quality of the light seemed to change – although whether this was an objective feature of the corridor, or some trick my mind was playing, I couldn't say. To leaven the sound of feet plocking on the hard corridor floor, I cleared my throat. 'Really enjoyed the Gollancz-Bragelonne party, Saturday evening, by the way.'

'Thanks! It *was* good, I think.'

'It was.'

Conversation died.

We walked on. There was nobody else around, now. The corridor stretched to infinity before us. There were no more coffee or noodle franchises. A dreadful monotony and blankness defined the structure. Odd creatures seemed to slither, or lollop, along the floor – always visible only in the corner of my eye. When I turned my head there was nothing there. We marched on. 'What sort of food does this place do?' I asked. 'This restaurant we're heading for?'

'Burgers,' said Simon, in the dull voice of a man trying without hope to persuade himself of the truth of his own assertion. 'Beer.'

'I'd like a beer,' I said, in a raspy voice.

'Yes,' Simon agreed. 'Beer.'

We walked on. The roof above us seemed to be moving, flowing with a glimmering, uncanny motion, somehow simultaneously fast *and* slow. Speckles in the granite floor sparked like meteors, fled away into impossible petrific depths. The walls pulsed. Step followed step followed step. There flashed upon my inner eye a true vision, gifted me by the weird topography of the corridor – of Simon and myself emerging from the west entrance, bearded, our clothes rags, into a future that didn't recognise us – or, perhaps, into a deep past, where megalosauri grazed mesozoic ferns, lifting curious heads to observe our intrusion. There was no going back now.

We walked on.

Also from Steel Quill Books

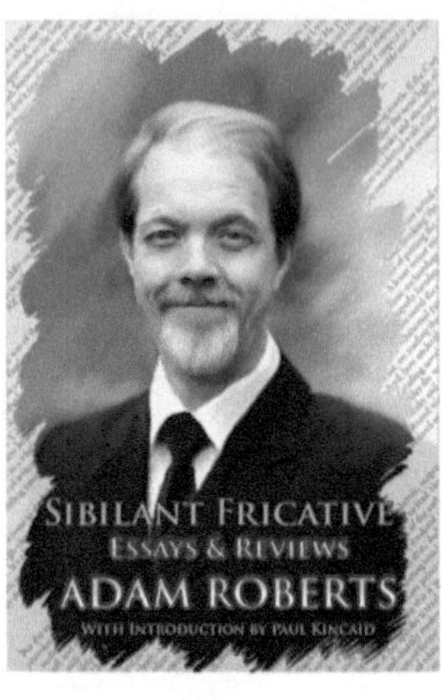

In ***Sibilant Fricative*** Adam Roberts considers a broad spectrum of speculative fiction, from fantasy to science fiction, from literature to films. The book opens with insightful consideration of Philip K Dick's oeuvre followed by Ridley Scott's *Blade Runner*, and closes with a volume-by-volume analysis of Robert Jordan's *Wheel of Time* opus. One thing the author never loses sight of is the need to entertain.

"*Sibilant Fricative* is undoubtedly one of the finest collections of essays that genre criticism has ever produced."

– Jonathan McCalmont, BSFA Vector magazine

"…the essay on the "Two Hobbits" is worth the entry ticket alone, and there is so much more entertainment within… Erudite, entertaining, intelligent collection of essays and reviews."– *The Bristol Book Blog*

"Adam Roberts makes everything wonderful. If he wrote non-fiction about drying paint, I would still be the first in line to read it."

– Jared Shurin of Pornokitsch.

~

"*Titan* is one of the blandest pieces of fiction I have come across in four decades of reading novels. If the Campbell shortlist is a high-class curry restaurant of delicious, spicy and stimulating food, then *Titan* is a single slice of white bread and margarine on a white plate under the neon light of a truck drivers' café." *on Titan by Ben Bova*

"I challenge you to read 'similar to what one might find' without thinking 'the play what I wrote'… He piles stuff upon stuff, and at the end we're presented a hardback-bound big pile of stuff. And all of it rendered in dead, humourless, grey prose…" *on The Edge of the World by Kevin J Anderson*

"Let me see if I can boil down *Crossroads of Twilight*'s 700-pages for you. Drivel. There you go." *on Crossroads of Twilight by Robert Jordan.*

Lifelines and Deadlines

James Lovegrove

Selected Nonfiction

Released September 2015

James Lovegrove is the *New York Times* best-selling author of more than fifty novels and novellas. James also writes nonfiction, his reviews and articles having appeared in numerous venues in print and online, including a regular review column for the *Financial Times*.
Cover Art by Adam Brockbank

Never timid, often contentious, sometimes amusing, ever insightful, and always entertaining, ***Lifelines and Deadlines*** features the author's selection of his very best nonfiction from the past twenty years.

"As a survey of the field over the last few decades this collection really can't be bettered. Lovegrove knows how to temper his wide knowledge with wit, how to cut to the heart of a well-judged critical assessment, and he's simply incapable of filing dull copy. He's always fair, always readable, always wise. If there's a better reviewer of SF, Fantasy and Horror working today, then I'd like to meet them. Mind you, I'd like to meet anybody, really. I'm bitterly lonely." – *Adam Roberts*

www.ingramcontent.com/pod-product-compliance
Lightning Source LLC
Chambersburg PA
CBHW021218260626
47172CB00002B/492

* 9 7 8 1 9 0 7 0 6 9 8 0 2 *